MW01244855

ISBN-13: 979-8387297731

Acknowledgements

I came up with the initial concept for this novel in 2014, about a year after my mother passed away. The only notion I had was I wanted to do with this novel was to have a modern-day protagonist, grieving for their loved one, and they decide to take a road trip, meeting Jesus in the process. I didn't have any further ideas to take this story. Then, life happened—upheavals of life.

My Dad needed our attention due to his worsening dementia. We learned as we dealt with Dad's weakening memory, as he fought to hold on to his past the best he knew how. He struggled physically, and of course cognitively, as he lost his ability to walk, and then his ability to speak. You never were taught how to deal with managing a parent through illnesses, or even gave it a thought what to do when your parent needed your care liked they took care of you. We relied on professionals until his last moments of his life in December 2016.

It was six months later when my sister was diagnosed with ovarian cancer. It was a very hard punch to the gut. Cancer was another disease I had to learn about, although I'm learning now with my good friend, Mel's, battle with cancer, my sister shield me from the hidden struggles of chemotherapy and radiation. Martha fought like hell for two and a half years.

I couldn't help but wonder why God didn't take me instead of my sister. She had a family of her own—a husband and two grown children. I did not. I thought as myself as dispensable; nobody needs me in this world, as I have athetoid cerebral palsy and need daily physical care from others. What was this life all about? I really wanted to ask God this question. What was my purpose? I didn't really know, truly.

In early 2020, the pandemic hit. I was home, working on putting new virtual instruments on my Christmas CD I had originally done in 2010. It was during this time that the wheels started turning, as I was slowly started to shape the plot this story with this protagonist who meets Jesus on a road trip. It all came together within three months, and I was off and writing this story in August 2020. I am convinced that couldn't have written this novel without the tremendous losses over the past nine years. With the tremendous worldwide loss of life due to COVID-19 really frightening and heartbreaking. I thought a lot about the first responders, the medical professionals, the general caregivers that were putting their lives on the line to care for these people who had this novel, respiratory virus. A pandemic. We lived through a pandemic, that we as a country, certain officials of our government, handled very poorly at the start. God seemed to put a spotlight on the inequities of our society and other societies across the world that need all our attention. If we stay silent, our Earth, freedoms, and our rights will be lost. Everybody has a voice, and every voice must be heard. Truth must win out over disinformation.

With this novel, I wanted to demonstrate that Jesus and God are accessible to all of us who are believers. I might get a lot of criticism for portraying my protagonist as somebody who doesn't attends church very often, but who wholeheartedly believes in God, Jesus and the whole of Christianity. I also portrayed Jesus (Jay) as a very modern, hip Man because, again, I wanted to demonstrate His accessibility to the masses.

When I was 18, I was going to school at Crotched Mountain, a residential school for children with developmental disabilities in Greenfield, New Hampshire. On weekends, our group took trips to various places around southern New Hampshire, and very often Boston.

One Saturday, we went to Keene where there was this mill-style shopping mall. Everybody in our small group was encouraged to go off and explore things on our own. I decided to take the elevator up to the second and third floor. Whatever was on the second floor didn't impress me much, so I got back on the elevator and up to the third floor I went. I don't know what possessed me to go up to the third floor, but I did. I got off the elevator and saw this expansive space of office cubicles. Everything was white—white walls, a white, high drop-ceiling, and even the cubicles were white. At first glance, no one was in the immediate area, which gave me the opportunity to cruise down an aisle or two. Out of nowhere, he appeared—Jesus—well he certainly looked like Jesus. His face, his beard, his long brown hair, and he wore this white robe with this white, rope around his waist. In my mind, all I saw was Jesus. As he passed me, going in the opposite direction in the same aisle, I tried not to freak out. Passing him, I smiled at him and went along my merry way, like I knew where I was going. When I felt I could look back, I stopped, I turned, and he was gone. I booked it back to the elevator, went back down to the first floor and told Nestor, one of our counselors, that I saw Jesus up on the third floor. Did Nestor believe me—I don't know. Today, Nestor is a pastor in Pennsylvania.

Since 1985, I have been a huge fan of the musical group, The Hooters. In 1995, one of the front men, Eric Bazilian, composed, *One of Us* for Joan Osborne. I love the song, and the lyrics make you think. I don't know exactly when I thought of that song as a springboard for this story, but it certainly had an influence.

Listening to music while I write is a gigantic lift to my spirit, and when my spirited is lifted, I feel I can do anything. Writing this book, I listened to Steve Winwood's 2017 Live at least three times a week. All the other times I wrote, I jacked myself up on Billy Joel, Live, Sarah McLachlan, The Hooters and various other artists. In July 2021, I discovered The Dave Matthews Band. I have always liked his big hits that played on the radio, but I never dug deep and listened to more of his songs. After listening to his Essentials Playlist on Apple Music, I was completely hooked. I needed to listen to listen to these songs because they have such a spirituality that complimented the story I was writing. I have always loved music and I get very moved by certain songs. And I always have songs in my playlist that happen to mention God or Jesus, not because I listen to Christian music, but it's what I have been hearing

—

practically my entire life. If my novel ever gets turned into a motion picture, I definitely want a say what goes on the soundtrack!

First, I would like to thank my brothers, Peter and Paul, and my sister-in-laws, Sue and Karen, who had no idea what exactly I was doing, or writing, but had the faith I wasn't goofing off on something silly. Thank you to my nieces and nephews, Sarah, Thomas, Grace, Sam, Ben and Jack for just being the wonderful people who you are. I love being your aunt. To my brother-in-law, Glenn, who loved Martha so much, and being the perfect husband to her. Thanks for trusting me with Gracie when you're working. Thank you to Aunt Pat who asked me questions about the novel that I would not reveal. Shhhh! It's a secret…

Thank you, Mel for being my sounding board when I needed to bounce an idea off you, and for keeping me sane, grounded and laughing. Thank you, Hazel for narrating all kinds of stories you've read or watched, keeping my imagination going nonstop. Thank you, Jen for keeping my spirit and body nourished and keeping me on track. Thank you, Ray for your constant calmness and your knowledge or firearms. Thank you, Melissa for being another sounding board, especially about how the human mind works. Thank you, Candace for your energy and spirit and your strength. Thank you, Kim for not knocking my belief that this might be a New York Times Bestseller, and for all our therapy sessions. Thank you, Kathy for your friendship and constant support. I could not have done this without out you all!

A special thanks to David Sandretto for assisting me with editing this novel. Your kind words will stay with me forever. And a very special thank you to Michelle for her personal sacrifices to make sure I was well and happy during the second half of 2022. You blow my mind constantly with your strength, kindness and sense of humor. Thank you for assisting me with minor adjustments to this novel.

I would like to give Lewis and Meg Randa a special shout out to the lessons I have learned from them since they bestowed the Courage of Conscience Award to me in November 2015. They taught me about the incredible stories of civil disobedience in history. I even had a chance to practice civil disobedience in January 2017. I hope my novel makes you very proud.

I would like thank Debi for our 41-year friendship. If I didn't know you, I don't think this book would have been possible for me to write. Your soul is the true essence of kindness and acceptance. You understand life so beautifully, and death so significantly with grace. You have taught me so much throughout the years and I treasure every lesson. I have no doubt that God knew what He was doing when He made our paths cross. Even though we are two, small states apart, we always have that ability to get together every once and a while. I am very lucky indeed.

Enjoy!

For Mom, Dad and Martha

Departure

Another morning broke. Rain or shine—it didn't matter, Alex was still in her gray and saddened haze. *Fifty-eight days.* A growing number started her every morning. She knew she had to get up out of her bed to perform the normal bodily functions, but she would rather lie in bed for the rest of her time on Earth. It was a monumental feat to get her feet on the floor every morning, not because she suffered from some dreadful disease, nor did she have creaking bones and stiff muscles due to an advanced age. Alex was a healthy 26-year-old with her life in front of her. The only obstacle she had to overcome was the loss of her brother, Nathanial Ryan Roma, who was three and a half years her junior—Alex's little brother.

Working groups of muscles, she sat up on the edge of her childhood bed, in her childhood bedroom. She should have had been ashamed of her current status, but she really wasn't. She looked for her iPhone. Her Dad had developed a new habit of sneaking into her bedroom at night and moving her phone from her nightstand to her tall, walnut bureau across the room. She hated that she slept so soundly. Her feet were on the floor. Before she stood, Alex took a deep breath, knowing she would have to get through another day.

Alex finally stood and walked over to her tall bureau. She grabbed her iPhone and checked her messages. There was only one message from her friend, Conrad. Alex had many friends, but 58 days in, he was the only friend who hadn't become annoyed with her withdrawal from human interaction. Conrad had texted he was going to pick her up at noon. It was 11:09 a.m. The background photo behind the time was her favorite of her and Nate, three years prior, at a tavern in Wellfleet. Nate was smiling and seemingly happy. Alex knew Nate could put on a good face when he had to. A tear rolled down one side of her face. She caught it before it dropped down to the Heart Pine floor. Suddenly, she pulled herself together and gathered up her clothes for the day.

Getting showered and dressed before noon was definitely progress. Some days, Alex could sleep until three o'clock in the afternoon and return to bed before seven. On this day, she found her dad reading *The Herald* in the breakfast nook.

"Where are you off to?" asked her father, shaking the paper but not looking up.

"Conrad is picking me up in a few minutes."

Her father shook the paper, but only more forcibly. "When are you going back to work?"

Alex tired of hearing this question. It took the air out of her lungs as she closed her eyes, facing the white kitchen cabinets as she fixed her tea in her travel cup. "I don't know, Dad."

He sighed heavily. "That's the same answer you have given me for the last week."

"If you don't like my answer, stop asking the question," Alex snapped.

Her father sighed heavily again. "You have to return to your residency."

She heard Conrad's car horn. "I'll be back later." Alex left the austere, Victorian house before her father could rattle off another question. She got into Conrad's silver Honda Accord, and they drove away.

Alex enjoyed feeling the late spring air whipping through her black hair. Her eyelids closed over her dark green eyes for a moment or two. She felt that she could sleep forever.

"Are you going to talk to me or what?" Conrad asked, as he quickly gazed over at her in his passenger seat.

"Talking is overrated."

"Well, that's rich, coming from you." Out the corner of his right eye, Conrad saw Alex giving him the middle finger. "Do you want to go for a run? Let's go for a run!"

Alex looked at him. "Really?"

"Really," he said with fervor. "It'll be good for you! Get all those muscles moving; release all those fantastic endorphins; get those lungs exhaling!"

"You sound like a doctor." Alex smirked.

"Well, I am a doctor! And guess what?!"

Alex, once again, looked over at Conrad, knowing what he was going to say.

"You're a doctor!" Conrad said with great emphasis.

Alex did not speak; she couldn't, as her emotions overwhelmed her. Tears fell from her eyes as she rested her chin upon her palm. Her eyes were staring out the side window, but she wasn't seeing anything but her own grief and failures. Alex became a doctor so she could heal and help people. She couldn't help Nate—she had failed Nate, she had failed her parents and she had failed herself. Alex had been living in her world of failure for 58 days; tomorrow would be 59 days; the day after that would be 60 days—two full months of failure. Even before Nate's death, she was failing him, she believed. Day in and day out, Alex knew he was sinking down and down, but he disguised it really, really well until he couldn't anymore. Recalling all those times Nate went missing—it was pure hell thinking he was dead in a ditch somewhere. Sometimes he was gone for two days, sometimes he was gone for two weeks. Those long weeks were chaotic and nerve-racking. When Nate finally appeared, unhurt and unaffected, Alex's first instinct was to scream at him, but she understood his disease, so all she could do was hug him with all her might. At times, Alex probably hugged him so tight imagining that her love could heal him. She had tried everything.

Soon, Conrad pulled into the *110 Grill* parking lot in Hopkinton. He shut off his car. "Hey, I'm sorry," he said, his voice gentle and kind.

Alex took a deep breath and exhaled fully. "Nothing you said was wrong. I just have to get a handle on things, you know." She looked at him, relaying she heard his words.

"I really think you ought to talk to someone; I know a few good therapists."

"A few good men?" Alex commented with some humor. "I don't know, I don't know. I'd rather just talk to you."

Conrad chuckled. "I am just an ER doctor."

"We all took psych?"

Conrad smiled at her as he watched her sweep away another tear. He put his hand on Alex's shoulder. "Of course you can talk to me; I just worry about you sometimes."

"Yeah, I know." Alex sniffled again. "How is Justin dealing with you spending all your spare time with me, trying to put Humpty Dumpty back together again?"

"Are you kidding? He loves you as much as I do. He knows this is not forever." In an instant, he leaned nearer to Alex. "This is not forever."

Alex nodded.

"Let's eat, I'm hungry." Before Alex had time to react, Conrad emerged from the driver's side. He watched Alex follow his lead. They walked into the restaurant.

On this day, Alex ate more than the previous day. Unknowingly, she was making little strides here and there. Conrad noticed them. The tab was paid, and they exited the restaurant. He had every intention of driving her home, but Alex wanted to walk. He wasn't going to argue. It was a late April day, sunny but surprisingly crisp from the breeze. Conrad, with tight, curly, strawberry blond hair and a closely shaven beard, handsome and built, had a physique women craved but possessed a soul only for men. He had a heart bigger than the sun. Conrad was her best friend. Conrad stated he would pick her up the day after next. He also reminded Alex to call him when she got home. They had a long embrace before going their separate ways for the day. They both spoke, "I love you."

With her travel mug in her hand, Alex started walking in the opposite direction of home. She watched Conrad pull away and then wave goodbye. Instantly, she felt sadly alone again. She had a destination in mind where it was peaceful. With no plans for the rest of the day, she could do what she wanted. As she walked, Alex took in everything around her: the scenery, the people, the smells, the sounds. Surrounded by everything Earthly and real, she felt so detached, like a figment of her own imagination. She had all the makings of a human being, but she felt far from human. All her movements were human, but she felt mechanical. She felt like an object, walking in some space, and maybe in some other time.

She reached the entrance of Saint John Cemetery. It was the place she spent most of the past 52 days in. Even days when the skies opened, or when the New England winds off the Atlantic howled and pierced, this was the place that calmed her soul. Alex walked to Nate's gravestone and sat down on the newly grown grass. Nate's gravestone wasn't the biggest around, but it wasn't the smallest either. Her parents had spared no expense. His portrait was engraved on a five-by-seven-inch piece of granite inset into the stone, which displayed Nate's full name, birthdate, and date of death. Alex suspected that when strangers walked by his gravestone, they probably surmised he died of some form of cancer, a fatal car accident, or some genetic, childhood disease that ended his life early. Strangers would never think that a handsome man like Nate would ever end his own life. Alex knew the cold and hard truth; there was darkness that overtook his mind, eating away at his confidence, eating away his happiness and joy.

Alex pulled up a blade of grass, playing with it between her fingers to give herself an activity.

"I never learned to whistle with grass," Alex stated out loud, figuring Nate's spirit might be listening. "I can play the flute, or I should say, used to play the flute, but I can't make a sound with grass." She threw the blade forward, giving up the task. She wiped her hands on her sweatpants, giving her hands something to do. Looking around, Alex learned she continued to be alone.

"Today, Conrad reminded me I was a doctor, but I don't feel like a doctor, Kiddo." Alex plucked more grass out of the ground and began to fiddle with the blades with her fingers again. "How can I save strangers when I couldn't save you?" This time, her voice was calm, although quiet. She exhaled a long breath from her lungs. Through the tree canopy above, Alex gazed up and saw the patchwork of blue sky, realizing how infinite the universe was and how insignificant she was. The grass between her fingers became insignificant also; Alex let them drop back onto the ground. Her chin found the palm of her left hand, as she took in the sheer number of gravestones that surrounded her. Soon, Alex crossed her arms over her knees, and she fell asleep.

Her iPhone awakened her gently. She picked a ringtone that wasn't obnoxious or loud, but soothing, with a violin musical measure.

As Alex slowly awakened, she was surprised she had fallen asleep. She looked at her phone—it was Conrad. She didn't notice he was parked about 75 feet away; she didn't notice he was walking up behind her until he got about 10 feet away. She stood up quickly, a little embarrassed she let so much time elapse. "I guess I'm kind of easy to find these days."

Conrad stood and slowly smiled at his dear friend. "Yes, you are." Stepping forward, he extended his strong arms around her. In their embrace, Conrad rocked her from side to side, as if they were dancing a simple dance. "Let me take you home," he whispered softly. In the crook of his shoulder, he felt Alex nod her head.

Before leaving, Alex kissed the tips of her middle three fingers and placed them on Nate's granite engraved portrait. "I'll be back soon."

The house was dark; it was only 7:30 p.m. Alex walked around the downstairs, but nobody was there. She turned on a few lamps. In a few minutes, Alex found herself tiptoeing around upstairs, searching for any signs of life. At the end of the hall, she noticed her father's office lamp on. "Alex, is that you?"

Taking a deep breath before she answered, Alex thought how she would explain her day's activities, realizing his question was more of a request to go see him. "Yes." She walked into his office and saw him reading a textbook.

His eyes met hers, as he leaned back in his caramel-colored, leather office chair. "Sit, please," he said in a more caring voice than earlier that morning.

Alex sat down on the matching, caramel, leather couch. "Is Mom still at her conference?"

"Yes. She should be home tomorrow," he said easily. This was a question he could answer when there were a million questions he could not. A professor of Gerontology at Harvard Medical School, his alma mater, Michael Nathanial Roma was a brilliant man. He knew how to cheer on his students, he knew how to teach, and he knew how to speak, although he was struggling to find words for Alex. His eyes gazed at his daughter a little longer than usual. "Did you have dinner?"

Hesitating for a split second, Alex didn't know what to make of his still look upon her. Her father was a handsome and fit man of 59 years old. He had a full head of salt and pepper hair. A 60th birthday had been planned but her mom promptly cancelled after their only son took his own life. "I ate earlier; I'm not hungry." She prompted herself to offer to make him something.

"Oh, no. Thank you, Al. I ate about an hour ago."

"Sure, sure," she said, looking at her clasped hands. Finding nothing else to say, Alex stood and wished her dad a good night.

"Goodnight, Al."

Day 59. From the direction of the sun, Alex sensed it was much earlier than 11 a.m. Again, her iPhone had mysteriously leaped to her tall bureau, but it really wasn't a mystery. It was another day she would have to figure out how she would spend her time when just about all her motivation had been decimated like a tidal wave taking out a small island in the Pacific. She did not want to think about anything, do anything or feel anything; all of it was too overwhelming and heavy upon her soul. She had grieved before but not like this. When she was 19, she lost her grandmother to heart disease, which she had for years and years. Her death was sad, although not surprising. Nate's death swept her into a swirling cyclone of water, only allowing her to breathe when it was absolutely necessary. Constantly her arms flailed, as they searched for something to grab onto. There was just water, and sometimes air, which allowed her to sustain life. She grew very tired very fast, as she couldn't tread water any longer. In that moment, Alex suddenly jolted awake, gasping for air.

She had no choice but to get out of bed and just breathe, realizing she was having a horrifying dream. Several minutes dragged by, as she steadied herself at the end of her bed, finally sitting on the floor with her face in the palms of her hands. Sobs came quickly and cruelly, much like Day Two. This was Day 59 and the growth that she thought she was making experienced a violent shove backwards. Alex's soul felt defeated, as if she had been in a boxing ring for the entire 59 days, with her opponent just wailing and wailing on her with no mercy, and with no empathy. The only possible way she might be able to make it would be to accept this new reality. Alex didn't know how to escape from this infinite darkness, and cavernous space. There had to be a source of light that led into the openness where she could just breathe easily again. If she found a way to breathe again, she might, just might, be able to live again.

Unknowingly, day 60 snuck up on her without warning. Alex's mother, Joanne, got in after Alex went to sleep, as she stayed in bed the entire day. With a swift knock on the door, Alex's mother entered her room like a whirlwind, disrupting everything in her wake, including her daughter.

In a moment, Alex's bed covers were ripped off. "Mom! What are you doing?!" she asked with much frustration in her voice, as her eyes were still closed. Alex rolled onto her side, signaling to her mother she had no desire to get out of bed.

Placing a hand behind Alex's calves, Joanne moved them off the edge of the bed. "Come on, you have to get up," her mother demanded.

It always surprised Alex how strong her mother was with her small stature. She tried to protest her actions, not quite awake yet, although Alex knew this fight to have her own autonomy on this day would be futile. It boggled her mind why her mother's grief was so different from hers. Suddenly, Alex was sitting up on the edge of her bed, forcibly pulled up by her right arm. She reluctantly engaged her back and core muscles and sat independently. "Are you happy now?" Sarcasm protruded into her voice.

"I'll be happier if you would go take a shower so we can go for a run," Joanne announced. "I'll go make us some smoothies."

"Are you serious? You want to go for a run?" Alex was dumbfounded by this crazy idea.

"Yeah, I want to go for a run with my daughter," her mother repeated, looking into Alex's deep green, sad eyes.

There was a tear in the corner of one, ready to roll across the bridge of her nose and then gravity would have its way with it. Alex watched her mother catch her tear before gravity grabbed it. Her mother was a beautiful woman with platinum-blond hair by choice. Her hair was a little bit longer and grayer than she would have liked, but it was difficult times and keeping up physical appearances took a back seat. Feeling her mom's hand lift her chin, she kissed her on her forehead. "Okay."

"I love you, you know," her mother softly stated.

Opening her arms, leaning to the left, Alex hugged her mother tightly. "I know."

"We're going to get through this, I promise."

Alex gave her mother a strong embrace. "I'm happy you're home, Mom."

"Me too, Honey. Me too."

One lap jogging around the track at Hopkinton High School just about did Alex in, as she rested the heels of her hands above her knees, as she bent, breathing heavy. *Boy, I'm out of shape.* Creaking her neck down, Alex saw her mother jogging up behind her, on her second lap. *Are you kidding me? I'm half her age and had slept for the last 18 hours.* Finally, she stood up, as she could breathe again. Alex walked slowly around the track; she lost track of how many times her mom passed her on the track, making Alex feel terribly inferior. Her mother was a physio trainer for the Boston University Sports Program, and when you are a physio trainer, you'd better be physically fit.

Two months prior, Alex would have been able to keep up with her mother; of course she hadn't run any marathons, but she could run at least four miles without much trouble. She was truly amazed how much two months of just sitting on the couch or lying in bed, having your motivation being sucked out of you like air being sucked out of a balloon, does to a human body. Yes, Alex was a doctor—she had read all the textbooks on this very subject, but experiencing it for herself was altogether a different monster. Her overwhelming sadness and Nate's manic-depressive paranoid schizophrenia only supplied her with a sliver of his life-altering illness, the darkness that fogged his mind so cruelly.

Her Mom touched her on the back of the shoulder. "Do you want to walk the path with me?"

"Sure," Alex answered without hesitation, looking forward to getting some shade from the warm June sun. Hopkinton High School had a state-of-the-art campus for athletics. Being the daughter of the physio trainer for BU gave Alex perks statewide, especially in her hometown.

"How are you feeling?"

Under the grand tree canopies of the path, Alex wanted to give her mother a hopeful answer, but she knew she would see through her. "Umm…," Alex began, trying to delay the honesty. She walked as she held her travel mug with both index fingers, bouncing off her thighs.

Her mother resisted the urge to press her for an answer, although she wanted to confirm what her husband reported.

Alex searched for words. "I guess I just feel lost, you know," Alex admitted. "It has been years since I didn't wake up and worry about Nate, worrying if he was going to have a good day or a bad day; I worried if he was going to take off again, and if he did, I was terrified what we would have to deal with. I searched for anything that would be an answer for him."

Suddenly her mom stopped walking and started sobbing. "What a horrible mother I have been." Tears dropped to the dirt walk.

"Oh no, Mom! Don't think that!" Alex softly demanded. With her arms around her mother's shoulders, Alex guided her off the path and onto a nearby bench. "I didn't mean to make you so upset."

Between her tears, Joanne hugged her daughter very tightly. "I'm so, so sorry. I failed both of my kids." Tears came easily. "I should have known you were struggling to find a way to help Nate; we all were."

This was the first time Alex really saw the mutual pain in her mother's eyes; she knew this horrible pain all too well. Finally, she felt some validation with someone else, a solidarity, a common bond; she didn't feel so alone anymore. Alex wrapped her arms around her mother and held her close. "What do I do now?"

Gently squeezing her daughter's upper arm, Joanne delighted in this time with Alex. "Take it one day at a time, Sweetheart." After Joanne spoke, she immediately thought her response was weak—she wanted to give her daughter a better sense of direction. "We must ask ourselves what Nate would want us to do." Joanne sat up straight and grabbed one of Alex's hands; she wiped her eyes clear. "He would not want us to wallow; he wouldn't want us to be stuck, as we are."

"Are you kidding, my middle name is 'wallow'," Alex said, smirking.

Turning her torso to the left instantaneously, Joanne smiled. "You made a funny!" Her face lit up like a ray of sun, as she grazed her hand upon Alex's outer thigh. Joanne chuckled.

Alex gazed up to the treetops with a slight smile. "Oh yeah, I'm a laugh-a-minute," she said with playful sarcasm. Alex continued looking upward, enjoying this time with her mom. "Dad is becoming frustrated with me. He thinks I should get back to residency…like yesterday."

Joanne sighed. "He's just as lost as we are. He just wants the best for you." She rested her arm on the back of the bench. She wanted to give all her attention to her daughter.

"I know…but almost every day he hounds me and hounds me— I don't feel like I'm ready yet," Alex admitted.

"If you're not ready—you're not ready, Alex. This shouldn't be a race to see who can get back to any kind of normal first. It's a process, and everybody has their own process."

"How are you coping so well?" Alex asked her mother.

"Oh Sweetie, I have my days," Joanne solemnly admitted. "Some days are so heavy I can barely breathe."

Surprised, Alex looked skeptically at her mother.

Joanne returned to sitting straight on the bench. "I believe over many years of Nate's illness, and with him not making much progress, I think I fortified myself to deal with what might come our way, you know. I didn't want to think about what if something would happen to my baby boy, but I think it was in his eyes; I saw he was struggling for many years." Tears fell from her eyes.

Lifting her right hand, Alex wiped away her mother's tears with her fingertips. "I think I understand that." Once again, she held her mother closely.

"You know, you are a lot stronger than you think you are."

"Strong like my Mom?" Alex rhetorically asked with a breaking voice.

"Yep."

Weeks passed, and Alex got stronger and stronger. Nearly every morning, she ran the track with her mom, benefiting her mind, body, and spirit. Finally, she could keep pace with her mother; even in the early summer, New England heat, she started to feel alive again. Her dad stopped asking Alex about returning to her residency, probably due to the urging from her mother. On some summer nights, they drove to the beaches along the South Shore. As they looked out on the Atlantic, they walked barefoot in the sand. The night sky was magnificent on clear, moonlit, summer nights, as the waves decided on their ferocity every minute of the day and night. The sound of the ocean was loved by whoever listened to it and gave it their proper attention. The resonance of the humbled waves brought peace and renewal of souls. Not all souls seek out restoration when visiting the ocean. Everyday visitors just seek out the ocean for the relaxation, for the love of the sound of the waves advancing and retreating with the tides. They seek out the warmth of the sun, balanced by the coolness of the coastal breezes. Alex was using the ocean to heal.

It was nearly July. Life had become a little bit easier to navigate, as a ship finding calmer seas. Where there were dark gray clouds, turning up seas and winds, whipping rains around and around, knocking anyone off course, finally there were breaks in the clouds, as the direction could be recalibrated. Alex needed something else, but she wasn't sure what exactly it was to restart some kind of normal existence. She still felt stuck, as if she was standing in mud up to her calves, struggling to walk forward.

She could see the pink, orange, and violet horizon in front of her, but Alex couldn't seem to reach it, to touch it and to feel it. Desperately, Alex wanted to move forward but figuring how to do so was difficult.

On another humid July evening, she took a ride to Duxbury Beach with Conrad and Justin. Duxbury Beach was the favorite beach of many in Massachusetts and throughout New England. Most of the beach was an isthmus, jutting out about four and a half miles southwest into Cape Cod Bay. The width of the beach, 50 yards wide, acted as a barrier against all the storms that blew in from the Atlantic. The three friends walked part of Duxbury Beach and continued onto the isthmus. It was the coolest place to be on hot, humid, New England nights, as the wind blew off the ocean. The moon, amber in color, was gloriously bright and pronounced. It lit the backs of passing, thin clouds, as they gave dimension to the dark, golden night. Alex remarked that she hadn't seen the sky so beautiful for a few years.

"It has been so long since I have been to this beach. It's beautiful," Justin remarked out loud. "We should come here more often." He felt Conrad squeeze his hand, as they looked out into the Atlantic. Tiny waves advanced on the beach in a steady cycle.

"We should," Conrad agreed. He began walking the beach. The other two followed.

"I love it here; this is my favorite beach." Alex walked with her two good friends, as she took in everything around her.

Conrad caught her eye while they continued to amble down the beach. Alex's gaze was coming back to life; the sparkle that had temporarily vanished had finally returned. Conrad smiled and winked at Alex. "It's nice to see."

"What are you talking about?" she asked, smirking a bit.

"The sparkle."

"The sparkle?" repeated Alex.

"Yeah," Conrad said. "The sparkle in your eye is back."

Alex looked at Conrad inquisitively. "I have a sparkle?"

"Of course, you have a sparkle in your eye," Justin spoke up with gusto. Unlike Conrad, Justin was tall and a bit lanky. His black hair was thick with a wave that complemented his olive skin and boyish face. Many people called Justin, 'Doogie', because not many believed he was old enough to be a doctor.

Alex stopped in her tracks. "Who knew." She scanned the ground and found a soft spot to sit.

Conrad and Justin followed suit. They were sitting, facing the ocean. "The sparkle is back," Conrad said softly, reassuring her.

Sitting on the beach, Alex rested her arms across her knees. "How do I begin again?"

There was a long silence between the three friends. They looked out beyond the ocean to search out the answers. "I think you should take yourself out of your comfort zone for a while," Justin suggested.

"Like take an origami class?" Conrad asked his husband with a bit of humor.

Justin playfully and lightly slapped Conrad's right upper arm. "No, no, not an origami class." Justin sat up straighter to give himself more of a stand. "I mean, take a trip somewhere that you have never been, and spend a good amount of time there."

"Where would I go?" Alex looked upward to the visible stars. "I can't picture myself going to the Bahamas and being waited on hand-and-foot. I'd get so bored."

"How about going on a road trip?" Conrad blurted out.

"A road trip?" Alex repeated. "I don't have a car, so that is a big problem."

"I can get you a car, cheap," Justin announced.

"Your brother?"

"Yeah, he can get a good deal on a good car." Justin looked to his right at Conrad, and then over at Alex.

Alex took a deep breath, and then exhaled all the grief from the day. This was a big step—whether she decided to go on road trip, or something else, Alex knew she had to make a move, a move forward. Then, memories came flowing back of the childhood trip, a road trip, she attempted to take with her parents and Nate. They only got to Philadelphia when they had to stop because Nate came down with a severe stomach bug, where he had to be hospitalized for a few days. After his hospitalization, her parents decided to return home.

"We went on a road trip about nine years ago. We didn't get too far because Nate came down with some weird stomach thing; he had to be hospitalized in Philly."

"Where were you headed?" asked Conrad.

"We were supposed to drive across the country to see all the sights."

"Never made it across the country?" Justin inquired.

"Nope." Alex still was amazed by the magnificent ocean before her. "I looked forward to that trip; I really wanted to see the country, especially the Grand Canyon."

"The Grand Canyon is incredible," Justin enthusiastically stated.

"Hmmm," Alex reacted. "How long would it take to get there?"

"Oh God, it would depend on if you wanted to drive straight through, sleeping at night, or if you want to make stops along the way," Justin explained. "You have time; I would take my time if I were you."

"Sure," Conrad agreed.

"Is this a crazy idea, guys?"

"I don't think so," stated Justin. "If you want to do this, go for it."

Conrad agreed, nodding.

Alex returned her gaze to the Atlantic, really contemplating this trip. "I could camp out every night." She wanted to see how Conrad and Justin would react to this idea.

"I am woman! Hear me roar!" Justin expressed humorously.

Alex and Conrad looked over to Justin and broke out into unbridled laughter. Soon, laughter reached Justin and all three melted into the sand. She couldn't remember when she laughed so hard, for the tears running out of her eyes were due to laughter instead of sadness. It felt good to laugh, although she felt guilty for feeling a level of normalcy.

"We have all the camping gear you'll need," Conrad announced, trying to control his lasting laughter.

"You guys are not going camping this summer?"

"We don't have vacation time until Thanksgiving," Justin explained.

"Lucky you," Alex replied with emphasis.

"I know, right," Conrad reciprocated her gratefulness. "We are going to Justin's parents'."

Instantly, Alex realized Nate would be absent at the Thanksgiving table, absent on Christmas morning, absent at New Year's Eve, and absent at every holiday, birthday, anniversary, family reunion and every other future event not yet known in her life. Alex got quiet and reflective while looking out on the vast, moonlighted ocean. She felt suddenly alone.

Conrad moved nearer to her, putting his hands on her shoulders, and kissing her temple. "It's going to be hard for a while," he stated loud enough for his husband to hear. "Know that Nate will always be with you; he is here now."

Taking Conrad's cue, Justin rose and walked to her other side. Gently, he sat back down on the sand. "You know, you can come with us."

Though his offer was tempting, Alex knew she couldn't abandon her own parents. "I don't want my parents to be alone, but I thank you for your offer."

"Yeah, absolutely," Justin said with strength, strength that he wanted to reach her. Justin leaned over and embraced his friend.

A single tear ran down her cheek. "Wow, all this love. I'm a lucky girl to have friends like you," she said, grabbing both of their hands. And she was utterly grateful, so much so she felt her heart leap with joy. On this night, Alex took another step forward.

The 2012 black Toyota Camry was packed to its capacity with everything she would need for a cross-country adventure. Alex was nervous and excited for this trip; she didn't know whether this trip would influence her, or just be something to pass more time. She had to find out. Her mom and dad helped her get the last of her things in the car.

Her dad was holding another cell phone in a box. "Listen, this is an extra iPhone, just in case something happens to yours. It's all activated." He placed it in her soft hand.

This very generous gift made a lump in her throat. "Thanks, Dad." Alex immediately embraced him. "I'm going to be fine."

"I know you are," her father replied, struggling to let his daughter go. "I love you."

This was a declaration she hadn't heard in a very long time. Alex couldn't help but to embrace him again, only this time even tighter. "I love you too," she said softly. She felt a tear fall from her eye. Regaining some control, she caught her mother's gaze, as she tried to hold it together.

"Here's some tea for today," her mother announced, handing her travel cup to Alex.

Alex smiled, as she took the cup and placed it in the car.

"Will you be alright?"

Alex heard the anxiousness in her mother's voice. She gently embraced her mother and held her close. "I'm going to be fine, I promise." She determined her parents were having their own unspoken contest to see who could squeeze her tighter. She thought her mom just edged out her dad for the win. "I'll call every night."

Her mother had tears running down her face as she stepped back, standing next to her husband. She grabbed his hand tightly. "Please be safe."

"I will," Alex promised. Again, she gave each of her parents a quick kiss on their cheeks. "I'll see you soon." Alex got in her car. As she drove off, she waved goodbye.

Before she could leave Hopkinton, she had to make one more stop. Pulling her car under a big oak, she got out and walked the short walk to Nate's headstone. Wearing light blue jean shorts and a gray tank, she squatted in front of the familiar stone.

"Hey Bud. I apologize for not visiting you for a few weeks," Alex said into the air of another humid, summer day. "I'm taking a trip—a road trip across the country." Shuffling on her sneakers, she looked around the peaceful cemetery. "I'm not sure what I'll find, but hopefully I'll find something." Alex watched another car drive by hers and disappear around the corner. "I'll be back soon, Bud. I'll be back." After her proclamation, she stood and kissed the tips of her two fingers, placing them on Nate's granite portrait. "I love you."

Soon, she found herself driving west on I-90, heading toward the Berkshires. Once she got past Worcester and Springfield, the traffic dispersed, leaving Alex to breathe a little easier. The Berkshires was the home of Norman Rockwell, who famously captured the quaint, New England life portrayed in his art and paintings. Rockwell's art made many, many people want to live in Stockbridge and live that perfect life, where holidays were always perfect, children were always bundled up, gleefully sledding in the angel-white snow, and everybody always had gigantic smiles on their faces. Was life so good and perfect during Rockwell's prolific lifetime? Alex was skeptical, but it was refreshing to think about. Alex realized life isn't perfect; she knew this firsthand.

Turning off on the Stockbridge exit, she wanted to take a short break from driving, stretch her legs, and maybe get a snack. Stockbridge seemed like an inviting place to stop, even if was to grab some snacks. She had to drive a few extra miles to get to the center of town. At the first convenience store Alex spotted, she turned in and parked. As she imagined, the store was a traditional, three-story gabled building; it had been restored during the last twenty years. Its color was light mustard, trimmed out in colonial white. Everything was colonial in this town, down to its blades of grass needling their way through the brick laid sidewalks. Alex stepped up onto the sidewalk and made her way into the convenience store. Entering, her eyes easily adjusted the artificial lighting inside. Alex looked around the rustic wood-clad interior to get her bearings. She started walking up and down the narrow aisles, picking stuff to munch on while she was on this first leg of her road tip. She cradled some Chips Ahoy cookies and black Twizzler licorice as she headed for the refrigerated section toward the rear of the store. So many options to choose from, as she sauntered back and forth, searching out what she really wanted to drink. Her indecision was starting to get to her own self. Alex finally settled on three 16-ounce bottles of Nestea iced tea. With her arms, she carried her goods like a newborn baby to the cashier, setting everything down gently. Alex looked upon the cashier. The image of him caused Alex to lose her composure; the young man, although younger, resembled Nate. It took all her strength not to reach across the counter and pull him to her and not let him go. Alex couldn't help but to lock her eyes on him, but she was aware if she stared for longer than she should, it would probably unnerve him. Swiftly, she brought her eyes down and scratched the divot above her lip. She noticed he had a nametag pinned to his maroon, collared, short-sleeve shirt. His name was Rob. Alex felt the need to speak.

"Rob is a nice name," Alex spoke, wanting to hear his voice.

"Thank you, ma'am."

It was the very first time someone had called her 'ma'am'. She didn't know quite how to react. Suddenly, Alex recalled the soft tone of his words instead the content. It was eerily similar to what she could remember of Nate's voice. She wanted to hear it again. "I bet this town gets busy around Christmastime."

"It usually does, ma'am," Rob answered while ringing up the last of her items. "You should come back at Christmas. I think you'd enjoy it."

Alex hesitated for a moment, waiting for him to end another sentence with 'ma'am'. He did not. "That sounds wonderful, Rob." She handed him a twenty-dollar bill and watched him make change. Alex caught another long glance at him when he was doing his job.

"Here you go, ma'am," he said, handing back her change.

When their fingers touched, Alex felt an indescribable sensation she had never felt before. The sensation was of great peace and love. Alex had no words—all she could do was to stare into Rob's light blue eyes, Nate's eyes. With change in her hands, Alex picked up her bag of snacks. "Thank you, Rob." She exited the store. She jumped in her Toyota and took a deep breath, but oddly enough she wasn't upset; she kept on feeling the peace and the love. Alex was ready to continue her journey.

Driving about four more hours, Alex found herself in Quakertown, Pennsylvania, her first nighttime destination, headed to a campground. Alex stopped at a local market and picked up food to cook for dinner. Alex's car engine was running sluggish—not the way she wanted to finish her first day of the road trip. She was about two miles away from the campground. The engine gauge told Alex to pull over to give the engine a drink of water. It was pitch black on this winding road; the last thing she wanted to do was pull over, but she had no choice.

Alex's mind started playing games with her fears, as she waited for the engine to cool. She left the headlights on for comfort, for as little comfort as she could muster up. Flashes of scenes from horror movies made her heart race. Feeling around on the backseat, Alex found the flashlight. She psyched herself up to grab the water, open the hood, remove the cap, dump the water in, and then do everything in reverse in record time. Alex grabbed the flashlight and the water, and she opened the car door. She lifted the hood and looked for the cap on the radiator. Pouring the water in as fast as she could, Alex continued to look around in the darkness that surrounded her. *I'm crazy to be out here in the middle of nowhere by myself.* With the water gone, she twisted the cap back on and dropped the hood. She jumped into the driver's seat while closing the door. Breath exhaled from Alex's tense lungs. "I did it."

She attempted started the engine, eager to continue on to the campground. Alex's body froze when she saw a figure walking into the car headlights. She locked the doors. Fear paralyzed her; all she could do was to keep her gaze on the figure. It was definitely human—no alien strange stature. The human was a man; she couldn't scream because her lungs were hardened. He didn't appear frightening, instead oddly tranquil. She was still scared out of her wits. Alex realized the engine had stalled. Her palms started to sweat, not to mention every other part of her body. On total adrenaline, Alex turned the key, but nothing happened.

The stranger stood in front of the car. *Do I dare get out?* Before she knew it, he stood beside the car.

"It looks like you are having some engine trouble," he said through the glass.

Alex stared at him, not knowing how to answer. She could lie and tell him the car is fine. She could let him help her before he hacks her up into small pieces. "I think it needs a little time to rest; it should be okay."

"I'll take a look under the hood if you'd like," he said politely.

What could it hurt? I'll stay locked in the car, and he'll look at the engine, trying to rationalize the situation. *He could also kill my engine.* Inasmuch as Alex could see of his face, it looked kind. "Okay." She never took her eyes off him. He opened the hood. A few seconds later, he asked Alex to turn the key. The engine started.

He closed the hood. "It should be okay."

She rolled down her window just enough so her voice wouldn't be muffled. "Thank you so much," she said sincerely. "Is there anything I can do for you?" She reached into her pocket for some money, extending a ten-dollar bill through the window.

"Oh no, I can't take your money."

At that moment, words came out of Alex mouth before she could reel them back. "Can I give you a ride somewhere? Where did you come from anyway?"

The stranger stepped closer to her car. "I'm staying at a campground up the road. I just wanted to take a walk."

"What campground?" she asked with the intent of seeing if he was straightforward.

"Tohickon Creek Campground."

It was the same campground she was going to. Alex was about to break the biggest cardinal rule of any lone traveler—she was about to offer a stranger a ride. "Let me give you a ride back. It's the least I can do for your help."

The man stood there in quiet thought. "I'll walk back, but thank you for the offer."

"Okay," Alex said with hesitation, leaving the door open for him to change his mind. "Are you sure?"

"I'm sure," he said.

Putting the car in drive, Alex pulled away, leaving her stranger in the darkness. Guilt filled her soul leaving him behind. She didn't even ask him his name. Alex felt worse than dirt—she felt like the sludge that came out of the car when the oil was changed. She continued to berate herself until she arrived at the campground.

Fighting her tiredness, Alex fought to hammer in the last tent stake into the ground. There were people scattered everywhere on the reservation, all of them more adept at erecting a tent—20 minutes faster than she could. Hunger began to drive her efforts to start a fire. Food was in her cooler. Alex didn't have a lighter because she didn't smoke. She couldn't find the matches in her car. Scared that the million pairs of eyes that surrounded her were watching, Alex slowly raised her head to have a peek. If people were staring, it wasn't apparent.

In the lantern light, she began to rub two sticks together. If cavemen could start a fire with two random sticks, Alex figured she could. But it wasn't working; even when exerting enough energy to electrify a small town, she couldn't start her own flame. Alex truly believed she was going to starve. Not the kind of person who liked to give up easily, she continued to create great friction between the sticks, but still no flame. The muscles in her arms were exhausted; she had to devise a new plan. The easiest thing to do was to go see if any of her fellow campers had a match. When Alex returned with a matchbook, he was hovering over her pile of wood and sticks. It was the same man who helped her with her car. The sight of Him stunned her, as she temporarily forgot how to breathe. For what seemed like an eternity, Alex stood in her silence, in what felt like a divine universe of her own, as she watched this man wave His hands over her firewood. In an instant, there was a blazing fire. Alex's mind tried to make sense of it all but couldn't quite wrap her scientific brain around what she was seeing. She told herself to walk closer, to investigate. Her legs obeyed.

The same peace that she felt earlier in the day engulfed her once again. Fear was light-years away. As she kneeled, Alex noticed His hands. She reached out in amazement as she took His hands in hers. Alex could see the fire through the jagged holes of His hands. Suddenly she looked at His face, which Alex hadn't seen clearly before now.

"Are you…?" She had trouble finishing her question.

"Do you want me to be?" He asked, looking straight into her eyes.

Alex didn't know how to answer His question. She looked around trying to figure out whether she was still where she thought she was. "Am I dead?"

The Man chuckled. "No, you're not dead."

She continued to look around to see if there were any people in the woods holding video cameras, taping the next episode of *Punk'd*.

Looking Him up and down like a newly discovered entity, Alex studied Him closely. She still had His hands in hers. Alex's eyes glanced to His feet; similar wounds were in each foot. She found His face again. "How can this be?"

"Do you believe in Me?"

"I would be crazy not to as I seem to be staring into the face of Jesus Christ." Again, she looked all around. "How come other people don't notice You?"

"I choose the people who I allow to see me," He answered with conviction. "All they see is a regular old Joe, helping you start a fire."

"Why me?" She had a sinking feeling that she had disappointed Him at some time in her life.

"It's my experience—and I have a lot of experience," He paused to smile, "that people who take road trips by themselves are looking to find something missing from their lives, or to discover something." Embers floated into the night. "What are you in search for?"

Alex didn't know the answer to that question, not at that moment anyway. "It's too soon to tell," she said quietly. Tears started to flow down Alex's face, as she wiped them away.

"What do those tears signify?"

"What don't they signify might be the better question," she answered quickly with laughter through tears.

He looked at Alex with compassion. He gently put the back of His hand to her cheek. "Let's cook up some food; your stomach's growling."

After Alex ate, she said *goodnight* to her unexpected guest and retired to her tent. She still had many more questions, although she was exhausted and needed sleep. With the fact that Jesus Christ was just outside her tent, Alex slept easily and deeply. No dreams surfaced in her unconscious. When Alex finally awoke, He was nowhere in sight, and her heart saddened. Alex grabbed a change of clothes and walked to the communal bathrooms and showers. Upon returning to her tent, He was sitting around a smoldering fire.

"You're back," Alex said in an obvious fashion.

"I'm never too far away."

That was the obvious answer, she thought. He pointed at a cup of tea for Alex on a nearby rock. She looked at His hands; His wounds were barely noticeable in daylight. She sipped the tea, kneeling beside Him. "Are you going to join me on this road trip, wherever it takes me?"

"Would you like Me to come along?"

She chuckled, looking at the ground. "I would be kind of crazy if I turned down Jesus to accompany me."

"I don't know," He replied, "people have done crazier things," reciprocating her smile.

Putting her cup of tea on a rock, she began to pack things up in the Camry. The tent came down in no time flat; Alex presumed she would be able to erect it in ten minutes by the week's end. In all of Alex's activity, her eyes continued to go to Him, as she tried to confirm if what she was seeing and feeling was real. His appearance looked familiar but not as stereotypical as all the pictures throughout time made Him out to be. He looked like a modern man that anyone would run across. He looked like a biker dude without the bike, wearing very-worn jeans and a navy blue hooded sweatshirt over a beige t-shirt. On His feet, He wore ratty, old, Kelly-green Converse sneakers. His black hair was in a short ponytail; He had a day-old beard. Alex offered Him a bottle of water.

"Oh, no need—I'm fine."

"That's right, you're not really there," she said with a spot of sarcasm.

"I am really here!" He said, standing up quickly. "I choose the people who I want to see me, and I chose you." Without speaking another word, He got in her car.

Oh great, I pissed off Jesus. Alex followed suit and got into her car. She started the engine and began the second day on the road.

The morning was clammy and gray. Alex looked at her mangled road map to determine what direction she wanted to head in. Alex noticed He was staring at her, sitting sideways in the seat.

"What?" she asked nicely.

"Why don't you use your GPS?"

She looked at him, confused. "How do you know about a GPS?"

He smirked. "You're acting like I just stepped out of 33 A.D. I am as modern as you are—I get to see everything."

"Well, that's a little scary," Alex replied. "What address should I enter into my GPS?" She watched Him take the GPS and enter in an address like an old pro. "Where are we going?"

"Laurel Caverns in Farmington."

She thought that location was out of the blue, but she went along with it. "Okay. I've never explored caves before."

"I am aware. I thought you'd enjoy it."

Alex grinned.

At the entrance to the campground, the female, synthetic voice on the GPS told her to take a right. Alex obeyed. For the first few minutes, there was no dialogue with her co-pilot. She glanced toward Him several times, quickly, to try to comprehend His presence. She wanted to reach out her hand to touch Him again, but she didn't dare. Alex didn't want to show her disbelief once again. Something told Alex He was reading her mind—He did say He knew everything.

She broke the silence beyond the rumble of the car engine. "What do you want me to call You?"

"Uh?"

"Names," she replied. "Would you prefer I call you Jesus, Christ, J.C., Dude…?"

He smirked. "Jay is fine." He adjusted Himself in the seat. "What should I call you?"

"For somebody who claims to know everything, do I need to tell you?"

Sighing, He turned to her, "For somebody who has Jesus as her co-pilot, you are very brash."

Alex cocked her head away from Him while she kept her attention on the road. "It's just my nature." She breathed out. "Just trying to scope You out."

"That's fine, Alex."

She smiled. "So, you do know my name."

"I've known your name for hundreds of years," Jay said with confidence.

His statement took her by surprise, as Alex glanced His way. She had more questions than answers. "Can you predict the future?"

"No, neither God nor I can predict anybody's future," Jay said formidably. "Although We might be able to influence souls that might be a little lost."

"Am I one of your 'lost souls'?" She didn't take her eyes off the road.

"I have encountered more aimless souls than you in My journeys," He replied.

Oh great. I have Jesus Christ as my shrink.

"I heard that."

She looked at Him with frustration. "Is anything that comes into my head sacred?!"

"Nope, not on this trip."

Alex sighed a long sigh. "What if I turned around and said, 'to hell with this trip'?"

"Do you believe in hell?"

His question derailed her immediate thought of going home. "Hell is for murderers and rapists—child beaters, pedophiles, and big-time thieves!"

"Please—don't let Me stop you."

"What?" she asked, glancing over at Him. "You don't agree?"

"Oh yes, I agree, but hell is not this fiery, hot place where bad people go for all eternity." Gathering His thoughts, Jay continued. "Hell is more of a black hole effect. If somebody lives a life of darkness and betrayal, he would really see the bad choices in life, in death. If somebody lives a life in the light of God, he or she will experience the love of Heaven."

"It sounds like a cold place, Hell."

"It's a very cold place."

"Am I bound for Heaven?"

Jay laughed. "Such a question, such a question."

"I thought it was a legitimate question!"

He continued to laugh. "Do you really think at age 26, you are going to turn bad all of a sudden?"

"Well, no."

As Alex and her co-pilot rode along, the conversation ceased for a few minutes. She was alone in her thoughts, or at least she perceived to be. She knew Jay was radioing in on her every thought and in on her every emotion. She tried to void her mind of everything and concentrate on the journey, wherever it took her. The only problem was that Alex didn't know where she was going; the original route she had planned was not hers anymore. She had turned it over to this Man that no other mortal could see. Was He sitting beside her, or was He a figment of her fragile state? One thing for sure was that she felt definably safer with her co-pilot. She didn't know if that was a sure sign she was going nuts or if she was experiencing something that few ever had. When Alex looked over at Him, He was as real as she was.

Tower of Voices

After driving three hours on the highway, Alex needed food, gas, and a restroom. She pulled off at an appropriate exit that had all three. As she didn't want to be rude, Alex asked Jay if He wanted anything. He didn't, as she expected. The afternoon was hot and humid in State College, Pennsylvania, not unusual for a mid-July day. When she returned from the 7-Eleven convenience store, Jay was reconfiguring their route on the GPS.

"What's ya doing?" she asked, with a half-eaten Devil Dog in her hand.

"We are taking a slight detour."

"To where?" Chocolaty crumbs fell on the ground.

"Shanksville."

Alex looked at Jay, trying to keep her jaw from falling. "Why are we going there?"

"Call it therapy," He replied with a grin. "Must respect your doctor."

With that, she ate another Devil Dog and got back into her car.

Alex didn't say too much to Jay as They headed toward Shanksville. She was nervous about going there and seeing the site where 40 people lost their lives, as they attempted to regain control of their airplane. Her spine tingled, reliving that horrific day. She had just begun her junior year in high school. By ten o'clock on that Tuesday morning, everyone was back home, consumed by their televisions while the United States was being brutally disfigured. Nobody could make sense of it, only the terrorists who sacrificed their own pathetic, inconsequential lives. *How much hate does someone have to commit such a horrible act?*

With each mile that ticked away, Alex's apprehension grew like a rising tidal wave. The voice on the GPS began giving an increasing number of directions—she knew the destination was getting closer. "If you know where this place is, why aren't you giving me directions?" she asked abruptly.

Always the cool one, never upset by her occasional grumbles, He didn't flicker. "I guess I could. Would you like me to?"

"Yes, please. The voice on the GPS is getting on my last nerve," she said with a little more calmness to her voice. She listened as Jay told her where to drive. He did have a soothing voice—the most soothing voice she had ever heard. Within ten minutes, They were on the outskirts of an expanse open field. Alex parked in the second of three Flight 93 National Memorial parking lots.

"Grab your water."

The sun was as hot as the day was long. They started walking down the tree-covered path which led to the main memorial that displayed all the crew and passengers of Flight 93. Prior to entering the memorial, there were several informational displays that told the facts on what happened on that horrendous day. Alex traced her right index finger over the flight path, and instantly looked upward to the cloud-filled sky, frighteningly imagining this airplane descending into the sacred ground very close by. Her body quivered.

She took a mouthful of water to quench her thirst. They walked under the small linear concrete bridge, entering the area that exhibited the mammoth slabs of white marble with gray veining, positioned in a zigzag pattern, all connected. Sometimes wreaths or small flower bouquets sat along the bottom of each stone. Each marble slab was devotedly engraved with the name of a crew member or passenger who became an American hero on that very cruel day. Alex fought the urge to touch the marble. She wasn't a family member or friend of any of these brave souls. She had no right to touch any of these massive stones.

"These are all your brothers and sisters. Even though you didn't know any of these people, they're still your brothers and sisters."

Standing in front of the zigzagged marble, with her hands on her hips, all Alex could do was look to her left, and then to her right, taking in every one of the names. The names of those who were alive one moment, and gone the next. This fact angered Alex deeply. These deaths could be avoided if hate wasn't in the picture. She walked back, standing at the wedge-shaped wall, which overlooked the large boulder placed about two hundred yards out in the field at the crash site. A hand touched her shoulder. "How could God let this happen, Jay?"

He looked at her with mournful eyes. "It was God's will."

"God's will?" Alex said, turning to Him. "It was God's will to allow ten extremists to kill 3,000 Americans that day? I don't believe that for a second, Jay!" she said forcibly.

"Did God create man?"

"Of course, He did. He created You."

Jay squatted to His heels. "That's right, and how did I die, Alex?"

"You died on the cross."

"I died on the cross—I was killed on the cross by My enemies, by the people who were afraid of Me, who were jealous of Me," Jay said with conviction. "I don't think God was happy I died in the way I did. I was His son!"

"Why didn't these people rise up from the dead like you did?" she demanded.

"They did! They are in the paradise of Heaven!" He exclaimed, lifting His hands toward the sky. "They are with God."

"Did they want to die this horrible death and have their lives cut short because of these fucked-up terrorists?" Alex asked angrily. "Did they have a choice?!"

"Did I have a choice, Alex?!" Jay said, agitated. "Did I wish to be so brutally killed on the cross?"

She looked at him mournfully. "Why do people hate, Jay?" Alex asked, now in tears. "It doesn't make any sense."

"Human beings all develop into their own creatures. We are influenced by our environments, our families and friends, our upbringing, our beliefs, and on and on. Just like everyone has their own fingerprint, each one of us is so undeniably different," Jay explained.

Alex listened intently. "I get that. But what about the hate? Why do people hate so much?"

"People are frightened by others who don't look like themselves, or think different ideas, or have different values, different circumstances, and that is what people fear—they fear the unknown."

"You were killed because people feared you."

Jay looked at Alex, as a tear slipped down His cheek. "People didn't know any better."

"Extremists fear us—kill us." Alex looked out to the massive boulder. "What was the reward? They killed themselves in the process."

"These people believed they would be rewarded in the afterlife."

"Were they right?"

"Nope."

They drove down a short way where the Tower of Voices stood grand in another open space. At 93 feet tall, the concrete open cylinder had vertical grooves punctured all over its surface to allow the wind to move the chimes. Alex stood near Jay in the center of the tower and looked upward toward the untouchable sky, blocking the strong southwesterly sun with her hand. She had to squint to gaze up toward the 40 different-sized polished aluminum chimes that spoke for all the lost voices that would never speak again. A strong wind swept up the valley, initiating the internal strikers to sound the chimes, resonating haunting but beautiful sounds.

"They are talking," remarked Jay.

Alex brought her head downward to look at Him. "What are they saying?"

He looked upward to better understand all the voices. "They are all talking, sounding happy like a big family; I can hear the love they have for each other." He smiled.

"You can't hear conversations?" she asked, intrigued.

"No, not really."

Alex didn't inquire why and continued to wander around the center of the tower and listened to the chimes. Aware of what happened on the flight, Alex thought about all the cellphone conversations that took place before the presumed end came; her heart wrenched out of her chest imagining what it felt like saying goodbye to loved ones when you couldn't change what was about to happen. The crew and passengers had a plan but there were no guarantees they would succeed. They had resolve in whatever consequences their heroic actions resulted in; their efforts might save several lives other than their own. They didn't think of themselves as heroic; they had a task in their sights, and it had to be dealt with. "Hate," Alex whispered angrily.

They stopped at a diner before figuring out the next destination. The diner, Kings Family Restaurant in Somerset, was a family eatery, average to American life. Alex entered and found the restaurant fairly empty. A young girl with long, straight, blond hair and light blue eyes greeted Alex with a wide smile. The girl asked Alex if she would like to sit at the heightened counter or in a booth. Alex chose a booth in the far-right corner, sitting facing the entire space. The walls of the restaurant were bright yellow, which contrasted with the booths, tables, and counters, all Mahogany. Having total view of the restaurant, Alex searched out Jay, but He wasn't visible. She sensed He was close by.

The young girl returned to take Alex's drink order. She only wanted water with ice; Alex was parched from the day's events. It felt good to be in air conditioning. Alex's waitress returned with the water, condiments, and a four-leafed, folded, plasticized menu. Alex made a point to take note of the waitress' name.

"Thank you, Hope," Alex said with elation. "That's a very pretty name."

"Why, thank you," replied Hope, with a light and friendly voice. "And your name?"

She took a quick sip of water. "My name is Alex."

Hope smiled at her patron. "Are you from around here?"

"Actually, I'm from the Boston area," she explained before getting entangled in her next words. "I'm sort of seeing the sights."

The city of 'Boston' lit up Hope's eyes. "I am going to be a freshman at Boston University in September!"

Alex displayed enthusiasm, relieved Hope didn't ask follow-up questions of which sights she had visited. "No way?! Alex said excitedly. "My Mom is the chief physio trainer at BU!"

"It is a small world!"

"It is! It is!" Alex took another quick sip of water. "Well, good for you, girl! What are you majoring in?"

"I'm going into the Pre-Med program, with a minor in music," Hope replied with total joyfulness.

Gasping, Alex looked at Hope in utter excitement. "Oh wow— you're going to be a doctor." Once she spoke the word 'doctor', tears pooled in her eyes. "Wow—a doctor."

Hope noticed her patron's tears, as she demonstrated her caring personality. "I see tears." Slowly, Hope sat on the other side of the booth.

Quickly, Alex tried to sweep away the tears about to break free. "Believe it or not, I am a doctor; an emergency room doctor." She lightly sniffled. "I see a lot of myself in you."

Hope smiled at Alex once again, but this smile was her own, not a generated smile put on for hungry patrons ready to fill their bellies. This was a genuine smile, shot up from her soul. "It's very nice to meet you, Dr. Alex."

"Thank you, Hope."

"You look hungry, Doctor. What can I get you to eat?" Instead of the giddy and perky teenager she portrayed herself to be, now she exhibited her adulthood so important for a physician.

"What would you recommend?"

Hope, sitting up straight, perused the menu she knew all too well. She closed the menu and halfway stood, as she leaned on the table. "Do you like chicken Caesar salad—my dad makes the best chicken Caesar salad."

Alex smiled, looking up at her, grateful for her kindness and amazed at her empathy. "I would like that very much, Hope."

"I'll be right back," Hope replied, still smiling.

Alex sat quietly, with her hands clasped in front of her. Taking account of her emotions, she dug down deep and recognized she really did hold onto her teenage dreams of becoming a doctor. There was still a thread, more like a vein, connected to her younger self—the younger self who believed she could do anything, believed that she could conquer all, and believed she could help Nate. This was where the thread became tight, as it was always about to break. Alex realized her limitations, even if she despised these shortfalls. She remembered wanting to save the world, as well as to save Nate.

"Here you go!" Hope set down a very large plate of fresh spinach, Bibb lettuce, cherry tomatoes, yellow peppers, mushrooms, shredded Radicchio, a host of various onions and tender grilled chicken strips, sprinkled with Romano cheese.

"Wow—this looks great, Hope," Alex announced, staring at the beautiful bounty.

"Can I get you anything before I leave you in peace to eat?"

"No, no, no—I'm all set. Thank you, Hope."

"If you need anything, I'll be around."

"Thank you," Alex happily replied. She began to eat the plentiful Caesar salad, finally aware of how hungry she found herself. Her tastebuds blossomed after each forkful she took. Soon, the Caesar salad, so abundant when it landed on the table, now was almost gone. Alex didn't need anything else to nourish her strengthening body; she was quite content, sitting quietly, looking out over the rather empty restaurant. There was an older woman sitting diagonally from her, two tables over. She was solitary at a table for two, appearing very forlorn and lost. Out of the corner of Alex's eye, she saw Jay walk over to the table to sit across from the gray-haired woman. Taking His hands, He placed them over hers, sitting so quietly, as if He was radiating His love and strength into the woman's soul. Alex realized she was observing a remarkable act that very few mortals would ever see. The rejuvenation of her soul wasn't suddenly apparent, but Alex concluded she would probably feel a lift in spirit by the following morning. At once, a man, dressed in all white, approached her.

"Hi," the energetic man said. "You must be Alex?!"

It was a quick change-up going from Jay to this bald, very fit man. Alex placed him around age 50. "I am Alex," she said enthusiastically. "You must be the dad cook!"

"Yes, I am. My name is Joe!" He extended his right hand. "Nice to meet you, Alex!"

Alex extended her hand to meet his handshake. "Nice to meet you too, Joe."

"Was your Caesar salad okay?"

"It was delicious, Joe!" Alex expressed with excitement. "I can't even make a good peanut butter and jelly sandwich for myself." Through the light laughter, she noticed Hope walking up beside him.

"You have met my future doctor here," Joe stated, as he proudly put his arm around his daughter's back. "She's so bright!" Joe was so animated in his physical mannerisms.

"As you can see, I'm his favorite child," Hope expressed with natural humor, as if she was born an amateur comedian. She sat on the edge of the seat opposite from Alex.

Bending slightly, Joe neared Hope. "You're my only child." He laughed, causing her to laugh.

Alex was enamored by their loving father-daughter relationship. "What kind of doctor would you like to become?"

"Oh my," Hope reacted, not really prepared to have a good answer. "I go back and forth between a neonatologist or a pediatrician."

"Wow, those are pretty hefty choices," remarked Alex with great admiration. "You like kids?"

"I love kids."

Joe sensed the conversation could go on and on. "Alex, it was a pleasure to meet you!" Once he saw her stand, he took a step back. "I hope we will see each other again sometime! All the best!" He grabbed Alex's right hand, squeezing it tightly. "Hope, don't talk her ear off. Alex has people to see and places to go." Joe swiftly strolled back into the kitchen.

Laughter filled Hope's core; she took her father's cue. "It was so nice to meet you today."

"I'm so glad I met you as well," Alex gleefully stated.

"Where are you headed?"

Caught on the back of her heels, she thought about her answer. "Actually, I just started this road trip across the country."

"Alone?!"

Alex didn't know how to answer this question either. "Yeah, by myself."

"That's wild, and crazy," Hope expressed with astonishment, and a little bit of envy crumpled up inside of it.

"Yeah, a little bit," Alex freely admitted. Before leaving, she asked Hope where the restrooms were located. When she returned to pay her bill, Hope was waiting for a goodie bag for the road. "What is this?" Kindness permeated her voice.

"Dad put together a bag of road-friendly snacks for you."

Quite overwhelmed by their generosity, a tear sneaked out from one of her eyes. "Oh my, you two are too nice." Alex snuck in a hug for Hope, embracing her tightly. That feeling that Alex felt after skimming the cashier, Robert's, hand the day prior, had returned—a feeling of peace radiated over her, like everything was so right in the world, so calm and so fair. Alex could not explain it.

"Have a safe trip, my friend," Hope said.

"Wait," Alex replied before she walked away. "I need to pay my tab."

"No, you don't," Hope announced, signifying she had given her so much more in the past hour and a half.

Quickly, Alex grabbed a folded twenty-dollar bill out of the back pocket of her jean shorts and handed it to Hope. "Please, take a tip."

Hope nudged Alex's hand away. "No."

"Hope, yes."

The way Alex looked at her sternly made Hope acquiesce; she took the tip.

"You have a cellphone?"

Hope reached behind her and pulled it forward.

"Let me put my number in it." Alex watched her key in her code and open her contacts. Alex input her number. "If you ever need anything, anything at all, just call."

"Really?!"

"Of course! Boston is far from Somerset, you know."

Unexpectedly, Hope gave Alex a last, warm embrace. "Drive safe."

"Thank you." With a final wave, Alex exited the restaurant. The Camry was baking in the hot, summer sun.

Jay was leaning on the driver's side door. "How was lunch?"

Chuckling, Alex winked at Him, as she unlocked the car.

Her thumb was keeping time with the beat of the music on the radio, having found a station that played classic '90s tunes. It was an activity that kept her alert while driving east on Interstate 76. Alex was becoming a little weary from traversing what seemed like the entire state of Pennsylvania throughout the day; loud music was what she needed. Soon, Joan Osborne's *One of Us* came on the radio, giving her a chuckle. The lyrics were ingenious and thought-provoking—indeed she was living out the song. It was getting to be evening and the heat from the day's sun was slowly dropping; she put down the car windows to get some kind of breeze through the car. It was just enough to liven her senses a bit. Alex looked over to Jay; He seemed sound asleep. *I guess Jesus sleeps.* Within a moment or two, He stirred, awoke, and gave Alex directions.

It was getting to be near dusk, as They neared Gettysburg. It was a long day of driving and emotion, and Alex just wanted to get to a campground to unwind. Jay had different plans. He began to give more directions to Alex. Not surprisingly, she resisted the idea of lengthening this leg of the road trip any longer. Jay persisted, and she abided by His wishes. Soon, They found Themselves on a solitary road surrounded by vast Civil War battlefields. They pulled over and exited the car. Alex took the opportunity to stretch muscles after being confined in the car for two and a half hours. Whether it was in daylight or darkness, the battlefields in Gettysburg emanated a surreal, haunting feeling. The hallowed ground always seemed like it wanted to talk—talk about the horrors that took place here just over a century and a half ago. The tortured silence went on for miles and miles.

Jay started walking up the road like He was on a mission. Alex followed. About 20 yards up, Jay turned and walked further inward toward the field. Again, she followed without questioning His motives— she was too tired to think. Suddenly, Jay stopped and squatted to His heels, as if He was searching for something out in the vast open field. Jay reached down to the dirt to pick some up in His palm. Within His palm, the dirt had turned into blood.

"Touch My shoulder," Jay requested.

"What?" Tiredness was in her bones.

"Put your hand on My shoulder," He whispered.

Alex obeyed and touched His shoulder, and in sheer amazement, she, without warning, was staring at a Civil War soldier, dressed in his State-issued blue, wool, shell jacket, his forage cap, his blanket roll, and his blue infantry trousers. On his feet, he wore leather Army boots. He held a rifled musket in his hands. On further investigation, he had a gaping wound in his chest, displaying what was left of his mortally injured body. Seeing this, Alex reached out and attempted to see if she could save him.

Reaching for her right hand, Jay grabbed it before she could touch him. "He's already dead, Alex. He died in 1863."

She was breathless at the vision. "Who is he?"

"What was your name, young soldier?" Jay asked in a strong voice.

Waiting for an answer, Alex was able to take her eyes off his mortal chest wound, and onto his boyish face. He didn't look older than 18 years old, with his short, blond hair and his icy blue eyes. Alex knelt on the ground next to Jay.

"My name was Private Millis Stone, Sir," the figure stated, looking straight forward. "I was in the 97th New York Infantry."

"Very good, Private. You are dismissed," Jay commanded.

Alex watched the young soldier salute, and then, vanish. "Where did he go?" she asked excitably, as she stood, looking all around. "Did he know he died?"

Jay followed her lead and stood. "He knew he died."

"Did You call him down from Heaven?" Alex was trying to make sense out of everything.

"Sometimes spirits descend from Heaven to check up on the living, or to places that held some meaning to them," explained Jay. "I intercepted Private Millis Stone."

Alex, through her weariness, had to mull over this concept for a moment or two, feeling the amazement of this affirmation she had just witnessed. "All of this is real, isn't it?"

"It is real," He confirmed.

With the breeze and the morning sun coming through her tent, Alex awoke just a little past seven o'clock. It wasn't too early to call her parents; she was supposed to call them the night before, but exhaustion caused her to sleep soundly again. It was good to hear their voices, and she could tell they were ecstatic to hear her voice. As she recited all the previous day's events, omitting the fact about travelling with Jesus and bearing witness to seeing a Union soldier on the lands of Gettysburg, Alex's voice was getting stronger, more joyful. What the rest of the journey held for her, she didn't know, but Alex wanted to continue. Alex didn't fear the unknown—she welcomed it and wanted to own it. Alex told her parents she loved them, always promising she would call when she got to her next destination, wherever that might be. Her next call was to Conrad and Justin, knowing that they would be eager to hear from Alex as well. She wasn't wrong.

Operating the zipper on her tent, Alex peeked her head out to get the lay of the land, which wasn't much different from the last campground: the same trees, same rock, and the same people. Alex stepped out, donning her cheap, neon pink flip-flops, and walked around her designated area. Searching for Jay, Alex saw Him, about 50 feet away, looking over a short rock cliff. She decided to go get cleaned up before setting off on the road again.

Alex returned to her area and found Jay tending to morning tea. When she had finished putting her laundry and toiletries away, Alex sat in her nylon camping chair. "Good morning."

"Good morning," He replied, handing her tea. "Sleep well?"

"I slept like a rock once again." She sipped on her tea. "It's gorgeous out here."

"It's gorgeous everywhere."

Alex found His eyes and understood His insinuation. "That it is." She sensed He had something on His mind. "What's ya thinking about?"

He paused, and then glanced at her. "When are you going to start talking about Nate?"

She instantly looked away from Him, not knowing how to respond. "I'm not ready."

"I think you are ready, Alex," Jay confidently expressed.

"And how do you know that?" Alex said angrily, walking off near the rock cliff. There was an incredible breeze moving through the small, narrow canyon before her. In the deepest crevasses of her soul, she knew He was right; she was ready.

Jay approached Alex gently. "What are you afraid of?"

Exasperated, more with herself than the questions, she exhaled a long breath. "I don't want to be angry at You and say something I can't take back."

Jay began to laugh uncontrollably, clapping His hands a few times. "That's really great!"

"What?!"

"Do you realize the millions of people around the world who take my name in vain because they're mad at me?" He asked rhetorically. "I hear the cries every day, Alex, every day."

She looked at Him to make sure He was serious. She saw it within His eyes that He was, but still resisted something that was uncomfortable. "Nate had a beautiful heart and a crazy good voice, you know." Tears came easily.

"I know."

"Crazy good," she repeated, as she stared out into air. "He could have made a name for himself." Alex sipped on her tea. "His mind betrayed him."

"The human brain is so powerful, full of mysteries for which modern medicine doesn't have a handle on yet."

"Yet?" Alex shot back. "Will we ever have a handle on all the workings of the human brain?"

"Well," He started, "You doctors have gotten this far. I am rather confident you will crack the code someday."

She looked at Him with slight disappointment. "That's a really piss-poor, crappy answer."

Jay suddenly grinned wildly. "That's good, that's good—I'm getting under your skin."

Having the urge to flip Him off, she resisted the action, figuring it wasn't an act she wanted to show off to Jesus Christ. Alex finished the last of her tea. "Where are we headed today?"

"Hawksbill Mountain. It's within Shenandoah National Park."

Driving through southern Pennsylvania, They crossed over into Maryland, West Virginia and then Virginia. Alex had been to New Hampshire, Vermont, and Maine; she had seen several mountain ranges, but these mountains, the Blue Ridge Mountains, were bold and expansive, as they looked like they went on forever. She imagined if a giant existed, two thousand feet tall, this giant would step on all the mountain peaks and make it to California within a half an hour. What would the giant do once he got to the California coast? She didn't quite know, although the giant probably would dive into the Pacific to swim into eternity.

Sperryville was a small town of 700 people. Driving through the center took a total of 15 seconds—it was small. They spotted a sandwich shop inside a shopping plaza. Alex was hungry; she parked and went into the shop. Jay remained in the car. As a natural observer, He spotted a man standing outside of the local market. The man, tall and dark-skinned, seemed to be waiting for a ride, as he was holding numerous bags of groceries. He constantly looked out to the parking lot, looking for a specific car which would bring him home. The car didn't come, and the refrigerated and frozen groceries were thawing fast in the warm shade. Jay noticed the man look worried.

Alex emerged from the sandwich shop and got into her car. She noticed Jay staring at something and looked toward His gaze. "What's going on?"

"This man needs a ride home," Jay explained, quickly pointing toward him.

Taking a bite of her chicken wrap, Alex observed, and concluded the same idea. Grabbing a napkin, she cleaned off her hands and got out of the car again. "Sir," she said, approaching the man. "Can I help you?"

The man, somewhat surprised at her offer among a slew of people walking by him time and time again, looked very kindly at her. "My wife was supposed to pick me up; our other car is in the shop."

"Can I drive you home? I don't want your groceries to go to waste."

The man looked down at his bags of groceries, realizing she had a point. "If you wouldn't mind. I only live three miles away," explained the man.

"Sure, sure," Alex remarked. "My car is right over here." She walked quickly back to her car, making room. Jay was already in the back seat. "May I ask your name?"

"My name is Greg," he answered with relief in his voice. "It's awful nice to do this…"

"Alex. My name is Alex. It's nice to meet you, Greg." She opened the passenger side door. "Please, get in."

"Thank you," Greg said with sincerity.

Walking back to the driver's side, she got in, moving her sandwich to her dashboard. "Greg, this is Jay. Jay, please meet Greg." Starting the engine, she witnessed Them shake hands, trading pleasantries. Alex put her car in reverse. "Okay Greg, point me in the right direction."

Raising his right hand, Greg pointed forward, to the far side exit of the parking lot. "You can get out over there."

"Thanks," she replied.

"This is so nice of you, Alex and Jay," Greg repeated his gratefulness. Riding through the parking lot, Greg felt and saw the eyes on Them. "Ignore the onlookers." Greg had gotten used people staring at him and his white wife. Given he was in a strange car with a different white woman, people would stare.

Looking around quickly, she didn't notice the 'onlookers' until she really looked and finally understood. "Really?" Alex rhetorically asked with ire in her gut.

"Really," Greg replied, signaling that this was his reality. "You can take a right."

Stopping at the intersection, Alex looked at Jay in the rearview mirror, witnessing tears in His eyes.

After a three-mile drive on a two-lane road, Greg told Alex she could take the next right. Once driving about 100 feet on this asphalt road, it suddenly became all dirt. The drive became windy and bumpy. They were driving through woods. Greg promised his house was not far up, on the left. A few minutes later, Alex drove up a similar dirt driveway and faced a small, ranch house that was a bit run down. Two young boys came running out of the gray house, followed by an attractive woman with dirty blond hair, chasing the boys, to make sure they stayed in the sparse grass-laden front yard. Alex hoped the boys had more grass in the backyard. Greg got out of the car quickly to act like a magnet to keep the young boys near him.

"Hey, Little G," Greg said excitedly, "Take a bag into the house for me." Greg gave the taller boy a paper bag of groceries and touched him lovingly on his shaved head.

Both Alex and Jay emerged from the left side of the car.

"Julia, this is Alex and Jay," Greg announced to his wife as she held the front screen door for Little G. He grabbed onto the littlest boy and lifted him. "Are you calm now, are you calm?" Greg kissed the boy, as the boy started to scream and push away from his loving father. "Okay, okay, Kyle, I'll put you down, but I have to hold your hand."

"Oh, thank you so much for driving Greg home," Julia said gratefully, walking toward Greg and grabbing bags of groceries from him. "Please, please, come on in. I'll make you both something to eat."

"Come in," Greg reiterated, still holding onto Kyle's hand.

Alex and Jay followed the young family inside. Under her breath, Alex asked Jay what He was going to eat. Jay chuckled. Inside, the small space was cluttered with toys and laundry, either going into wash or coming in from the clothesline. Alex watched Julia try to pick up as fast as she could. "Oh, please, please relax," she told Julia.

Sweat started to trickle down Julia's forehead after trying to get back to the kitchen to tend to her company. "Alex and Jay, what can I get you to eat?"

"I just ate, thank you, Julia," Jay kindly said.

Alex stared annoyedly at Jay. "I'm good, but I would love to have a glass of water." Her stomach looked forward to chowing down on her chicken wrap baking on the dashboard.

Julia poured cold water from the refrigerator into a glass. "Please, sit."

Both Alex and Jay sat down at the small, walnut veneer, wall kitchen table. With her thirst secretly out of control, Alex sipped a long stream of water into her gullet.

"Hon, Alex here is a doctor up in Boston," Greg divulged while he put away the groceries.

"What do you practice?" Julia inquired.

"I'm in emergency medicine," Alex answered. She watched Jay walk into the den where the two boys were playing. He sat on the floor.

"Don't let them drive you crazy, Jay, especially Kyle. He can get a little rambunctious at times," Greg announced with a watchful eye.

"I'm not afraid, Greg," Jay replied, sitting on the tan carpet. Jay was very aware of Kyle's condition. He observed the young boy stand next to the old, rust-orange sofa and stare off aimlessly at the ceiling, shifting his weight back and forth between both legs. Kyle held a plastic, red block in his right hand. "What do you want to do with that block, Kyle?" Jay gave Kyle a quick scratch on his back. "What do you want to do, Kiddo?"

Alex, along with Greg and Julia, looked onto the interactions between Jay and Kyle, curious to see what would transpire.

"He can't talk," said Little G easily, giving the facts to Jay.

"He can't?" Jay rhetorically asked Little G with a kind voice. "I believe Kyle is going to talk someday."

"Is it autism?" Alex asked for either parent to answer.

"Yeah. He was diagnosed when he was just about a year old," Greg explained. "We have Kyle enrolled in an intensive therapy program during the week, about two hours away."

After looking first at Greg, and then at Julia, Alex's eyes grew inquisitive. "You have to drive two hours each way to Kyle's day program?"

"Yes," answered Greg. "Luckily, I work in Richmond, where his program is, so it's not too bad. If he gets sick at the school, then Julia has to go pick him up because I can't leave work, so…" Greg stood against the door jamb between the kitchen and the den. "We can't afford anything closer than Richmond."

"Boy, that's tough," Alex commented and sighed. Soon, all of them were again looking into the den. Something amazing was happening there that made Julia stand to join her husband at the doorway. Alex stood to get a better view.

"Oh my God," Julia quietly cried out, as she watched her little Kyle begin stacking two blocks. Tears started to fall from her eyes. Julia noticed her autistic four-year-old making eye contact with Jay. "Look at him, Greg."

Emotional much like his wife, Greg grabbed her right hand, and then squatted on his heels. Greg was mesmerized, as Kyle just stared into Jay's eyes. He watched Kyle observing all of Jay's face, even reaching out to touch His scruffy cheek. "Kyle has never done this before, not even to us."

As Kyle felt Jay's scruffy face, he gently climbed into Jay's lap and sat quietly, as He held his small hand. Quite content, Kyle looked around for a few seconds, and then found his mother's tearful but happy eyes, and then his father's. Kyle just stared at his mother and father, like he had just discovered their eyes for the first time. It was then that Kyle stood and approached his parents kneeling in the doorway. With one look back at Jay confirming his intent, little Kyle reached his mother, staring right into her eyes.

"Oh my God," Julia repeated, hugging Kyle for the first time without Kyle screaming and fighting with all his might to get out of her arms. "Oh my God," she cried, as she held Kyle. She could have been happy holding Kyle for the rest of her life, but she knew she had to let him go to Greg. Without a struggle, without screaming, Julia lifted Kyle forward and into her husband's arms.

Greg reached and grabbed his son, as he sat down on the tan linoleum kitchen floor, clutching him to his chest. Tears streamed down his face. "How did you do this, Jay?" He had to see it for himself. With both hands, Greg held Kyle around his chest, holding him out so he could have a glimpse into his son's eyes. It was real—his son was looking back into his eyes. "Hi, Bud!"

"Why is everybody crying?" asked a little voice.

"Oh, come here, G," Julia said, reaching out to her eldest son. She wrapped her arms around his hips. "We're just happy because your brother is making eye contact with us and Jay." Julia looked for any indication that G comprehended this miraculous thing that just occurred. He needed to witness it for himself. Julia stood and asked G to follow her. Standing behind Greg, Julia squatted on G's side. "Look into your brother's eyes," she said quietly. G obeyed and stared into Kyle's eyes for what seemed like forever.

"I see it, Mama."

Julia grabbed onto G's arm so tenderly, as tears flowed freely.

"This might be the best day of our life, Jay," Greg happily admitted. "You're truly a godsend."

Jay humbly smiled, not speaking any words.

Somewhere in the background, Alex stood, having a front row to this magnificent event. Only she knew who Jay was. She had happy tears already soaked into her skin. Sometimes she had to remind herself that what she was witnessing was real; every undeniable second was absolutely real. *What a gift.*

"What do you say, Alex, are you ready to leave these good people in peace?" Jay asked, standing up from the floor.

Before she had a chance to respond, Greg interrupted. "Wait a minute—you don't have to leave just yet, do you?"

Alex looked at Jay and left Him to answer. "I don't know, Jay—do we?"

In a playful look, Jay smiled toward Alex. *Touché.*

It was an experience Alex had rarely known before, being in the company of strangers and being in a strange place for the night. It was just about three days since she had met Jay. In all circumstances she couldn't call Him a stranger anymore. She had already witnessed a few of His achievements with mortals They had crossed paths within the short time. The achievement with Kyle, bringing him out from his own little world, trapped inside himself, and then finally freed, awakened, and unleashed was truly amazing. As the night wore on, Kyle continued to emerge like a butterfly wrestling out from his cocoon, ready to flutter his wings, to show people his true colors. Alex was sure it was going to happen.

After the kids were in bed, Greg and Julia cooked their triumphant guests a hearty meal of chicken, baked potatoes, and green beans. Alex and Jay were very grateful for the bounty. This was one of those times Jay would halt His fasting and eat out of respect out of the situation. Jay offered to say Grace before the meal. Alex had to pinch herself just for the notion that she was in the presence of Jesus—it was simply mind-blowing. During Grace, holding the hand of Jesus, Alex, once again, felt that radiant peace engulf her like a warm blanket, as she listened to Jay's tranquil voice. His voice was like music—hitting the right note at every turn of the prayer; Alex realized she could listen to His voice until the end of time. The prayer concluded with a collective, "Amen." It was the first real homemade meal she had enjoyed in a few days. It felt good not to be eating in her car, or in her tent. She was grateful.

Early the next morning, Alex awakened to a small hand touching her face. It was Kyle, with his bright, new curiosity to the world. Admittedly, she was concerned with what a night's sleep would do for Kyle, apprehensive that Jay's work would fade away during sleep, but it did not. Alex sat up on the edge of the couch in the den, holding onto Kyle's hands while looking into his big, brown eyes. Wanting to speak, although not possessing those skills just yet, Kyle extended his left hand toward the kitchen and grunted. Alex was amazed with what this little boy was doing. She wanted to run to get one of his parents, but she didn't want to startle the boy. Rising to her feet, still holding onto Kyle's hands, Alex followed him into the kitchen. Focused on the beige refrigerator, Kyle touched it with it his free hand, and grunted once again. It was then that Greg appeared in the kitchen.

"There you are Little Man," Greg said in a caring voice, picking Kyle up in his arms. "I hope he wasn't bothering you too much."

Self-conscious of her disheveled appearance, Alex tried to tame her wild, morning hair. "Oh no," she answered. "I think he wanted something from the refrigerator, as he was making me follow him."

After these words ricocheted around his head for a few extra seconds, Greg's facial expression turned to wonder. "He did that?"

"Yes, he did," Alex affirmed. "I think he'll show you."

Like a child on Christmas morning, Greg instantly put Kyle back down on the floor and asked him to show him what he wanted. Greg watched his son walk to the refrigerator and grunt. He stood there in amazement until he heard a second grunt. "Wow."

Alex watched as Greg opened the refrigerator for the young son. "I guess this is a new thing for Kyle."

"Oh yes," Greg excitedly answered, as he witnessed Kyle point to the carton of orange juice. "Do you want orange juice—he wants orange juice!" Greg announced like he was announcing it to the entire world. Greg hurriedly filled Kyle's purple sippy cup and sat Kyle at the table, positioning himself across from Alex. "You're a doctor—have you seen anything like this before: an autistic child just turning around like this?" Greg never took his eyes off his son.

Alex sat at the table. "Autism and child development are not my specialties, but I know there have been cases where kids just emerged, if you will." In Kyle's case, Alex knew exactly what had improved Kyle's condition, although if she revealed Jay's true identity, Greg would probably throw Them out of the house, thinking They were freaks preying on vulnerable souls.

"Where is Jay anyway?" Greg inquired, as he got ready to cook Kyle some eggs.

Sitting up, looking up out of the front screen door, Alex tried to see if He was walking around the property. "He likes to go for walks early in the morning; He's an outdoorsy kind of guy." Alex easily noticed Greg, still amazed with his son, who was altogether content, drinking his orange juice.

"Can I ask you what your deal is with Jay? Are you a couple or something?"

Alex had to chuckle for a moment. "No, no," she spoke. "We are just friends embarking on a road trip across the country." Pausing, she debated whether to divulge more information. She decided she would. "I lost my younger brother a few months ago, so this is like a healing journey."

"Oh Alex, I'm so sorry."

Alex was relieved Greg didn't ask the cause of Nate's death. She wondered if she would be truthful or make up another cause to avoid the stigma.

Jay entered through the front screen door. "Good morning."

"It is a good morning, Jay," Greg said with unbridled happiness. He gently squeezed Kyle's arms. "Look at this boy, Jay—he's telling us what he wants and grunting. He never did that before."

Jay stepped closer to Kyle and squatted beside him. "How are you doing, Kyle?" Patiently, He waited for a response, which He knew would come. As a few seconds passed, Kyle looked toward the right, and he locked eyes with Jay. Out of the blue, the boy cooed at his new friend. "Listen to him talking!"

Delayed a day, for healing a child of his ailment was priceless, Alex and Jay got back on the road, headed toward a day of hiking on Hawksbill Mountain. The events of the past day still had a hold on Alex, like an awe-inspiring new medical procedure she might have witnessed with her very eyes, scrutinizing every part of it, understanding every step and every action from beginning to end. It wasn't so easy to scrutinize the feats of Jay. She continuously had to remind herself that the man sitting in the passenger's seat was Jesus. She knew that He could vanish anytime He wanted; He was, for some reason, with her, seeing her through this journey she was on. Was she worthy of His accompaniment? Alex did not know. She did not know when, where or how this journey would end. She felt a bit apprehensive. At this moment, she didn't want it to end. Everything seemed so up in the air; everything seemed so fluid, and so nonchalant. Alex was going to let things just happen.

A mountain was waiting. Hawksbill was that mountain. It was another warm, but cloudy day. Before They embarked, Alex slathered her arms, legs and all her exposed skin with sunblock. She brought water and snacks. It felt good to get outside after a day with Greg, Julia and the two boys—Alex needed to do something physical. They began their trek up Hawksbill. The forecast called for the possibility of rain and thunderstorms later that afternoon, keeping the trail rather uninhabited. It was peaceful having only the trees, dirt, rocks, birds, insects, and clouds above listen to her breathing, as Alex remained in step with Jay.

He didn't hike any faster than her pace, which was fairly quick. Over the last month or so, Alex had gotten her stamina up to close to where it once was before Nate's death, although climbing a mountain worked those hidden leg muscles that didn't show themselves walking on flat surfaces or on the occasional single-flight staircase. Alex soon recalled the long days working at the hospital, taking the stairs at least twenty times a day. That was when she was really in good physical shape, she thought, surmising that if she hiked similar mountains for the next seven days, she would be where she wanted to be, physically.

The sound of a waterfall made Jay pause, pointing it out to Alex. It was a small waterfall, about ten feet high, as the water torrented off the smooth rocks, pooling in a shallow, natural basin below. Alex took advantage of the pause, and water, as she cupped palmfuls of it, drenching her hair, face, and neck. The clouds did nothing to remove the humidity from the air, only serving to block some of the sun's strongest summer rays. Alex's fingers combed back her soaked, black hair, as she prepared to continue the trek up to the top.

An hour later, They reached the top of Hawksbill. The view was stunning, even with the clouds engulfing the Sapphire-blue mountain tops, sprinkled with green highlights. Out in the distance, a heavy cloud of gray set off lightning strikes in various slopes and valleys. Alex was mesmerized by the display of lightning crashes, something about the randomness of it—she had never witnessed anything like it before. They were too far away to hear the accompanying thunder. Then a thought— a realization—entered Alex's head. It probably would not have occurred to her if she hadn't witnessed this spectacle of nature.

"This is what it was like inside of Nate's brain, isn't it?" she asked, still struck by what she was seeing. "All these synapses firing off at once. He couldn't control them."

Jay saw a tear travel down her face. "No, he couldn't."

"And all the drugs Nate tried didn't do a fucking thing, did they?" Alex questioned angrily.

He remained silent so she could process her thoughts, and her anger.

Frustration gripped Alex around her chest, as if she had a leather belt restricting her respiration, pacing back and forth along the stone wall of the summit. Tears streamed down her face with each step. "I should have pushed his doctors to try something else."

"I have no doubt that you researched every drug, every therapy, every possibility you could find."

"I did, you know," she replied, as she finally sat on the stone ledge. Alex turned and stared out at the lightning show. "Lightning within his mind was making him suffer so much, and we could do nothing to help him." She hunched over, holding her head in her hands, sighing. "All I wanted to do was to make him better."

He sat down beside her on the ledge. "You know, you did help Nate. Not in the way that you expected to help him, but you helped him by sticking by him when he was having episodes. You slept on the floor beside his bed to kept him safe. You spent hundreds of hours just talking to him to get him through the bad times."

Raising her head, Alex gazed at Jay. "That wasn't enough," she spoke, turning her head away from Him. "Did You see his eyes, angry and full of rage, every time we had to admit him in the psych hospital? Did You hear Nate tell You he would hate You forever if You left him there? Those were the worst times of all."

Jay sighed, feeling Alex's sadness. "You know he wasn't in his right frame of mind when he said those things." The sky was beginning to darken, as the wind blew around Them. "An ill mind is often times irrational."

"Yeah, I know, but Nate's words still crushed my soul," Alex admitted softly. She looked up and saw the dark clouds, intimating and bold, getting closer. "I think we had better get going." She wiped the last tears away.

"Yes, we should go."

It started to mist when They began hiking down Hawksbill. When They got to the car, the sky opened up, soaking Them down to the skin. Alex looked over to Jay in the passenger seat, already as dry as lace fluttering in a dry, summer's breeze, while she was as wet as a common store receipt dropped in a street puddle. She couldn't help but to stare at Him for a moment or two just to realize once again she was in the presence of Jesus. Reaching out her hand, Alex touched His sweatshirt, and suddenly, her clothes were dry. The same feeling of peace and warmth flooded inside her entire body, providing Alex with some restoration, and some hope for the days to come. For the next hour, while the rains came down, while the winds blew, sometimes with ferocity and stamina, and while the skies thundered and flashed, Alex caught up on some sleep that had escaped her from the night before. Beside a sleeping Alex, Jay prayed, as He did every day. He reached out to all the souls who were asking for His assistance.

Reflection

They located Oak Ridge Campground, on the outskirts of Washington D.C., to catch some shuteye. Alex awoke early to catch the sunrise and to take advantage of the quietness of the morning just to walk in solitude. The sunrise, magnificent in its beauty, gave the clear sky horizontal paintbrush strokes of bright fire yellow and honey, on each side of the giant ball of light, announcing to everyone that a new day has arrived once again, right on time. Pink streaks of color gave the Heavenly sight some purpose and definition. Alex felt grateful that she had witnessed such a beautiful display of nature, remarking she did not witness sunrises nearly enough.

Alex pulled out her cellphone to check the time, and yet again, viewed the background picture of her and Nate. Bringing her attention back to the time, Alex suspected it wasn't too early to call her parents—she knew their routine. After several seconds of the phone ringing, her mom picked up. Alex was not prepared to feel pure joy once she heard her mother's voice, almost bringing her to tears. Joanne could hear it in her daughter's voice, panicked until she knew everything was okay. Alex informed her where she was, and what she did the previous day, minus the fact she still had a co-pilot named Jesus, convinced Joanne would demand she come home. She told her mom about her hike up Hawksbill Mountain and seeing the lightning show down below in the valleys, explaining her realization that the same thing had been happening inside of Nate's brain—the misfiring of all those synapses he couldn't control, that sent him down in the darkest episodes that controlled him. Noticing that her mom was becoming upset, Alex stopped talking about Nate's illness, and began talking about the good times. This discussion lifted both of their hearts and spirits up high. Joanne passed the phone to Alex's Dad so he could hear his daughter's voice. Their conversation was more about the facts of the trip: how was the car? Was she eating enough? Was she being safe? He was comforted that she was fine; he was happy to hear her voice. Before Nate's illness, Alex was always his little girl. He was struck by her strength and confidence even if he rarely expressed it. Now, things seemed to be different. In the chaos of caring for Nate, he kind of lost sight of his daughter. Now, her dad was recognizing Alex again. He deeply wanted the best for her. Alex heard it in his voice.

Like most dads, he gave the phone back to the mom. Alex didn't really ponder this typical habit—it just happened. They moved forward to talk about plans for their respective day, but unlike Joanne, Alex wasn't sure where the wind would take her. The call lasted for about another thirty minutes. Mother and daughter found it very easy to just enjoy a good chat even if it consisted of nothing important. It was a marked difference when Nate's illness consumed much of their conversations, never really knowing where his next episode would lead him. Alex was now getting to know her mother much more deeply than any other time in the past, and she felt her mom was getting to know her on a different level as well. To feel happy about this revelation brought the feeling of profound guilt to Alex. To her, feeling happy was to accept Nate's death without consequence. Then she remembered what Jay said to her on Hawksbill, about trying to solve Nate's illness when there were no answers. Alex was resolved to have these feelings for the rest of her life. The call ended with a promise to talk later, as they exchanged I love you's.

Alex returned to her campsite; Jay had just prepared her morning tea. It was beautifully cool at that time of morning, but the weather was expected to get hotter throughout the day. She sat quietly, contentedly reflecting on her conversation with her parents, feeling at peace, which had been elusive for longer than she had ever realized. The day was ahead; Alex asked Jay what He had planned. He wanted to see some of the National Capital sights. Would They be actual tourists, she wondered, but quickly reminded herself that Jay was set on continuing her therapy, as He referred to it. Alex would have liked to refer to it as her restoration, as she hoped.

They took a tourist shuttle into Arlington and stopped into a diner. Alex got her fill of eggs and home fries. About a mile away sat Arlington National Cemetery, where many of the nation's soldiers are buried. Alex had spent a few days in Washington D.C. on a class trip when she was in the eighth grade. Like on all school trips, teachers try to pack in so many activities in a span of 72 hours that everything becomes a blur. The eighth-grade trip was like that for Alex—one big blur. With no schedules to keep, without having anything set for days to come, Alex looked forward to taking in everything that she could.

The temperature had risen 30 degrees from early that morning, as now it was getting close to noon. Entering the gates that protected the hallowed grounds, Jay and Alex gazed upon the thousands of white marble headstones that ran in conjunction with the hills and scoops of the lush, green grass. Behind Alex's Ray Ban knockoff, black sunglasses, tears welled in her eyes.

"War. What is it good for?" she asked rhetorically.

Jay's physical appearance never changed from day to day, but he still had all the human characteristics and expressions any mortal human would have. "War is humanity's greatest fault—their greatest weakness," He said with despair. "Humans are equipped with rationale, and the ability to contemplate their actions and words. I am aware people are better at restraint, understanding and acceptance, but no one should ever take another life, for any reason."

"What if someone is coming after you? Can you defend your life?" she inquired, hanging on His every word.

As He walked next to Alex, He considered the situation. "No one should take a life, but I know every situation is different."

"Every situation is different," Alex retorted, "but we, as a nation, are obsessed with guns, if you didn't know that already."

"I am very well aware of that."

Alex continued to saunter in the blazing sun. She took a gulp of water from her water bottle. "I have done my share of rounds in the emergency room; GSWs are not nice. Bullets tend to ricochet all around the torso, tearing everything to shreds." Scratching her itchy right eyebrow, Alex drew a heavy sigh. "In med school, we had to look at photographs of wounds of victims after being shot with AR-15s; barely anything is recognizable."

"Guns serve no purpose," Jay relayed with ferocity.

"You'll get no argument here," she said. "When kids are shooting each other in schools, something really needs change. When politicians rely on the NRA for campaign funds, things really need to change." When she didn't hear a response, Alex looked toward Him, finding tears in His eyes. "I apologize."

"Oh, don't apologize for stating the truth," He reassured, and continued. "Truth is severely lacking these days, especially around here." Jay saw some shade. "Let's sit."

Following Jay's lead, Alex sat on the grass under an elm. "This is quite a place," expressed Alex, looking out over the marble headstones.

"It's a sad place," Jay softly specified, scanning outward. "Most of these men had their lives cut too short, in the most violent of ways, often not knowing life during true adulthood, and not realizing their ultimate potential."

"Many people believe these soldiers are heroes, sacrificing their lives for our freedoms, our liberties."

"I can't argue with that," He agreed, "I just have a difficult time with governments not practicing diplomacy, and so easily jumping into military engagement. Military engagement always results in death."

"I know you want to preserve life as much as possible, but are there exceptions? For example, the roundup of Jews by Hitler, where he exterminated six million just because he deemed them inferior. He also euthanized over 200,000 of his own people with disabilities because they didn't 'fit' within his 'perfect society'; would diplomacy have ever worked with his crazy thinking?" she exclaimed. "One philosopher, Bentham, I think, said do the greatest good for the greatest number."

"Look at you, being all scholarly," Jay said, smiling.

"Yeah, I can come with the goods on occasion," Alex chuckled back at Him. "I find war repulsive also, but sometimes it's a necessary tool to protect groups of people who might be in grave danger."

"That's what I'm talking about—people can rationalize all different circumstances; why do people kill?"

Alex sighed. "It was believed Hitler was mentally ill; I guess he had a tough upbringing."

"The workings of the brain can be staggering," Jay replied with sorrow. "Like fingerprints, everybody has a unique mind."

"Very true." Even though this was easy to understand, Alex had never related the idea of brains being like fingerprints, being so different than the next. The lightning storm on Hawksbill returned to her consciousness. Nate's brain was unique, like his fingerprint. Leaning on the trunk of the big elm, Alex began to play with some grass blades beside her, not plucking too many from the hallowed grounds. "Life is so random, you know. Once you are conceived, anything can happen, depending on everything that surrounds you, and what's in you. You could live to be 102 and be a very renowned scientist who finds a cure for some dreadful disease, or you can be born too early and not even survive to see a day full of sunshine. Randomness."

Lifting His head, Jay found her eyes and nodded. "Randomness, with a little help from above."

She soon agreed. "Yes."

"Okay, we sat here long enough." Jay got to his feet. "Let's go."

Alex followed suit and stood. "I'll follow you."

Several minutes of walking brought Them to the Tomb of the Unknown Soldier. It was the place where first-time visitors come to witness. It was a sacred American ritual that began in 1937, five years after the Tomb was completed. Alex and Jay followed the crowd to the viewing area: concrete tiers, behind solid, horizontal, metal railings. Everybody stood silently. Alex, remarking to herself, noted that this must be the quietest place on American soil where people gather to watch and remember. The only sounds heard were the footsteps, the clicking of the soles of the black leather shoes which the unranked Army guards wore. Also, there was the rattling of the workings of the M14 rifle. Every move of the honor guard soldier was meticulously performed, in any kind of weather, in full uniform.

Much like her fellow onlookers, Alex was transfixed on the soldier and his precision maneuvers, his unrelenting concentration to every movement, and his fixed gaze that never faltered. Respect filled her soul, as she attempted to surmise if she possessed that kind of discipline, that kind of concentration. Alex realized she had never been tested before; would she fail? She did not know.

Twenty minutes passed without any disruptions or outbursts from the crowd. Inscribed on the West panel of the marble Tomb read, *Here Rests in Honored Glory an American Soldier Known But to God.*

Far enough away from the area where the ritual continued, Alex relaxed her muscles. "I suppose you know who lies in that Tomb."

Jay looked downward, positioning His left ear near Alex. He lifted His eyes and met her gaze. "I know everything," Jay stated once again, smiling.

58

Admittedly, Alex didn't expect Jay to reveal any names, she only wanted to confirm He knew who rested in the Tomb.

They walked across Arlington Memorial Bridge, bringing Them to the Lincoln Memorial. The upper level of the Memorial, which held the colossal statue of Abraham Lincoln sitting in a circular, ceremonial chair, seemed like a cool place to take refuge in the shade from the hot, summer sun. Alex climbed the many steps to get relief. Jay followed and sat next to her. They didn't need to speak; all They had to do was look out and see the many monuments that recalled the profound history of the nation. Alex glanced behind her, really taking a long look at Lincoln, who was staring out toward the Washington Monument on the opposite side of the reflection pool, as if stating he stuck to his morals when half of the nation opposed him. She couldn't help but to consider the state of the nation now, just as much divided, and so raw with tension. At any time the dam might burst. When or where, Alex didn't know, but it was bound to break.

Jay reminded her that at the bottom of the very steps where They sat, Martin Luther King Jr. gave his historic *I Have a Dream* speech in 1963. Alex kindly told Him she was well aware of that speech. In grade school, she remembered the book report she did on Rosa Parks. She still possessed great admiration for the woman who wouldn't give up the seat in the front of a Montgomery city bus so that a white man could sit down. There needed to be more Rosa Parks in the world, Alex deduced.

Once their break was over, They descended the steps. Seeing the engraved stone where King stood to deliver his speech on that famed August day, she stopped and crouched down to touch his name with her fingertips. At thirteen, she didn't have the presence of mind to give such a response, but knowledge, experience and time had changed her, making her aware of the many struggles that people must endure. This knowledge created a better person, and a better physician—even if being a physician wasn't a high priority at that very moment. Her priority was to reconstruct herself, much like contractors reconstruct a building with a damaged foundation, cracked by a devastating blow.

Not far from the Lincoln Memorial perched the Vietnam Veterans Memorial, set into an embankment, in a wide V-shaped layout. Alex was the first to reach the western half of the memorial. Like everywhere else They had been earlier, there were several people in the vicinity. The path along The Wall was a middle strip of horizontal limestone pavers, flanked on both sides with natural light stone squares with soil between. Lights, about eight feet apart, shine up to the Heavens from the ground at night. Alex could only imagine how moving this place might be after sunset. Walking a little bit further down the path, she started to see names on the reflective surface of the black granite slabs. The black granite gradually rose from the Earth with each step, leading up to the apex. As the wall rose, the names of the dead filled the black, mirror-like surface from top to bottom. It had been days since she had seen her own reflection; Alex didn't recognize herself at first, but then realized it was indeed her image. It was the same image she looked at every time she turned on her cellphone. The only difference was that she didn't possess a smile, and her arm didn't wrap around Nate. Shifting to the right, Alex cloaked her nondescript expression against names of the dead. Jay was standing next to her, but she didn't see His reflection in the black polished granite, stirring up an unsettling feeling. Alex was still getting used to Jay turning Himself on and off like a lightbulb. All the names, over 58,000, were overwhelming at times. Alex gazed to her right and saw several visitors holding white pieces of paper, sometimes large, sometimes small, over chosen names, and rubbing the graphite of a common pencil, causing the name to be engraved on the paper. *How many times do they come and engrave their chosen names,* Alex silently wondered. She imagined thousands of rooms across the country, each with walls displaying one or more paper engravings taking from The Wall, remembering the dead. Some people probably had these engravings on ragged strips of paper to have them close to them—close to their hearts, for as long as they walked the Earth.

A light breeze came across the site of The Wall. Alex turned and saw a man sitting on the ground, on the grass, beyond the roped walkway. Observing him, it was clear that he had difficulty sitting, let alone standing. There was another man, kneeling beside the sitting man, seemingly trying to help him to his feet. Alex walked toward the two men and ducked under the rope. Whether compelled by a feeling that she could help, or by her Hippocratic oath, for which she never made a distinction, Alex began her assessment.

Crouching down, she needed to get closer. "Hi," Alex expressed in a friendly tone, "my name is Alex—I am a doctor. I've noticed you might be having some difficulties standing." The sufferer, being big and stocky, had a puffy face and gray, unkempt hair with a matching beard, was confused, unaware of his state. His eyes were bloodshot and weary, and his breath smelled sweet. The odor of urine, feces and general body odor permeated the immediate area.

"He's been here for a few minutes," the man on the opposite side spoke. "He comes here almost every day."

Alex listened carefully. "Do you know his name, Sir?"

"Oh, oh, please call me Henry," he kindly said. "This is Gene."

"Thank you, Henry," she said. "I'm just going to ask Gene some questions."

"Okay."

"Gene, do you know where you are?"

Holding his head off the ground, Gene looked aimlessly around, not speaking.

"Gene, do you know what year it is?" Alex pursued. She glanced into his vacant eyes and knew Gene needed medical intervention.

"Henry, what can you tell me about Gene?" she inquired. She guessed Henry was about 65 years old, with a slightly gaunt face and a thin stature. He wore worn khakis and a checkered short-sleeved shirt, and had short, blond hair.

"He's homeless."

Alex quickly looked up at Henry. "Did you say he's homeless?"

"Yes, Ma'am, he's homeless."

These words had to process longer than most. "You said Gene comes here almost every day?"

"Yes, Ma'am," Henry answered, rotating himself toward The Wall. "These are our brothers in arms. We never leave our brothers."

Alex speculated if Henry needed medical care as well. "You and Gene fought together in Vietnam?"

"Yes, Ma'am," confirmed Henry. "Gene was my C.O. At first, I was a spitfire, little shithead from Louisiana who didn't much like taking orders from a Negro, as they used to call them back then. But, one day he just put me in my place, and I didn't give him any more shit."

Alex had to come to terms with his use of the word, 'them', in his context.

"Back in 1990, I had just gotten a job as a Mall patrol officer and lo and behold, Gene was here one day, and we just started hanging out."

"Henry, I'm going to call 9-1-1 now; Gene is pretty sick, and he needs to go the hospital."

"He doesn't like hospitals!" Henry nearly shouted. "He has never gone. He says once people go into hospitals, they don't come out!"

Seeing the anxiety upon Henry's expression, Alex knew she had to be creative to put his mind at ease, as she waited on the phone. "What if I go with Gene to the hospital? Would you like to come with us?" Finally, an operator answered her call. Alex gave them the information and their location.

"I don't know." Henry stood and paced near his friend.

Alex knew she had to keep calm. "Henry, you helped me so much with Gene. I could still use your help."

Henry quickly kneeled. "What do you need?"

"Tell me more about Gene," Alex spoke swiftly to keep him engaged. "What was Gene doing when you ran into him back in 1990?" Quickly, Alex gazed out around the memorial to try to see Jay. She spotted Him about fifty feet away, comforting a visitor still grieving from a tremendous loss.

"Back then, he was homeless," Henry stated.

The surprising, heartbreaking answer brought her attention back to Henry. "You're saying Gene has been homeless all this time?"

"Yes, Ma'am." Henry touched Gene's hand gently in his. "When I had my apartment, I tried to get Gene to stay with me. A few times he stayed, but he didn't like to be confined."

"Henry, do you still have your apartment?" she asked, filled with apprehension.

"No. When I lost my job, I lost my apartment."

Alex sighed long and deep, frustrated with the system, frustrated with war, and frustrated at the lack of humanity and basic decency in the world. "Where do you usually stay?"

"I usually stay at the homeless center, especially if it's cold out."

What was frustration suddenly turned to sadness. Alex knew meeting these two Vietnam vets would remain in her memory for the rest of her life. Far in the distance, Alex could hear the approaching sirens. Time escaped her, as Alex was tending to the gentlemen. Soon, Alex spotted the first responders, one man and one woman, dressed in Navy uniforms and matching caps. Alex sprang up and waved down the two responders. It was easy to spot the small group on the adjacent lawn; they approached them. They easily lifted the school-bus-yellow stretcher with the black mat over the rope; they would have to find an alternate route with an occupied stretcher. Alex knew she had to be the communicator. "Hello," she extended her hand. "My name is Alex—I'm a physician." She turned to face Gene. "I found Gene lying here; he seems to be a diabetic—probably ketoacidosis. He has cognitive difficulties."

The woman paramedic spoke. "Do you know his full name?" She soon joined the other paramedic in assessing Gene's condition.

Alex pivoted toward Henry. "Henry, what is Gene's last name?"

"Dobbs. His name is Eugene Dobbs," Henry answered, visibly concerned about his friend.

"What's his address?" the female paramedic asked.

"Gene is homeless," Alex disclosed. "I just came across Gene and Henry while I was visiting The Wall." She swayed back and forth, as she watched the male paramedic start a line drip into Gene's left hand. Alex bent down so both paramedics could hear her. "Henry tells me Gene isn't fond of hospitals. I promised Henry I would stay with Gene, and I believe Henry needs medical attention also."

Collectively, both paramedics glanced up toward the clearly agitated Henry, as he paced in his small area next to Gene. They both agreed with her assessment. The paramedics prepared the stretcher to receive Gene. Soon, a few men who were visiting The Wall took heed and stepped in to help get Gene onto the awaiting stretcher. Gene moaned in pain, or maybe it was fear, as he was lifted.

"Don't hurt him!" Henry cried out.

Alex, Henry's newly designated caretaker, stepped in front of the distressed man, looking to engage his eyes. "Henry, Henry," she said calmly, "they are not hurting him. They are not going to hurt him, I promise." It was difficult to keep his attention. "We can go with Gene to the hospital. Do you want to go accompany Gene to the hospital?"

Henry continued to pace, as his eyes didn't leave the activities surrounding Gene. "Will you be there?"

"I will be there," Alex promised, looking directly into his eyes. In a surprising move, she felt his clammy hand, like a child would grab their mother's hand in an unknown situation. Walking with the paramedics, pulling and pushing the heavy stretcher over the plush green grass until they got to the walkway, Alex turned back to find Jay. After a few seconds of searching among the several people at the memorial, she locked eyes with Him, mouthing 'come with me'. Watching His lips, Alex saw Him reply, 'I'll be there soon'.

They reached the emergency entrance of the Washington DC VA Medical Center, a little north of the U.S. Capitol. The ride was brisk but controlled. Fully stopped, the rear doors of the ambulance seemed to open automatically until she saw the receiving medical staff dressed in the usual blue scrubs. Alex signaled to Henry with a light touch on his arm to allow the medical staff to take Gene out first. She thought she would exit the ambulance first to assist Henry down off the high step. It was very weird, almost foreign, to enter a hospital after five months. Haunting memories of that fateful night came rushing back to her skull like a train wreck. All the blood, every forceful chest compression she performed to attempt to save Nate's life nearly brought Alex to her knees, but she knew she couldn't crumble on the ground when she had Henry to look after. Somehow, from somewhere deep within her core, she kept herself breathing, which kept her moving forward until she discovered where Henry needed to go to be evaluated, still having the presence of mind to request that Henry stay near Gene, at least within earshot. A young nurse's assistant directed them to an empty exam bay, across from where Gene was being evaluated. The nurse's assistant asked Henry to undress. Alex used this opportunity to step out and asked the assistant where the restroom was located. The assistant pointed her in the proper direction.

Once Alex locked the door to the unisex bathroom, with royal blue tile on the floor, and gray subway tile on all four walls, she felt her stomach start heaving, without mercy, as she just made it over the white, wall-hung toilet, expelling everything she ate for breakfast. She felt those hidden stomach muscles violently contract only when humans vomit or cough deeply. They became sorer with every muscle contraction. When Alex felt like there was nothing more that needed to be expelled, she sat back on her heels and began to sob uncontrollably. It had been weeks since she had had such an emotional break—an unadulterated, full on wave of grief—she chocked it up to stepping foot into an emergency room, the frustration of the day, and the very disturbing memories surrounding Nate's death. One step forward, three steps back. Alex honestly thought she was getting a handle on this grief thing, finally, but brutally she found out that wasn't the case, cursing herself repeatedly that she had failed.

Alex, realizing where she was, and what she needed to do, was able to pull herself together, used the toilet as intended, and got to the sink to wash up. Turning on the cold water, Alex cupped her right hand and sipped water into her foul-tasting mouth, then spit it out. She did this repeatedly until she could drink some water. With her mouth flushed out, Alex needed to work on her face; whether the task would be more challenging, she did not know. She wanted to add more hot water to the mix before she splashed it on her face. When the water was lukewarm,

Alex used both of her hands to get the water onto her reddened face. The water felt good while she drenched her face, as she did it a few times, to wash away her tears. Finally, she looked into her mirror and saw what she was unable to see in The Wall. She saw her own clear reflection, tattered in spots, but mostly intact. Moving closer to the mirror, Alex searched out wrinkles, temporarily forgetting her young age. Figuring she looked adequately presentable, she grabbed a few sheets of brown, rough, cardboard-like towel. Alex gently dabbed her face dry, especially around her bloodshot eyes. They looked tired and drawn, but she believed she could pull off leaving the bathroom, as she didn't want Henry to worry that she had abandoned him.

Stepping back, Alex adjusted her jean shorts and gray tank top one last time; she exited the bathroom, not expecting to see Jay standing six feet away. "Oh my..." she jumped back, not finishing her exclamation.

"God?" Jay humorously inquired.

She looked at Him for a few fleeting seconds before looking to her left, and then to her right, like she expected a speeding car to fly by. "It might be silly to ask but how did you know where I was?"

Pushing Himself off the royal blue, cinderblock wall, Jay stood upright, with His hands still in His pockets. "I always know where you are."

She cocked her head upwards and to the right, smirking. "Of course."

Jay followed Alex to wherever she was going. "Are you alright?"

Pushing her lips upward, in a silly manner, she mulled over her answer. "I'm okay."

"You don't sound very convincing."

"Do I have to be convincing?"

Jay chuckled. "I guess not."

Alex found Henry in the same place, only this time, he was wearing a hospital johnny.

"I thought you weren't coming back," he expressed with angst.

"No, no, I just had to use the bathroom," she reassured him.

Henry nodded. "I guess the doctor is coming to look at me."

"That is true," Alex confirmed.

"Why?" Henry replied, tensely. "Gene is the one who's sick!"

"I know, but I, as a doctor, wanted you to be checked out just to be on the safe side."

In utter exasperation, Henry threw up his hands before he grabbed the back of his head. "I'm not sick!"

Holding onto her composure, Alex was able to grab his frightened blue eyes. "Henry, what if I go check on Gene for you? Would you like me to do that for you?"

Henry looked away from her. "Yes."

At that time, one of the residents walked into the curtained-off exam room. "Hi, my name is Dr. Sacco," he announced. "And you are…" Dr. Sacco looked at the red folder in his hand. "You are, Henry Philips."

"Yes," Henry confirmed.

She was put off by the manner Dr. Sacco, who appeared to be a pompous individual, regarding himself above his patients, as he couldn't even have taken the time to know the next patient's name. Under his white coat, Dr. Sacco wore blue scrubs. Alex put him around 30 years of age, slightly balding on top of his dark hair. Tall and lanky, sitting on a low, rolling stool   Dr. Sacco's average gaze turned to Alex. "And who is this?"

Alex didn't like the way he looked at her up and down, as if he was a high-class, fashion designer, observing a disastrous outfit. Before she had time to reply, Henry spoke.

"That's Alex. She's a doctor."

In his vain gaze, Dr. Sacco looked back at her. "Alex, the doctor?"

Alex had the inclination to speak something snide and cutting, but resisted. "Yes, I am an emergency room physician at Tufts in Boston."

"You're a New Englander," Dr. Sacco said, in an obvious tenor. "What brings you down here?"

"I'm on vacation," she answered quickly. He did not need to know anymore. It was time for Dr. Sacco to tend to Henry. *Do your job!*

Discerning she had had enough of his idle banter, Dr. Sacco turned to Henry. "Henry, where do you live?" Dr. Sacco started his physical examination, first feeling the structure and lymph nodes in Henry's neck, and then listening to his heart and lungs.

"When it's cold, I stay at the homeless center."

"When were you last seen by a physician, Henry?"

In the far corner of the examination bay, Alex quietly sat with her legs crossed on a metal chair, as she rested her elbow on her opposite arm across her legs. With her ever-improving bloodshot eyes, Alex watched Dr. Sacco's bedside manner, which she was not impressed by yet.

"It has been a long time," answered the patient.

"Do you eat regularly?"

"What do you consider regularly, Doc?" Henry inquired with just the right pinch of sarcasm.

Alex had to catch herself quickly before she chuckled out loud.

"Do you eat three meals a day?" Dr. Sacco clarified.

"I usually eat one meal a day, before the rats get to the food people throw out in trash cans. Sometimes I don't eat at all."

Henry's reality didn't surprise Dr. Sacco, although he gave Henry no indication that he understood his plight. "I am going to have Stacey draw some blood. I'll be back in a little while." With that, he was gone.

"A little while. How long am I going to be here?" Henry asked into the air.

Quickly, Alex stood, trying to distract Henry from his current circumstances. "Henry, I'm going to go check on Gene for you. I will only be twenty feet away. If you need me, just call—I'll be able to hear you."

"Yeah, okay," Henry answered.

"I'll be right back," Alex reiterated to him. Walking past the yellow privacy curtains, she found the exam bay where different doctors and nurses were tending to Gene, whom Alex still considered was in serious condition. Out of the corner of her right eye, she saw Jay standing over Gene's very ulcered feet and toes, so ulcered that she saw right down to the bone in some areas, black tissue in others. She didn't know how he walked if it wasn't for the diabetes that probably numbed his lower extremities. Her eyes were locked on Jay, as she expected Him to do something. Once the medical staff left the bay, Alex stood at Gene's bedside and watched Jay conduct His calling. Holding His crucified hands above Gene's battered feet, Alex witnessed a glow of the bright amber light pouring down, engulfing the affected areas. Alex, struck by this loving, glowing light, felt forced to look to see if anyone else saw this glow—a glow she considered brighter than sun. Her sunglasses—not needed.

"Don't worry," Jay spoke, still working on Gene's ulcers, "nobody can see this light at this moment."

How sad. Everybody should see this light.

Intentionally, although slowly, Jay dimmed this great light, as He prayed for healing.

Stepping closer, she studied Gene's feet. The ulcers were still present.

"It's going to take a few days to improve," Jay explained.

All Alex could do was to nod and stare at Jay in amazement. A struggling voice broke her static gaze.

"Henry," Gene said with a tired voice. "Henry."

Returning to the middle of the side of his bed, Alex saw Gene open his eyes a little. "Hi," she said gently, "My name is Alex. Henry is here. Do you want me to get him for you?"

Gene, seemingly confused from his medical circumstances and his unfamiliar surroundings, swallowed hard, as he moaned, clearly in pain. "Henry!"

"I'm going to get Henry for you," she reassured Gene, as she touched his right arm. Walking back to Henry's exam bay, Alex found him exactly where she had left him. "Throw your pants and shoes back on—Gene is calling for you."

Henry, a little slow to react, looked at her with a quick look, and then another. He caught on and jumped to his feet, putting his pants and shoes on. He followed Alex to where Gene was located, as he looked at his friend with great angst. "Is he going to be okay?"

"Come over here and let Gene see that you are here." Alex directed Henry where to stand. Giving Henry space, she walked around to the opposite side of the bed. "Let him know you are here, Henry." Like a spectator, Alex observed the interaction between the two friends. Henry was obviously unprepared to see Gene in this particular state, with all the tubes and wires going in and out of places. He was overwhelmed with the beeps and sounds, wondering if the sounds were good or bad. Once Henry settled down, he started speaking to Gene, which put Alex more at ease. When Gene heard Henry's gentle voice, so soft and light in tone, Alex noticed Gene's heart rate get to a more normal range. Alex noticed Henry take Gene's hand into his—Gene's heart rate settled even more. She smiled. "You're doing a good job, Henry." Glancing to her left, Alex saw Jay, still standing at the end of the bed where Gene lied. Jay was smiling.

Alex's stomach began to growl after a while. She and Jay found the hospital cafeteria so Alex could get something to eat. Gene and Henry would be admitted into the hospital; it was critical for Gene to get the medical attention he needed to live. Things were different for Henry since his physical condition was much more stable. It had been years since either man had received sufficient medical care, which had only compounded Gene's diabetes. Henry was underweight and malnourished from his homelessness. Thinking about their circumstances only made Alex angrier and angrier; she could only imagine the struggles they probably had gone through daily. Not having any experience being a soldier in foreign lands, Alex had to rely on her book and film accounts of the wars which American soldiers fought. The mindset of soldiers who fought and survived was much different from that of non-military folks. Doing their job meant taking lives of the enemies. It was done in the most brutal of ways: gunfire, hand grenades, bombs dropped from planes, and hand-to-hand combat with knives. It was kill or be killed. Alex didn't imagine there were courses for soldiers on how to maintain their sanity after having taken the life of another. Alex couldn't help but to contemplate that a wartime soldier's duty was to kill the enemy. Her Hippocratic oath was to do no harm. The dichotomy was dumbfounding.

After Alex had a salad, Jay suggested They spend the rest of Their time in the hospital's chapel while They waited for Gene and Henry to get admitted. Alex didn't object. By this time, it was getting close to 8 o'clock in the evening. Entering the chapel, Jay held the door for Alex. They were the only two in the small room. There was a set of candles, set into red, glass vases; Jay lit a candle. Following His lead, Alex did the same, thinking about Nate. Exhaustion started to seep into her bones from the day's stresses. Jay was already seated in one of the wooden benches that lined the chapel. Behind the plain altar, a stained-glass mosaic depiction of Jesus was embedded into the plain, painted, white wall.

"That doesn't look like You," Alex said quietly, off the cuff.

"He is wearing much better clothes than I am."

Alex burst out into laughter, all along, trying to be quiet. Jay joined her in her laughter. "Is it sacrilegious to be laughing in church?" Alex asked, stretching her neck and shoulders in a backwards motion.

"Not at all. I love to hear people laugh, of course when it's in good taste," He explained easily. Jay looked Alex over with a careful eye. "You look exhausted."

"I am that." The very thought of exhaustion made her rub her eyes with her thumb and index finger.

"Want to take off?"

"I can't," she replied quickly. "I want to talk to the social worker to make sure these guys get the services they need."

"That's fine," Jay replied. "You really care about these guys."

"Yeah, I do." Sinking in thought, Alex looked around the chapel. "I think Henry and Gene are more than just friends." She returned to Jay; her hands were clasped her lap.

"They are," Jay confirmed.

"And you're okay with that—God is okay with that?" Alex asked with skepticism pouring out of her skin.

Sitting forward, Jay put His elbows on His legs and clutched His hands together. "You know God and I are all about love, right?"

Her eyes switched back and forth. "Yeah."

"In Our eyes, love is love between two people who care for each other. Love is love. Love is happiness. Love is joyfulness. Love is caring. Love is devotion." With every love equation, His voice gained strength. "Love is love, Alex."

At that moment, she sighed, relieved. "We have a pretty progressive Pope now, you know."

"I know—We created him."

"I still don't understand why women can't be priests. It would solve a bunch of issues," Alex commented.

"Those are the Catholic Church's rules."

"Yeah, but they are a bit antiquated, don't you think?" she asked.

"I guess," Jay replied. "Why? Are you looking to change professions and become a priest?"

Raising her head, she looked at him and smirked. "Oh, you're funny," Alex announced. "No, I don't want to become a priest. I just want the world to be fairer, that's all."

"Ditto to that, my friend." Jay leaned back on the bench. He looked at the stained-glass image of Himself while considering His next question. "Have you been in love before?"

This question ricocheted around her brain, bouncing off the gray matter until it found a soft spot to sink into to be processed. "Have I ever been in love? Is that what you asked me?"

"Yeah. Have you ever been in love?" Jay repeated.

Not knowing that answer without some critical thought, Alex looked vacantly into the far corner of the chapel. "Oh wow," she paused, still not knowing what the answer was. She straightened her back to stretch her back muscles, seemingly to gain some more time. "I can't believe you asked me that."

"You are avoiding my question," He said, smiling.

Taking a deep breath, Alex exhaled for a few extra seconds. "I know," she said, admitting the overt stalling. "I did date someone when I was in college—med school—but it didn't last for more than a few months; it wasn't anything serious." Scratching her nose, she looked downward. "Once I got occupied with caring for Nate, he told me it would never work out anyway." Realizing she hadn't thought about him for these last few years, she concluded their relationship really didn't mean anything. "He was kind of a jerk."

Looking at Alex with profound sympathy, Jay reached out to touch her hand. "I'm sorry."

She was a bit surprised that she didn't feel anything else with His hand on hers. He must have times when He avoids using His gifts, she deduced. "To answer your question, no, I haven't been in love before." A tear, solitary in nature, streamed down the left side of her face. "Isn't that sad…I'm twenty-six years old and I have never been in love." More tears fell, as she glanced at Jay. "I don't think I'm that ugly or anything," Alex slightly joked, wiping her tears with the underside of her right wrist.

"Is that the way you see yourself?"

"Oh God, I don't know how I see myself," Alex surmised. "All of these years, I have been so consumed by Nate—making sure he has this, making sure he has that. With him gone, I really don't know what my purpose will be." Tears came easily.

"Have you ever thought about having your own family?"

Something about that question made Alex laugh. "Of course, I haven't," she answered with her eyes on Jay. "I haven't been in love."

"You were a little girl once, long before Nate became sick," Jay reminded Alex. "How did you see yourself when you got older?"

Shifting on the bench, Alex crossed her legs toward Jay, as she attempted to reach back into the memory crevasses of her mind. "I always wanted to be a doctor, no doubt about that," Alex recalled, still with tears in her eyes. "Sometimes I wanted to be a rock star but given the fact that I can't hold a tune to save my life, that put an end to that dream." A laugh escaped. "I can't remember having any visions about being domestic and having a family."

"You did," Jay interjected.

Alex met His eyes. "I did? When?"

Jay grinned. "You were eight. Your cousin, Jake, and his wife, Izzie, dropped by with their newborn. They let you hold him, and you were completely enthralled with him. He slept in your arms for about an hour. It was then you really thought it might be cool to become a mother."

The memory flashed in her head like a spark, finally remembering that very moment and feeling. "He was a little cutie." Then she sighed. "I was eight—I probably wanted a pink pony too."

Exasperated, Jay stood. "Come on, let's go back upstairs and talk to this social worker."

Alex knew she could make Jay wrap up conversations if she began joking around. This time, He seemed a little curter with her.

The elevator took them to the fifth floor, and they followed the signs to Room 524. Alex was pleased they placed Gene and Henry in the same room. Gene was in the first bed, sitting up and eating a bowl of chicken and vegetable soup, a vast improvement since she had first set eyes on him. Henry was having the same soup, with a roll, pork, and chocolate pudding for dessert. Both men were eating ravenously, which was not surprising to Alex. They didn't even notice she was in the room until she spoke Henry's name. At once, Henry looked up, seeing Alex standing between the two beds. Henry swallowed his mouthful of food in haste and introduced Alex to Gene, speaking about the young woman who saved his life. Alex quickly tamed down that notion. She kept her attention on Gene, waiting to see if he would acknowledge her presence. Even though the bowl of soup kept his attention, Gene managed to grumble a 'hello'. Returning his 'hello', Alex moved toward Gene to take his empty bowl. Sitting on the food tray on the hospital table was a small, plastic container, filled with lime, sugar-free Jell-O. Alex offered to peel off its lid. Seeing Gene interacting with her, a vast contrast to the condition in which she found him seven hours prior, made Alex's heart soar, especially when he responded with a 'thank you'. Gene started eating the green Jell-O at once. Henry looked on, commenting that Gene was a very hungry guy. Alex concurred.

After Alex had watched nearly two episodes of *Friends* with the guys, the social worker finally arrived. Alex put her in her mid-40s, with long and wavy strawberry blonde hair, with a slightly Rubenesque form. She entered Room 524 with a bubbly voice, introducing herself.

"Hi guys," she spoke to her new audience. "My name is Shay Reynolds. I'm going to be your social worker."

Both men remained silent.

Standing up from the chair in the corner of the room, Alex stood and sauntered closer to Shay. "Hi, my name is Alex Roma." The two women shook hands.

Without looking up from his meal, Henry added his familiar follow-up. "Alex is a doctor."

His response made Alex chuckle. "I am a doctor. Thank you, Henry."

"No problem."

"Are you a doctor here, or..." Shay inquired, leaving the question open-ended.

Alex crossed her arms across her chest. "I'm from Boston; I'm just here on vacation." But it wasn't a vacation.

"I understand you came across Gene and Henry?" Shay prepared to take notes.

"I did, I did. They were over by the Vietnam Memorial," Alex recounted once again. "Gene was lying on the grass; it was obvious Gene presented signs of diabetes—probably ketoacidosis. Henry presented with some cognitive difficulties."

"Which was all confirmed here," Shay shared.

"Yes." Alex made sure she continued to talk softly.

Rustling paperwork she held in her hands, Shay flipped through a few. "I did manage to get their discharge records. They were released from the Army in June of 1972, a week apart—Henry being released first. That's all the information I have."

Alex didn't want to make any conclusions based on this sparse information. "Can they be admitted into a residential program, together?" Alex asked Shay.

At first, Shay didn't catch on to her peculiar inquiry at first, but the pieces all started to fall into place. "You think they are a couple?"

"I do," Alex answered. She also answered with her eyes.

"I understand," assured Shay.

Once Alex knew Shay understand, she exhaled a long, relieved sigh.

"You look exhausted."

The word 'exhausted' ushered in a huge yawn that Alex tried to hide. "I really am," she easily admitted. "I think I will go."

Reaching into her folder sleeve, Shay pulled out one of her business cards. "Here's my card; please call me when you get home. Maybe we can FaceTime once they get settled. I know you went above and beyond what any average human would ever do for these guys."

Overcome with gratitude from Shay's words, Alex shied away, not feeling she was worthy. "That's very nice of you." Gazing up, she saw Gene and Henry were fast asleep in their beds, beds that weren't concrete or grass, protected from the elements outside, with their bellies full of food they didn't have to compete with rats to eat. "Will you be here tomorrow?"

"Absolutely," promised Shay.

"Will you say goodbye to Henry and Gene for me?"

"I will."

"Thank you," Alex replied to Shay, as her tired eyes thanked her too. With one last look toward the resting Henry and Gene, she hoped for the best for them. Leaving Room 524, through the corridors and down the elevator, she exited the hospital and found a warm night outside. Just around the corner, Jay stood, waiting for her. Alex walked close to Him, wrapping her arms around His shoulders. "I need to go and sleep."

Jay embraced her. "I know."

The bright morning sun slinked in from an open window, shining onto her face. Alex turned over and started to awaken. Stretching her arms up over her head, she slowly opened her eyes to realize she was home, in her bed. Sitting up quickly, Alex felt something strange, feeling she wasn't supposed to be there. Getting out of bed, she searched upstairs. Her parents were already up. She jogged down the stairs to find the living room, den, and dining room all quiet. Sounds were coming from the kitchen—normal sounds, cooking sounds. Alex peeked into the kitchen and saw Nate making breakfast. *Nate!* She could hardly believe her eyes. Alex walked close and wrapped her arms around his shoulders. She vowed that she would never let him go; never again. Their embrace, so profound and so strong, immersed Alex with a sensation of divine peace and adoration which she had never felt before. It was the greatest feeling, so warm and restorative, Alex believed she could live the rest of her life in this very state. There was no need for words.

She heard a dog barking nearby. Sleep ended—her dream ended. Alex opened her eyes to find herself inside of her tent, already feeling the heat of the day. Before making a move to get up, Alex remembered her dream, recalling the incredible feeling she had just experienced with her arms around Nate. It was truly the greatest sensation she had ever felt.

Running her fingers through her dark, messy hair, she sat then rose to her feet, squatting to gather everything she needed to take a shower. Outside, she found Jay, sitting by the small fire, as He already had her tea ready. She told Him she would hurry back.

The tiredness of the previous day still had a tiny hold of her muscles, but more so of her mind. In the semi-private women's bathing-and-toilet small, concrete building, droplets of lukewarm water awakened Alex's senses a bit more. It was another warm day, so she didn't mind the temperature of the water. Suddenly, she remembered her and Jay's conversation in the hospital's chapel, realizing their conversations were becoming more profound, more meaningful. Alex condemned herself for the way she joked about wanting a pink pony. In all actuality, she probably didn't want a pink pony, she wanted not to think about the tough stuff—her future, flaws, and everything in between that created an entire spectrum of who she was. She knew her heart, and she knew her head. Breaking free of the guilt from not being able to save Nate still gripped her so damn tight, much like a cobra gripped its prey. She wondered if she would escape this imprisonment that suspended her life and her growth. Growth was mandatory, she demanded for herself.

It was amazing how fast her hair dried in the summer sun, as she walked back to her site. The tea was still waiting for her. After putting her used items away from the shower, she sat in her nylon camping chair. "Thank you for the tea again. You take good care of me."

Jay was sitting quietly, oddly enough, doing a Sudoku puzzle. "You're very welcome," He said, giving His full attention.

Alex sat forward. "Hey Jay, I…" She paused to gather her thoughts. "I would like to apologize for the off-the-cuff remarks I made in the chapel. They were uncalled for, and I apologize." She sipped her tea.

"Yesterday was a tough day," Jay reminded her. "You don't need to apologize."

Looking left, over the tent and into the trees, Alex contemplated her next words. "Yeah, I need to apologize." Sipping her tea, she returned her eye to Him. "I know you are trying to draw me out of this," Alex paused to find the correct noun, waving her arms around a bit, trying to make the word come faster. "Defeatism! This defeatism that I'm in."

Jay couldn't help but to laugh out loud. "Well, that's a word!"

She laughed along with Him. "That is a good word, isn't it?"

Seeing the smile on Alex's face, Jay kept His smile. "Absolutely!"

Quickly, Alex glanced downward toward the ground, as if the entire world was judging her missteps. "I have never pictured myself as one who gives up very easily. Maybe those words are incorrect." She continued to think out loud, quietly. "Like I said last night, I don't really know where I go from here."

"The biggest issue for you is that all your desires before Nate died have disappeared from your sight," explained Jay with great passion. "But I clearly see them within you; they are so ready to emerge again from your heart but you, My friend, need to allow them to be unchained."

Alex nodded in agreement even though she was frightened out of her mind just to think what it would take to reach that stage. "Do I have it within me?"

Jay saw this was a serious question from Alex. "Of course you do, Alex." He sat up straighter as He sat on the bare ground. "You have the capacity to do a million amazing things. Don't be afraid just to try."

Looking into His eyes, she found it hard to pull away, but her insecurity overwhelmed her, as a tear fell. Swallowing hard, she quickly wiped it away, looking into the trees again. "So, where are we heading today?"

"Myrtle Beach," Jay answered.

"Myrtle Beach?" repeated Alex, surprised. "Isn't that like seven or eight hours away?"

Jay rose to His naked feet, putting on His Converse sneakers. Jay noticed her eyes, focused on the sneakers. "What?"

"You need new sneakers, Dude."

"No, I don't," Jay replied. "I have had these for forty years."

A chuckle snuck out of Alex. "They look more like fifty years old."

"Oh, very funny," Jay chortled.

Undertow

Jumping on I-95 South, already stocked up with the food essentials she would need to satisfy her appetite, Alex was excited to be going to somewhere new. She had a natural curiosity for people, places, and things. She always wanted to know the way things worked, and how things progressed. She possessed the perfect attributes for a physician.

Having miles and miles ahead of her, Alex took the opportunity to chat with Conrad and Justin, and then her parents, on speakerphone, always mindful to not give away that she had a co-pilot by her side. They would probably have been ecstatic to know Jesus was in her passenger seat, although convincing anyone of this might have been mystifying, to say the least. Though she had left home only six days prior, it felt like she had left two months ago, having witnessed many incredible things, which not many mortals get to see. Enjoying the easy banter with Conrad and Justin, catching up on all the news going on at home, led Alex to feel a bit homesick, but not enough to end this journey. She knew the positive impact it was having on her broken soul. Nate was constantly in her thoughts, and especially within the depths of her heart that were only reserved for him. It was obvious that the listeners in Massachusetts were aware of the new revival to her voice—light and hopeful; it was more than a revival, it was a metamorphosis, which Alex didn't even notice.

Almost seven hours had passed with a single pitstop. It was getting close to dusk when they reached Myrtle Beach. As luck would have it, or maybe it was Jay's divine interventions, Alex had secured a campsite at Myrtle Beach State Park earlier that day. It was a long road into the campground, but once there, greeting her was a magnificent sight of the Atlantic Ocean that she knew well. Unpacking what she needed for the night, Jay helped her set up the essentials. Alex picked up food at the nearest Piggly Wiggly. She just had to step into a Piggly Wiggly just to say that she had.

The salmon cooked well over an open flame, along with the red potatoes and fresh carrots. It was a beautiful night on the campsite grounds, with a light breeze cutting through the muggy air. Even though it was late, Alex looked forward to taking a quiet walk on the beach. That was where she could feel relaxed, very in tune with her head and her soul, finding a true symphony within. The breezes, wherever they came from, cleared out all the lingering dust in all her brain creases and valleys, as she let her thoughts, concerns and all the negativity sleep for a while.

After everything was cleaned up and put back into their proper places, Alex took a beach towel from the backseat and walked to the beach. Jay remained watching over the smoldering fire. Stepping on the warm, South Carolina, white sand, all of Alex's muscles became pacified, understanding that she wasn't driving miles and miles in her car. Walking further onto the beach, Alex dropped the beach towel and removed her flip flops she had changed into before she ate. She loved the feel of sand surrounding her feet and toes, aware of every grain and a stray pebble here and there, and feeling the different temperature spots in different areas of the beach. Alex got closer to where the tide ebbed and flowed in intervals calculated by the Earth and Moon, and all their forces.

Glancing up and down the beach, there were just a handful of people scattered. Some were lovers, and some were simply enjoying the night air. Forgetting about time and place, as if the world disappeared for a second or two, Alex sauntered along the inside edge of the tide, until she grew weary. Finding her towel where she had left it, Alex spread it out and curled up on it. Soon, she would be fast asleep.

As He touched Alex's exposed shoulder, Alex slowly stirred, finally opening her eyes, and realizing where she had slept.

Seeing Jay, she shot up quickly. "Was I here all night?" Rubbing her face and eyes, she realized she had indeed been.

Jay, with his never-changing appearance, laughed. "I have come to the conclusion, my friend, that you can sleep almost anywhere."

Alex looked around to get her bearings. "What time is it?" Oddly enough, there was nobody else on the beach within a few hundred yards.

"It's nearly 7 o'clock," He answered, stepping closer to the tide.

Regaining all her senses, she could tell another hot day was in store. As Alex stood, she gazed out onto the Atlantic and saw Jay actually walking on the water. If nothing had convinced her that Jay was indeed Jesus, this feat solidified it for her. The sight of Jay playing around on the ocean mesmerized her like every other feat she had witnessed. "He walks on water." For the five minutes He spent on the water, Alex stood, without moving, without taking her eyes off Him.

After she drank her tea, Alex decided to take advantage of the early morning hours and the sheer fact that the campground had laundry facilities. It had been six days on the road, and things were piling up in her back seat. The building which held the washers and dryers was a nondescript concrete structure with a metal roof. Steel doors closed it during the night. Alex loaded up a washing machine and inserted six quarters to begin the cycle. It was apparent there wasn't any sitting area, so Alex stepped outside and squatted, leaning on the front right side of the building. She was amazed that the hot summers she had experienced in New England came nowhere close to the intense heat and humidity of the south. It was almost unbearable in the shade, let alone in the sun. Alex just had to breathe to sweat. Taking a big gulp of water from her Contigo bottle, Alex suddenly heard some commotion from a little further down the road. A few more seconds past, and voices became louder, angrier. Alex stood and hesitantly walked toward the antagonistic quarrel. Looking around the immediate area, Alex noticed others giving attention to the commotion. Would somebody else, a stranger, have her back? Alex didn't know that answer.

Slowly she approached the scene, seeing an older and a younger male, brutishly walking on the main side of the camper. Before they noticed Alex fifteen feet away, both men violently slapped their hands on the adjacent camper, uttering racial slurs that were profoundly offensive.

"What's the issue here, guys?" Alex asked with a forceful voice.

The older man, unshaven and unkept, wearing blue jeans and an unbuttoned white shirt, approached Alex with obvious liquor upon his breath. "Little Lady, please go and mind your own business."

After being addressed as 'Little Lady', Alex suddenly realized being called 'Ma'am' didn't seem all that bad. "May I ask your name, Sir?"

"You can ask. It doesn't mean I'll give it to you."

The younger man, with wavy, dark hair, and wearing only jeans, walked closer to Alex. "You want something; I can give you something sweet."

"Move away from me," she demanded instinctively, as her unwavering eyes locked with his stoned eyes. It was then, out of the left corner of her eye, she noticed a family of three emerge from the adjacent camper. Sensing Jay's eyes upon her, Alex knew she wasn't alone.

The African American man stepped forward, slowly walking toward Alex. "Ma'am," the gentleman said. "I don't want you to get hurt."

Seeing the genuine concern in this man's sorrowful eyes, Alex couldn't help but to intervene. "What's the issue?"

"He and his black kin have to move to some other spot. I don't like their stink!" exclaimed the older man, as he stumbled around his area.

Stepping forward, Alex finally saw the blue square banner representing the current President. "Why don't you request a new spot, Sir?"

"Because I was here first!" the old man shouted. "I worked my entire life to buy my RV when I retired," he touted in his drunkenness. "I expect to go on vacation and not to be subjected to share space with those kinds of people."

Ire grew in Alex's chest. She was very aware that whatever she said wouldn't penetrate his inebriated consciousness. "Don't you think this man worked hard to buy his RV?"

"He probably stole it."

Her first instinct was to punch the old man, but she knew she couldn't for several reasons. Alex glanced to the left and stared into the face of the crying son. "What's your name?" She put out her hand, walking toward him.

Wiping his eyes dry, he struggled to make eye contact. "Danny."

Alex squatted to her heels. "Hi Danny, my name is Alex," she said softly. "Would you and your mom like to come hang out with me at my campsite, while your Dad gets things straightened out at the office?" She looked up to Mom's eyes and saw her gratitude.

Danny also looked to his mom to know how to answer. "Okay."

Wanting to get the young man out of that particular situation as quickly as possible, she held his hand and directed them closer to the laundry facility. She turned to tell the dad her campsite number. Once he pulled their RV out of the spot, Alex continued to direct her guests to her site.

"You know what you are?!" yelled the old man.

Rushing Mom and son out of ear shot of the old man, Alex sadly knew what was coming, and it did come, clearly. Alex cringed and tears filled her eyes. Without saying anything, they finally reached Alex's campsite. "Somebody sit in my chair, please." Alex got the soft sleeping pad from her tent, folding it in thirds. "Here you go, Danny, sit on this."

"Thank you," Danny expressed kindly.

"I apologize," said Alex to Danny's Mom. "I didn't get your name before."

"It's Ana, Ana DeFranco," she replied, as she extended her hand to Alex. "There's no need to apologize."

Ana was still standing. Ana was a stunning, beautiful woman, with long, wavy black hair, and rectangular, black-rimmed eyeglasses. "Please sit," Alex almost begged. "Can I get you anything to eat? All I have are Twizzlers and an apple."

Ana, already full of gratitude, didn't want anything more.

"I have water," Alex offered. "Come on, it's hot out here—you have to have water."

They both agreed.

Rummaging through everything in her back seat, she found a package of yellow cups. She filled them to the brim on the back seat. "Here you go."

"Thank you, Alex," Ana replied.

"Thank you," Danny said before taking a big gulp.

"May I ask where you are from?" Alex sat on the ground.

"Do you want this chair?" Ana asked, as she started to stand.

"Oh, no, no. Please sit, Ana," she begged again. "After six days of camping, I've sort of gotten used to sitting on the ground."

"We are from Philadelphia," Ana replied. "I'm the CEO of First Bank of Philadelphia, and my husband, Mark, is one of the coaches for the Philadelphia Eagles. We had time to get away this weekend before everything gets busy again."

"I bet things do get a bit hectic with both of your jobs."

"And what do you do?" inquired Ana.

"I am an emergency room doctor," Alex was uncomfortable to admit inwardly.

"You are a doctor?!" Danny said excitedly. "You don't look like a doctor!"

"Danny, please," Ana scolded her son gently.

"Out of the mouths of babes," Alex chortled out loud. "I really am a doctor, Danny."

"That's so cool!" Like the curious young man that he was, his mind started to wonder. "Did you ever have to cut somebody's leg off?!"

"Danny!" Ana's voice became bolder.

All Alex could do was laugh. "Umm, no, I haven't had to amputate someone's leg, thankfully, but I do know how." She smiled.

"Where do you practice?" Ana asked.

"I practice at Tufts in Boston," replied Alex, nodding her head.

"And you're here on vacation?"

"Actually, I'm driving across country, seeing the sights and things like that."

"You're doing that alone?" Ana asked, while her eyes expanded.

Alex chuckled. "I get that reaction a lot when I tell people." Before she continued, Alex recoiled a bit. "Yes, I am alone on this trip. It's sort of a restoration journey." Feeling vulnerable, she bowed her head in embarrassment, as her thoughts boomeranged back to Nate.

Sympathy filled Ana's eyes, as she stood and gracefully knelt on the ground next to Alex, wearing a gorgeous yellow and rust, mosaic sundress. "I don't know what brought you here, but just knowing you this short time, you are the strongest person I have ever met."

Somehow Alex held it all together in front of young Danny. Alex grabbed Ana's hand and held onto it tightly. "Thank you. That means everything to me."

"May I give you a big hug?" Ana posed.

With tears welled in Alex's eyes, she glanced to Ana. "Of course."

Ana bent over Alex and squeezed both sides of her back. Soon, Danny would be joining his mother, lightly embracing Alex.

Grabbing onto his arm softly, Alex wanted to display her gratitude. "Thanks, Bud."

Figuring it was warm, too warm for lengthy embraces, Ana ended hers with a light circular touch to Alex's back.

"Mom, Alex is crying," Danny announced.

"Don't worry, Kiddo, these are happy tears," explained Alex, wearing a gigantic smile.

"Danny," Ana started, "Do you think Dad would object if we asked Alex to join us for a little fun in the sun today?"

Her son looked directly at her, sporting a typical teenage grin. "Nope!"

"Danny speaks!" Ana declared. "You are our guest today!"

Looking back and forth, between mother and son, Alex tried to comprehend what just happened. "What?! I can't do that!"

"Why not?" implored Ana.

"Yeah, why not?"

Hiding her smile, Alex giggled. "I have six days of laundry to finish up—that's if it's still there."

"Well, go check things out."

Alex stood and wiped the dirt off her legs. "Stay here, and I'll be right back." She started walking toward the laundry facility.

"Mom, I think I want to become a doctor," Danny said loud enough that it reached Alex's ears.

Stopping in place, her heart nearly exploded from her chest, with great pride and resolution, as happy tears accompanied Alex through her walk.

Approaching the laundry building, Alex instinctively glanced to her right. The RV was gone. She looked down the road in both directions—Alex still could not spot the vehicle or the two men. Not knowing much about RV or campers, she concluded she would not have the ability to spot it amongst the hundreds of similar vehicles surrounded her. But the question remained—*where were they?*

She stepped into the open-air building, finding Jay finishing up her laundry. The sight of this made her laugh. "What are you doing?" she asked, smiling.

"I am keeping my eye on things while doing your laundry."

"Nice cover, I guess," Alex humorously stated. She looked around the shaded inside, gauging who was nearby. "Is there anything I should know about?" She helped Jay put the rest of her clothes in the gray, mesh laundry bag.

"No," answered Jay.

"Nothing at all?"

"I have things under control, Alex," He reassured. "I want you to go have fun with the DeFrancos today."

Throwing the mesh bag over her left shoulder, feeling like Santa Claus for a millisecond, Alex kept scanning the area. "What are you going to do for the rest of the day?"

"Don't worry about me. I have many things that will keep me occupied."

"Okay," said Alex without reservation. Alex made her way out of the concrete building. "See you later, my Friend."

"I'll be here."

Spending the day with the DeFrancos was the first time in a very long time Alex actually had fun. If someone ever asked Alex what she did for fun in the last 15 years, her answer usually was spending a quiet night at home watching a movie. On these occasions, she would get partway through the movie, and then fall asleep. At times, she would go out for "drinks" with Conrad and Justin after working a 16-hour shift in the emergency room. None of them actually drank anything stronger than lemonade, typically opting for water just to rehydrate. It was more of a way to unwind, and to get friend therapy because they all knew the rigors of their chosen profession—life-and-death decisions that had to be made on the fly, working on threads of sleep. This was Alex's so-called fun.

Mark, a very nice and personable man, waited on Alex for the entire day, as he was very thankful for what she had done earlier in the day. He was a tall man, standing about six-foot-four, about eight inches taller than her. He was bald, and his physique matched his profession. The DeFrancos' RV was pristine and air-conditioned. On Ocean Boulevard, Mark knew where to park this very large home on wheels.

To Alex's surprise, one of their planned activities was to take an hour-long helicopter ride over Myrtle Beach. Instantly, Alex felt nervousness flare up in her stomach. In her senior year of high school, she flew to Europe, but that was in a big, big airplane, she reminded herself. Mark saw the apprehension in her eyes. He confessed that the first time he went up in a helicopter, he threw up beforehand. With a comic's relief, Mark asked her if she wanted to do the same. Appreciating his inborn tendency to be funny, Alex chortled and passed up the offer to throw up. The fact that Mark's friend of fifteen years, Zion, was the pilot, and that they had three tours in Afghanistan together, made her decision to get on the helicopter that much easier. In the back of her mind, Alex knew she had Jay's blessing to have fun.

She was the third person to board the helicopter. Alex belted herself like she was going on an upside-down, all-around rollercoaster ride at any amusement park across the country. Seated across from Mark, Alex noticed him laughing at her uneasiness, but all along reassuring her that everything would be okay. Following his lead, Alex put on the headset and moved the microphone boom into position in front of her mouth.

At last, the rotors began to turn at a furious speed, cutting through the heavy air like a sharp knife through paper. The helicopter lifted off the ground, getting high enough to hover over 18-story buildings, powerlines and the SkyWheel, Myrtle Beach's modern Ferris wheel. Alex grabbed onto the leather loops where she could reach them. As they got higher in the sky, everything got smaller on the ground. Alex glanced across to Mark; he gently moved both of his hands up and down to signal to her to just relax. Once they began to fly forward, hugging the South Carolina coast, Alex's nervousness changed to exhilaration. To her left, she had the endless blue Atlantic to adore. To her right, she looked down at the miles and miles of endless, sandy coastline, peppered with people all along the way. It was the first time Alex felt a cooler breeze. It was that very breeze that exhilarated her soul. Sitting beside her was Ana; once Ana knew Alex was enjoying the ride, she started indicating out points of interest. Zion had his own points of interest he wanted to get across to Alex. She tried to take everything in because she was alive, and Nate wasn't. The gravity of this idea made Alex reflect on the past six days, all the things she had seen and done, and it weighed heavily on her shoulders like it had been since that horrible night. She had gotten too lost in thought to realize they had landed.

Everyone had an appetite after the flight. Mark drove back down to the center of town and parked across the street from Mrs. Fish Seafood Grill restaurant. Mark invited everyone in for a nice meal in a semi-private room he reserved when they were in town. Alex, feeling underdressed and unworthy of the special attention she was getting for doing a thing any caring person would do. As the guys and Danny headed into the restaurant, Alex politely held up Ana and asked if her very casual jean cutoffs and teal blue tank were appropriate clothing. Ana laughed and let Alex in on a little secret: Ana's brother owned the restaurant. It was then that Alex breathed freely.

Francis Burks, a hearty and kind-hearted gentleman, greeted everybody at the entrance, embracing them one at a time, especially his little sister.

"Frankie," Ana got her brother's attention over the constant din of the restaurant. "This is Alex. This morning, she came to our rescue when these two jerks were bothering us in our RV at the campground."

Frankie immediately looked into his sister's eyes. "No?"

"Yes," she reiterated to her sorrowful brother. "They were really, really without mercy."

Clearing a tear from his eye, he hugged Ana. "This stuff has to stop, man. I can't wait for 2020 to kick that guy out of the White House." He walked closer to Alex. "Alex, I'm very pleased to meet you. I can't thank you enough for doing what you did." Another tear rolled down his cheek. "Can I give you a hug?"

Alex couldn't say no. Alex noticed Frankie was so tall he had to bend his knees as he gently threw his big burly arms around her back. Feeling his embrace, she suddenly felt that amazing feeling of warmth and peace that was becoming a regular occurrence, but never insignificant. "Thank you," Alex expressed, patting his back.

Frankie wore a blue short-sleeved dress shirt and nice blue jeans with brown leather shoes. "Did Danny hear any of the commotion, Sis?"

Uncommonly shaken, Ana's expression turned serious. "He heard quite a bit of it, yeah."

Placing his hands on his hips, exhaling hard, Frankie gazed to the floor. "I'll have a talk with him later, if Mark is okay with that."

"Of course he is," Ana replied, hugging Frankie around his lower back. "I'm going to use the powder room. Alex, do you wish to join me?"

"Oh, sure." Alex followed Ana to a very nicely decorated powder room with four separate stalls. The white 8-inch hexagon tiles complimented the navy-painted wainscoting, with white wallpaper with blue swirls all over. "Wow, look at this bathroom."

Ana was already in a stall. "Frankie has some great taste. He even put a water feature in here."

"That's a smart feature, I must admit," Alex said from two stalls down.

Ana exited her stall and was at one of the sinks. "Do you have any brothers or sisters, Alex?"

For a very common question, it stopped Alex cold. She finished up in the stall and exited. "I had a younger brother, Nate." Thinking about her next words, Alex debated she was strong enough to say them. "He committed suicide at the end of February." Replaying the last eight words repeatedly, Alex could hardly believe she had uttered them. Alex leaned on the sink counter.

"Oh my God, Alex, I'm so, so sorry," gasped Ana, drying her hands in a frenzy.

Yes, Alex said the words. Already washing her hands, she gazed into the mirror. "This is the first time I have admitted that out loud." Shaking the excess water off her hands, she grabbed some brown paper towels. "He had pretty severe schizophrenia, so yeah."

Seeing the overwhelming sadness in Alex's gaze, Ana began to cry. "One of our cousins committed suicide about two years ago, in 2017."

Immediately, Alex brought both hands together in front of her nose and lips. "I'm so sorry." Alex stepped forward and hugged Ana tightly.

Ana reciprocated Alex's sincere embrace. "Curtis, who lived not too far away from us in Philadelphia, was falsely excused of dealing drugs to some kids. He never did drugs in his entire life!" Ana passionately emphasized. "We know what happens to black men when they are falsely excused of something—they are always presumed guilty. Curtis was 22, just out of college, with a wife and a young baby girl." Ana shed more tears. "They wouldn't let up on him, so one day he decided to get some pills and swallowed the whole bottle's worth."

With her hands clasped in front of her, Alex closed her eyes, as chills rushed up and down her spine. "I'm so sorry," she repeated, as tears welled in her eyes.

"That's what we call 'living black in America'." Ana swallowed hard. "I'm so scared for Danny."

Seeing the sheer terror within Ana's eyes, Alex threw her arms around her new friend. "Jesus will protect Danny—I have no doubt."

She found Jay reading by a small fire. Although physically and emotionally weary from her day, Alex wanted to take a midnight stroll on the beach to unwind. She promised Jay she would return in a little bit, touching Him on the shoulder. Unlike the previous night, there were rain clouds moving in, but she didn't care—Alex loved the peace and tranquility of it all. Like all other walks on the beach, she tried to unburden her mind from the heaviness of the day. Carrying her flip flops in her right hand, she left her other hand to feel the drizzle in the ocean breezes. Because of the pending mist, the beach was mostly barren as far she could tell in the darkness of midnight.

After walking for about ten minutes, Alex started to hear rustling behind her. Listening for several more seconds, all her hairs on her neck started to rise, as her breathing changed.

"Jay?" she inquired without turning around. There was no response, only louder rustling. Alex's pace got faster, matching her heartbeat. Knowing she had to make a move, she remembered to breathe. In a brave move, she stopped and turned, finally seeing what she didn't want to see. "What are you doing, guys?" she cried out, only recognizing one of the men from earlier.

"I spent my whole day looking for you, bitch!" the one she recognized seethed, spitting as he talked. Violence was in his drunken saliva.

Paralyzed, Alex had never been so frightened. "What are you doing?"

He grabbed her upper left arm hard and squeezed. "I'm gonna do to you what the campground did to us—screwed us over!"

Blood drained out of her left arm. In an instant, Alex began to kick her feet furiously. "Let me go!" She kicked at the air and nothing else, as the other guy grabbed her other arm. "Jay, help me," she uttered to herself.

Within seconds, Jay appeared. "Stop what you are doing," sternly He spoke.

Stunned by Jay's appearance, the two perpetrators let Alex drop down to the soft, white sand. They attempted to run, but they couldn't. They attempted to talk, but they couldn't. All they could do was to look at this Man that had them in His sights.

Alex lied on her back, taking the deepest breaths into her lungs, as Jay rushed to her, helping her sit up. Easily, she sobbed with all that she had.

Jay surrounded her with His arms, rocking her back and forth. "You're okay, Alex." He continued to comfort Alex until she calmed a bit. Looking at the two standing still, He stared into their eyes. "The police are coming to arrest you both," Jay explained. "It's not My doctrine to not give people second chances, but from what I know—and I know a lot—it will serve you both well if you spend time contemplating your sins."

Still trapped in an unexplainable force field, both sinners could only observe what was happening. Once the police arrived, the men were released from their invisible confinement, making every attempt to run, but their legs appeared to be made of lead. They listened to their Miranda rights before the police rushed them off the beach.

She felt safety within His arms. As her adrenaline levels dropped off, Alex felt her upper arm throb. She knew the drill being a physician; the thought of going to the hospital to be checked out, and to have the police take photos was standard protocol. All Alex wanted to sleep—sleep for days upon days, nights upon nights.

"You can do this," Jay uttered in a sweet, calming voice.

It was close to noon. Alex was finally starting to stir. As she flexed her left bicep, the harrowing memories of the previous night came rushing back. The heat of the day was already making her sweat, as it was very bright in her royal blue tent. She turned over and grabbed her iPhone; it confirmed how late it was. She had three missed calls which made her increasingly anxious as to how she would hold it together when she eventually spoke to her parents, and to Conrad. Buying some time, Alex decided to message them, priming them that she would call them later. Maybe she was priming herself. There would be no FaceTiming if she could help it.

Alex unzipped the tent, ducking her head out into the bright sun, finding Jay within four feet, with His nose in a book. "What's ya doing?" she asked lightly. Rising to her feet, she stretched out all her muscles.

"Just sitting here, reading," He said, closing the book. "How is your arm?"

Just the mention of her arm made Alex massage it again with her right hand. "It's still sore."

Standing, He took a few steps closer, and then gently touched her arm. With both hands, Jay infused her bruised, sore muscles with His seraphic light, healing it with all His might. "Am I hurting you?"

Drawn by His sacred abilities, Alex watched in absolute amazement, as she could feel the tissues in the injured areas of her arm begin to mend. She gazed up into His eyes and looked at Him with wonder. "No, You're not hurting me."

"Good," Jay remarked. Within a few minutes, His task was completed. "It should feel better in a few hours."

Out of pure instinct, Alex's right hand returned to her injured arm, as she chuckled a bit, recounting the characters from *The Karate Kid*. "Thank you."

"You're very welcome," Jay sincerely spoke.

"So, where are we heading?"

"If you're feeling up to it, I thought we would go to Savannah."

"I hear Savannah is a beautiful city," Alex said with more lift to her voice. "I'll go shower."

"It is, it is." Jay made sure Alex was ready to continue the journey, studying her expression and her state of mind. It was a bit tattered but unbroken. "I'll start packing up the car."

"Thank you," she returned.

They were on the highway, heading south again, to a slightly hotter climate. The events of the previous night preoccupied her thoughts, and her nerves, as things could have gone so much worse. As she, Conrad and Justin were emergency room physicians, she knew all the wrenching and frightening accounts of rape victims coming into the hospital, with a wide range of injuries caused by their perpetrators—if they came into the hospital at all. Alex was not raped, although the very thought of the possibility that she could have been, brought her core to a standstill, with a crippling terror that would be with her for years. Humans were unpredictable; some men, whether it was their upbringing, or being victims of abuse themselves, devalued women, using them how they saw fit. Rape was more about power than sex. Power. The feeling of power of one classification over another had been the greatest sin in humanity. Power men had over women, power of whites over blacks and other minorities, power wealthy had over the poor and disenfranchised—all of it wholly unfair and immoral. Alex, again reaching for her left arm as it rested on the steering wheel, realized she was one of the fortunate women who escaped further, more intimate, trauma. Turning her eyes to the Passenger who sat beside her, Alex was very grateful for Him.

The thought of calling her parents and Conrad pierced her psyche for the entire hot ride to Savannah. They arrived in the city after 6 o'clock, where there would be about three more hours of fading sunlight. Since she hadn't splurged during the trip, Alex decided it was time to do so, and Savannah fit the bill. The Marshall House, in the heart of Historic Savannah, was a long, brick building, with green shutters surrounding every window. The first level was equipped with a long portico, with ornate, green iron arches holding up the green metal overhang above. Alex wanted one of those rooms so she could relax on the portico, and maybe feel a Savannah breeze.

She was in luck—one of those rooms was vacant. The room, Victorian and decorated in that Southern appeal, was just perfect. She ordered room service and decided to call Conrad first. She stepped out onto the portico and waited for him to pick up. A little part of her hoped that he was still at work, but a big part of her wanted to hear a familiar and kind voice. The Savannah breezes she had looked forward to turned up, blowing her dark, straight hair in the same direction as the breeze. Conrad answered his phone, giddy it was her. Giggles turned into tears, as she failed to hold it together. After hearing his shaken voice, Alex hurried to tell him that she was okay. Immediately, Conrad told her he was going to FaceTime her. Pressing accept, Alex saw his worried expression, looking for guarantees that she was definitely okay. Sitting in almost complete darkness, only the light from her iPhone partially illuminated her face. Conrad was at home in his well-lit kitchen.

"Hi," she quavered, holding the back of her wrist to her lips. Alex breathed in and then out. "I am okay."

"Why don't I believe you, Girl?" Conrad squawked over the small screen.

Emotions grabbed her tightly. It was so hard trying to be strong, strong enough not to worry her best friend—she failed. Alex sobbed. "I'm okay."

"Do you want us to come get you?" Conrad asked sincerely. Justin entered the frame. "What's going on, Al?"

Somehow, she was able to calm herself down. "I got a little banged up," explained Alex, trying to clear the tears from her face.

"Banged up?! What do you mean 'banged up'?" Conrad wanted answers.

"Well," she began and swallowed. "Yesterday, I kind of pissed somebody off, and later on, he found me, and wanted to do bad things." Alex grew upset once again.

"Did he succeed?!" angrily Conrad inquired over a thousand miles away.

Gasping, and then exhaling out her anxiety, she pulled it together. "No, no, he just umm…" Alex paused to breathe. "He just squeezed my arm hard, you know."

Relief drenched over Conrad and Justin; they could breathe. "Did somebody call the cops?"

"Yeah, yeah, the Guy who stepped in called the police," replied Alex, as she looked to her left to look to Jay, touching His shoulder.

"Well, thank God for him," Justin spoke before Conrad got anything out.

"You can say that again."

"Thank God, thank God, thank God," said Conrad, as he stood straight up again. "Just promise me that you're okay. Where are you anyway?"

Telling Conrad about the frightening encounter lifted a great weight off her shoulders; she had the ability to move forward. "I promise you, I am okay," she reassured Conrad. "I just got to Savannah from Myrtle Beach; I decided to treat myself to a couple of nights at an inn. Room service should be coming soon."

"We are so jealous," Justin said smiling.

"I wish you guys were here with me."

"Us too, Al. We miss you!"

"Oh God, I miss you too," she reciprocated the feeling. "Conrad," began Alex, "would you be so kind to call my parents and just gloss over the scary parts, tell them I'm okay and that I'll call them in the morning, please?"

"Sure, my friend," Conrad promised. "Hey Alex, who did you piss off in Myrtle Beach?"

Quietly smirking, she rubbed her exhausted eyes. "Two guys from the far right."

Conrad smirked. "Oh, I get it."

Alex was efficient in narrating the events of the previous day, not leaving many details out. This would give Conrad and Justin some context of what led to her attack. After about five minutes, she wished Conrad and Justin a good night, and avowed her love for them. They did the same.

It was morning again. Instead of waking up in a tent, sleeping on a firm, foam, yoga pad, she awoke in a room with walls and a ceiling, and on a fluffy, queen-size bed, which she blissfully enjoyed sleeping on. Alex grabbed her phone; it was 7:32 a.m. She got up to find Jay. He was rocking easily in one of many rockers on the portico the inn supplied for their guests. He seemed like He was enjoying the early morning sunrise and the quietness of the new day. After a quick visit to the adjacent bathroom, Alex returned to sit on the soft bed, as she found her inner resolve to call her parents. She didn't know what exactly Conrad had told them, but she had to call. It only took one and a half rings before her mother picked up. Judging by Joanne's very relieved tone, Alex also remembered she had to breathe, trying to combat her need to receive a mother's love and empathy for her child. If Alex fell completely apart, she knew that this trip would be over, as her mother would insist she come straight home. Alex knew she was on some kind of unparalleled journey, not to be compromised by any small setbacks, not to be compromised by fear or selfish wants or needs. She needed to know how this trip would end, how she would come out on the other side of it. Would it change her, or would it leave her in the static, numb state she found herself in after Nate's death? Alex knew she would need to convince her loving parents that she was indeed okay. She did just that.

Alex didn't want to spend any more time in the room; she wanted to explore what Savannah was all about. Walking on the street, Alex asked the first gentleman she crossed paths with where she could find some good breakfast. Young in nature, he didn't know too much about the area. She saw another gentleman, a little bit older than the last. He was well-dressed—indeed it was a Sunday—wearing off-white trousers along with a white button-down shirt and red suspenders. Sweat was already forming on his forehead from the heat of the day. Alex was wearing her usual variety of denim shorts and tanks; a pink tank was the color of the day. She asked the gentleman if he had any recommendations. Very kindly, he stopped and listened. From his back pocket, he pulled out a white handkerchief and wiped the droplets of sweat from his forehead. When he spoke, his voice was booming, but altogether gentle. He mentioned a place called The Collins Quarter, a few blocks north. His laugh was delightful. Alex extended her hand, thanking him for his time. The gentleman bowed his head, bidding her a good day.

The Collins Quarter, with its typical brick façade, already had people seated outside. Alex and Jay went inside. There was no such thing as a table for one, so she had to settle for a table for two. The hostess sat her at a table in the far corner of the restaurant, in front of a large window. Alex was the only being who could see Jay at this moment, learning that He preferred to be invisible in restaurants. Quietly, she sat, waiting for service, observing the people inside. It seemed like the usual Sunday crowd, dressed up and prepared to spend time with family. Jay excused Himself when the young waitress was approaching. Alex focused on the young lady's white nametag; it read, 'Rehani'.

"Hi, my name is Rehani. I'll be your server today." In her hands she held a wrapped-up knife and fork, along with a menu and a pitcher of water.

"That's a beautiful name, Rehani," Alex replied, smiling. "Hopefully I pronounced it correctly."

"You did, you did," enthusiastically Rehani spoke. Rehani was a tall young woman with a tremendous spirit. Her dark hair was wavy and long, which complimented her tall stature. She wore black pants and a white shirt. Silver hoop earrings were perfect for her oval-shaped face. "May I bring you a beverage?"

"Oh yes, certainly," Alex began, "I'll have some regular tea please, Rehani. Earl Gray is fine."

"One Earl Gray coming up," Rehani confirmed. She set off to do her task.

Picking up the plasticized menu, Alex perused the breakfast choices. Wanting to keep it light, she decided on the avocado toast and a bowl of fresh fruit containing blueberries, strawberries, cantaloupe, and kiwi. Alex raised her head and glanced around the restaurant, spotting Jay about four tables ahead, sitting with an older gent who was seated alone. Alex didn't have time to surmise anything about the gent because Rehani had already returned with her tea. "Oh, thank you, Rehani."

"You're very welcome," Rehani returned. "Do you need more time looking over the menu?"

"Oh, no," Alex answered, "I'll have the avocado toast and an order of fresh fruit please."

Rehani didn't have to write anything down. "Good choices," she commented. "I'll return shortly."

"Thank you, Rehani." While Alex waited, she sipped her hot Earl Gray. She observed the street outside; people walked back and forth, as each of them had some destination. Watching the sparse foot traffic relaxed Alex's mind and body, so much so that the events of two nights prior all but vanished. She happened to put her tea on the table, laying her arms on the surface, and crossing them in front of her. It was then that Alex's right fingers touched the injured bicep, massaging it with some pressure, causing her to finally look downward. The bruises, black and blue in various shapes, had disappeared. She pressed harder and the soreness was gone. What wasn't gone was that feeling of paralyzing fear. Alex hoped that would fade with time.

Rehani returned with the breakfast order and placed everything on the table. "Can I get you anything else?"

Looking over the bounty, Alex was satisfied. "I am good, Rehani. Thank you."

"You're very welcome again," replied Rehani. "If you need anything, just wave me down."

"Okay, Rehani," Alex resolved. Wasting no time, she dug into her avocado toast, waking up her tastebuds. After a few bites of fruit, Alex's mouth watered enthusiastically. She didn't realize she was so hungry. Within twenty minutes, she had devoured everything.

"Wow," Rehani said, returning to Alex's table. "Somebody was hungry." Rehani began to clear to table.

"Yeah, well, I have a very hearty, New England appetite," Alex explained. "When it snows, we tend to eat." Laughter sprang out.

"Oh, you are from New England?" Rehani uttered. "May I ask where exactly?"

"I am from Hopkinton, Massachusetts, very close to Boston," detailed Alex. "My name is Alex," she clarified, extending her hand.

Rehani reached out to reciprocate the handshake. "It's very nice to meet you, Alex. I'll be right back." She quickly brought the dishes back into the kitchen and returned. "So, you are from the town where the Boston Marathon begins?"

This question puzzled Alex a bit; she wasn't sure where Rehani was heading. "Yes," she hesitantly answered.

"Oh, oh, I apologize," Rehani started, "I'm a criminal justice sophomore at Southern University nearby; we have been studying the Boston Marathon Bombings in class recently."

Clearing her throat, Alex took a sip of her tea. "Yep, that was a very sad and tense five days up there."

"I bet."

Alex wanted to change the subject quickly. Memories came flooding back of a very paranoid Nate thinking the bombers were coming after him. It was his first lengthy hospital stay. "So, what do you want to do with your criminal justice degree?"

Suddenly, Rehani squatted down on her heels. "I'm going to go into law enforcement for like three or four years, and then I'll go to law school."

"Law school—good for you," spoke Alex, excited. "We need more women in these traditionally male professions."

"God, I hear you," Rehani agreed, smiling widely. "What do you do, if I may ask?"

"I am a physician," Alex admitted, clearing her throat once again.

"Oh wow, that's so cool!" Rehani shifted on her heels. "I thought about going to med school, but I didn't think I could handle the intense schoolwork."

Quietly pondering how tough med school was, Alex also knew how intense law school was from her friends who had chosen that path. "I hear law is pretty intense as well."

"Yeah, people say that too." Rising to her feet, Rehani adjusted her clothes. "Can I get you anything else, Alex?"

"Oh no, Rehani, I am fine," Alex answered, grateful.

"I'll be right back," announced Rehani.

Alex finished her tea, and then pulled out her iPhone out of her back pocket.

"Here you go," Rehani handed Alex the check. Seeing Alex pull out her credit card, she politely took it from her. "I'll be back."

Standing, Alex stood and adjusted her own clothing. Jay was still sitting with that gent otherwise sitting alone. The gent's eyes spoke volumes about his loneliness. Rehani returned with the two paper receipts on a small plastic tray. "Thank you, Rehani." Sitting back down, Alex did a quick calculation and signed the main slip. The restaurant crowd had dwindled down to just a few.

Rehani returned, noticing Alex's gaze toward the older man. "That is Mr. Wyatt; he lost his wife about two months ago. He comes in here every day."

"Boy, that's sad," Alex said with sadness in her voice. "Do you know if he has any family around?"

"I believe he has a daughter who lives in California," answered Rehani.

Alex stood, placing her iPhone back in her back pocket. "Do you think Mr. Wyatt would mind if I sat with him for a few minutes?"

Rehani's eyes returned to Alex, amazed by her generosity, which was sorely lacking in the world. "I think he would enjoy that very much."

It just took Alex about eight steps to reach his table. Grabbing the corner of the table, she squatted to make eye contact with Mr. Wyatt's downward gaze. "Hello, Mr. Wyatt," she initiated, speaking softly, "my name is Alex." Waiting for him to respond, Alex saw him lift his eyes. "Can I sit here with you for a few minutes?"

His right hand directed her to the chair across from him. "You can sit there," Mr. Wyatt offered.

Watching Jay get up from the same chair, Alex sat. "I hear you are quite the regular around here."

Raising his head, Mr. Wyatt grinned all he could. "That's right, I come here every morn. People are nice here," he uttered and then looked back down to the daily newspaper. Mr. Wyatt had a round head full of untamed, gray hair. His gold-rimmed, square eyeglasses certainly weren't new—far from it. The beige-striped, Polo-like shirt seemed the same age as his glasses, along with his matching beige pants. For his age of eighty or so, Mr. Wyatt was a little overweight.

"Yes, they are very nice in here," Alex agreed. "Do you live close to the restaurant?"

"It's not far," replied Mr. Wyatt with his nose still in the newspaper.

Alex struggled to engage the old fellow in mutual conversation. "Have you lived in Savannah long?"

Looking over his eyeglass frames, Mr. Wyatt glanced at Alex with a querying eye. It was then he noticed her friendliness. He folded his newspaper. "I am Savannah-born and -raised," he began. "My father was the harbor master; worked there all his life. He met my mother, married her, and they had five children—I was their second."

Her eyes opened wide while she listened to Mr. Wyatt. "You must have all sorts of nieces and nephews," Alex commented. "Do you have any children?"

A big smile emerged upon his face. "Yes, we have a daughter who lives out west, out in California, you know. She's a professor of Music up in San Francisco." He paused for a moment. "She and her family just returned home from her mother's funeral. She sang like an angel during the service."

"Oh Mr. Wyatt, I am so sorry for your loss of your wife."

To find some comfort, he gazed out toward the street. "She was sick with cancer, you know. For many years, she fought like the dickens." Mr. Wyatt turned forlorn and introspective. "You don't know how much strength you have until something like that hits, and then a different kind of strength rises up."

Alex's eyes filled, as she looked out the same, familiar window. "I lost my brother a couple months ago from mental illness," Alex revealed. "Does it ever get easier?"

Mr. Wyatt met her eyes in solidarity, sorrowful solidarity. "As I see it, through people's sickness, they demonstrate how important life is, and how not to take anything for granted, no matter how small something is, whether it is a smell of a cup of coffee or a quick rain shower." His words were so poetic. "Our time on Earth is what you make of it. We just have to figure out what our best path is, and it's different for everybody."

Clearly moved, and a little astonished by his quick turnaround from introvert to extrovert, Alex was calm. "You're a preacher, aren't you?"

Smiling, Mr. Wyatt tipped his head. "I'm a retired preacher. I preached for nearly forty years."

"You're still a preacher," she concluded.

Leaning back in his chair, Mr. Wyatt grinned. "I guess I am," he said, and then rested his arms back on the table. "I don't know if this will help or not, but before my wife passed, she told me I had to fill my heart with love, all the love I could stuff into it, every day. She said if I did that every day, no hate, no regret, no loneliness could ever sneak in."

She didn't look away, as tears escaped her eyes, truly appreciating his words. "That's beautiful."

"She was an amazing woman," Mr. Wyatt said about his beloved wife. "So, Alex," he started, chuckling. "What do you do?"

"I'm a physician up in Boston." Maybe if she said it enough, she might believe it again.

"Isn't that something," he said proudly, and then recognized the doubt in her vacant glance. "You have lost faith in yourself, haven't you?"

The outside gave her comfort once again; she looked but saw nothing. "Yeah."

A long, uncommon sigh escaped from Mr. Wyatt. "You know what?"

"What?"

"God never makes mistakes," he announced with the passion coming from his soul. "He wanted you to be a doctor for reasons you don't even know about yet. Your gifts will come to you soon enough, I'm sure of it."

"You think so?" tearfully Alex implored.

"I know so," Mr. Wyatt said with ferocity. "Listen, I have service to attend at noon. Come with me." This was more of a command rather than an offer.

Alex pondered his offer, as she cleared away her tears, still looking at the outside world. "I'm not dressed for it."

"Is that the best you have?" Mr. Wyatt humorously asked. "Do you think God cares what clothes people wear in church? Have you looked at me?"

Wanting to laugh, she tried to read him, holding back her laughter until Mr. Wyatt began to laugh his deep guffaw. Alex started to laugh. "You're a very funny man."

He smiled at his new friend. "Come with me."

Knowing Mr. Wyatt probably wouldn't take no for an answer, she agreed. "I'd love to come."

"Great," Mr. Wyatt replied, smiling. Like a young boy, he got to his feet in a flash. "That's my car," he said, pointing at the powder blue Chevy Impala on the other side of street. Where's your car?"

Following his lead, Alex rose from the iron chair and pushed it back under the table. "My car is back at the hotel."

"You can come with me," Mr. Wyatt announced. "See you all tomorrow."

A chorus of voices around the restaurant bellowed out to say goodbye to Mr. Wyatt as he exited.

The First Baptist Church, a Greek-Revival building, was founded in 1800. Southern Live Oaks covered with Spanish moss surrounded the church, and provided adequate shade from the hot, Savannah sun long enough to enter this old church. Alex followed Mr. Wyatt into the church. The wide center aisle was flaked with wooden pews, which all had red vinyl cushions on them. Mr. Wyatt slinked into one of the left, rear pews without calling attention to himself, and invited Alex to sit next to him. She accommodated Mr. Wyatt. Looking across the aisle, Alex spotted Jay also taking a seat, figuring no one else could see Him but her. If there was any more appropriate place for Jay to be, she couldn't think of one.

Their service was about to begin. The doors opened wide at the rear of the church, and a young pastor, dressed so smartly, as any big city lawyer would be, clutched his Bible to his chest. As he reached the altar, which wasn't nearly as elevated as altars in Catholic churches, he cleared his throat. He introduced himself, like he did at the beginning of every service, just in case there were any newcomers. The voice of Pastor Benjamin J. Samuels resonated around the church, ricocheting off the marble walls and into the owners of ears who might have been half asleep. Everyone was awake now. Mr. Wyatt quietly chuckled, feeling so proud of his protégé. Alex turned to her new friend and smiled. Pastor Samuels stood about five-foot-eight and was very physically fit. Good looks blessed him. As he began speaking his message of the day, his audience was enthralled. The message of the day was germane to the struggles that were heavy on his listeners' souls, feeling like their own country was against them at every turn, and at every step forward, only to get pushed back. With years of progress, suddenly they were moving in reverse, just because of the color of their skin. Pastor Samuels, reaching down into his Heavenly soul, spoke passionately about being resilient, and being smart. Being smart took on a new level of understanding, with which only black and brown-skinned families were all too familiar. One's ethnicity and the color of one's skin could become a life-and-death risk, especially for men from their teenage years to middle age. Then Pastor Samuels pleaded with his congregation to allow him to recount the last four hundred years of the greatest sin.

Alex listened carefully to Pastor Samuels words. From her extensive medical training, she knew that each and every body, only differing based on sex or medical defects, possessed the same neurological, circulatory, immune, muscular, and nervous systems. Blood runs through everyone's veins; everyone breathes; everyone has a heartbeat. These facts cannot be denied. Pastor Samuels continued his sermon by talking about how humans differ in their physical appearances based on the different areas of the Earth where they originated. African people had darker pigment of skin due to the warmer climate in which they lived, and still live. It cannot be ignored, Samuels continued, that all communities throughout the world want the same things from life: every human being wanted to be purposeful. Having a purposeful life was what brought people happiness and satisfaction. Wanting to have a family, and having your children succeed in their life was also universal throughout civilization, Samuels mentioned passionately to his congregation. Suddenly he became quiet and reflective, as he walked around the pulpit. He looked downward to the floor, trying to piece together his next thoughts, finally speaking the truth of which almost everybody was aware, all but the youngest. Pastor Samuels spoke about the country they called home—the country that after four hundred years still viewed them inferior to their white counterparts. Samuels vowed that all men and women were created equal—that was what God wanted. He broached the topic of slavery, and wondered that if slavery had never happened, would the white man see them differently—as equals. That question could never be answered, Samuels concluded. Their future was in their own hands, but God was walking with them through this life. If you want something, Samuels stated to the church, all that was needed was God's wisdom, His foresight, and His love. God would deliver, Pastor Samuels concluded.

After the service, and once half of the congregation had left to go about the rest of their day, Mr. Wyatt walked toward the pulpit, where Pastor Samuels remained. Alex followed him. As the young pastor spotted his teacher, Benjamin's eyes lit up with his smile. His arms rose to embrace his dear friend.

"Ed," Benjamin gleefully said. "It's so nice to see you." He chortled again. "How have you been?"

Mr. Wyatt kept his hand upon Ben's shoulder. "I've been okay," Mr. Wyatt said with a little sorrow. "Some days are harder than others, you know." A tear dropped from his eye, seeping into the red carpet. "Ben, I would like you to meet my new friend, Alex. She is a physician from Boston."

Ben extended his right hand. "It's so nice to meet you, Alex." He lied his left hand upon hers.

"It's good to meet you as well," kindly replied Alex. "Your sermon was powerful—I really enjoyed it."

Situating his hands in a wai pose, Ben touched both thumbs to his lips and bowed. "I thank you very much. God bless you."

Instantly, Alex didn't quite know how to respond, leaving her tongue-tied. "You're welcome." She caught a glimpse of a very amused Jay on her right.

"So, what brings you to Savannah?" asked Pastor Ben.

The answer was more difficult to put together, given the fact she was on a road trip with Jesus. "I'm just seeing the country, driving."

"May I?" Mr. Wyatt asked Alex with a soulful look.

Hesitating for moment, Alex trusted his eyes. "Sure." She grew somewhat anxious.

"A few months ago, Alex lost her brother to mental illness." Mr. Wyatt turned to a resolute Alex, and then looked back to Ben. "Alex has lost her faith in herself."

As Ben listened to his wise teacher, he grew melancholy. "Alex, I'm so sorry for your loss." Ben ushered her to the closest pew where they all sat. "What was your brother's name?"

"Nate. His name was Nate," she quietly stated.

Ben clasped his hands together across his lap while he thought. "The greatest gift God has given us, as humanity, is our ability to hope. Sometimes there are people out there who get knocked down time and time again. These are the people who think hope is all lost. Hope is never lost. People just need to look up to the sky, whether in a light or dark sky, and search out those strands of hope, strands of light, you can reach.

I like to think our loved ones drop down these strands of hope so they can connect with us on Earth. I believe these strands of hope, which can be singular or many, are the ways we can keep them in our minds, our hearts and our happiness."

"Oh wow," Alex exclaimed, as she pondered that concept.

"What would Nate want for you?" asked Pastor Ben.

Compared to all the other questions she had been asked, this question was easy to answer. She looked away, steadying herself to speak. "Nate would want me to be happy," she replied, struggling with that idea.

Ben recognized that answer was difficult for her to accept. "Why are you fighting with that idea? Why can't you allow yourself to be happy?"

A more difficult question. Alex glanced upward to the white ceiling, counting the lights, trying to hold it together. "He, umm, he took his own life, and I, I couldn't save him."

Hearing this, Ben understood her conflict within herself. Sensing her deep grief—soul-deep—that had nearly drowned her, in her soul's pool, he wanted to throw her a lifejacket. "I have counselled many people whose loved ones committed suicide, and all of them blamed themselves, which is a very heavy burden to bear," Ben started. "With you, it's a heavier burden to carry because you are a physician. You have this knowledge that God has supplied you to help people, to heal people." Breathing deeply, Ben continued. "Even though I'm not a physician, I serve people with their spiritual growth. God has also given me this knowledge. I have failed a handful of people, including my sister." Tears came easily.

Mr. Wyatt patted his friend on his back.

Alex's attention turned straight to Ben.

"My sister was drug-addicted for many years. Myself, my other brother, and my mom tried, tried, and tried to get her help, get her into a drug program. Do you know how hard it is to get a black woman into a drug program instead of prison?"

"Unfortunately, I do," Alex spoke honestly.

"Yeah, well, that task was unattainable for our family and for many black families." He paused to gather himself. "She got pregnant, had her baby girl very premature, and my sister passed away four months later." Out of frustration, Ben's right fist gently pounded his right thigh.

"What was your sister's name?" Alex asked softly.

Raising his head proudly, Ben smiled. "Her name was Carol. My mom loves *A Christmas Carol*."

"It's a classic Christmas tale," she replied.

Quickly, Ben stood and cleared his eyes. He turned back to his guests. "Hey, can I invite you back to my home for a little lunch? On Sundays, we have big lunches. We love to have some company."

Alex turned to Mr. Wyatt to gauge his intentions.

"I would love to come see your family," Mr. Wyatt happily said. "I hope you have enough food for me."

With a clap of his hands, Ben broke out into unbridled laughter. "Oh, we always have enough for you, my friend." Grabbing his right hand, Ben gave Mr. Wyatt a shoulder hug. "We would love to have you too, Alex."

Alex smiled at his offer. "I think I would like that very much, Pastor Samuels."

"Please, please, please, call me Ben."

Chuckling at his boyish plea, she acquiesced. "Okay."

Pastor Samuels lived south of the First Baptist Church, in the Savannah suburbs. His house was ranch-style, shaped in a "U" layout, and on a corner lot. Painted light green, the house was trimmed out in white, trying to get to that Craftsman's-style look that didn't quite reach that classification. Pastor Samuels parked his maroon Dodge SUV behind an older, blue, Volvo sedan, while Mr. Wyatt parked behind a light gray Dodge minivan that looked a few years newer than the Volvo.

They followed Pastor Samuels inside, through the front door and into the living room. Voices were coming from another room. Pastor Samuels walked into the kitchen where his family was gathered. It was just another Sunday; sometimes he brought home guests, sometimes he did not. On this Sunday, Ben brought home a familiar face and an unfamiliar face. Cheers rang out when Ben's family saw Mr. Wyatt. Ben introduced everyone to Alex, as all welcomed her like just another family member. Ben's mom, Yvette, was the first person who embraced this stranger, Alex. Yvette was nearing 60, although she looked ten years younger. She stood about 5 foot, 5 inches tall and was Rubenesque. Splashes of gray streaks within her thick, brown, and wavy hair only accentuated her beautiful facial features. Yvette wore bright purple pants and a yellow, flowery blouse to match the beautiful flowers outside. At first touch, Alex sensed Yvette had a heart of gold.

After Ben's wife, Tina, gave Mr. Wyatt a gigantic hug, she welcomed Alex with the same warmth. Tina, taller than Yvette, but shorter than Mr. Wyatt, was very thin, almost gaunt. She had short black hair, and she wore a black-and-white summery dress that was almost as thin as her.

Leaning on the pale-yellow Formica counter, stood Ben's brother, Mike. Unlike the others, Mike was a bit shy and seemed to keep things close to the vest. Alex wondered if he had always been shy or if life had just tossed him around a bit, like life had done to her. He smiled and waved at Alex when Ben introduced him to her. Mike wore jeans and a navy-and-white wide-striped shirt. Mike had short dark hair with a thin stature and average looks. Suddenly there was a small cry from a back room.

"I'll get her, Mom," Ben said in a caring voice. He left the kitchen.

"Alex," Yvette got her attention, "please let me get you something to drink."

"Oh, water will be fine, Yvette," she replied, politely stepping toward her. "Can I help you with something?"

Like any southern host, Yvette swung her gaze back on Alex. "Now girl, you are our guest; you will not lift a finger in this house."

Alex instantly smiled at Yvette. "Okay." Listening in on Mr. Wyatt's short conversation with Mike indicated that Ben's brother was uncomfortable in his skin.

As soon as Yvette handed Alex her ice-cold water, Ben emerged carrying a child on his chest.

"And this is Ruby," announced Ben toward Alex. He manipulated the little girl's rigid body for her, turning her around so she could face everybody. "Come on, girl, say hi to everybody." Sitting down, Ben held her on his knee.

"There's my baby girl," Yvette said, as she caressed Ruby's constantly moving jaw.

"Where's her chair, Mom?"

"I think it's in the den, Hon," Yvette answered Ben.

"Mom, I'll get it," said Tina.

Quickly, Alex noticed Ruby had some type of developmental disability, most likely athetoid cerebral palsy. She walked closer to Ben and Ruby and crouched down in front of Ruby. "Hey Kiddo, what's ya doing?" asked Alex in a very bright voice. "It's good to meet you." Reaching for Ruby's closed fist, and being as gentle as she could, Alex

104

tried to have Ruby grab onto her index finger.

Ben, moved beyond words, watched the loving nature of Alex interact with Ruby, and shed a tear. "Many people are afraid to interact with this little, sweet girl."

Validating his words, Alex's heart indiscernibly dropped—she recognized his frustration, noticing the quick look he gave his brother. "Will Ruby come to me?"

At that time, Tina returned with Ruby's push chair that resembled a toddler's stroller. She sat next to Ben.

"Oh, sure," Ben acknowledged, as he held Ruby under her arms. Once Alex had a good hold of his precious niece, Ben let go.

Within her arms, Alex held Ruby close and stood. "How's that, Ruby girl?" It didn't go unnoticed that she had all eyes on her, as she was still a stranger to most of her captive audience. "I am a physician from Boston," she revealed. "During med school, I did a dissertation on cerebral palsy, including all three types. I was inspired by Rick and Dick Hoyt, the father and son who ran the Boston Marathon for over 30 years; Rick has severe athetoid cerebral palsy."

"I think I heard about them," Mr. Wyatt spoke up. "Isn't Rick in a wheelchair and his dad would push him?"

Holding a very content Ruby, Alex enjoyed every second. "Yes," she replied.

"God love that man," Mr. Wyatt exclaimed proudly.

Taking a glance around the kitchen, Alex looked for Jay, giving Him a quick wink. "Rick studied at and graduated from BU, majoring in special education."

"He did?" inquired Yvette. Skepticism doused her question.

"He absolutely did," Alex said with happy affirmation. The little girl squeaked like a little bird getting prepared to let the world know she was listening.

"What was that, Ruby Tuesday?!" blurted out Ben. He stood and walked to where he could see her sometimes-distorted expression, as uncontrolled muscles frequently had their way. "She's smiling."

This revelation pleased Alex. She decided to sit and try Ruby in a different position. "Do you want to look at everybody?" Turning Ruby around on her lap, Alex held her around her narrow torso, as she could nearly touch her fingertips together. She looked at her pale pink shorts and her white top. "How old is Ruby?" Another happy squeak came from the little girl.

"She's very vocal today," Ben proudly stated. "Is she sitting steady on your lap?"

Sensing Ruby's legs slightly between hers, Alex knew the girl was comfortable. "Yes, she is."

"Ruby will be five in a few months," Yvette directed toward Alex. "She was born at 29 weeks at just barely three pounds. Her Mom, Carol, passed before Ruby was released from the hospital." Yvette finally sat down, next to her granddaughter.

"Ben told me," Alex sorrowfully expressed. "I'm so sorry for your loss."

Sighing heavily, Yvette reached out and held Ruby's small hand. "We're grateful we have this little, beautiful child."

"Mom, I gotta take off, I'll call you later," abruptly announced Mike. He walked out, not saying another word.

Stifling his obvious anger, Ben took a breath and stood. "Please excuse me everyone—it seems my brother has forgotten his manners." Instead of going out the side door four feet away, he walked into the back den and through the living room to get to the front door.

"Please excuse Mike," Yvette cut the tension, "he hasn't been the same since Carol passed."

The kitchen remained silent. Alex continued to hold little Ruby on her lap. She knew what Mike was going through losing a sibling, although she wasn't as angry as Mike seemed to be five years out. Hopefully, Alex thought, in five years, she would be in a better place— a place where she would be satisfied and happy. That day was getting closer and closer. At that moment, she realized how much she missed her parents, Conrad, and Justin. Ruby happily squealed once again, bringing a smile to Alex's face. "This girl wants to talk!"

"She might be hungry," Tina suggested. "She hasn't eaten in a while."

"Would you like me to put Ruby in her stroller?" asked Alex, very willing to help wherever she could.

Yvette was already at the refrigerator getting her milk drink ready. "I usually feed her on my lap." She put a plastic eyedropper on the table.

The appearance of the eyedropper unnerved Alex. Not wanting to step on any toes, Alex also had a responsibility to Ruby. "Does Ruby eat any solid food?"

"Oh no," Yvette quickly responded, "she doesn't have the ability to chew, and she coughs a lot."

Growing increasingly anxious, Alex realized she had to witness how Ruby got her nutrients. Now cradling Ruby, Alex tenderly gave Ruby to her grandmother. As expected, Yvette rested her arm on the table, placing Ruby's neck in her arm crevice, as she balanced Ruby's legs on her lap. Yvette picked up the eyedropper with the arm, which was supporting Ruby's neck, and carefully squeezed the milk droplets into her mouth. Out of pure concern, Alex couldn't help but get to her feet to watch this bothersome method, her eyes cringing at every turn.

Yvette sat Ruby straight up every time she started coughing. "Okay baby," Yvette reassured Ruby. Once the coughing stopped, Yvette began the feeding method again.

Anxious for Ben to return, Alex continued to watch the never-ending cycle of Ruby taking in some fluids, and then aspirating. "Yvette, do you mind if I try feeding Ruby her milk?" she kindly asked.

Not expecting this question, Yvette studied Alex's intentions, not knowing what to expect.

"Mom," Tina spoke out, "let Alex have a shot; she might have a better way to feed Ruby."

Alex had a surprising and welcome ally in Tina; she turned and mouthed 'thank you' to Tina. "Ruby will be safe."

Reluctantly, Yvette allowed Alex to try feeding Ruby. "How will you feed her?" she inquired with trepidation.

"Oh sure, sure," Alex replied, as her voice exuded positivity. "I thought I would put Ruby in her stroller so she's sitting more upright, and I'll see how it goes with the milk." Watching Yvette's expression turn from despondency to enlightenment was gold for Alex, as she allowed the child to leave her arms.

Rushing downward, Alex slowly took Ruby into her arms. "Come on, Ruby girl." Alex got another happy squeak out of her, making her chuckle. She made her way to the stroller sitting in the small dining room. Gently, Alex sat Ruby in it and buckled her in. "Let's go sit next to Grandma," she stated, pulling the stroller through the kitchen.

"Here's the towel."

With gratitude, Alex smiled at Yvette. "Thank you." She held the towel as she prepared the eyedropper, filling it halfway with milk. "I'm going to put a few drops under her tongue to see if she can move the milk to her throat."

"Okay." Yvette's voice was anxious, as she observed.

Kneeling on the floor, Alex squeezed a little milk under her tongue. The towel she held just under Ruby's chin absorbed the milk that flowed out. Not discouraged, Alex would try again. "This time, I'm going to support Ruby's chin." Sticking a few more drops in, Alex held Ruby's chin. "Show me how you can swallow," Alex joyfully said to the little girl with the big brown eyes. Several seconds passed, and suddenly, Alex noticed she swallowed. "You did it, girl!"

Immediately, Yvette started weeping. "Oh Lord, she did it."

Smiling at Ruby, Alex was elated. "Want to try it again?" she excitedly asked Ruby, seeing the excitement in her eyes. "Okay!" Alex put more drops of milk into Ruby's mouth and gently held her chin until she swallowed. "Good job, Ruby Tuesday!"

"My Lord, God is good!" exclaimed Yvette, as she put both of her hands on Alex's shoulders. "God Bless You, Alex."

At once, Alex felt that same warmth and peace running through her entire being like the few previous instances during the past week. She would never tire of the incredible jolt of grace and satisfaction. As this magnificent feeling faded, Alex embraced Yvette's hand. "Would you like to try it?"

"Sure, sure," answered Yvette.

Standing back up, Alex moved the stroller closer to Yvette, giving Yvette full access to her granddaughter. Stepping to the opposite side of the stroller, she noticed Yvette a little apprehensive. "Don't worry, you'll do fine." Alex sat on the nearest kitchen chair.

Filling the eyedropper with milk, Yvette put the eyedropper in place and squeezed some milk into Ruby's mouth. Hesitating a little with holding her chin, some milk dripped out. "Oh, I didn't do that right," Yvette berated herself.

"Ruby still has milk in her mouth; you'll sense when she swallows," Alex kindly explained. Continuing to observe, she saw Ruby swallow. "There she goes!"

Looking admiringly at Alex, the smile on Yvette's face spoke volumes. "I felt her swallow." Giddy about this new discovery, Yvette couldn't help but to chortle. "This is so wonderful."

"What is so wonderful?" Ben asked, walking back into the kitchen.

"Alex got Ruby to swallow her milk sitting up," Yvette explained, wearing the biggest grin.

"Is that true, Ruby Tuesday?" Ben gently peppered the child. "I have to see this." Stepping around the table, he softly put his hands on Tina's back, showing her his love for her. "Let me see this."

Wasting no time, Yvette followed the method she just learned.

She held Ruby's chin closed until she swallowed. "See that, Uncle?!"

Alex knew he was an emotional man but once he witnessed Ruby's sudden progress, he broke into tears. "Oh Ben, I didn't mean to upset you," pleaded Alex, as she stood up.

"Oh no, these are happy tears," Ben said happily. "We have been through doctor after doctor to get this child some therapy, and we get so much pushback." Ben cleared his eyes, as he sat next to Mr. Wyatt. "It's just so frustrating."

"How much therapy does Ruby receive?"

"Like two hours a month."

This was like a punch to the gut for Alex, knowing how critical early intervention was for children like Ruby. "That's it?" With her heart breaking, Alex sat back down.

Defeated himself, Ben rested his elbows on his legs. "That's it."

Alex cleared a tear from her left eye, sighing deeply. "I'll make some phone calls tomorrow."

"What else do you think Ruby could do?" seriously inquired Ben.

"How much time do you have?" Alex answered candidly.

Remaining at Ben and Tina's until well into the evening, Alex enjoyed the company, the conversation, the bounty of food Tina and Yvette prepared, and the genuine love they all showed her. Most of the topics of conversation through the warm Southern evening were about Ruby and her future care. By no means was Alex an expert on cerebral palsy, although she had concrete knowledge of it—the most common disability in childhood. Alex was careful not to overstep on suggestions, knowing how deeply this family loved Ruby, but she had to stress the importance of getting more nutrients into the youngster even though that was a scary proposition for some, especially Yvette. Alex had to make the connection that if Ruby was able to swallow liquids, she would be able to swallow solid food. It would be a process of finding the right types of food they could chop up small and mix with soft food that Ruby could swallow easily. When Yvette and Tina put Ruby down for the night, Alex quickly discovered that the child didn't sleep well. In her mind it was because Ruby was hungry, with her small stomach craving something more substantial. She mentioned this to Ben, and she saw that invisible lightbulb flip on in the back of his mind. He promised he would do what was best for Ruby, understanding he had to make his mom more comfortable with the changes the child needed.

The evening was growing late; Mr. Wyatt was set to call it a night. After using the bathroom one more time, Alex stepped into Ruby's bedroom, where she was finally sleeping in her oversized crib. There was a small lamp still on; the illumination was enough to see a sleeping Ruby. Alex carefully and quietly rested both arms on the side rail. What Alex didn't notice was Ben just outside the doorway, listening to all the great things Alex was gently whispering to his precious niece. So profoundly moved by Alex's words, then and there, he quietly recited a special prayer for Alex, in the name of God, Jesus and all the angels. Knowing Mr. Wyatt was waiting, Ben hurried to offer to drive Alex back to her hotel. For Mr. Wyatt, it had been a long, but enjoyable day. He took Ben up on his offer and went home.

The child was still fast sleep when Jay walked into Ruby's room and leaned on the crib's bottom rail. "This was all you, Kid," He announced, gratified.

Turning right, Alex grinned at His praise for her. "You think?"

"I know it, Alex," strongly He remarked. "It is not every day that I see this kind of pure compassion out of people. Obviously, there is compassion all over the world, but some people tend to not slow down anymore; everyone's racing to get nowhere."

"I didn't have anywhere to be today," Alex concluded with her tired eyes.

"You needed to be here," Jay said with conviction. "You're tired, you can leave."

In all reality, Alex didn't want to leave; it was the first day in a long time she felt that she was useful. Reaching down with a very tender touch, Alex softly stroked Ruby's cheek as she slept. "Will she be okay?"

"Yes," Jay reassured her.

Still looking at the child, Alex finally realized she could leave. "Goodnight, Sweet Girl."

The following morning, hot and humid as the day before, Alex woke up early. She went out onto The Marshall House portico to take in another bright Savannah morning. Opening her iPhone, she recalled exchanging phone numbers with Ben the night before. Once he had seen Nate's image upon her screen, he had inquired if that was her brother. After she had confirmed his question, he had shown Alex a photo of Carol. It was a horrific situation they had in common—an exclusive club that members never wanted to join. They understood each other's grief. Ben was a man of God, and he, by nature, accepted God's will, even it was painful. God always had a plan, Ben had justified for Alex.

FaceTiming with her parents almost every morning became a ritual that steadily gained importance to Alex. When her mom answered her calls, Alex recognized her happiness just knowing that she breathed life in. On this day, Joanne's reaction remained the same, as she reveled in seeing her daughter's beautiful face. They talked about their previous day and what they had done. As Joanne listened to Alex recount her day with Ruby, she brimmed with immeasurable pride; how she loved seeing her daughter's spirit again, which had waned a bit since Nate's death. During their conversation, Alex's dad appeared, receiving the summary. Joanne gave Alex some suggestions of who she could call to establish the proper services for Ruby. Gratitude shone all over Alex's face, as she would follow up on her leads. Needing to leave the call, Michael excused himself, telling his daughter he loved her, and he would talk to her the following day. With an exuberant voice, and with a smile as bright as the sun, Alex reciprocated her love for her dad.

Alone again with her daughter, Joanne gently touched upon what happened in Myrtle Beach, needing assurance that Alex was indeed okay, carefully watching her eyes for any deviations away from the truth. Alex promised her mom she was coping well. Instinctively, her mom believed her daughter, but so needing to hold her daughter, as if she was still seven years old, suffering from a knee scrape. But this wasn't a knee scrape, or even a sprained ankle; it was three frightening minutes that could have turned out very differently. Joanne was incredibly thankful her daughter wasn't seriously hurt, knowing she would have lost her mind if something did happen to her daughter. Unfortunately, Joanne already knew the indescribable grief of losing one child; she didn't want to lose another. Oh God, how she wanted to hug Alex. Joanne had to continue reminding herself Alex would be coming home soon. With that thought on her mind, she wished her daughter a good day, letting her know she loved her to the moon and back. Again, Alex easily expressed her love for her mom.

With just a small carry-on to put in the car, Alex and Jay got on the road in no time. She absolutely enjoyed her two days in Savannah and vowed to return someday soon, very motivated to visit the Samuels family again. Montgomery, Alabama was their next destination, and with the nearly six-hour travel time, that gave Alex plenty of time to make the calls she needed for Ben.

Jesus and The Butterfly

Taking Martin Luther King Jr. Boulevard, Alex and Jay merged onto I-16 heading west. When Alex felt comfortable within the flow of traffic, she began to make calls. Earlier that morning, she had gathered all the phone numbers she may possibly need and programmed everything into her iPhone. Using voice commands, Alex requested a phone number to be dialed. Jay sat quietly, watching Alex's faculties come alive, with every word she professionally spoke, with every question she asked, never being intimated that she didn't know everything. A few times Alex caught Jay glancing her way, as she communicated very well what she was seeking for Ruby. She saw His smile.

Being a physician in just one state, dealing with the insurance policies, and figuring out what would and would not be covered was one of those things Alex figured out, slowly. Now she was in uncharted waters, dealing with Georgia's medical system and understanding just how Ruby was covered. It was mind-boggling and frustrating all at the same time. Alex must have talked to Ben ten times on this Monday. Every conversation with Ben, sometimes brief, sometimes long, helped Alex put the enigmatic pieces together. She realized this process might take more than a day or two, or possibly five. With strands of information accumulating, that she had to hang onto, she had to find a way to record everything. She had a personal recorder at home, and without having an address for the rest of the trip, she had to find a store that sold a digital voice recorder. Being familiar with the Best Buy stores in New England, she set out to find one close by. There was a Best Buy coming up in Columbus, Georgia. It seemed like a good place to stop for some lunch.

With no one left to call, Alex dialed Conrad. It was always a gamble of sorts whether he would answer or not, given his screwy work schedule. On this late Monday morning, he answered.

"Hello," Conrad spoke over the iPhone's speakerphone.

"You're not at work yet?" Alex teased.

"Ha ha," he sniggered. "How are you doing, Girly?"

"I am doing pretty okay," she replied with positivity.

"You're driving; where are you headed?"

Nearly turning 'I' into 'we', Alex narrowly avoided going down that rabbit hole. Quickly, she turned to Jay and slightly winced. "I am headed to Montgomery, Alabama, to see some sights and things like that."

"That sounds cool," remarked Conrad. "Didn't they just open a new museum in Montgomery? It has something to do with slavery and lynching. I know it won't be the happiest of subjects, but it might be interesting."

"Yeah, yeah, yeah, I'll check it out, most definitely," Alex affirmed. "How's Justin doing?"

"Justin is at work, but he told me to tell you, if you called, he sends his love," Conrad said lovingly. "Actually, tomorrow, we are meeting with the woman at the adoption agency, so…"

Hearing this, Alex gasped with joy. "No way?!"

"Oh yes!" said Conrad, trying to remain calm. "It's a baby girl."

Alex could hardly contain her enthusiasm. "Oh Con, wow. Finally!"

"I know, I know," he mirrored her happiness. "I am so damn nervous though."

"You? Nervous?" Alex echoed. "You don't have anything to be nervous about. Come on, Con, you and Justin are two great guys, you are emergency room doctors. What else more would they want?"

"For us not to be gay," Conrad obviously spoke.

As she watched traffic, Alex sighed slowly. "Well, you can't really get around that little factoid."

Conrad reflected her exhale. "I know, I know."

"I'm going to be an auntie to a baby girl," she giggled with glee. "I'm so excited."

"Yes, yes, hopefully very soon."

"Oh Conrad, I'm just so happy for you guys."

"I know you are, Sweetheart," sincerely he spoke. "Hey, I'll call you tomorrow and tell you how everything went."

"I'll be waiting for that call with anticipation," Alex expressed exuberantly.

"Stay safe, and I love you."

"Love you too. Bye." Alex ended the call. "I'm going to be an auntie!" she aimed at Jay.

"I heard," Jay returned.

Startled by Jay's tempered response, Alex grew nervous. "Will they get the baby?"

"Don't you want to be surprised?"

"No," Alex answered quickly. "Not if they're not going to get the baby, I don't."

Jay chuckled. "You're funny, my friend."

"I'm glad I can be your entertainment for the day."

Turning in the passenger seat, Jay faced Alex directly. "Do you know what's really entertaining?" He inquired humorously.

Turning her head to look at Jay, she saw His grin. "What might that be?"

"I'm waiting for the moment you slip up and say something like 'we are' instead of 'I am' to your parents or Conrad. How will you explain that one?"

Glancing back at Jay, wearing a smile as big as the day, Alex knew she had to mull over this for a while. "You caught that, huh?"

"Yep, I did," He replied, still smiling, awaiting her answer.

Not taking her eyes off the road, her mind searched out for the proper solution. "I can't exactly lie, even if it was just a little fib." In her mind, Alex worked out the possibility of teaming up with her car as a 'we', but that would also be false. She didn't have any four-legged companions in the car that she could pair up with herself. If she didn't think about an answer, Alex knew that it would come to her.

"Your President lies," Jay reminded her.

"Yeah well, he's an egotistical maniac with no soul," she expressed fervently.

Jay continued to watch Alex work through her thoughts.

"You are enjoying this, aren't you?"

"I just want to know how you would handle it, if you were to 'slip up'." Jay sincerely inquired playfully.

Sending her eyes to the road again, trying to think of a perfect solution to an issue that might not even arise. "I'll think of something." Alex looked at Jay. "Do you trust me?"

"Of course, I trust you, Alex," Jay reassured her.

Nodding her head, feeling relieved His trust was with her, Alex again looked forward. "Thank you."

"You're welcome."

Twenty minutes later, Alex drove up to the Best Buy in Columbus. Not surprising for a Monday early afternoon, the big box store was not crowded. Alex asked the first associate she came across where she could find the digital voice recorders. The young man, not much over 18 years old, politely requested that she follow him. He brought her right to the items she was looking to purchase. His nametag read 'Isaiah'. Isaiah noticed Alex's very unfamiliar accent and dared to ask her where she was from. Of course, she answered she was from

Boston. Very taken Alex was from Boston, Isaiah started to chat her up, about anything and everything, but mostly about sports, namely football, instinctively about Tom Brady. It was a common occurrence when people found out she was from Boston—Tom Brady frequently became the topic of conversation. The funny thing was Alex wasn't all that much into football. Of course, if Alex went over to a friend's house, on a Sunday during football season, she would occasionally watch a game or two. She knew who Tom Brady was, the legend, although she had other things to think about. She would rather spend Sunday afternoons, if she happened to be off, going to art museums, going on long hikes, taking walks on the beach or just curling up with a good book.

Attempting to find the right digital voice recorder, preferably on with voice activation, Alex found a similar recorder to the one she had at home. She grabbed it off the chrome hook and carefully looked over its features. Yes, this was the one. She thanked Isaiah for all his assistance. Oddly, he continued to follow Alex to the checkout. At times, Alex had to remind herself she was mature for her young age, and there might be times that older teenagers might find her attractive. She guessed this was one of those times. After she paid for her recorder, she left, got in her car, and pulled away. As luck would have it, there was a restaurant across from Best Buy. Alex went into Pita Mediterranean Street Food and ordered a Gyro Bowl, skipping the extra carbohydrates. As she ate, Alex set up her new voice recorder, all the while observing Jay's movements, as He visited a few souls in the establishment. He only had to touch people on their hands for His power to affect them, easing their worries, and sometimes, their fears.

With just another hour and a half until they got to Montgomery, Alex put her new voice recorder to good use, recording all the things she wanted to remember for Ruby. Before they made it to Montgomery, Ben called her one more time that afternoon, mostly to thank her for all the work she had accomplished that morning. She had to let him know that there was more leg work left to be done. Never naïve of anything in his life, Ben knew things just didn't happen without advocating or a little grunt work. Ben wished Alex a good and safe night. Alex did the same.

Dirt

Prior to arriving in Montgomery, Alex discovered there weren't many campgrounds around the city, therefore she decided to stay at an inexpensive hotel: the Capitol Inn and Suites. It was within walking distance to the Alabama State House, the Dexter King Memorial Baptist Church, led by Martin Luther King, Jr. from 1954 to 1960, and the National Memorial for Peace and Justice. Parking the Toyota in front of the hotel's entrance, Alex walked inside to check in. The lobby was square and nondescript. Nobody else was in the lobby but the desk attendant, a middle-aged man who looked like he wanted to be anywhere but there. Tall and husky, he wore a blue vest, beige shirt and pants that matched the paint on the building. He had a soft voice. It was in her nature to greet people kindly, with sincereness, because in her profession and with her personal experience, she never wanted to assume what kind of day someone was having.

"Hi, do you have any single rooms available?" Alex inquired cordially.

Like he was running on fumes, he pecked at the computer keyboard one finger at a time. "We have a few singles available upstairs."

"How much, Sir?"

"Singles are 56 dollars a night," the man squawked.

"That's fine, Sir," Alex answered. Reaching into the pocket of her jean shorts, she grabbed her iPhone, taking out a credit card. "How has your day been, Sir?"

The question registered in his brain, but he didn't really want to answer. "Hot."

His reply didn't surprise her given his underwhelming energy level. Alex noticed the very old air conditioner in the window behind him. "That air conditioner doesn't work?"

The man looked at it quickly—the only thing he did quickly. "If that worked, I would have it on," he said gruffly.

Obviously, he was not having a good day. "Sir, can I get you some water?"

"No, I don't want water," growled the man, as he returned to his task at hand.

Alex was resolved to leave the desk attendant to his task, answering the questions she needed to answer to get the room. Unceremoniously, the room key appeared on the counter with the receipt and a hotel pamphlet. "Thank you, Sir."

Not surprising, the man did not respond, but simply sat down to await his next customer.

Alex got back in her car and searched out Room 232. Slowly, she drove at the top speed of 5 mph while switching her eyes between the parking lot and the blue doors on the second level. The building was L-shaped; she turned at every corner. After three corners, she finally spotted Room 232. She parked and gathered the minimal things she would need for the night. As Alex exited the driver's side door, she felt like she kicked something that was on the ground. Looking downward, she saw something against her back tire—a toy or something similar. Crouching down, she picked up a plastic action figure that looked like Jesus. It was Jesus! Before she could say anything to Jay, Alex started laughing uncontrollably, unable to stand up.

Jay appeared toward the rear of the car. "What's so funny?"

Still leaning on the side of her car, laughter had a hold of her, as her entire body joggled in hysterics.

"What do you have in your hand there?" Jay asked, smiling.

Holding the plastic Jesus up enough so He could see, Alex suddenly realized she hadn't laughed like this in a very long time. "I think it's You!"

Taking the plastic figure from her hand, Jay studied it well. Dressed in a white robe, along with a brownish-red sash, his face and hair depicted the historical portrayal of Jesus. "I think you're right," He surmised, as He began to laugh. Seeing all the scrapes and dirt on the tiny, Holy figure, Jay held him in His hand. "He looks kind of beat up."

Recovering from her amusement, Alex stood up again, smiling from ear to ear, taking little Jesus back, looking closely at the miniature figure. "You're right, he looks a bit rough." Opening up the back door, Alex found her Clorox Cleanups and dutifully wiped off all the dirt on every small surface. "Look," she giggled, as she realized the figure had poseable arms, "his arms move!"

Never in the last eight days had Jay seen Alex so carefree, so childlike. "What are you going to do with him?"

It was then and there, right in downtown Montgomery, Alex realized what she had her hand. "He will be my substitute for You, if I happen to say 'we' instead of 'I' in front of my parents, or Con, they won't think I have lost it." The plan made sense. "You are always in my car; he will be in my car. I talk to You—I can talk to him. Your name is Jesus—his name is Jesus. You are a little bit taller than he is, but height doesn't matter much in this situation."

All Jay could do was burst out in laughter, as He listened to Alex's loopy but logical rationale. "You're funny, you know that?"

"Yeah, I have my moments," Alex returned, "but You should have known that already."

"Touché, my friend," Jay expressed.

Before going upstairs to check out her motel room, she tucked plastic Jesus under her driver's seat, and then locked the car. "I'll be right down."

Alex got word that the Irish Bred Pub & Restaurant was a place with good food and a good vibe. It was also within walking distance from the hotel, so that also made it that much more appealing. The weather hadn't changed since they left Savannah; it was still hot, sticky, and cloudy. The Irish Bred Pub was less than a mile away, just seven blocks west and two blocks south. Alex walked casually on the sidewalks that held so much American history. The dichotomy of Montgomery being the first Confederate capital, where Jefferson Davis set up the White House in 1861, then one hundred years later becoming the birthplace to the Civil Rights Movement, when Rosa Parks refused to give up her seat on a bus for a white man, was astounding. It was a difficult concept for

Alex to wrap her head around. It was even more difficult to fathom that it took all that time for African Americans to receive any semblance of civil rights; Alex knew existence in America was far from equitable for African Americans.

The façade of the two-story brick building blended in with the other old brick structures on the adjacent streets. Close up, the interior of the restaurant looked inviting. Alex walked inside and the rush of cool air enlivened her. One of the male hosts met her soon after and confirmed she was a party of one, which she hadn't gotten used to yet because her comrade was almost always invisible to others. The host asked Alex if she preferred to sit at the bar or at a table. On this evening, she chose to sit at the nearly empty bar. Inside, the restaurant was industrial, with exposed black conduits for air circulation. The walls were a cleaner brick, not worn from the outside elements. Not far, to her right, was a boisterous table of five—a happy, lively, joyful group. Lots of laughs were coming from the group of three men and two women. Alex couldn't help but overhear their lively banter, as it was obvious some were in town for a class reunion.

Soon, the bartender, in his mid-thirties, with a slender build, approached his latest patron. "Hello," he said with a Jamaican accent and a welcoming tone, "my name is Rick; may I get you something to drink, Miss?"

What she wanted to drink, she didn't know. "Do I want a beer, Rick?" It had been months since she had an actual alcoholic drink, not because she was in recovery, but because life had gotten so heavy. "Do you any IPAs?"

Rick snickered. "Girl, this is an Irish pub—we have every kind of beer you can think of."

"Do you have Harpoon?"

Upon hearing her request, Rick's face grimaced. "Oddly enough, we don't have Harpoon. Sorry, Girl."

Immediately, Alex giggled. "Alright, I'll have a Sam Adams."

"One Sam Adams, coming right up," Rick proudly announced, as he went to retrieve a Sam Adams and a beer glass.

With her elbows on the bar, Alex stared blankly at the television above the thousands of bottles of alcohol. Peculiarly, it was tuned into a Red Sox game. Rick returned; Alex watched Rick pour the beer into the glass. "Do you always watch the Sox play?"

Raising his arm, Rick pointed at the party of five. "Some of them are from Boston. Gotta keep our patrons happy."

Upon hearing this, Alex turned and observed them. "Small world, isn't it?"

"Are you from Boston as well?" Rick inquired, smiling, as he folded a white dish towel.

"I am," Alex asserted. She took a sip of her Sam Adams.

"Listen up everybody," Rick announced with a booming voice, "Boston is in the house tonight!" With both hands, he pointed to the party of five and Alex, causing some muffled cheers to come forth from the back of the restaurant. Seeing Alex's cowering reaction to her sudden 15 seconds of fame, Rick laughed. "What? Did you rob a bank or something?"

"Do you really think I rob banks, Rick?" Alex played along with his humorous character.

Chortling and chortling, Rick still handled the white towel. "No, no, no, not at all, pretty lady. May I ask your name?"

She appreciated his endearing humor. "My name is Alex."

"Alex—what a lovely but strong name that is," sincerely Rick stated. "Let me grab you a menu."

Taking another sip of her Sam Adams, she heard a voice coming from the table of five. "Oh, hi."

"Are you alone, Honey?" the woman with Irish brogue asked.

"Yes, kind of," she answered.

"Would you want to come sit over here with us? Come sit over here with us."

The question turned into a directive. "I don't want to impose; you look like you're catching up," politely said Alex.

"Ahh Honey, we have been catching up for the last three days," the Irish lady spoke, "if we haven't caught up with everything yet, we have a bigger problem." Laughter broke out over the entire table, as the party of five all urged Alex to join them.

With the entire table pleading for her to join, Alex couldn't say no. Standing, she grabbed her beer and iPhone, and sat with the very welcoming group. "I thank you very much," Alex proclaimed.

"What is a sexy young thing like you sitting at a bar all alone?" one of the gentlemen brazenly uttered.

"George!" bellowed the Irish woman. "Your wife is sitting next to you!"

"Yeah, I see her," George dryly expressed, taking another drink sip swig of whatever he was drinking.

The Irish woman rolled her eyes. "George, grow up, will ya!" The entire table laughed. "By the way, my name is Nuala Jameson." She extended her hand for Alex.

"Hi Nuala," Alex met her hand with Nuala's. "My name is Alex Roma."

"It's very nice to meet you Alex," Nuala replied in a friendly voice. Nuala, with her short red hair to match her very round porcelain face, wore a flowery yellow blouse with a white tank and matching white pants. Her shape matched her age perfectly. "Do you want to meet these other ballbusters?"

There was no other choice for Alex but to laugh. "Absolutely!" She took another sip of her beer.

Nuala started on her immediate left. "This is my loving husband, Jeff, then we have George's very patient wife, Maribeth, you know George, and next to George is Frankie. We all went to Alabama State University, and we all became teachers."

"Well, good for you all," Alex replied, smiling.

A voice from behind the bar became louder. "Alex girl, where did you go?"

Raising her arm straight up, with a flailing hand, she got Rick's attention. "Over here, Rick."

Coming out from behind the bar, he walked over to the party of six now, carrying a menu. "Did they suck you over here, willingly?" Rick playfully interrogated Alex.

Before Alex could answered, George wanted to speak. "Hey, we can be very stingy with our gratuity tonight."

The entire table laughed.

"I think I came over willingly," Alex replied, chuckling.

"Ahhhh, I don't know, I don't know," Rick said with his wide grin. "Just be careful of Georgy, over here, Alex girl."

"Oh, I know all about George," confirmed Alex, as she glanced quickly at the menu Rick handed her.

"Remember Rick, gratuity, gratuity," George teased, as Rick went off to tend to other customers.

"You all have been here a lot," Alex remarked.

"Oh yes," Nuala spoke up first. "Jeff has family down here, so we are here at least twice a year. Sometimes George and Maribeth come along. Frankie lives in Montgomery."

"Very nice," Alex spoke, facing Nuala, and then everybody else. "Where do you all teach in Massachusetts?"

"Jeff and I teach in West Roxbury, and George and Maribeth are school administrators in Dedham," Nuala narrated. "And what do you do, Alex?"

"I'm a physician at Tufts."

"No shit!" Frankie exclaimed. Frankie, a grayish-haired, balding gentleman, dressed in tan shorts and a plain short-sleeved navy shirt, finally spoke.

"Yes Frankie, they do give medical degrees to women," George said sarcastically.

"But she's so young?" added Frankie.

"Well, thank you, Frankie, I am 26," Alex revealed.

"See!" Frankie loudly exclaimed to the entire table.

Alex chortled at his hidden exuberance. She sipped her beer.

"Well, good for you, girlfriend," Nuala proclaimed, with everybody else at the table nodding in agreement.

"What brings you to Montgomery?" asked Jeff. Jeff was one of those men who adored his wife, as he always had part of his hand on her. His brown eyes spoke volumes on how much he loved Nuala. Jeff was the only African American at the table. With a full head of hair and a beard, he had an easygoing personality. Wearing a tan suit with an electric-blue dress shirt, he looked like he was going to teach a class.

Not surprising this question would come up once again, she still had to answer it in a way she felt comfortable. "I...ahh, I...ahh, I lost my younger brother at the end of February, so I'm trying to regroup, and I'm taking some time for myself; I'm driving cross country."

It was dead silence at the table of six. Some eyes were focused on Alex, while other eyes looked around the table at the others.

Jeff cleared his throat. "I'm very sorry for your loss. I just lost my brother to cancer a few months back."

"I'm very sorry for your loss, as well," Alex addressed Jeff.

"Fred was such a good man," Nuala said with sadness.

Feeling like she sucked the air out of their gathering, Alex felt horrible. Suddenly, she stood, grabbing her beer and the menu. "I think I'll return to the bar."

"No, no, no, you must stay," demanded Nuala.

"Oh, no one told you," George directed towards Alex. "You're picking up the bill tonight; you are a doctor—way above our pay scales."

Alex burst into hysterics. The entire table could be heard chortling throughout the place. "George, you're definitely a funny guy."

Nuala stood and clutched Alex to her. "Don't worry, you're going to be fine."

"People keep telling me that," Alex admitted.

Letting Alex free, Nuala made sure to look into her eyes. "You can believe it."

These words connected with Alex in a way not many others had up to this moment. Whether it was the time she had spent with Ruby, or some other reason, she believed things would be okay. Grabbing Nuala's hand, squeezing gently, Alex wanted her to know she heard her words. "I'm getting there, I really am."

"I have faith you are," Nuala spoke wholeheartedly.

Alex remained with the five people who welcomed her to their table, quickly realizing that they were embracing in their friendship. They ate, laughed, and delighted in conversation as if they had known their guest for many years. For that one night, the party of five brought Alex in from the invisible storm, giving her protection and her soul nourishment that it was seeking; her soul was sucking up this nourishment like a sponge, hanging on every word that was spoken, but Alex just enjoyed the laughter that surrounded her. She realized she missed laughing.

With a new person at the table, the five friends had every reason to tell and reminisce on stories about their college days during the late '70s and early '80s. They had been young adults trying to figure out life and everything else. The more poignant stories came from Nuala and Jeff, as they had had to deal with the prejudices of being a mixed-race couple, desperately in love, and desperately trying to find a community where they would be accepted and not vilified. They found that community in Massachusetts. George, being the big jokester that he happily portrayed, could also be a teddy bear, explaining that he and Maribeth had moved to Massachusetts to get to a state where he could have the freedom to teach freely. Frankie just enjoyed living in the heat of the south. After the first snowfall in New England every year, George packs up a shoebox full of snow and sends it to Frankie. George admitted that his mail carrier was not his biggest fan. Without missing a beat, Frankie suggested that George stick a lobster in the box every once in a while, causing the entire table to erupt in fits. Again, Alex joined in on the amusement of these old friends. The atmosphere was electric.

Once the meal was complete, and the ice broken, attention soon returned to Alex. Some wondered what her plans were going to be while she was in Montgomery. She mentioned that she planned to visit the National Memorial for Peace and Justice. Faces that surrounded her turned solemn but altogether tranquil. Jeff was the first to speak about the newly completed structure. Some of the words with which he described the memorial were 'haunting', 'moving', 'sobering' and 'chilling'. Jeff also strongly suggested that every American should experience it for themselves, ultimately thanking Alex for her commitment to visit the memorial. She understood the gravity of the memorial.

It was obvious that the evening was ending; Alex would never forget the fun she had with her new friends. Alex exchanged phone numbers with Nuala and Jeff, as they promised to pass it on to the others. One by one, Alex hugged each of the five who had supplied her with happiness. The last was Jeff, and as he gave her a light embrace, Alex again sensed the spectacular warmth and peace that engulfed her soul. As many times as she had felt it in the past eight days, she would never tire of it. Nuala and Jeff offered Alex a short drive back to the hotel, but Alex very politely turned it down. They debated this offer until they agreed to a compromise: Alex would call Nuala once she got to her hotel room. Before leaving the restaurant, Alex made sure she said goodbye to Rick, as she loved listening to his Jamaican intonations.

Outside, suddenly feeling alone, Alex checked around two corners of the restaurant—no Jay. Waiting a few more minutes, she tried not to look altogether strange, especially if Rick spotted her.

"Looking for Me?" Jay asked, promptly appearing.

Catching a glimpse of Him, she startled. "Holy shit!" she blurted out. "You like scaring the crap out of me, don't You?"

Smiling and giggling, Jay leaned against the brick façade. "Sometimes it's fun."

Putting her hand against His shoulder, Alex kiddingly pushed Jay toward the direction of the hotel. "This night was jammed with funny guys."

Jay started walking. "Did you have fun tonight?"

"I did, I did," Alex replied before she yawned. "I had dinner with this group of friends who went to college down here; most of them live up by Boston now."

"Really?" Jay inquired, although He already knew.

"Yeah, it was cool," she expressed, fulfilled. "And what did You do with Your time tonight? I didn't see You anywhere in there." They were halfway to the hotel.

"I was doing My thing not too far from here," Jay answered. "There's a riverfront park close by; I find people who are upset, or just sad—a lot of people are sad these days."

"I know," she concurred. Alex walked a few more steps, debating whether to ask the question that was on her mind. "How do you think I'm doing?"

With Alex walking on His left, Jay looked back to catch her gaze. "How do you think you're doing? I mean, you're the doctor, and the patient, aren't you?"

"Yeah, I guess."

He looked at her again. "You guess?!" Jay needed a better answer. "How do you feel, Alex?"

With every step she took, as the muggy, Alabama air surrounded her, Alex evaluated how she truly felt. "Today, I felt I had a purpose; it felt good, you know."

"You always have a purpose, Alex. Everyone has a purpose."

With her eyes to the concrete sidewalk for a few seconds, she thought about His words. "I wonder if Nate felt he had a purpose. I'm not sure he could hold onto his purpose for very long, you know." A hard exhale came from her lungs.

"I can tell you that if Nate had a hard time holding onto a purpose, I can guarantee that it was important for Nate to know you and your parents continued to love him through all his ups and downs," Jay narrated.

"Oh God, did he worry about that?" Alex poignantly inquired.

Jay liked what He was seeing from His mentee. "You are not human, especially if you don't have complete control of your mind and your thoughts, if you don't have that fear that the people whom you love could suddenly disappear. I'm not saying Nate feared that, but many people who have mental illness have a very real fear of people abandoning them."

"I get that," Alex uttered. "Nate knew we loved him, and he knew we would do anything to help him." Alex felt tears forming in her eyes.

"He knew that," Jay confirmed, as They arrived at the stairway to Room 232. "Go get a good night's sleep."

Sniffling, she cleared her eyes. "You'll be around?"

"I'll be around," He assured her. "Goodnight, and don't forget to call Nuala."

Quickly, Alex glanced back at Him, giving Him a funny stare. "Thanks for the reminder," she spoke, as she started up the stairway. "Goodnight, Jay."

It was a cheap room, especially compared to The Marshall House in Savannah, although it gave her shelter for the night. She awoke to some thumping from the adjacent room, thinking it was mighty early for such activity. Jumping in the shower, Alex assumed the thumping would stop by the time she got out. It did not. *Rabbits.* She would have to call her parents from her car, the only quiet location she could think of. She dressed, packed up her small bag, and left the room.

The air was surprisingly hotter than the day before. She had to remind herself she was in the south in summer, as she started to sweat instantly. Opening her car, Alex threw her bag in the backseat and sat down on the front seat. Whether or not it would help, she rolled down all the windows, hoping for a breeze, a passing gust, or maybe just a puff of air. Such things were hard to come by.

Alex touched her mom's number in the FaceTime app. Seconds later, Joanne appeared on the small screen, so very happy to be looking at her precious daughter. Humorously, Alex had to explain why she was sitting in her car and not in a hotel room, or at some campground watching the sunrise. They had a good chuckle over the 'thumping' aspect to her situation. Joanne offered to put more money in Alex's account for some upgrades, but Alex refused the extra funds, although she thanked her mother. A child of privilege, Alex was never one to flaunt her affluence—quite the opposite—she supported many causes, namely the National Suicide Prevention Alliance. The monies that were sustaining Alex on this journey were strictly hers. Alex had obtained a full scholarship to Tufts Medical School. She knew the value of money and what it could bring. When Nate died, she needed to be close to her parents.

Her dad got on the call as usual. Alex smiled seeing his face light up, knowing she was still his little girl. He asked all the typical dad questions: how was the weather? How was the car running? Was she being safe? He probably knew about her attack on Myrtle Beach, but he avoided bringing it up with Alex, knowing that if he did, he would break down in tears. Joanne was his rock—even more so these days. Every day Alex was away, her dad missed her more and more. Saying 'I love you' to Alex became inherent, as he took nothing for granted—not anymore.

126

Soon, Alex wished her parents a good day, ending the call with 'I love you'.

Before continuing with her day, Alex went to check out. Walking into the familiar lobby, she saw the same man, wearing the same clothes, sitting behind the same desk. She approached the desk, wanting to know if he had worked all night. Alex hoped he got to go home, as she explained to the detached man she was checking out of Room 232. It was obvious to Alex that the man didn't remember her from when she checked in the evening before. He only spoke the words he needed to speak to complete the transaction.

"Have a good day, Sir," Alex spoke, stepping away from the desk.

"What did you say to me?" the man asked abruptly.

Hearing his voice stopped Alex in her tracks. She slowly turned back to him. "I said, 'have a good day, Sir,' Sir." She wondered if she sounded like an idiot.

"Nobody says that anymore," the man barked, as he stared out the window at nothing. "Nobody says hello, or goodbye, nobody thinks about anybody but themselves nowadays." Getting these words off his chest seemingly helped him breathe a little easier. "Thank you for saying that."

Alex made sure to look directly into his eyes. "You're very welcome."

The man nodded, displaying a tiny smile.

She reciprocated his smile. Alex exited the lobby, smiling inside, knowing that she had connected with the desk manager.

They stopped at Prevail Union for Alex to get a cup of tea and something substantial to eat; she didn't know how long they would spend at the memorial. They walked down Montgomery Street, passing by the Rosa Parks Museum. A visit would have to wait for another day. Soon they parked on the expansive grounds, a full city block, of the National Memorial for Peace and Justice. One hundred and sixty years prior, it was the popular square for whites to sell slaves in Montgomery. It was an unfathomable transaction Alex struggled to comprehend, as people had disregarded the fact that slaves were human beings, with hearts and minds just like their owners; but their owners considered them property—property such as vehicles or tools. Humans were not property.

She bought a single ticket; Jay, invisible to almost everybody, didn't need a ticket. There weren't many visitors on this day, so if Alex wanted to chat with Jay, she could, whispering.

Walking the grounds of the memorial, they came across the sculpture by Kwame Akoto-Bamfo, of seven shackled figures, ranging in age and gender, terrorized, after having traveled across the Atlantic where so many of their fellow passengers, piled up on one another, had perished from illness, hunger, or fear. Once captured, they became numbers instead of names; they immediately lost their identities as men, women, children. They left their professions in their homelands, and suddenly were the property of others—slaves. The fear on the faces of the sculptured figures was palpable, for all to see.

Entering the main part of the exhibit, the large square, there was a flat foot with shortened walls, leaving the upper section open, bringing in all the light and air from the outside. Steel poles were attached to the inside surface of the flat roof, moored the coffin-sized, rusted steel rectangular cubes, representing the more than 4,000 documented African Americans lynched between 1877 and 1950. Historians believed many more lynchings occurred, going unnoticed or just ignored. Each coffin-sized chunk of rusted steel represented each county which had documented lynchings in the United States, 805 counties in all. Visitors had to look up to read the names of deceased African Americans on each steel block, as if visitors were looking up to the tree branches, street poles or jerry-rigged gallows used for lynchings. Alex immediately saw trees differently, very much aware that crowds of white men, women and children would gather in town squares to witness these horrific practices against blacks, who had rights on paper, but practically none in reality. Since lynchings were an accepted practice, photographs were taken, and many even turned them into postcards. African Americans were often lynched for minor infractions, for sexual assault accusations, to enforce white supremacy, and for economic struggles of the white man. Black terrorism and intimidation were the methods whites used to control blacks. When the accused couldn't be located, the oppressors didn't think twice about lynching one of the accused's family members, including wives. Often, after lynchings, oppressors dragged their victims through black neighborhoods, demonstrating their unrelenting power. For this reason, many African Americans fled the south, moving either north or west.

Overcome, Alex took a few deep breaths to allow what only stopped happening sixty years prior to horrifically seep into her consciousness. She strolled slowly, constantly peering upward to all the hanging steel blocks, with all the names and dates of their lynchings—their deaths. The names represented human beings, human beings who probably lived in fear for most of their lives, all because of the color of their skin.

"This is unbelievable, Jay," Alex said softly, still looking upward.

"This is what greed does to people; it makes people lose their virtues, makes people lose their humanity. All these lives wasted. All these lives who didn't have children; imagine the possibilities," Jay spoke, heartbroken.

"I don't understand how people could do this. How can people just kill people? They were savages. Weren't these people Christians?"

Crouching down, Jay clasped His hands together. "Many of them were Christians. Sometimes fear, whether contrived or real, makes people come up with justifications why some actions are acceptable, accepted even by God."

Continuing to look up, Alex let out a heavy sigh. "This wasn't okay, this was not okay," Alex protested.

"No arguments from Me, My friend," Jay replied. "It is my hope that people learn from their transgressions, to learn from history so that they will do better with time."

"What makes me different from the people who think all this was okay?" pressed Alex, clearly agitated.

"Knowledge. Your experiences. Your faith," Jay uttered, standing back up. "You're a healer, not an annihilator."

Alex chuckled. "When you say 'annihilator,' I automatically think of Arnold Schwarzenegger in the Terminator movies."

"Boy, you have watched a lot of movies."

"Yeah, I did," Alex replied, forlorn, looking up to the steel blocks. "When Nate slept a lot after his doctors switched his meds, he stayed with me sometimes; I watched a lot of movies." Alex continued to walk, slowly and with purpose, studying every steel cube and reading each name and date. The number of the names overwhelmed her.

Jay began walking toward the rows of glass jars, jars that contained dirt from some of locations where the lynchings occurred. Written on the glass bottles, in white ink, were the names of lynching victims and the locations where the bodies crashed down to the ground. With His right index finger, Jay touched a few of the bottles.

"I will never look at dirt the same way ever again, Jay," Alex remarked, just staring at the numerous bottles. All of this was very heavy.

Turning to His left, He stepped toward the clear tray of dirt positioned where visitors could touch and feel the sacred dirt, freely opened. Jay put His Holy hands into the dirt and lifted it, and then allowed it to cascade back down into the tray. "Join me," He urged Alex.

Following His lead, Alex stood next to Him and began touching the dirt with her fingertips. Together, They ran their fingers through every inch of the dirt, cupping some into the palms of Their hands, holding it, feeling it with the gravity it possessed. Finally, to Alex's right, through the space underneath the steel cubed rectangles, people started to appear, dressed in squalid clothes from the olden days, some drenched in sweat, some of them drenched in blood, most barefoot, as they stood under their names. "Whoa..."

"They are present every time someone touches this dirt. You can see them because of Me," explained Jay.

Immediately, Alex studied their faces—young and middle-aged, and mostly men—boys. Their expressions were practically the same: motionless and scared. Their eyes were still—life had been drawn out of their bodies too soon and so violently. Words escaped her, as sadness seeped into her bones. "What is existence like in Heaven for them?"

"They have been reunited with their loved ones," explained Jay. "There is no fear, no hatred, no pain in the Kingdom of God."

Instinctively, Alex's thoughts went straight to Nate, liking the notion that he wasn't in anymore pain, although she missed him so very much. "Will we ever have a better existence on Earth?" she summoned from Jay.

"That is solely up to humankind," remarked Jay quickly. "You know how the world works; you know that people perceive things so differently. I can tell you one thing—it only takes one voice, one singular voice to make change happen."

"You think I have that voice?" Alex inquired hastily.

"Everybody has a voice," Jay pointed out. "It all depends upon how people use their voices. History has taught you that much. People are speaking out all over the world; the pendulum swings back and forth. It is always a struggle to put forth a common goal the population can get behind, but that shouldn't deter people from trying to provoke positive change."

Enthralled by Jay's sensible commentary, Alex hadn't noticed the dirt had slipped out of her hands, causing the apparitions to vanish. "They're gone."

"They will return when somebody else touches this sacred soil."

"They won't be able to see them," Alex rhetorically commented.

"They won't be able to see them, no," Jay confirmed.

Alex returned to the vast space under the steel county markers. There were only a few other visitors at the memorial. It was a very sad, but consequential place to see. "Jeff was right," she announced. "Every American must see this place."

"Every person should see this place," reconstructed Jay.

"You're right," she agreed. Before her, suspended from above, were 805 steel forms, with over 4,000 names and the dates of their deaths engraved into each block. History would not forget such a dark time in America.

Returning outside, they continued to walk, coming across the sculpture by Dana King, depicting three women: a grandmother, a teacher, and a pregnant woman, signifying the silent activists of the Civil Rights Movement, past and present. The grandmother figure, often associated with Rosa Parks and the Montgomery Bus Boycott, celebrated the women behind the scenes who worked so fearlessly during that period. Teachers, both past and present, taught children to the best of their abilities; they possessed the ability to teach history and create an environment where children could explore ideas and grow as individuals. The pregnant woman represented all the possibilities that each new child presented. She held the idea of hope.

Alex couldn't help but to touch the figure of the grandmother, thinking about her bravery and tenacity. People during those times had reached their limits and pushed back. The movement grew and grew until they were finally heard. One voice turned into many voices. Alex imagined the struggle for African Americans to remain cool and collected, as Martin Luther King, Jr. preached the essence of non-violence. They were fighting for their civil liberties, as the populous white government continued to resist the movement. Civil disobedience ignited the movement with strength and conviction. African Americans took part in sit-ins, which often resulted in assaults by whites upon blacks, while blacks resisted the urge to fight back. Fighting back only gave the opposing whites supposed proof that blacks were uncivilized and uneducated. African Americans fought to discredit that very notion by obeying the civil obedience decree: do not engage in violence. The world was finally watching through their black-and-white televisions, apropos for the times. Soon, Americans everywhere had a visual account of what was transpiring in the south, opening the eyes of the shielded and unknowing.

The last of the sculptures, a piece by Hank Willis Thomas, depicted ten black figures encased in a block of concrete from which their foreheads, arms and hands were visible, indicating the racial profiling by law enforcement in America. It was the very visible part of systemic racism that most of the public saw when it was captured on surveillance footage or cellphone recordings. Statistics show that 1 out of 1,000 black males will lose their lives during their lifespans during encounters with law enforcement. Statistics also show that Native American men and women, and Latino men and women, were more likely to be killed than whites during similar encounters. Alex understood the meaning of the concrete which surrounded these ten figures. The concrete was systemic racism, not only in policing, but in all aspects of life: education, health care, economic opportunities, and so on. It was ingrained in our society since the first ships, jam-packed with Africans, captured, stolen, and converted to use as property. The question didn't leave her mind how people, supposedly God-fearing people, could ever consider that people of Africa were not people at all. Greed was the ultimate sin that catapulted slavery into motion. Cold, hard greed. This idea made Alex's skin crawl.

After a light lunch, Alex wanted to drive just an hour west to Selma, to walk across the Edmund Pettus Bridge. It was the bridge that on March 7th, 1965, the Civil Rights demonstrators attempted to cross, marching to the Alabama State House that was still in sight, partially. Jay concurred. Soon, They found Themselves on US-80, traveling west. There was not much exciting about US-80; it was just a road to get from one place to another. Alex was used to walking, and sometimes jogging, a few miles here and there, but the thought of walking 54 miles, with or without breaks, from Selma to Montgomery, made Alex's legs ache. Now she really understood the Civil Rights Movement and the momentum it had in the south. African Americans demanded the right to vote because they were Americans, whether or not others perceived them as such.

Alex's phone rang. It was Ben. "Hello, Ben," said Alex contentedly.

"Alex!" Ben uttered excitingly. "Where are you headed?"

"I was just visiting the National Memorial for Peace and Justice."

"Oh wow," Ben replied, knowing the experience of visiting the memorial. "I visited there last year...I cried my eyes out after I left."

"I know what you mean, Ben," said Alex. There seemed to be a natural moment of silence before either spoke about the now. "How's Ruby?"

"Today we tried feeding her oatmeal for breakfast; she ate the entire bowl!"

Gasping from happiness, Alex suddenly became invisibly emotional. "She did not?!"

"She did!" Ben confirmed, giddy.

"Oh wow, Ben," said Alex. "Have you heard from anybody I reached out to yesterday?" Her eyes were concentrated on the road.

"I heard from a physical therapist from Memorial Health. They need to see Ruby, evaluate her…"

"Make sure she has cerebral palsy and is not faking," jokingly Alex said.

Ben laughed on the end of the phone. "Exactly, exactly."

"If you need me to make any more phone calls, or anything else, please don't be afraid to ask—I'm just a phone call away," Alex asserted. "I love that little cutie."

It took Ben a few extra seconds to suppress a lump in his throat. "I think Ruby feels the same way about you." There was another distinctive pause in the conversation. "Let me let you go, and I'll talk to you soon."

"Of course, of course," she uttered happily. "Maybe one of these nights we can do a FaceTime or a Facebook video call, something like that."

"That would be great, Alex. Ruby would love that!"

"Sounds like a plan!"

"God bless you, Alex," Ben prayed.

Intuitively, Alex turned to Jay with a smile. "Thank you, Ben. God bless you, as well." She stumbled over those last words as if she was stumbling over a boulder in plain sight. The call ended.

Jay busted out in unquenchable laughter. "You are too funny!"

Faking a grin, she knew exactly what He had in His head. "I don't want to speak for God."

"Is that your defense?" He inquired, still chuckling. "I bet you're figuring because you're not a 'woman of the cloth', you're not allow to say, 'God bless you'?"

"It seems like We are reading each other's minds," Alex spoke.

"You're avoiding answering My questions again," Jay pointed out.

Continuing to devote most of her concentration to driving,

thoughts began to run back and forth, around in her mind. "It doesn't come naturally to me," she offered.

"Why is that exactly?" Jay asked shrewdly. "People say, 'God bless you' every day—people just like you."

"Yeah...I know, but..." She kept her hands on the wheel and eyes on the road. "I just feel awkward saying it." Quickly, she found Jay's astute eyes.

"You don't feel worthy, do you?"

She turned back to Him. "No, I don't," Alex admitted.

Seeing a single tear fall from her cheek, Jay leaned in closer. "You know what," He led, "I believe you are worthy. God believes you're worthy."

Inhaling and exhaling a deep breath, as she took in all the sights surrounded her, Alex held back tears.

"Do you know what else?" Jay asked.

"What?" returned Alex, drying her eyes.

Surprising Alex by picking up little, plastic Jesus from the car floor, He held the miniature version of Himself up. "He thinks you're pretty worthy too." Jay, with His hands, made plastic Jesus dance around a bit, child-like and laughing.

Catching a glimpse of plastic Jesus, and then Jay's goofy expression, Alex broke out in fits, smiling. "Oh man!"

They reached Selma within an hour. Driving through Selma, it was like every populous American city—it had its nice parts and its rundown areas. Selma's population was 80 percent African American. Once Alex spotted the Edmund Pettus Bridge, she found an open parking lot and parked. The air was warm and muggy, with sprinkles of rain falling from the gray, dense clouds. Alex grabbed her water mug and locked her car. The light mist falling felt good on her exposed skin, which was warmer than her shower that morning. Alex looked forward to the walk across the bridge and back again, as she hadn't had a long walk since the last night on Myrtle Beach. The events of that night still ran through her consciousness more than she wanted, although Alex was resolved to get passed it.

Feeling her leg muscles wake up, as she began ascending the curve of the bridge, Alex liked the sensation of her body moving and her heart rate increasing. Occasionally, she looked over toward Jay, noticing His ease about His physicality. *He is Jesus.* At the crest of the bridge, Alex paused and leaned on the metal railing to overlook the Alabama River, very tame and still, except for the tiny droplets of rain piercing the surface of the river. Droplets of the same rain fell onto her skin, especially on Alex's arms and shoulders.

"John Lewis was beaten on this bridge in 1965," she spoke to begin the conversation, looking onto the murky river.

Jay nodded. "I am aware."

"They are talking about changing the name of this bridge to the John Lewis Bridge soon, which would be awesome. John Lewis is awesome," announced Alex.

"John Lewis is an angel on Earth," Jay said sincerely. "It would help humanity if there were more John Lewises on Earth."

"Absolutely," Alex spoke down to the river. Deep in thought, she attempted to imagine what that Bloody Sunday was like, trying to feel the apprehension of the unknown, not knowing what the peaceful protesters would face at the other end the bridge, especially being frightened about their physical welfare. They were approaching Americans, while they were Americans. They weren't in a civil war; they weren't in any foreign land, but they were ready to lay down their lives for what they believed. "They were marching to gain the right to vote, and they were beaten," Alex grumbled in frustration. "That was so wrong."

"I agree."

Alex sighed heavily. "News cameras again brought the whole of the country to this bridge; a picture speaks a thousand words."

"Shall we continue to walk? It's going to start pouring soon," Jay pursued.

Still in deep thought over the brutality on the bridge, Alex barely heard His words; her eyes were fixated on the river. "Yeah, okay."

They reached the other side of the bridge, and immediately crossed back to the other side to run into the car, just as the skies opened up. Raindrops forcibly pelleted the exterior of the Camry while Alex took the time to find a campground close to Memphis; Memphis would be the next destination, she was informed. Memphis was five hours away, although she didn't feel like driving all that way, especially if it was going to pour the rest of the day. Alex found a campground in Fulton, Mississippi, about three hours away.

An hour into the ride toward Fulton, the rain let up to a light drizzle. Alex looked forward to getting to the campground at Whitten Park to chill by the water. She also looked forward to sleeping under the stars again. In her mind, sleeping under the stars meant she was a little bit closer to Nate. Without the clouds in the sky, it gave her a direct line that made it easier to talk to him. The atmosphere was a big space, and Alex knew his spirit was out there, drifting. It was an emotionally exhausting day and all Alex wanted to do was to be still.

It wasn't out of the ordinary for her and Jay not to have a conversation for miles and miles on end while she drove. Often, Alex would look over to Him, as He seemed to be asleep, and she didn't quite know why He had to sleep. For all she knew, Jay didn't eat, so why would He have to sleep. After a heavy day like this, Jay always wanted to give her the opportunity to reflect, and to give her thought processes time to absorb reality, and all the humanity and evils that accompanied it. This was His game plan for Alex, to get her in a better place; she had gifts that couldn't be wasted; she had compassion that couldn't go unnoticed; she had love that couldn't be restrained. Everything that she was bottling up, her doubts, her fears, and her sadness, had to escape for her to thrive.

Still asleep in her tent, as dark persisted before the Mississippi sunrise, Alex was roused by her iPhone. Trying to shed the slumber zone, with her right hand, Alex searched the dark space around her until she located it. Opening her eyes slightly, she saw it was Conrad calling.

"Hello," Alex managed to wrangle out of her mouth. Still coming out of her sleep coma, she questioned what she was hearing—a baby crying. "Are you watching something on television?"

"No, I'm not watching anything," Conrad spoke, bordering between laughter and bewilderment. "We have a baby!"

The word, 'baby', woke all of Alex's senses up. "You guys got a baby?!" Alex asked at a normal decibel level. "You guys got a baby?!" This time, the entire campground must have heard her. Realizing her loudness, she instantly threw her free hand over her mouth to stifle the raw emotions.

"Yes, we have a baby!" Conrad confirmed. "FaceTime us back."

Trying to locate the zipper to exit the tent and having the presence of mind to throw on her flip flops while shining the light to find the way out, Alex managed to get out. Her heart raced with excitement as she pushed the appropriate buttons to FaceTime Conrad and Justin, but the first face she saw was the precious, little face of a newborn baby with sparse, dark hair. "My God, she's beautiful," cried Alex. Happy tears rolled down her cheeks.

"Say hello to your Aunt Alex," Justin spoke, as he changed his voice to a higher voice to mimic a child. "Tell Aunt Alex I haven't slept all night, keeping my Daddies awake."

Emotions still consumed Alex, as she walked along the water's edge in slow circles, trying to get all the happiness out of this very moment and tuck it away. "What's her name?"

Justin still spoke. "My name is Lila Alexandra."

Once Alex heard that the precious, little girl had her name for a middle name, she was overwhelmed with tears. "A beautiful name for a beautiful little girl." As the sun came up in the Mississippi sky, she strolled out on the nearby dock and sat to chat with the brand-new dads.

"We wish you were home to hold her," Conrad replied, as he took Lila into his strong arms. "She's just so cute."

"I can see that," Alex expressed with genuine love and affection. "Someone's going to be spoiled." As she cleared her eyes and face with the bottom of her Pearl Jam, white, concert t-shirt, the sun brightened up the morning sky like an orange ball of fire. The surface of the lake, placid as it waited for the day's activities, steamed upward through the air. Alex couldn't recall a more beautiful morning in her life.

"Oh yes, this little girl is going to be very spoiled," Conrad agreed, taking a bottle of formula that Justin handed to him. "Where are you now?"

"I'm in Fulton, Mississippi. Just stopped here to sleep. Going to drive up to Memphis."

Lila was quite content, in Conrad's arms, having an early breakfast. "Oooh, you can visit Graceland," he suggested, laughing.

"I don't think so, Dude," replied Alex humorously, readjusting her legs on the rough wood of the deck. "How much time do you have off?"

"I have three months off; Justin has six weeks off. My Mom will babysit after the three months."

Alex loved watching Conrad hold his infant daughter. "When I get home, I'll babysit anytime you need me to, Con."

"Oh yes, no doubt, Al," Conrad concurred. "I can't wait for you to hold this little cutie." The simple notion of having a child of his own moved him to shed some glorious tears.

"I'll be home soon, Con," Alex reassured, as she nodded to make that concrete. "I'll talk to you guys tomorrow."

"Be safe, Al," Conrad spoke. "I love you."

"I love you, Alex," Justin reiterated.

"I love you too," she returned. "Bye."

"Bye," Justin and Conrad said in stereo. The call ended.

Alex carefully let the iPhone drop on a board of the dock. Leaning back on the palms of her hands, she felt such pure joy, she felt the warmth of the morning sun, and she was smiling without the guilt of feeling happy. This was a monumental step of feeling happy while Nate lay on her conscious. It was a fine line for Alex's psyche between feeling happy and feeling guilty for allowing herself to feel happy. Nate was still dead, although Alex was beginning to feel joy. It didn't seem right, like she was disregarding his life, his existence. There was a ping pong match going on in the game room in Alex's head. It was a match that would start time and time again; every now and again, the players, joy and guilt, took timeouts, but the game, the never-ending game, would always restart.

Obviously aware that this was a head game, Alex knew she was in control, but sometimes the guilt was stifling, always pushing her happiness back when she only wanted to move forward, even though Alex was a co-conspirator to her own imprisonment. She needed to find the key so she could release herself.

Leaning forward again, Alex grabbed her iPhone and gaped at the background photo of Nate and herself, the same photo she chose as her background on the day after he died. She missed Nate so, so much. Opening FaceTime, Alex pressed to call up Mom.

After a few seconds, Joanne appeared on the small screen. "Good morning, Sweetheart. What's the matter? Where are you?"

It was the response Alex expected, as she laughed and cried at the same time. "I'm in Fulton, Mississippi," Alex answered the simple question first. "Conrad and Justin just adopted a little baby girl...They named her Lila Alexandra." She cried easily now.

Immediately, Joanne happily gasped. "Oh Sweetheart, that is so wonderful." Joanne held her excitement at bay until she got to the root of her daughter's tears. "Are those happy tears?"

Nodding was the easiest to do at that moment. "Mostly," Alex pushed out, feeling her chest tense up from her emotion. "All I want is to feel happy, Mom, but the very moment I feel any kind of joy, I feel so, so guilty."

All Joanne wanted to do at that very second was to reach through the phone and hug her daughter. Soon, she began to get tearful. "Oh my girl..." Joanne began, "you are allowed to be happy—there's no law that says you can't be happy." Joanne cleared her eyes for the moment. "This is the process of grief. You never know when it'll rise to clutch you in the throat. It's different for everybody."

"Do you feel any happiness these days?" Alex asked straight away.

"I'm always happy when I can see and talk to you," honestly Joanne answered. More tears came. "You and your dad make me happy."

A fleeting chuckle arose from Alex's raspy throat. "Oh yeah, I'm doing such a bang-up job right now." Sarcasm was all over this statement.

"I live for these moments with you," initiated Joanne with fervor. "You are my world, and you are my inspiration! I brag about you to everyone I possibly can." She paused to take a breath. "You are my daughter and I love you…so, so much."

Alex had full-on tears running down her face. She used her t-shirt again to dry her face. "I love you, Mom."

Emulating her daughter, Joanne grabbed some paper towels to dry her face. It was then that Michael walked into the kitchen. "Hi."

Once he saw his wife's red eyes, Michael grew concerned. "What's going on?"

Walking over to him, Joanne grabbed her hand on his opposite shoulder, resting her head on his nearest one, sharing her phone with him. "Alex is fine; we were just talking about things that make us happy."

The dichotomy of the present situation puzzled him. "Okay." Taking a few more seconds to dissect the scene, he focused on his daughter. "Alex?"

"Hi Dad," Alex smiled. "Conrad and Justin adopted a baby girl yesterday—they named her Lila Alexandra."

Hearing this name nearly brought him to tears. "Oh my God, that's fantastic, Al!"

"It surely is, Dad," she asserted. "How have you been?"

"I miss you like crazy, Al," Michael easily admitted, as he felt his wife squeeze the right side of his neck. "It looks like you're sitting on a dock."

"Actually, I am," she confirmed. "When Conrad called, it was right before sunrise, so I got to watch the sun come up while meeting Lila."

"God, Al—that's beautiful," Michael assert, looking intently at his daughter. "Hey Alex, do me a favor?"

"Yeah Dad?" Alex expressed.

"Don't go swimming in that lake," begged her father. "You're in the deep south; there could be crocs or gators lurking around."

Very enthusiastic laughter sprang out from Alex. "You know what, Dad? I was contemplating taking a swim before I take off to Memphis, but now, I have to reconsider."

"Please do," Michael commanded quickly.

She chuckled. "Okay, I won't go swimming."

"Thank you."

"You're very welcome, Dad." She finally stood, stretching out all her back muscles while yawning. "I think I'm going to go get ready and get on the road."

"Okay Sweetheart, please be safe," Joanne spoke up.

Combing her fingers back through her semi-tangled, dark hair, Alex felt grateful for this time. "I will, I will. I love you guys."

"We love you too, Honey," Michael said tenderly.

"And Alex," Joanne got her attention. "Don't be afraid of feeling happy."

These words brought the lump back into her throat. "Thanks, Mom."

"Bye, Kiddo."

"Bye." Alex ended the call, feeling slightly alone for a moment or two. She turned and began walking back up the deck, seeing Jay waiting for her. As she approached Him, Alex embraced Jay spiritedly. "Thank you."

Not really expecting this action from her, Jay gently touched Alex on her back. "For what?"

Alex stepped back. "For this morning."

Crazy enough, there was a breeze in Mississippi during the dog days of summer. Alex had all her windows down in the Camry while she enjoyed the wind blowing her hair in all directions. The radio was on but at a low volume. Remembering the early hours of that morning made her smile inside, as she still struggled to smile on the outside. The forces within her were at odds, and she knew it. Alex didn't know what it would take to feel truly happy again, but she knew it had to be significant. She scolded herself for failing to remain happy minute to minute, hour to hour and day by day, especially over the presence of a new baby girl in her life. Yes, she was over-the-moon about Lila Alexandra, although the profound weight of Nate's death consumed her. Alex's grief was unpredictable, just as her mother said it would be. She wanted her mother's strength even though Alex couldn't piece it together. Allowing herself to think out of the box, Alex really wondered how her parents were coping with the loss of their child. Were they being brave for her sake? Were they crying every night? Was she being selfish? A new reality set in—she was being selfish. She really didn't like herself at that point. Sadness suddenly turned to anger and aggravation, questioning if she should call her parents back to apologize for all this shit she was putting them through. With many miles to go before Memphis, Alex decided to wait until then.

For the rest of the drive, Alex was very tough on herself, as she mentally put together what she was going to say to her parents. She wasn't afraid but determined to express her wishes to not be a burden; she wanted to be on the same level of support with her parents. Thinking back on the past several months, Alex recognized her drain on the people that surrounded her, the people who blanketed her with love and understanding, namely Conrad and Justin. Remembering back to the first few months after Nate's passing, recalling her dad's constant questions about going back to work, Alex finally looked at it differently, considering that her father knew her well. Maybe he knew that getting back to work would keep her mind engaged, instead of assuming that he just wanted to not look at her day after day, doing nothing. Putting herself in her father's shoes was an eye-opening exercise. What if Alex had a son with severe mental illness? What if Alex's boy took his own life? What if she had a daughter who was a doctor? What if Alex's daughter found her brother with his wrists cut and very close to death? How would Alex feel when her daughter failed to save her brother? It was an overwhelming feeling of guilt of failing her children. That was what Alex's father must have felt and continued to feel. This revelation struck Alex like a punch to the gut, as she tried not to disdain herself to the point that she could not recognize her worth. They were only fifteen miles from Memphis, but Alex couldn't wait to talk to her parents. Alex got off at the next exit and looked for an appropriate area to park. She found a big, empty parking lot and threw the Camry into park.

Pressing her dad's icon in FaceTime, four steps below her mom's, Alex knew he would jump to the worst assumptions. "Hi Dad. Are you busy?" She could tell he was in his work office.

"Al? What's the matter, Hun?" Michael was obviously concerned.

As quickly as she could, Alex gathered her thoughts and spoke, "I need to apologize to you..." she paused to breathe, trying not to crumble into dust. "I apologize for not seeing Nate's death from your point of view."

Michael became suddenly emotional. "Oh Alex, baby," he cried. "You don't have to apologize."

"But I do, Dad," she strongly appealed. "I never put myself in your shoes...I never considered how you, or Mom, were coping through all of this."

"Oh Al," softly spoke Michael. Tears filled his eyes. "We're coping the best we know how." Clearing his throat, Michael pondered his next words. "Mom and I were aware of the severity of Nate's illness, and we had to accept the fact that Nate wouldn't improve beyond where he was, and we knew that this could be a possibility." Michael wept openly. "Alex, we love you so much; we'll never forgive ourselves that you were the one who found Nate."

Alex sobbed in unison with her dad. "You had no control over that, Dad."

"I should have, Al," Michael proclaimed. "You don't need to apologize for anything, Honey."

"That's not true," Alex portrayed, with a soaked expression. "I want to apologize for being so curt when you would ask when I was going back to work; that was inappropriate."

"Oh Al, we just didn't know how to communicate back then," Michael admitted.

Alex gave a slight grin. "We are making up for it now, uh?"

"We are, we are," he smiled. "What brought this all on?"

Changing positions in her seat, putting her right foot on the driver's seat, Alex got more comfortable. "I just realized I was a shit to you, and I was very into myself, so much so, that I didn't really consider what you and Mom were going through." She took a sip of water. "This morning, I got to thinking about Conrad's and Justin's new baby girl, thinking about the future and all the good times they'll have with her. Then I thought about you, and how much we've all changed in the last six months, for better or worse."

"Al," Michael lovingly spoke, "losing Nate was devastating for all of us; nobody should experience this kind of pain." Taking a deep breath, he looked away for a moment. "These last months with you home with us have been very special. I have thoroughly enjoyed having you under our roof. I like looking in on you in the middle of the night, like I did when you were young. I'd move your iPhone to the big bureau, so you'd have a reason to get out of bed every morning, because I know how much you love that picture of you and Nate."

More tears rolled down her face before her fingers cleared them away. "I figured," Alex said, smiling.

"Where are you, anyway, Honey?"

"I'm like 15 miles away from Memphis," she answered. "I just couldn't wait to tell you all of this…it weighed heavy on me."

"I'm glad you called, Al," Michael replied without hesitation. "I'm very proud of you, Kiddo."

"Thanks, Dad," she said, wiping away the last of her tears with the inside of her left wrist.

"Tonight, I want you to go listen to great blues, eat some great food, and just have some fun, but of course, be safe."

"I will, Dad."

"Okay, Honey," Michael said affectionately. "I love you."

"I love you, Dad." Alex ended the call, taking a deep breath. She understood Jay was observing her throughout the call. "Thank you again."

"That was all you, my friend," Jay established. He handed her a hand towel He retrieved from the backseat.

It was still early in the day; Alex decided to head up to Meeman-Shelby Forest Campground to check things out. Just north of Memphis, she figured she could set up the tent and take an Uber into the city later. She checked into the campground for one night, although Jay didn't give any hints as to what their plans would be the next day, and He didn't ask her to extend her stay for a second night.

Once at her designated camping spot, Alex didn't waste any time setting up the tent in fine fashion, being utterly surprised at the remarkable headway she had made within the past nine days. Growing up, Alex had only gone camping a handful of times with her parents and Nate, always somewhere close to home. A few times in the recent past, she had camped with Conrad and Justin. During all those times camping, Alex observed more than she participated in setting up a tent, and all the gear that went along with it. She had instant access to YouTube if she didn't know how to do something. It was still a battle to get a fire started without some modern amenities such as a matchstick or a charcoal lighter. Never in her life had she witnessed anybody start a fire with two sticks, almost doubting if cavemen had the ability to do the two-stick method.

The day continued to be very comfortable for an early August afternoon in Tennessee. Alex decided to take advantage of the perfect weather and walk the trail within the campground, knowing a long walk would do her good. After changing into olive green, cargo pants and hiking boots, spraying Deet around her ankles, Alex grabbed her water bottle and left Jay to do what He did when He was not with her. Wooden signs pointed Alex toward the direction of the trail, which she found easily. Not seeing any others on the trail, the peacefulness settled into her bones while her legs propelled her forward. Gazing her eyes upward, Alex was amazed how tall the trees were, observing several bird species hang in the wind above. She never tired of seeing all these creatures and woods that surrounded her and enlivened her soul. Still feeling the effects of crying with her father through FaceTime, Alex attempted to rub the fatigue from her eyes, recognizing she felt somehow lighter, unleashed from her earlier albatross, having released its talons from her shoulders. The air flowing in and out of her lungs reminded Alex that she was very much alive and well and being mindful of her lungs taking in the air she needed, and of the blood running through her veins, and of the things she was observing. She listened as the ground beneath her hiking boots rejigged itself with every step. With all of Alex's senses being utilized, it solidified her current existence. This wasn't walking on a beach, where she would love to be, but walking in the woods still was valuable to her psyche.

Once the sun sank behind the tall trees, Alex resolved that it was time to get back to her campsite even though she could have walked a few more miles. When she got back to her site, Jay was preparing more of the gear she hadn't gotten to yet. Alex thanked Him, as she began to change back to sneakers. Whether Jay was bored or knew something she didn't, Alex noticed He was staring as if she wore a funky hat upon her head. Being very secure with Jay, she flat out asked Him what His concerns were. Apparently, He didn't have any, and confident with that, Alex began the process of beckoning an Uber. She was hungry.

It was approaching 7 o'clock when the Uber showed up at the campground. The driver, Jamal, had a 4.67 Uber rating—a good rating in Uber nation. Alex and Jay walked to the front entrance where Jamal parked his neon-blue Sentra, clearly visible to all. She knocked on the door and told him her name. After the usual exchange for a typical transaction, Jamal invited Alex to get into the car. Like every other time she had used Uber or Lyft, Alex sat in the back seat instead of the front, figuring the driver appreciated their personal space, and in fact, so did she. For a second or two, Alex felt slightly guilty because Jamal was unaware he had a second passenger along for the ride. Alex was sure, if Jamal believed in Jesus, he probably wouldn't mind giving Him a free ride into Memphis.

"Where are you going, Ma'am?" Jamal inquired cheerfully.

Here goes the whole "ma'am" thing again. "Memphis, Beale Street, please Jamal."

Jamal began to drive. "First time in Memphis?"

"Yes," answered Alex, feeling upbeat. "How could you tell?"

"I've been driving for a long time; I know my first-timers," Jamal spoke proudly. "Where are you from, if I might ask?"

"I'm from Boston," she divulged. "Have you ever been to Boston?"

"No, Ma'am," Jamal answered. He took the exit onto the highway to head south. "My boy keeps bugging me to take him to Fenway Park to see the Green Monster."

"Is he a Red Sox fan?" Alex put Jamal between 35 and 40 years old. His silver, wire-rimmed eyeglasses accentuated his slightly-chubby-to-match-his-body-type, clean-shaven face. Even though he had a receding hairline, his dark hair covered his head.

"He loves the game of baseball, although he doesn't have a favorite team. It's weird—kids are weird today," he mentioned, shrugging.

Alex chuckled for more than a few moments. "How many kids do you have?"

"I have four," Jamal announced while holding up four, chubby fingers on his right hand. "From three to twelve, two boys and two girls—they are all wild and crazy, but they are the lights of my life," he expressed with a great passion and a great, resounding laugh.

"Oh, that's great," Alex chortled.

"And they all want to be lawyers," Jamal exclaimed, smiling from ear to ear.

"Even the three-year-old?" humorously she inquired.

A thunderous, robust laugh erupted from Jamal's core. "You don't know the half of it!" he insisted. "My wife is a prosecutor and she's the kind of person who talks a little shop at home. My three-year-old daughter is already attached to her older siblings; she learns so much from them." Jamal became a bit more serious. "My kids want to save the world, you know, with all this division stuff going on—all this police brutality happening; it's just crazy."

"It is very disturbing, that's for sure," agreed Alex.

"I have to talk to my kids all of time about presenting themselves far above the bar compared to their white classmates, and I'm so angry that I have to do that, but I have to do it because it could be a matter of life and death one day."

Giving Jamal her undivided attention, Alex searched for the most appropriate words. "I'm not going to say I have personal experience being racially profiled, although I understand systemic racism."

"Yes! Yes! Systemic racism is the issue that we struggle to get passed," passionately proclaimed Jamal. "My older two understand systemic racism, can you believe that? My wife and I try to show them this wasn't God's plan for humanity."

"It sounds like you have a blessed house," Alex sincerely commented.

"I do, I do," Jamal repeated. "I'm very blessed, very blessed."

Naturally, she gazed to her left and grinned at Jay. The traffic got heavier as they approached the city. "Jamal, where would you recommend first-timers go to get good food, and listen to great blues?"

"Ma'am, what's your name if you don't mind me asking?"

"It's Alex," she joyfully replied.

Briefly, the conversation got off topic. "Wow, that is such a strong name," he declared vibrantly.

"So I hear," she relayed, laughing softly.

"Wow, such a great name," Jamal ruminated out loud. "Yes, good blues clubs...I would have to go with B.B. King's Blues Club. The best barbeque ribs around, hands down!"

With nothing to do but laugh, Alex so appreciated his exuberant enthusiasm. "Okay, I will trust you."

"Yeah, that's a good time right there, Alex," Jamal underscored. "May I ask you what you do, Alex?"

Strangely enough, Alex balked at this question. "Ah, I'm an emergency room doctor." At once, she felt Jay stare in her direction, feeling His disappointment.

"No way?!" Jamal spoke with excitement.

"Yes, I am," Alex reassured Jamal, and herself. Bravely, she looked toward Jay, confirming His dismay with her, sensing the gnawing in the bottom of her stomach.

"Well, your parents must be so proud of you," Jamal surmised.

Still feeling her stomach trying to calm, Alex sighed quietly. "They are very proud."

Reaching the beginning of Beale Street, cars were bumper-to-bumper, which was not unusual. "I'm going to have to drop you off here, Alex," said Jamal.

"That's fine, Jamal. Are you available to come back around ten?" Alex inquired, poised.

"Of course, Alex. I'll be right here."

"Thank you, Jamal! You're wonderful!" she expressed, as she got out of the car.

"Thank you, Alex," returned Jamal. "Have fun!"

"Thanks." Alex shut the rear car door, and then stood up, seeing waves of people walking up and down the landmark street. When the car had passed, Alex and Jay began to walk Beale. It was a beautiful night in the city and Alex wanted to enjoy it—the atmosphere, the electric vibe and the music that surrounded her. "Are you angry?"

"I don't get angry, Alex," Jay stated clearly, "but I do get discouraged when people don't think much of themselves, or their abilities. You know yourself better than anyone."

"I know," she acquiesced. Not really having a follow up, Alex continued to walk amongst the dispersed crowd.

Swiftly but gently, Jay held her right arm, causing Alex to put all her focus on Him. "Believe in yourself, my friend."

Surveying everything within His eyes, she saw His compassion, love, and all His goodness from the depths of His soul. "I am really trying, Jay."

"Okay," He returned, accepting her response. "Let's go listen to some blues."

His made her shrug, and then, chortle. "Okay, let's hear some blues."

She was definitely walking in Memphis, although Jay could only walk with His feet ten feet off the Beale. He didn't choose to do such a thing on this night. Everywhere she looked she saw neon lights inviting people into their establishments, visually broadcasting that their fare and music was the best in Memphis. She felt fortunate that she had a recommendation from Jamal; she didn't have to decide which establishment to descend upon. Making her way down Beale, Alex caught a glimpse of a young man doing somersaults down the center of Beale Street, much like the actor portrayed in the film, *The Firm*.

Searching the street, she spotted the young man's hat on the ground awaiting tips. Alex knew she didn't have any change; she didn't even know if she had any dollar bills. Alex checked the small slit on the back of her iPhone protector. No bills found. Alex approached the young man, asking him if he accepted Venmo payments. Surprisingly enough, the young man did. Spending about a minute with the tumbler, Alex secured the Venmo payment to him. The young man thanked Alex for taking the time to talk to him, and for her tip.

Passing every establishment on Beale, the music could be heard clearly mushrooming out of every opened door, sending out feelers to the thousands of ears that passed. Blues music, largely dependent on its lyrics, emerged after slavery was abolished. It was derived from African spirituals, then the genre transformed during the century and a half of living black in America. The evolution of guitars, basses, organs, and drums made blues exceptional. Alex couldn't recall the last live music performance she had heard, although it could have been Billy Joel at Fenway in 2016, digging some of the old school music her parents surrounded her and Nate with, growing up. Soon, they stumbled upon B.B. King's Blues Club. It was a toss-up whether Alex was more excited to eat or to listen to a live band. The growls from her stomach voiced its opinions quickly. Inside the entrance, Alex was met by a young man, dressed in Khakis and a black shirt embroidered with the establishment's logo and his name, Will. Far from being a taller chap, Will stood 5'9", just an inch above Alex. His dreads gave Will a little extra height. Kindly, Will explained the places where Alex could sit, either on the main floor, or on the mezzanine level. Taking but a second to decide, she decided to sit on the floor. It was unusually crowded for a weeknight, explained Will, but he had a single table available. Before he started to the table, Will grabbed a menu, and then showed Alex to her table, leaving her again, but not before giving her parting pleasantries, reassuring her that her server would arrive shortly. Alex thanked Will for his hospitality.

The band of five were doing their thing on the stage, which was elevated about two feet. They were playing a cover of *I'm a Man* by the Spencer Davis Group from so many years ago. Alex knew the song very well just because her parents were big Steve Winwood fans. She could listen to this music all night. Standing, taking a quick look around, Alex checked out if anyone else was recording the band, wishing to record just a few seconds for her dad. Alex decided to be bold and record about seven seconds of the set. Sitting back down, previewing the brief footage, she sent it to her dad. About a minute later, Alex's iPhone chirped, although it was drowned out by the live music. Believing her dad would respond rather quickly, picking up her iPhone, Alex saw he had indeed texted her back with a thumbs-up emoji, followed by a big red heart emoji. Another text followed with "I love you," followed by another big red heart. Alex returned her father's text with the same exact sentiment. At that moment, recalling the emotional conversation she had had with him earlier, Alex really missed her dad.

Ordering dill fried pickles as an appetizer and the B.B.'s famous lip-smacking ribs, Alex's hunger subsided quickly. Since she didn't have to drive later, she had a Sam Adams while enjoying listening to the magnificent, live music. Jay, as usual, went off to comfort people He found in need. There was a pause in the music, as a new band set up their gear. The house music, mostly B.B. King, began playing until the band was prepared to take the stage. Always an observer of life, Alex took in everything, the bustling of people eating and drinking, the methodical steps the band members took to set up the stage, and the people who were sitting quietly, as she was—but she was the only one sitting alone. Noticing a young man on the stage, he had a pronounced scissor gait—a prominent indication of spastic diplegia cerebral palsy, mainly only affecting the legs of the person. The young man was over six feet tall with a very muscular upper body with legs, not matching that muscle tone. He wore a rusted, but bright orange t-shirt that matched his knee-length shorts. Stylish dark sunglasses wrapped around his eyes and his hair stood like a perfect tuffet on top of his head. He concentrated on putting together the drum kit. From the way that he was so efficient at it, putting the bass, toms, snares and all the different types of cymbals in their proper places and angles, Alex was sure he was the upcoming drummer. Another gentleman had a different drummer's stool over his head, as he walked to the back of the drums, putting it down. Alex was more curious than ever to discover who was going to take a seat behind the kit, sipping her beer, waiting so patiently for confirmation. As she suspected, the young man took the seat behind the kit, like a pilot would take his seat in a cockpit of a 747 Airliner. A few tweaks here and there, and then it would be time to fire up the engines. It was the quickest soundcheck Alex had witnessed. The house music stopped, and the band began to play.

She was glad she had listened to her dad's advice to find some good blues. One could never underestimate what the power of music could do for the soul, even if it was draped in blues. Orange was just incredible behind the drums, as sometimes he would carry an entire song, having an amazing range on the drums, playing softly on certain measures, and staggeringly hard on others. He certainly had God-given gifts.

The set ended much too quickly for Alex even though they played for nearly an hour and a half. At some point, Alex recorded more than seconds of the last 84 minutes to send to her dad. He loved it. As Alex was paying her bill, the venue was clearing out. She began to hear a singular voice above the din of the usual activities of clearing plates, glasses, and silverware, and closing out the stage.

"If I knew you were a gimpy monkey banging on the drums, I wouldn't have come in to this joint!" the drunkard perversely exclaimed. "Go back to Africa!"

"Hey, you are the ones who brought my ancestors over here, Dude!" Orange verbally retaliated from the stage.

Once Alex heard these hurtful words, she glanced toward the commotion, seeing that there were a few guys surrounding the menace. Alex, blinded by ire, approached him. "What gives you the right to talk to him that way?!" She didn't realize she was shouting.

"What?" the imbecile blurted out. "He must do you good, white girl."

Her first instinct was to cause some physical pain to the 30-year-old, smart-mouthed asshole, but all the sudden, she remembered she was a doctor. "It's a good thing I'm a doctor. After kicking your ass, I would have had to give you medical attention, and I would have despised doing that."

The manager's voice erupted from the front. "Get him out of here, will you!"

"Go fuck yourself!" the drunkard shouted toward Alex, as he was being dragged out by the two designated bouncers.

The inside atmosphere got suddenly still. Standing in place, Alex took a few deep breaths before she started walking toward the exit.

"Hey you—Bad Ass Doctor, come back over here, please."

Hearing this new nickname gave her a chuckle. Alex turned and saw it was Orange beckoning her back. He took off his sunglasses.

"I'll be right down—don't move."

Alex complied, watching Orange getting help off the stage. Sitting at the closest table, he invited her to sit. She did.

"Wow, Bad Ass Doctor, you have some kind of Tyrannosaurus Rex backbone, man," he said, chortling. He stood to introduce himself.

"My name is Davis." He extended his hand.

Smiling, Alex shook his hand. "Hi Davis, my name is Alex."

"It's great to meet you," Davis replied, sitting back down.

"It's great to meet you, Davis," returned Alex. "That was a great set; you're pretty awesome."

"Why thank you, thank you very much," Davis said humbly. "I think I made a new fan tonight."

"Oh, of course!" Alex declared.

"I really wanted to thank you for standing up for me with that idiot. We get a lot of idiots in here that say the stupidest things." Davis caught something in his vision, close to the entrance. "Here's my girl!" Davis awkwardly rose to his feet again, taking the hand of his girlfriend. "Hi Sweetie," spoke Davis, hugging her. "Alex, this is Robin, my fabulous girlfriend. Robin, this is Alex. Alex, the Bad Ass Doctor, told this idiot off for me tonight."

Reaching across the small table, Robin extended her hand. "Nice to meet you, Alex."

"You, as well, Robin," Alex spoke, shaking Robin's hand.

"What happened tonight?" Robin inquired toward Davis, as if this was a frequent occurrence. She sat down.

"This guy was drunk, he called me some choice names, Alex told him off, and then the guys dragged his sorry ass out of here."

With her right elbow situated on the table, Robin held her chin up, as she looked at Davis, concerned. "I don't like this," Robin stated outwardly, "you being targeted. It's dangerous."

"The boys have my back, Babe," Davis reassured Robin, holding her hand. "They have my back. If not, maybe I'll offer Alex the position of my bodyguard."

Alex caught his wink, but Robin did not. "I don't know if I would fit that bill," she answered honestly.

"Are you from around here?" Robin inquired with interest and surveillance, wondering if she was in for a love quarrel.

"No, I'm from Boston," replied Alex, clearly putting her mind at ease. Robin, looking to be in her early twenties, had short, wavy black hair encircling her round face, as she had a slightly round figure.

"What brings you to Memphis?" asked Davis.

Alex wasn't sure if she wanted to completely reveal her reasons for visiting. "I'm just passing through town, and I was hungry."

"We have good food, don't we?" Davis uttered, smiling.

"It was great!" agreed Alex. When Davis and Robin didn't have their attention completely on her, she quickly checked the time on her iPhone. "I'd hate to cut this evening short, but I have an Uber coming at ten."

Quickly, Davis looked at his cellphone, and stood. "Oh yeah, we have to get going too." He dropped his cellphone back into his shorts pocket. "Alex," he said, reaching forward with both strong hands, grabbing Alex's right hand and wrist. "It has been a pleasure to meet you, and thank you, thank you for standing strong for me."

On her feet, Alex met Davis' eyes. "Oh, of course," she retorted, happy. "No problem at all." She pushed her chair back under the table. "Robin, it was nice to meet you."

Reaching for Alex's hand, Robin kindly shook it. "It was nice to meet you too."

Alex exited the club and looked for Jay. She spotted Him a little up Beale, His feet still on the ground. Alex picked up her pace and caught up with Him under the neon corridor.

"Did you enjoy your evening?" asked a relaxed Jay.

"I did, I did have a good time," Alex replied, smiling. "There was a brief, ugly scene at the end of the performance."

"I saw, I saw," He announced, scratching His right eyebrow. "You do believe in yourself."

Of course, Jay witnessed the scene. Why was she surprised over that fact? She didn't know. "I'm getting there," Alex concurred, grinning.

It was unusual to awake in a severe downpour with winds blowing in what seemed like 40 mph gusts. It was much more unnerving experiencing this kind of rainstorm inside a tent, only millimeters thick of nylon. Alex didn't take long to scurry to her car for better shelter. She scoured the area outside, seeing if she could spot Jay, but she couldn't, hoping He was safe wherever He was. Alex had no doubt He was safe and probably protecting others. Peeking at her iPhone, she discovered it was 6:07 a.m. on the east coast, so it was 5:07 a.m. in western Tennessee. Taking a moment to decide who to FaceTime first, she decided on Conrad and Justin, understanding infants need nourishment every couple of hours. Alex smiled when she saw Lila, asleep so contentedly, in Conrad's arms, figuring Justin was holding the phone. They kept their voices low, as they gave a very detailed account of Lila's day the previous day, recounting all her feedings, her diaper changes, her little, cute coos, her every yawn and every nap. When Alex had returned to the campground seven hours earlier, she had copious pictures from Conrad, and copious pictures from Justin, and she looked at every one before she drifted off to slumber land. Even if Alex was about 1,300 miles away from Lila, she loved being an auntie, easily imagining what the baby's skin feels like, the gentle smell of a baby's head, and what it would feel like to hold a baby, to hold Lila.

As Alex watched the quiet, adoring scene unfolding right before her eyes, she sensed the deepened love between Conrad and Justin now. They had always loved each other before Lila, but with Lila, their love suddenly had roots in the Earth that children had the ability to cultivate, to promote. Suddenly, they had a common bond, who was Lila. She was going to be their sunshine on rainy days. She was going to be their happiness on sad and tough days. Lila was going to be their strength when they felt weak.

The rain and wind had died down a bit, but she still couldn't see Jay close by. Alex wished Conrad, Justin, and little Lila a good day. Conrad reminded Alex that he was around anytime to talk if she needed a kind ear. Alex thanked her best friend and told him she loved him, Justin and of course, Lila. She was happy for the second morning in a row.

Alex then FaceTimed her mother. "Good morning," she said lightheartedly when seeing her mother's image.

Joanne smiled. "Good morning, Sweet Face," her mother began, "Are you in your car?"

"Yeah," Alex answered easily, "it's raining cats and dogs here, but I think it's letting up some." She looked out the windshield to confirm that statement.

"Did you just get off the phone with little Lila?!"

Listening to her mother give a little giggle was magical. "Have you seen her?! She's a little cutie!"

The fact that her daughter possessed a twinkle in her soul for this newborn baby girl lighted up Joanne like the bright, morning sun. "She is such a doll," excitedly agreed Joanne. "Conrad sent me pictures last night."

A giggle shot up from Alex's diaphragm. "You got those too, uh?"

"We did, we did," gleefully, her mother confirmed. She spent a moment or two longer to inspect Alex's unburdened eyes.

Alex heeded her mother's prolonged gaze upon her. "What? Do

I have something on my face?" she joked.

Widely grinning, Joanne, carrying the weight of her son's death for nearly half a year, finally felt an ounce of it just lift off. "You look so good today," Joanne revealed, as tears welled in her eyes.

"You do know if you start crying, I'm going to start, right?" Alex chortled, as she thumbed her tears away.

"Dad told me about the conversation you had with him yesterday," gently revealed Joanne. "He was very touched by everything you said."

She sniffled before she spoke. "I figured he would tell you." Looking through her windshield again, Alex swallowed hard, but remained composed. "I just realized that I wasn't thinking about you and Dad, and how Nate's passing was affecting you. I was just engulfed in myself." Looking out the driver's side window, Alex didn't want to show her mother her shame.

"Alex—baby girl, look at me," her mother begged and waited for her daughter to return her eyes to her. Alex complied. "There's no handbook for this pain we're going through. There's no light switch that God is going to flip to make things right again."

Alex chuckled, as tears trickled down, when her mom mentioned 'God'. "Wanna meet my little friend over here?" she asked, reaching down to find plastic Jesus.

"Your little friend?" Joanne mirrored, intrigued.

Out of habit, Alex brushed little Jesus off from anything that might have fallen on him in the previous days. "I found this plastic Jesus in Montgomery; he looked like he needed a home, and I figured it couldn't hurt having him in the car with me." She cleared her face of all the mucous. "Maybe Nate sent him to me to keep me company, to keep me safe."

"Nate would do something like that," Joanne granted sincerely. "Do you ever talk to Jesus?"

Alex grinned, realizing her mother might find this entire scenario strange. "Yeah, I talk to Jesus—sometimes we talk a lot." She worried she was scaring her mother. "Does that sound weird?"

"No, no, not at all, Sweetie," Joanne reassured her unreserved daughter. "All of your life you have never been into the whole church thing."

Getting comfortable, Alex knocked off her flip flops and lifted her right heel up onto the seat. She wrapped her hands over her knee. "I know, I know, but this doesn't have to do with church," she admitted.

"It has to do with Jesus, Christianity and just all of it put together." She knew she didn't have the language to explain things properly. "I'm starting to see things from His perspective instead of just what the church says, if that makes sense or not."

"Of course, it makes sense, Al," her mother expressed lovingly. "You can believe what you want to believe; nobody can tell you otherwise."

"Some people believe they are Christians but they're not," Alex determined, "and some people go about their lives not giving a thought to whether they are Christian or not, but they always do the right things."

"I'd imagine you are closer to the second group."

"Yeah, and that's not a bad thing," Alex surmised, as she surveyed the clearing sky above. "Jesus kind of picks me up when I am hard on myself, you know."

As Alex's mother, Joanne was completely engulfed with her daughter, while she spoke so forthright and freely. "You're pretty hard on yourself, no doubt about that."

"Well, I kind of have to be," Alex began nonchalantly, "I'm a doctor."

These words Alex just spoke were like an orchestra starting to play in her ears. Joanne wanted to jump up and down as though she was Alex's personal cheerleader, but she knew Alex would pull back if she did. "That's true."

The sun came out in western Tennessee to dry up the wet terrain below. Alex rolled down her car windows to get some much-needed air. "Where's Dad?"

"I hear him walking around upstairs; he should be down momentarily," shared Joanne.

"I just wanted to say 'hi' before I start getting ready," Alex uttered, stretching out her back muscles together with a yawn, while she combed her hair back with her hand.

"Where are you headed today?" Joanne inquired, sipping her tea. "Here's Dad." He kissed his wife.

"Hi Dad."

"Hi Hon, how are you doing?" Michael asked, stepping into the frame. "Thanks for the videos from last night."

"I'm glad you liked them."

"Al, where are you headed?" Joanne repeated.

"Oh, sorry Mom," Alex apologized, "I don't know…I know St. Louis is not too far; maybe I'll check it out."

Noticing his daughter so relaxed, sitting in her driver's seat, as if sitting on a couch just relaxing, made Michael's heart skip a beat. "You look so chill, Kiddo."

"That's because I am," Alex concurred, "and if I didn't have to pee and tame my hunger, I probably would stay here for a while."

Together, Joanne and Michael cracked up, smiling at their daughter, as it was vividly apparent she was emerging again. "Sweetheart, go get ready," Joanne gently directed. "We'll talk later, or tomorrow, or whenever you want."

Alex chuckled along with them. "Okay, sounds good...I love you guys."

"We love you too, Al," Michael easily announced, "stay safe."

"I will," Alex replied, smiling. "Bye."

"Bye," Joanne uttered tenderly. She ended the call, feeling grateful and alone at the same time.

After taking care of her hygiene, Alex had to take of her hunger. Upon returning to her campsite, Jay was there making her tea, and reading a new book, *Under the Tuscan Sun*. Almost immediately, Alex busted out laughing, thankful she didn't have anything in her mouth. Never in a million and one years would she have ever expected to be sitting across from Jesus, with a small campfire between them, as He sat quietly, so caught up in the story by Frances Mayes. As Alex ate some granola, she felt the need to tell Jay that the movie adaptation of the book was a romantic comedy. It didn't surprise Alex that Jay knew how the book was readapted for the film. What did surprise her was that He was so interested in the recipes in the book. When she pressed Him for why He had such an interest, Jay explained that He often looked through cookbooks to see how people used the bounties of the Earth, which God had supplied for consumption, and nourishment. This answer flooded Alex with many questions, but most importantly, were people eating correctly?

As a doctor, Alex was well-versed in nutrition and biochemistry, and what the human body needed to function. Vegetables, protein, legumes, and whole grains were the foods to eat. She asked Jay if humans were supposed to eat the meat of animals. Jay didn't make any judgments but reminded her that early mankind wouldn't have survived without animals to consume, reminding her that God was the creator of everything. It was with time, millions of years, that man had adapted food, good or bad, for what it was today. Sadly, Alex knew how well a person ate depended on their wealth and status within their communities. Inequities were pervasive, and with inequities come food insecurities which stifle black, brown, and poor people. With fewer opportunities making a living wage nearly impossible, the government attempted to solve the problem by keeping their heads above water by throwing money at the problem instead of creating opportunities for self-sustainability inside one of the richest countries. The more Alex ruminated over the facts, the angrier she became. Jay had done His job.

Siblings

They got on I-55 North just after 9 a.m. St. Louis was four hours away. Missing just about all the rush hour traffic, it was a smooth ride heading out of Tennessee. The day was a little hotter than the previous one, but not enough to throw on the air in the Camry; Alex liked feeling the air on her skin, especially at this time of day. She had gotten used to driving long distances by now, eleven days into the trip. It was a good time to allow her thoughts to go where they wanted, without destinations, and without tracking miles. Thoughts could come and go at a whim. Some thoughts stayed, some left, but returned, and some never came back. Alex loved the quietness and tranquility of being alone with her contemplation and reflection of what she thought this life was all about, and where she would be in another year or so. Alex also knew she had to complete this ride wherever it led her—wherever He led her. Whether or not she believed in herself, Alex believed in Him, and He believed in Alex.

It had been a while since Alex had talked to Nate at his gravestone; for some reason, Alex had believed that Nate only heard her when she was at the cemetery. This rationale didn't make sense anymore, now believing that if she could speak out loud, Nate was bound to hear, as his spirit surrounded her. With only Jay's ears near, if He was listening at all, as He was seemingly sleeping in the passenger seat, she knew He wouldn't pass judgment. She began with a simple 'hi Nate', and proceeded to inform him of her location, feeling slightly foolish doing so, because he most likely was aware. Next, Alex apologized for not visiting his grave, but then she knew she told him she was going away. Batting 0 for 2 at the moment, she felt she was failing to keep his interest up. She had to come up with something better. Maybe Nate wanted to hear something funny, so she decided to tell him that she could erect a small tent in under ten minutes. Was he laughing? Alex didn't know but she really hoped so, remembering how he laughed when he was in that right mindset. Building a campfire, Alex said freely and out loud, wasn't her strong suit. The scenery on both sides of I-55 wasn't too dissimilar to I-93 in Boston, Alex directed to Nate. Stepping in it right there and then, she associated Nate with Boston, which led her down that path of missing him. Before Alex got too deep, she managed to regroup, pulling herself up again. Taking a few deep breaths, determined not to go into that realm she had spent so long in, unable to feel anything but the heaviness of her grief and failure, Alex recalled that morning, observing Lila soundly sleeping in Conrad's arms. Lila suddenly became her holy grail.

It was approaching 1 p.m. when they reached St. Louis, as it was difficult not to avoid catching the view of The Gateway Arch. Alex must have seen it more than a hundred times on television or in images. Images could not give the Gateway Arch the magnitude of its actual size. People were able to go up to the top of the stainless steel rectangular clad arch, but Alex didn't feel the need to visit the top; she was more interested in getting something to fill her growling belly. The Blues City Deli was just off I-55; Yelp gave it good reviews. It would fit the bill. Given the time of day, the restaurant wasn't too crowded. Inside, Alex ordered the Feisty Tuna sandwich and sat at one of the umbrellaed tables outside. The sun tried to seep through the heavy clouds, but it didn't succeed, dropping the temperature down like two measly degrees.

"You did very well today, Alex," Jay spoke, sitting across from her.

Taking the last bite of her sandwich, Alex gazed curiously at Jay. "Huh?"

"I listened to you talking to Nate in the car," He revealed.

Nothing Jay said was a surprise anymore. She took a sip of her water. "Did I sound foolish?" she asked honestly, hoping for an honest answer.

"Of course not."

"Can Nate hear me?"

"Yes, he can hear you," Jay replied, locked into her eyes.

After several seconds, Alex unlocked her eyes from Jay's and took another sip of water, convinced that she could talk to her brother whenever she wanted. Remaining quiet for several more seconds, she debated what to ask next. "Did Nate send me plastic Jesus?"

"Do you believe he did?" Jay inquired, wanting Alex to come up with her own beliefs.

Out of the slightest frustration, giggling as she combed back her black hair through her fingers, Alex smirked at Him. "You can't just give me this one?"

"It is what you believe that is most important, Alex," Jay preached, "and not what I can tell you."

Sitting quietly, Alex mulled over Jay's words. "I'm going to say, 'yes, Nate did send plastic Jesus to me'."

"Okay, Nate sent you plastic Jesus," He repeated, smiling.

"Now that We have that settled," Alex spoke, and followed it up with a good, amiable laugh. "What should We do next?"

"I thought We could check out the Cathedral Basilica over on the west side."

"Point me in the right direction," Alex uttered, rising from the table, and disposing of napkins and paper plates. With her car keys already in her hand, Alex and Jay made their way to the Camry. Alex sat and immediately picked up plastic Jesus, clutching him to her heart.

The Neo-Byzantine Romanesque Revival Catholic Church was an impressive structure inside and out. Deemed a basilica in 1997 by Pope John Paul II, its structure was completed in 1914, although its numerous mosaic interior designs, encompassing 41.5 million glass pieces in 7,000 different colors, were completed in 1988. The church, with three domes and two spires, was built with a granite exterior. Alex walked through its front doors and immediately marveled at the sight of it all, as her eyes took in the beauty. Even from far away, as the dome structures reached 143 and 80 feet, she could see all the mosaic edges, as they fused together to forge all the religious scenes inside the domes and certain parts of the walls. Directly in front of her was the altar, under the crucifix simulacrum. Slowly stepping forward, down the middle of the wooden pews, she gazed from side to side, gazed upward to the domes and again, ahead of her, to the magnificent altar. Within a Catholic Church, Alex bent her right knee downward and made the sign of the cross. Not many people were in the church on Thursday afternoon, giving her preference as to where she wanted to sit. Alex chose to sit on the left, three pews back from the altar, sliding over about two feet to give Jay space to sit even though she was the only person who could see Him.

This never seemed to get old: sitting next to Jay, as she was in a church—it never got old. Alex just sat quietly, gaping at all the intricate mosaic work everywhere she looked, and imagining what painstakingly tedious work that had to have been. Human beings were amazing creatures, Alex formulized. Oh yes, she already knew this from her years in medical school, but the hands, eyes and hearts of the artisans who constructed this gorgeous structure were truly amazing, talented beyond words. She was taught not to talk in church but given the fact that the entire church was practically empty and that she was seated next to the Son of God had to give her liberty to whisper.

"This place is beautiful," she spoke softly, looking up to the brilliant, blue dome with countless glass pieces placed perfectly. "The human mind did all this."

Jay followed Alex's eyes to where she was looking. "Those are my Twelve Apostles that broke bread with Me the day before My crucifixion."

Alex was humbled. "I don't know how You could even eat when You knew what was coming the next day," she quietly commented. "I would have been puking my brains out."

"I was prepared for anything," Jay narrated, clutching His hands easily upon His lap, "I had faith that whatever—or whoever—came for Me the next day was My divine destiny."

When the next question popped into her head, Alex debated whether she wanted to know the answer. In front of her, she looked up at the crucifix simulacrum. She was bold. "What was it like to die?"

Turning to face Alex, Jay wasn't surprised at query. Surveying her eyes, He realized she was looking for solace that Nate hadn't suffered. "As you are aware, My death was torturous, brutal, and long. When My physical body died, My spirit was taken by the hand of God into His Kingdom." Jay paused for a moment. "Nate's death wasn't brutal like Mine; the hand of God took him quickly. He suffered far less."

One single tear fell from her right eye. "Was Nate frightened?"

"No," Jay replied attentively, "Nate was not frightened."

Again, it seemed that a great weight lifted off Alex. She gazed toward the altar. "They say that people who commit suicide don't get into Heaven. Is this true?" Returning her vulnerable eyes to Jay, she awaited His response.

"I can promise you Nate is in Heaven," He proclaimed, seeing the relief in her eyes. "Nate was sick; he didn't have the capacity to rationalize his actions."

Taking a deep, meaningful breath, the angst seeped out of her lungs. "He was very sick," Alex settled. And with that, she just sat quietly next to Jay, and just appreciated where she found herself, appreciated the company she kept, and appreciated all she had. Only days ago, Alex couldn't get through the day without weeping when her grief gripped her around her chest, constricting her ability to breathe efficiently, calmly, as though she couldn't rip herself from its grips. Whatever it was constricting was invisible. Recently, the invisible constricting, as it could have been a transparent python, seemed to be shedding away, bit by bit, leaving Alex more space to bring air to her chest. Alex liked how she felt and how she perceived things, she loved the way she was communicating with her parents, finding it a bit ironic she had to travel miles from home to get to that level of understanding and love which she hadn't experienced for many years. She knew she had no cause to blame Nate for this, and even if she wanted to, she couldn't. Alex also realized that if it wasn't for Jay guiding her through this consequential journey, she wouldn't know where she would find herself; she didn't know if she could have made it this far without Him. Savior was a big, gigantic adjective to describe anyone with, but Jay was her Savior, which fit Him accordingly.

It was late afternoon; the sky remained cloudy, and the air, humid. Alex decided to check in at Granite City KOA Journey Campground to get the feel of the layout. The campground was just over the line in Illinois, and an easy ride across the Mississippi River. After she retained her camping spot, Alex drove to it and parked. There were more RVs and campers than there were tents. At this campground, the trees were not as tall as they were at Meeman-Shelby Forest Campground, but they provided adequate shade. She opened her car windows and got some shuteye for a time. The late afternoon nap got cut short when her iPhone started making sounds, beckoning her attention. It was Ben calling on FaceTime.

"Hi Ben!" Alex proclaimed, waking up her eyes a bit. "How are you?"

"I'm good, I'm good," he replied happily. "Did I wake you?"

Quietly chuckling, Alex raked her hair back with her hand. "As my Dad says, I was just resting my eyes."

With his deep tone, he laughed out loud. "Guess who I have here who wants to say hi?!"

"Is that Ruby Tuesday?!" Alex's voice was bright and joyful, as the child came into the frame. "How are you doing, Kiddo?!" Alex watched Ruby's body become rigid with excitement, as her head turned unintentionally, all the while keeping her eyes on the screen. The girl was able to form a smile. "Oh, you're going to have a lot to say, Girl!"

"Yes she will," Uncle Ben said proudly. "Tell Alex what you ate for dinner last night—tell Alex." For a moment or two, Ben, demonstrating for the child that her thoughts did matter, watched his niece construct words in her mind. "Ruby had some mashed potatoes and chopped up some meatloaf and mixed it in with the potatoes, and then we cooked up some zucchini and she ate that." Ben couldn't help but to kiss the precious child on the forehead.

Purposely, Alex audibly gasped ebulliently, smiling. "You ate all that?!"

Ben laughed once again. "She ate a good portion of it, yes!"

"I'm so, so proud of you, Girl!" Alex asserted with immeasurable glee. "Oh wow—this is great, Ben."

"It certainly is, Alex," said Ben. "She's even sleeping much better."

"I bet she is, I bet she is with a full belly." All Alex wanted to do was to smile. "Have you been able to set up an appointment yet?"

"No, no, they haven't called back yet."

"Would you want me to call them tomorrow? Maybe I can shake things up a bit."

In his burly tone, Ben chortled once again. "You like to shake things up, don't you?"

"Yeah, I kind of do," confessed Alex, grinning widely.

"God bless you, Alex, God bless you!" Before she could respond, Ben started to speak. "If I don't hear from anyone tomorrow, we'll chat over the weekend, and make a plan for what to do next."

"Sounds good, Ben," Alex said. "Please give my best to Tina and Yvette."

"I will," promised Ben. "Ruby, say goodbye to Alex."

"Bye Ruby. We'll do this again very soon, Girl." Unlike before, Ruby squealed, completely overjoyed, making Alex giggle. "Alright, bye, Ben."

"Bye, Alex." Ben ended the call.

Sitting back into the driver's seat, Alex continued to smile, and remarked to herself that she might have the ability to smile for the rest of the night. She was so glad Ruby was eating solid food and sleeping better. It was what she needed to grow and to progress. She suddenly realized that she was doing the exact same thing—growing and progressing, but not as a child grows. Her soul was growing and evolving into something renewed, she hoped. Alex recalled watching the film, *Contact*. Jodi Foster's character, Ellie, an astronomer, was fascinated with the possibilities of communicating with people from faraway lands. As an adult, Ellie still struggled with her father's death when she was nine years old. If only she had gotten his heart medication to him sooner, maybe she could have saved her dad's life. Alex related to this fictional story. Even if the circumstances of the fictional story were altogether different, the extreme feeling of failure was constant, until Ellie found herself believing there could actually be a God. Alex had always believed in God, although with the death of Nate, she lost a bit of her faith—she lost faith in herself. It was slowly returning.

Managing to get over an hour of sleep in her car, Alex awoke to Lynyrd Skynyrd's *Freebird* blaring somewhere close by. It had been years since she had heard the well-known song, with its mournful lyrics, and its air of finality. The lyrics hit her hard, like a rogue wave knocking back whatever got in its way, knocking the breath out of her. Alex just sat and listened, as if Nate was singing these lyrics to her, trying to explain why he had to leave her. He couldn't change. He could not change even though he tried. With both hands upon the steering wheel, Alex leaned forward and quietly sobbed until the song ended. Through music, Nate was communicating with his sister, telling her what she needed to know and signaling that he heard her without question. Alex responded back with a peace sign to Heaven.

It was still rather early in the evening, as the temperature had fallen a bit, enough that she wanted to grab something to eat in the city, and then walk Forest Park. Alex found a place to park, and then the search was on for some food. Not shy, she asked some of the locals for food recommendations, and many pointed her to a food truck, Havana Cuisine, just a little ways up the street. Alex didn't mind the half-mile walk to the food truck; actually she welcomed it, after spending a good portion of the day in her car. Walking alongside Jay, passing people in either direction, Alex reflected on the day, as she attempted to compose a daily report in her head. She decided to shake it up a bit, figuring Jay could read her thoughts anyhow; Alex started speaking out loud, of course making sure no one else was within ten feet.

"Patient One, which is me," Alex clarified for Jay, "Patient One exhibited some growth today, eating properly, and seems to have higher spirits, as she spent most of the day with her friend, Jay."

Walking with His hands in His pockets and looking at the blocks of sidewalk in front of Him, Jay smiled. "I assume Jay is Me."

Sensing His humor, Alex gazed up toward a deep violet, painted sky, and let out a big laugh. "Yes," she replied gleefully. "Then at 5:48 p.m., Patient One, exposed to the song, *Freebird*, dissected its lyrics, line by line, and started bawling her eyes out when she realized her brother was indeed talking to her through the song."

"Tell me you don't write regular medical reports like that," Jay joked.

Turning, Alex looked at Him and snickered. "Ahh, no, I don't, and actually my reports are very detailed."

"I have no doubt," Jay exalted, enjoying this walk. "You know it's okay to cry," Jay stated, making sure He caught her gaze.

"Yeah, I seem to have made crying an art form or something these past several months," she bantered, looking around for signs of this food truck.

"Crying is the human response to sadness or happiness; it only goes to show you that you are human," Jay spoke without a doubt. "You are growing into a different person, a better person."

Alex looked up into the sky. "What kind of person was I before Nate died."

"You were a great person, and you still are!"

"Why, thank you, Jay," Alex quipped.

"What I'm trying to say is sometimes when people suffer loss, or have been through a traumatic experience, they morph into something better."

"Look at You, using a word like 'morph'," chortled a satisfied Alex.

"Sometimes I can hip," He retorted, grinning. "Do you know how caterpillars become butterflies?"

"I love butterflies," she proclaimed, "they are beautiful creatures."

One wink was all Jay needed to confirm His message. She understood.

Forest Park in St. Louis was one of the largest urban parks in the states, cranking out at 1,326 acres in all. After eating a Cubano sandwich and a small cup of black bean soup, Alex was eager to walk around the park before it closed at ten. Now the dark sky was filled with stars millions of miles away, and not familiar with any of the constellations, Alex just admired their beauty, often reckoning that Nate was one of those faraway twinkles of light in the big universe. Inside the park, people were enjoying rollerblading, cycling, jogging, and strolling in the evening hours. Some people just sat on the grass, giving all their attention to their smartphones, all the while the person sitting next to them was doing the same thing. Even if Alex was a child at the turn of the millennium, smartphones didn't come into existence until she was 14, and her parents didn't allow her to get a smartphone until she graduated high school. She did have a flip phone, but only for emergencies.

Emergencies began when Nate hit age 15, when his symptoms of manic-depressive paranoid schizophrenia began. His condition was severe, and the frequency of emergencies went from 0 to 30 in under six months, as Alex and her parents were thrown into an accelerated, chaotic state of reality, not knowing what to expect from one hour to the next. In the beginning, Alex's parents tried to shield her from those numerous emergency visits to the hospital—those times when Nate couldn't decipher truth from fiction; Alex didn't see all the drugs they were pumping into him just to get him calm. It wasn't until one day in the summer of 2011 that Alex was at home with Nate, only for a half an hour, while her parents went to the store, that she witnessed one of his episodes, as the voices began to run amuck through his already-fragile psyche. Alex figured if she spoke louder than the voices, she might hold his attention. That was her first attempt of settling Nate down, trying to distract him from the voices, and trying to keep his focus on her. She succeeded until her parents arrived home, and then the voices bombarded his every thought, his movement; there was no avoiding taking him to the hospital. It was the first time Alex experienced a trip to the emergency room. Her parents tried to have her remain in the waiting room, but Alex refused. She wanted to see everything, from the restraints to the series of syringes being injected into him, witnessing the drugs taking affect, as though he was a savage animal. The first time she saw this episode, jarring and paralyzing, Alex wept, secretly, away from her parents, for days on end, realizing Nate would not emerge out of it the same.

In front of the art museum inside Forest Park was Emerald Grand Basin; its shape was a half-circle attached to a large, slender rectangular water feature. The night reflections coming off the still water sheen were spectacular, especially the illuminations from all the lights around. Alex could only imagine what it would look like if the moon was out. This wasn't the ocean by any stretch of the imagination, but she loved gazing at water.

At once, a group of five appeared not too far from where she and Jay were standing on the square side of the basin. It was evident that this was their gig, whatever it was. They efficiently unpacked the two large duffle bags they brought, and quickly lit the black ropes with flames. With only the ends lit, the performers, some men, some women, began to twirl the ropes in all different motions. Watching the flames was hypnotizing and rousing all at once; as Alex watched, her eyes fixated on the kinetics of the flames, they lulled her entire being down to a level of placidity she had never experienced. Slowly, Alex sunk down to her heels, and melted her thoughts into submission.

On one side of her, Alex failed to notice a young gentleman, standing, and staring at the same rhythmic patterns of fire, fully enraptured, so much so that he seemed to not contemplate anything, or anyone surrounding him. Once the fire show was over, people dispersed, as it was almost time for the park to close. Alex stood up again and turned to her left, noticing the young man, walking in clumsy circles, and mumbling obscure words that made little sense. Before approaching the young man, she scoured the area, searching for anybody that might be with him, but there was no one. Alex decided to move in slowly.

"May I help you, Sir?" she inquired gently. He wore baggy, navy cargo pants, along with a long, white, stained t-shirt. The smell permeating around him signaled to Alex he hadn't showered in several days. "What's your name?"

Not drifting far from Alex, the young man's steps became more like hops. "The fire's gone," he told the sky, not willing to make any eye contact. "The fire's gone."

"They'll probably be back tomorrow," Alex positively stated.

Still pacing in front of Alex, he had non-stop energy. "The fire will be back tomorrow?"

"I believe so." Alex made sure she remained poised. "What's your name?"

"My name?" the young man repeated, as he continued to look up.

"I would love to know your name, yes."

He continued to pace, looking to the sky. "My name is Harrison."

"Harrison is a great name," Alex interjected confidently. "Where do you live, Harrison?" Now, she was suspecting Harrison had autism. "Harrison, can you tell me where you live?"

"I don't like where I live!" Harrison shouted more out of frustration than anger.

"Why don't you like where you live, Harrison?" Alex kept questions clear and concise.

Suddenly, Harrison's legs buckled underneath him, as he cried out. "No back! No back! Please no!"

The first instinct she had was to comfort him, but Alex knew there was a strong possibility that Harrison could become more agitated. Keeping her distance, Alex slowly sunk down to her heels. "I'm not going to hurt you, Harrison. I'm a doctor," she said, using a soothing voice. Alex looked up at Jay, disheartened by the situation, disheartened by humanity.

"Someone is coming," He announced to Alex.

Peering around Jay's legs, Alex saw a patrol officer coming nearer.

"What's going on here, Ma'am?" spoke the officer abruptly, like the presence of people in the park was disturbing his night.

Alex continued to crouch but she turned to face him. "Hello Sir," calmly Alex spoke, "my name is Alex and I am a doctor." Amazingly, she didn't give that statement another thought.

"The Park is closing in five minutes, Ma'am. You and your boy there need to leave."

Nothing about the officer's sentence gave Alex a warm and fuzzy feeling—quite the opposite. Against her better judgment, she rose from her heels, leaving Harrison in a fragile state. "Sir, if I may, I believe this young man has autism." Looking for the officer's nametag, Alex couldn't see one. The officer, husky, although not tall, wore issued dark green shorts and a shirt. He had a freckle-filled face to match his short, slightly wavy, red hair. He was sweating profusely. "I want him to receive medical attention."

"What's his name?" the officer inquired in a less combative tone.

"All I got from him was that his first name is Harrison," she announced. Alex watched the officer take a few steps back and use his radio mic attached to his right shoulder to call for a rescue.

"I have a bus coming," he relayed to Alex. One of his co-workers arrived, and he went off to talk to him.

Sinking down to the ground again, Alex studied Harrison's condition; if he was a piece of glass, and if the tiniest pebble struck him anywhere, Harrison would probably shatter. "Harrison, does anything hurt you on your body?"

Sitting on the grass, he held onto his knees, rocking back and forth. Harrison didn't answer.

With time, Alex grew more and more apprehensive about how Harrison would react to an ambulance. "Harrison, there will be an ambulance coming to give you a ride to the hospital. Have you been to a hospital before?"

Suddenly, Harrison looked upward to the star-filled sky. He continued to rock, as he was keeping time of his own rhythm. "Ambulances have lights."

"That's right, Harrison—ambulances do have lights," Alex reflected. "You love lights, Harrison. What else do ambulances have?"

"Sirens," Harrison responded quickly, as he unexpectedly made a siren sound childishly, as he accompanied the mock sounds with hand gestures.

"That's really good, Harrison," Alex excitedly stated. In the far-off distance, Alex heard sirens, getting louder and louder. "Harrison. Listen."

Harrison stopped rocking for a moment. "Siren."

"Yep, that's a siren," she concluded for him. Alex spotted the ambulance entering the Park. "Look. Here it comes," Alex said, as she followed it for him with her right index finger.

"Ride!" he exclaimed, standing up. He began to pace again. "Ride!"

Alex stood and met his eye level. "Want to go for a ride, Harrison?"

"Yes," he responded, standing still for a second. He touched Alex's arm with the lightest graze. "You?"

"Do you want me to come with you, Harrison?"

"Yes," answered Harrison, looking up to the sky.

"Okay, I'll come," Alex replied.

Happiness fluttered through his body, as he started hopping toward the flashing light of the ambulance. He was mesmerized.

Alex knew she would have to be his voice, his advocate for the night, a responsibility she was accustomed to. Taking aside the male paramedic, Alex explained the situation, and her suspicions. Harrison was already in the ambulance, enjoying the attention he was receiving from the female paramedic. "Meet me there," she mouthed toward Jay. All this felt very familiar—a déjà vu kind of familiar.

Jay nodded at Alex.

Not familiar with the St. Louis hospital system, Alex asked the paramedics where the best hospital for Harrison's situation was. Given his young age, between 15 and 18, they decided to take him to Cardinal Glennon Children's Hospital. The ride to the hospital was brief, as the driver put the sirens on for Harrison's entertainment until they reached the hospital grounds. He loved it. The ambulance stopped and the rear doors opened, as the paramedics lowered the stretcher down to the pavement. They guided Harrison into the receiving bay at a normal pace; Alex followed behind. Upon entering, Harrison was met by two female nurses who would do his initial assessment. One, Mary, stepped forward to talk to Alex, as the other took Harrison into an examination bay. It was obvious Mary took her position as a registered nurse very seriously; Alex saw it all over her determined expression. Mary was a little bit taller than Alex, wearing her blonde and brunette hair down below her shoulders. Her rounded, rectangular, wire-rimmed glasses fit her angular face perfectly. She walked with the slightest of staggers, which didn't seem to bother her. With the kindest of personalities, Mary engaged Alex with resounding respect. Not knowing Harrison, only what she had observed at the park, Alex stated her concerns to Mary. With the information relayed between the medical professionals, Mary had Alex wait in the nearby waiting room.

After using a nearby restroom, Alex took a seat. There was only one other person, a middle-aged woman, uncomfortably sleeping in one of the slightly padded, black metal armchairs common to waiting rooms across the globe. At the late hour it was, exhaustion seemed to hit her right there and then. She was that typical person that always liked to be doing something, whether she was at home or at work; Alex had to keep her mind busy, because when she stopped, she wanted to sleep. Alex chalked it up to learning to sleep in between classes during med school, finding an hour here or there during long shifts at work, or catching those hidden moments when she knew Nate was safe and sound after he experienced a psychotic episode. Memories came back of those times when she would just stare at him, as he slept, and just prayed he would wake, with his mind healed of all its ills. It was a miraculous wish that never prevailed; Alex never expected her wish to come true, but she wished all the same. At that very moment, sitting still, in a tan room, with fluorescent lights overhead, Alex lost the fight to keep her eyes open.

She had no idea how long she had been sleeping once she was awakened by Mary, asking her if she could assist them in trying to communicate with Harrison. When she approached the exam bay which she had seen Harrison enter, two police officers were present; one—a detective, wearing gray dress pants, along with a white shirt with a gray tie. Alex entered the exam bay, fully catching a glimpse of the magnitude of the situation. With only a brief on, Harrison was mostly naked, as his exposed skin revealed bruises nearly covering his entire body. It was an instant gape for Alex, struggling to comprehend what she was seeing. Harrison's baggy pants and shirt had hidden his skinny frame, as his bones tried to escape from under his skin. Soon, Alex walked to his side and found Harrison as joyful as he could be, as he ate a small cup of vanilla ice cream. Suppressing the usual human response of being outraged and saddened, Alex had to act like a physician. Mary took Alex aside for a moment to inform her that Harrison had bruising on his buttocks and genitals as well. Acknowledging the troubling, and gut-punching facts, Alex grabbed a nearby johnny and helped him put his arms through the holes. She pulled up a rolling stool and sat next to Harrison.

"Hey Harrison," Alex said with a lifted voice, no matter how difficult it was to lift, "are you enjoying that ice cream?"

"Yep," he replied quickly, staring into a mostly empty cup. "More?"

"Do you want more, Harrison?" Alex asked, looking for confirmation from Mary, who was now her temporary colleague. Mary would go find more ice cream.

"Yes, we'll get you more ice cream," promised Alex, gazing at his bruised chest when the johnny slipped downward. The detective entered the area. "Harrison, did someone hurt you?"

Slowly, Harrison rose his eyes and stared and pointed at the man in the suit. "Good?"

"Are you asking if the policeman is good?" Alex inquired from Harrison, studying his distraught expression.

Nodding, Harrison held his gaze upon the physically fit detective, with short, almost, white, blond hair. "Yes."

Alex saw his name was Detective Jaffery, and then found his green eyes. "Yes, Detective Jaffery is here to protect you, Harrison," she replied calmly, "he's here to help."

"Hello Harrison," the detective said, squatting next to Alex to appear less intimidating. "We're here to find out how you got those bruises."

Solemnly, Harrison looked downward and saw the dark patches of black-and-blue violence and pain over his thighs.

"Harrison," Alex spoke, grabbing back his attention, "how did your legs get hurt?"

Harrison seemed to get overwhelmed by this question; his hands began to fidget, trying to find something to occupy them. He picked up the blue, cloth edge of the light-green johnny, putting it between his teeth, gnawing on it.

"Harrison, could you take that johnny out of your mouth please," Alex formed this more as a kind demand rather than a question.

Staring at Alex, judging her resolve, her determination, Harrison complied with her request. "Like me?" he set forth in his own conveyance method, fearing he did something wrong to push her away.

"Of course, I like you, Harrison," Alex replied confidently. The urge to put a caring hand upon his shoulder was commanding, testing her humanity against the medical protocols not to touch a potential abuse victim—a privileged strife. "I want to help you, Harrison."

"Help?" inquired Harrison with a guise that would make anyone's heart stand still.

"Yes, I want to help you," Alex sincerely stated, not breaking the gaze with him. "Can you tell me how your legs got hurt?"

"Charlie," Harrison barely muttered, as he looked away.

Quickly, Alex turned to Detective Jaffery; her eyes were relieved, although she had more to uncover. "Does Charlie live with you?"

"Yes," he answered with the same forlorn expression.

It was difficult for Alex to hold onto her composure, as she stifled her outrage. "Harrison, you are doing great." She also had to remind herself she was doing great.

"Great?"

"Yes Harrison, you are doing great," Alex repeated with all the enthusiasm she could round up within her war-torn soul. "Do you think you can tell me your last name, Buddy?" She knew it was inappropriate to refer to him as anything other than his name, but at that point she didn't really care. All she cared about was the vulnerable human being, lying on the examination table beside her.

"Duncan," Harrison revealed, exhausted from the night he just experienced. "Sleep?"

Seeing the brutality displayed all over his body, the beating he had endured for one day or one hundred days, which was unknown, Alex could only imagine the emotional scars that lied within. All she wished for him was peace and happiness from this night forward. "Yes, you can sleep, Buddy." Alex asked Mary if there was a blanket around. Mary fetched one from a nearby cabinet and helped Alex cover Harrison. He was already asleep.

Detective Jaffery, Mary and Alex stepped out of the room while Harrison slept easily. "Forgive me, I didn't get your name, Ma'am," Detective Jaffery directed toward Alex.

"Oh, I apologize, my name is Alex Roma."

"Hon," Mary directed toward the detective, "I'm going to write my final notes and then meet you at the desk." Mary turned to Alex. "Girl, your awesome!" She was off down the hall.

The fact that Mary just referred to her as 'awesome' caused Alex to grin. "Mary's your wife?"

Jaffery instantly smiled. "Yes, she is! We've been married for 18 years."

"Congratulations," granted Alex.

"Thank you, thank you," replied the detective. "Do you live in St. Louis?"

"I am from Boston," she stated easily.

"I'm going to assume you didn't know Harrison before tonight?"

"No, I did not," Alex confirmed for the officer. "I was just hanging out at Forest Park, and saw Harrison after the twirling fire show, and I noticed he wasn't leaving, and he presented with autistic characteristics, and nobody seemed to be with him, so I stepped in."

"What is your profession?" Detective Jaffery inquisitively pursued.

"I'm an emergency room physician." This fact was becoming increasingly easier for Alex to state.

Hesitating for a moment, he smiled once again, with his hands on his hips. "Well, Harrison was very lucky you stepped up tonight," Detective Jaffery spoke. "Mary and I have a son with autism; you did an awesome job with Harrison."

"Thanks so much," replied Alex. "How often do you and Mary team up on cases like this one?"

Standing inches from a wall, Jaffery decided to take advantage and leaned on it. He crossed his arms. "A little too many," he regrettably uttered, "one is too many. The world seems very disjointed these days, you know."

"Oh yes, I know," Alex agreed, sighing heavily.

"Mary is just about to get off work—can we drive you somewhere?"

"If you don't mind driving me to my car over by Forest Park, that would be kind of great." Alex yawned, covering up her mouth with both hands, excusing herself.

"Follow me," ordered the detective. "Let's go find my wife."

Shadowing him as he walked through the different areas of the emergency department, Alex didn't have much time to observe what activities were happening around her. "Granted, I have watched many episodes of *SVU*, but what's going to happen to Harrison now."

"Well," Jaffery initiated, rounding a corridor corner, "we will look into whether Harrison receives any services from the state, will obtain his address and begin our investigation."

Alex stayed close behind the detective, as he weaved through obstacles like wheelchairs, hospital beds and portable sphygmomanometers along the way. "What is going to happen to Harrison when he can be released?"

"With Harrison's case being so severe, we will not release him until we have a safe place for him to go," explained Jaffery, as he rounded the main desk where he found Mary.

"Like a group home or somewhere like that?" Alex bluntly asked.

"Somewhere like that, yes," Jaffery indicated. "A social worker usually makes that call."

"Oh man," Alex murmured under her breath. The idea of Harrison being placed in a new and strange environment gave her pause.

Jaffery rested his arms on the surface of the large, nearly fully closed circle, off-white desk, tapping his knuckles, waiting for his wife to break free of work. "As a father of a child with autism, I know how important it is to have the right services in place."

Joining him at the desk, Alex rested her hands on the desk. "How old is your son?"

"He is 16; he's high-functioning," Jaffery retorted, watching Mary come around the desk. He put his hand upon her in the loveliest of ways. "We are going to take Alex to her car over to Forest Park."

"Oh, okay," Mary replied with pep only she could possess at 1:45 a.m., "do you have a place to stay?"

Following the couple out the hospital entrance, Alex kept up. "Yeah, I already have a spot reserved over at Granite City."

"Like a tent?" Jaffery asked, contorting his face.

"Yep," Alex replied, as she noticed the warm, morning air; it doesn't get cool in the summers of the south.

"Is the tent set up?" now Mary asked, still walking.

"Ahhhhhh…nope," Alex conceded. "Everything's in my car."

"You have to stay with us tonight," demanded Jaffery.

Noticing their steps slowing down as they approached a dark Lexus SUV, she matched their pace. "Oh no, I couldn't put you out; I'll be fine," Alex portrayed confidently.

Mary giggled. "Come on now, you wouldn't be putting us out— we have two spare bedrooms, each with its own bathroom. You can have your pick."

After Jaffery unlocked the car, they all got into the Lexus. "We'll take you to your car and you can follow us home."

It was evident they wouldn't take no for an answer. "I do thank you for your offer," Alex replied humbly, gracefully. "Have you already verified I am who I said I am?" Watching Jaffery through the center rearview mirror, she saw him grin widely. Alex started laughing.

"Perks of being a cop," uttered Jaffery, still grinning. He drove out of the hospital parking lot.

"So, what brings you to St. Louis, Alex?" Mary asked to bring noise to the car.

Evaluating her resolution at this late, or early hour, depending how one wanted to look at it, Alex was uncommonly calm. "I'm driving cross country; St. Louis seemed like a fun city to check out."

"Are you driving alone?" Mary asked, bothered.

Alex laughed, losing count of how many times she had been asked this question. "Well, yeah," she easily admitted. "Back in February, I lost my younger brother. I thought taking a trip would be beneficial, so…"

"I'm terribly sorry for your loss," Mary expressed with sincereness and warmth.

"Yeah, me too, Alex; I'm sorry for your loss," said Jaffery, giving her a look in the rearview as he drove.

"Thank you…thank you very much," a reflective Alex spoke, looking through the car windows at the city sparkling in the distance. "Have you both lived in St. Louis for a long time?"

"Oh yes," happily uttered Mary, "Joe and I went to both middle and high school together. We briefly lost touch while we were in college, then he called me up one day, and a year later, we were married." Mary squeezed his right bicep.

"Yeah, I was kind of idiot when I went to college," Joe muttered and laughed, paying attention to the road before him.

"Mr. Jaffery, my car is right up here on the left," Alex directed.

"The black Camry?" Joe asked, lifting one of his index fingers off the steering wheel.

"Yep, that's mine."

Joe pulled his Lexus perpendicular to the Camry and stopped. Watching Alex unlock the car, he found the button to open his window halfway. "Follow us."

"I will," Alex promised.

As Alex followed the Lexus, Jay was in the passenger's seat, as He was checking up on her, after not seeing her since she left on the ambulance with Harrison. He liked what He saw in her: confidence and determination. Jay didn't need to ask Alex any questions—He knew everything. Knowing Alex the way that He did after eleven days on the road, Jay was aware of her longing for His security, His strength, and Their heightened bond she had come to rely upon. Their time together was growing short, although Jay never would put a deadline on Alex's inclination to thrive again, leaving that all up to her. Jay believed she understood that component, even if she didn't care to dwell on it very much.

The Jaffery's driveway was large enough for two cars, side by side; Alex parked to the left of the Lexus. She grabbed her catch-all, black duffel bag from her backseat and followed Mary and Joe into their modest ranch, climbing up the curved brick stairs to the red front door. Inside, Joe flipped on the nearest light in the small foyer and walked directly into the kitchen. He dropped his keys on the gray, quartz kitchen counter and grabbed a beer from the stainless-steel refrigerator, reminding everybody it was Saturday morning. Joe offered Alex a beer or anything else that was available to consume in the kitchen. A cold glass of water was all she needed. Mary had Alex follow her to one of the two spare bedrooms and set her up for the night. As it was the wee hours of the morning, everyone hungered for sleep.

The hour was nearing 10 a.m., and Alex's iPhone was screaming for attention. It was Joanne chiming in on FaceTime.

"Hi Honey!" Joanne spoke gleefully, as she noticed her daughter was in a strange room. "Where are you?"

Unable to hold back a yawn, Alex tried to shield it with her wrist, trying to pry her eyes open. "Oh God, Mom—I apologize," she uttered, finishing the giant yawn. "The short version of it is I met this very lovely couple last night—I met them at the children's hospital here. They invited to put me up for the night."

Joanne looked inquisitively at her kindling daughter. "Children's hospital? What were you doing at the children's hospital?

Managing to sit up with her back against the white, wooden headboard, she tossed her hair back in the usual fashion. "They have this park in the city...Forest Park..." In typical Alex fashion, caring and detailed, she narrated the complete account, without mentioning Harrison's name, to her mother.

"There she is—my little world rescuer," Joanne uttered proudly, smiling, as she tried to hide the tears welling in her eyes.

"Why are people just so crappy to one another? Why can't people just be kind?"

"If you can figure that out, Sweetheart, God love you."

Alex stretched her arms up after she stretched her back, thrusting her core forward, as she quickly picked her iPhone back up. "And what did you and Dad do last night while I was saving the world?" she jovially asked, grinning.

For Joanne, when her daughter smiled, the world was right again—at least her little, shattered world. "We got brave enough to watch *Mr. Holland's Opus*." Joanne swiped away another tear from her wrinkled skin below her eye.

"Oh wow—Nate's favorite movie," Alex commented haphazardly, gently biting her bottom lip and looking away for a split second. "I haven't thought about that movie in a long time."

"Yeah, we cried a lot," Joanne admitted easily. "He loved that movie."

Alex had her own tears she had to wipe from her eyes. "I know he did."

Thinking it was time to change the subject, Joanne did just that. "So, who is this couple that you are staying with?"

"You mean, Joe and Mary?" she quipped.

Suddenly Joanne's tears turned to immediate laughter. "You're staying with Joe and Mary, and you have Jesus in the car." Staring away from her iPhone and holding her chin, Joanne chuckled at once. "Only you, my child. Only you."

"They even gave me a room too—can you believe that?!" joked Alex. Laughter consumed her, giving her stomach an extra workout. "No, no, no—they are very nice people, Mom." Alex threw her hair back once again, tossing it around a bit.

As she watched her child continue to emerge into a version of her former self, Joanne could only stop and stare for a few fleeting seconds, as if she was gazing at a shooting star. Alex was her shooting star. "I miss you, Baby Girl."

"I miss you too, Mom," she lovingly said, as she watched her mom's eyes erupt with love and gratitude. "Where's Dad?"

"Oh, he's golfing with some buddies."

It was difficult for Alex to smother a runaway giggle. "Golfing? When was the last time Dad went golfing?"

"It has been a long time, Al. A long time," Joanne easily uttered. "I'm glad he's getting out."

"Yeah, it is good," Alex replied, smiling.

"Oh look," Joanne joyfully interrupted, "Conrad just invited us to dinner tonight."

"Tonight?" Alex's voice extruded envy.

"Yes, tonight," Joanne repeated, as she smiled.

"Awww…You are going to hold Lila before I do," Alex stated the obvious.

"Is this a competition?" humorously asked Joanne, giving her daughter a funny, facial expression.

Giggling quietly at her adoring mother, she couldn't help but to realize how many moments she had miss out on these last months. "No, it's not a competition, but do you think somebody could FaceTime me when you hold her?"

Joanne chortled. "I think that could be arranged, Sweetheart. And what are you doing today?"

"I'm not really sure, although I hope to have a relaxing day," spoke Alex. "I should get up before Mary and Joe think something happened to me."

"Sure, sure—go get ready," Joanne pressed. "Please thank them for me for looking after my beautiful daughter, and I'll talk to you later."

Once again, Alex snickered, but this time, with humility. "Okay Mom, I love you. I'll talk to you later. Tell Dad I will talk to him later."

"I will. I love you, Al."

"Bye, Mom." Alex disconnected the video call. Right away, she got up and got ready for her day, feeling so thankful to be showering in a private bath. Dressing at her normal pace, which was quick, she cleaned up and made the bed in under twenty minutes. She opened the door and peered down the hall to see if there were any signs of life. Sauntering toward the kitchen, as quietly as her feet allowed, Alex heard hushed chatter, being met by Mary and their youngest son, Joshua. "Good morning, everybody."

Mary stood up from the kitchen island at once. "Alex, this is our son, Joshua. Joshua, this is Alex."

"It's so nice to meet you, Joshua," Alex stated happily. Joshua was tall and husky—a freckle-faced redhead with boyish looks. On this day, he wore long navy shorts and an oversized white T-shirt.

Joshua gave the stranger a quick look up and down. "Hello," blurted Joshua, returning his attention back to his mother. "Tad wants me to go to his house to check out what he just built."

"Okay, but just be back by 4 o'clock," Mary directed, "and be safe."

"Okay," Joshua spoke, heading out the back door.

Shaking her head easily, Mary snickered. "I guarantee that he will be talking your ear off later. What can I make you to eat?"

"Oh Mary, you don't have to worry about me," Alex protested, "I can go out and grab something."

"Girl, you are a guest in my house. Please sit," ordered Mary, pulling out a kitchen chair. "Do you like eggs?"

Before Alex answered, she acquiesced and sat down respectfully. "I love eggs, thank you."

Mary smiled. "I'm going to make you an avocado, cheese and tomato omelet," she announced, wielding a black, plastic spatula in her right hand. "Coffee or tea? You look like a tea person."

"I am a tea person, thank you, Mary," Alex spoke kindly, as she watched Mary gather up the ingredients for the omelet.

"Were you talking to your mom earlier? I was just passing your door when I briefly overheard," asked Mary, facing the stove.

"Oh no, were we that loud?" she inquired humorously, sprinkled with some embarrassment, obviously with nothing to hide. "Yeah, I was FaceTiming my mom; we do that every morning since I left on my road trip," Alex paused to reflect. "It's kind of funny how distance can make people become closer." The tea kettle started whistling on the stove. "I have always been close to my parents, but I don't know, we have just been communicating so much better."

Mary put a maroon mug, steaming with hot water and tea bag, on the table for Alex. "They miss you."

"Thank you, Mary," Alex politely expressed. "Yeah, they do miss me...I miss them." Alex sipped the hot tea.

"Do you have any other siblings?" gently Mary inquired, cooking up the omelet.

"No, no, there were only two of us," Alex replied effortlessly, "Nate was three years younger. He suffered from paranoid schizophrenia—pretty severe schizophrenia."

"That's so tough," Mary commented, taking extra air into her lungs.

Stretching her arms down upon her knees, Alex rubbed her palms together just to give them something to do. "Yeah, he...he took his own life," Alex revealed, nodding while exhaling, attempting not to crumble. She did not.

Instantly, Mary stepped in front of Alex, kneeling, grabbing both of her hands. "I'm so, so sorry, Alex," Mary spoke with genuine emotion that was plastered on her expression.

This was another astonishing feeling of warmth and peace that transfixed Alex into a quiet reverie, as she gazed to her right. "I have had a lot of practice saying those words over the past week, and for the first time, I'm not falling apart." A single tear trickled down her cheek.

"Let me fix this omelet for ya," Mary said, still holding onto Alex's hands before she stood up to tend to breakfast.

Vacantly staring and thinking about not much at all, Alex remembered what her father was doing. "My Dad is playing golf today— he hasn't played golf in years."

"Does he have a good swing?" Mary asked haphazardly, turning to Alex.

This question snapped Alex out of her inattention and went directly to her funny bone, wherever that might have been, sending her into hysterics. It must have been the morning for laughing because that was what Alex was doing—laughing.

Alex elected to stay with the Jaffery's on this Saturday; Mary was having a little get-together that evening with some of her co-workers—mostly nurses, a few physicians and physician assistants, and one or two certified nursing assistants. It was something this group of friends did, once a month, to keep up their friendships and the overall morale of the close-knit medical team. Alex wanted to feel that camaraderie again even if she wouldn't know anyone but Mary. It had been a very long time since Alex had any kind of social interaction with any of her co-workers, except for Conrad and Justin; she wanted to know if she could still communicate and associate with people in the medical field. She desperately wanted to know if strangers in the medical field would still think her worthy of her profession.

It was almost 4 o'clock when Mary realized she didn't have enough lettuce and tomatoes for the garden salad for at least eight guests. Alex offered to go to the market for Mary. Sliding into the hot Camry, Alex wasn't expecting Jay in the passenger's seat, being suddenly inclined to roll down the car windows. Jay thanked her even though He didn't need to since He had the ability to materialize at will. It was good to see Him. Starting up the Camry, Alex asked Jay what He had been doing while He had been out of sight, knowing full well He wouldn't give her specifics—she was lucky if she got any verbal answers. Alex set off to find Straub's Food Market. Mary gave her abbreviated directions, possibly forgetting she wasn't from St. Louis. Alex always relied on her iPhone to get her from place to place when she didn't know the area.

Ten minutes later, Alex parked at Straub's and entered the market with her invisible friend. For a Saturday afternoon, she was surprised that there was only a scattering of others shopping.

"So, why are you nervous about this evening?" gently inquired Jay.

Snapping her gaze to Him, Alex squinted her eyes, not understanding His question. "Who said I was nervous?" Produce surrounded her.

Jay smiled. "Maybe I should have said, 'apprehensive'."

Lightly scratching her left temple, Alex began to scrutinize the red, vine tomatoes. "Well, do you blame me?" she commented quietly. "I have been out of the loop for several months. I don't want to make an ass out of myself." She placed ten tomatoes into two plastic bags.

He laughed under His breath. "You are not going to do that," Jay said confidently.

"How do you know I won't?" Alex playfully inquired.

"I know you believe in yourself!"

A smirk grew across her face. "Okay, I believe in myself," easily Alex confessed, as she picked out three fresh heads of iceberg lettuce.

With His hands upon His hips, Jay shook His head. "Sometimes you make Me crazy."

She didn't believe His last statement. "Like I believe that," Alex uttered with humorous sarcasm, and headed for the checkout lines.

Again, Jay smiled.

Joshua was already home before the first guests arrived; Joe, too, soon arrived from putting in a full eight hours at the department. Mary had showered and changed into dressy clothes while Alex was at the market. Putting together the salad for Mary, Alex listened to Joe recount where the investigation was headed in Harrison's case, of course not mentioning Harrison's name. They were at a standstill trying to locate the suspect, frustrating Joe to his bones. By this time, Mary, Joe and even Joshua felt that Alex was a part of their family, as she offered any help she could give throughout the day to make the evening a success. It was easy for Alex to see Mary's enjoyment having her around on the Saturday she was hosting the dinner; whether it was a silly idea or not, Alex thought that Mary might have gotten a sense of what it would have been like to have a daughter, as they talked all day as though they had known each other for years. Spending time with Mary also cemented how much Alex missed her parents, even if it had only been twelve days since she had embarked on this journey.

Guests started arriving a little after 6 o'clock. Mary greeted them with her usual warmth, and she didn't need to show them where anything was because they already knew. She introduced Alex to everyone as the 'doctor from the north,' revealing only that she consulted on a recent case. It was up to Alex if she wanted to reveal any more about herself. There were hours to go before she became comfortable letting people in. For some reason, Alex took on the role of bartender when guests made their way out to the backyard. Maybe it was the fact that she had spent a good portion of the day helping Mary set up the magnificent and beautiful backyard for the dinner party. Maybe she wanted to make a good first impression. Alex recognized just a few faces from the previous night at the hospital, as they recognized her, praising her for what she was able to accomplish with Harrison. Very graciously, Alex took their compliments, thanking them for their kind words. As co-workers mingled and chatted, Alex sensed the good vibes they were releasing were about her; she was sure Mary was contributing to this tenor.

Nursing a beer, Alex heard her iPhone crave attention, seeing it was Conrad FaceTiming her. Alex had already warned several of the guests to expect cuteness overload when her mother would get to hold her best friend's baby for the first time that evening. Holding her iPhone at a distance, Alex allowed some of Mary's guests to share in this precious moment. With Mary standing behind her, Alex delighted in pointing out who was who on the small screen. Then it happened: Justin handed a very content baby girl to Alex's mother. Standing, Joanne swayed back and forth with Lila in her strong arms. The spectators in St. Louis gawked and awed over Joanne's overall physique, as they grew curious about her age. Alex was too preoccupied to let the sweet tenderness of this very personal moment overwhelm her; instead she pulled in the strength of her new comrades, as she enjoyed every precious second of what was happening back home. After a few minutes more, Alex said goodnight to everybody in Boston, throwing all her attention back into St. Louis.

As the sun went down on another day, some guests left while others stayed. After a delicious dinner of roasted chicken, red potatoes and the big garden salad, Alex helped Mary clean up when she saw the chance. She was still sipping her Heineken from three hours earlier.

Bob, one of Mary's friends, stood up from a crimson-painted Adirondack chair. "Can I get you another Heineken?" he asked Alex, using his right index finger to point at her beer.

Quickly, Alex lifted it, judging what was left. "I'm good, Bob, thank you."

"You've been sucking on that for the last three hours—are you sure?"

Nodding, Alex reached for her red Solo cup. "I have my water. Thanks, Bob."

"I thought you New Englanders knew how to drink," Bob griped, sounding disappointed.

Alex chortled. "I'm not one of those, Bob; I'm sorry to disappoint you." From one of her own Adirondack chairs, she watched Bob throw back the last mouthful of his Heineken and proceed to fetch another from inside. Bob, with a small belly on him, was average height.

Alex guessed he was approaching 40—a proud bachelor, with a balding head and average looks. On this evening, he wore a light green, plaid shirt with maroon shorts that oddly worked okay together. "Is he going to need a ride home?" Alex directed toward Renee, another one of Mary's friend's, sitting on her right.

"Nah," Renee uttered, "he should be fine. God forbid he gets a scratch on that Mercedes of his." Renee chewed on some small ice cubes. "How long are you in the city for?"

Leaning her head back against the chair back, Alex scratched the side of her nose. "I'll probably head out tomorrow."

"It sounds like you don't want to go home," Renee gently proclaimed. "Don't you have to get back to work?" Renee had a softness about her that made her an exceptional nurse. Her long, wavy black hair was pulled into a bun. She had beautiful features that complimented her perfect body frame of a forty-something-year-old woman, as she wore a navy-blue, linen jumper.

Pulling herself forward, Alex sat straight on the chair, crossing her arms. "I lost my brother back in February, so I am sort of on this restoration cross-country road trip, if I can call it that," she bravely explained. "Eventually I will go back to work."

Heather, another one of Mary's friends, was in Alex's captive audience, and before anyone else spoke, she did. "I'm very sorry for your loss, Alex," Heather put forward. All the others granted Alex their condolences as well.

Putting both of her arms upon the wide armrests of the Adirondack chair, Alex bowed her head slightly. "Thank you...thank you, everyone," she uttered without any signs of crumbling, which truly amazed her.

Bob returned with a new Heineken.

"Where are you headed next?" Heather inquired, curious and caring. She was also a nurse, although a little more Rubenesque in body shape than the rest, as she was the youngest of them all. Heather's hair, short in a hairdo from the '70s, was light brown, and she wore a white short-sleeved shirt and neon-pink shorts.

"Ummm...I'm really not sure," Alex easily admitted, knowing somebody else oversaw her destinations. "I go where the wind leads me, I guess." Alex sipped some water.

"That sounds kind of fantastic, to pick up and take off without a care," Heather concluded, smiling.

Instantly, Renee gaped angrily at Heather, finding her comment insensitive.

"I'm so, so sorry, Alex," Heather said quickly, "that came out wrong. I didn't…"

A long sigh came from Alex's lungs, as she turned her head downward to get her thoughts in line. "Well, I can tell you that I lost my brother to suicide, and I found him; I tried to save his life while his wrists were draining blood everywhere," she so vividly explained, choking back the raw emotion. "If I drove a million miles, it would never take away anything about that excruciating day." Alex stood and took a gulp of water. "I'll be back." Walking around the house, Alex found the sidewalk out front. Taking another deep breath, Alex judged her psyche and amazingly, it remained intact, for the most part. She didn't notice she had a tagalong gaining on her left until he was inches away.

"Heather sometimes can be less than appropriate," Bob uttered, still a little behind Alex's pace.

Turning to face Bob, she combed back her hair. "Are you afraid I might get lost?"

"Maybe," Bob replied.

Alex turned to walk forward again. "Are you drunk?" Humor engulfed her voice.

"Maybe," he chortled, as he tried to keep up with her pace. "Would you slow down? I'm old and fat."

"You're not that fat," Alex pointed out, slowing up some.

"Well, thank you very much, Alex," Bob expressed with the same humor. Bob stopped. "My brother put himself in the way of a train."

Alex stopped dead in her tracks, forgetting how to breathe, forgetting how to comprehend, turning back to face him. "Oh God, Bob," she cried, putting her hands up to her lips.

He walked closer to Alex. "I know what you're going through," Bob uttered, "the others don't have a clue what it's like to live in our shoes."

Tears fell from Alex's eyes, as she glanced at their surroundings; the neighborhood homes would soon have ears and eyes. "Shall we go back to Mary's? She has a front stoop."

Bob understood her suggestion. "Okay." Taking the lead this time, he walked back while Alex followed him to Mary's brick front stairs. Bob sat down on the right, while Alex sat on the left. "You don't have any cigarettes, do ya?" Bob checked his pockets.

Two minutes prior, Alex had tears, now she doubled over with laughter. "What makes you think I smoke?"

"Everyone has vices; I took a shot," Bob said, waving off mosquitos. A minute or so passed before they spoke. "I think it's cool what you are doing—driving across the country; at least you're doing something besides wallowing."

Chortling, Alex bobbed her head up down, as she clasped her hands together. "Oh, I wallowed alright—I wallowed for three months."

"I think I wallowed for a year," Bob uttered, looking up at the trees, swaying slightly with the wind. "I couldn't get out of my own way."

Turning, Alex glanced at Bob. "How old were you?"

"I was fifteen; my brother was 20, in med school," Bob revealed softly.

Suddenly, Alex breathed in, and then, released it slowly from her lungs. "Boy, that's tough." She rested her palms on her naked knees. "Were there any signs?"

Vacantly staring at nothing, Bob closed his fists in front of his lips. "Nope, no signs at all," Bob spoke, motionless. "That is what was so maddening."

Alex exhaled again. "My brother, Nate, had severe paranoid schizophrenia."

Bob turned his head to his left. "Boy, talk about tough."

Staring up at the same swaying treetops, Alex looked for any shooting stars, finding none. "Yep, it was tough." She came back down to Earth. "You know, I haven't asked you what kind of physician you were."

Without any thought, Bob began laughing. "I'm a psychiatrist, specializing in pediatric trauma and grief counseling."

Alex looked at him directly. "No shit?"

"Shit," he solidly confirmed. "What did you think I did?"

"I actually didn't really think about it," Alex confessed, smiling.

"Oh, thanks, thanks a lot," he kiddingly expressed, "now I really need a cigarette." Stepping down onto the brick walkway, Bob reached into the open passenger-side window of his silver Mercedes coupe and easily grabbed another pack of Camels. He stayed below and lit one up.

"You know those things kill you, right?" Alex rhetorically asked.

He blew out the residual smoke from his lungs. "Have to die of something; might as well go out happy."

All Alex could do was roll her eyes, shaking her head.

"I saw Harrison this morning," Bob announced between puffs. "Someone beat the hell out of that kid."

Sitting straighter, Alex hung on Bob's words. "What's going to happen now?"

"Well," Bob began, as he took another long drag. "On Monday, I'll start looking at getting him placed somewhere appropriate; me and my staff will keep close eyes on him and hope the son of a bitch who did this to him gets what's coming to them." Letting the cigarette butt fall to the driveway, he grinded it into the tar and picked it up, putting it somewhere in his car. "If it wasn't for you, he would probably not have survived too much longer."

Pushing her hair back from her face, Alex looked away, trying to accept the praise Bob was imparting on her. "Given he has autism, what are the chances of getting a conviction?"

Bob returned to the brick steps, sitting beside Alex. "Every case is different," he explained. "If the cops find a few witnesses, there might be a chance. If forensics find some trace evidence on his clothes, even better."

Alex pushed out a frustrated sigh. "The world is so fucked up; I don't get it."

"I don't get it either," Bob agreed. Hearing the front door open, Bob saw Mary stepping out. "Looking for us?"

Mary didn't let the screen door slam. "I kind of knew you two would be out here," Mary said, stepping down a few more steps, and sat behind Alex and Bob. "It's a beautiful night."

"Are you working tomorrow, Mare?" he asked, wrenching his head around to look at her.

"I'm doing a half shift later," Mary answered effortlessly. "We're having dinner around two—come eat."

"Is my nephew going to bust my balls?"

Mary giggled, as she grabbed Bob by the ear and playfully twisted it. "You know he will."

As Alex watched this close interaction between Bob and Mary, it dawned on her. "You two are brother and sister?" she asked, stunned.

Removing her eyeglasses, Mary caught the pooling tears in her eyes before they fell. "We are."

Emotion overtook Alex strong and hard. She stood, immediately embracing Mary. Instantly, for the second time that day, Alex felt the overwhelming peace and warmth that was incredibly healing. "Why didn't you let me know before?"

Mary reciprocated her strong embrace. "You were having such a good day; I didn't want to ruin it for you."

"Oh sure, sure, let your brother ruin her day," Bob spoke with a mix of humor and sarcasm.

Soon, Mary was hugging her little brother from behind, kissing him on his bald spot. "Let's go back in the backyard," she suggested.

Following Mary and Bob back through the house and into the backyard, Alex realized there might, just might, be hope that her life could be okay.

Bob remained after all the other guests had left. Joshua went to bed to get all the teenage slumber he could accumulate, leaving the four adults to talk the night away. They didn't dwell on the what-ifs—there was no point. There was no point to discuss the horrific details. Instead, they discussed the hot topics of the day, as they piled up without mercy. As a psychiatrist for children, Bob's hot button was how the current administration was separating children from their parents along the Mexico border. Even worse for him was seeing these children locked up in cages, with only mats to sleep on, with only Mylar blankets to serve some purpose, which he couldn't figure out. Bob was visibly moved by his knowledge of the devastating consequences of separating children, especially young children, from parents. The emotional toll would be with them all their lives. Most children would develop anxiety and depression issues that could persist throughout their lifetimes. This was his country who developed this hideous policy, treating children like animals, all because of where they came from, the 'shithole' countries as our president called them. At times, Bob hated to be considered American. Another night had passed.

There was a knocking on the mahogany door that soon became a pounding. At once, Alex sprang from her bed and twisted the pewter doorknob, revealing Nate behind the door, dressed in jeans and a bright yellow T-shirt. Panicked, he was holding his bloodied inner wrists toward the Heavens, begging for help. Alex directed him toward the bed, making him sit on the edge. She hurried into the adjacent bathroom to find needle and sutures, opening all the drawers and cabinets with speed and without accuracy. Amazingly, in her haste, Alex found a proper surgical needle and a spool of black thread. Alex surmised it would do for the situation, hurrying back to stitch up Nate's bleeding wrists. She found

Nate as she had left him, sitting on the edge of the bed with his wounds facing upward. At once, she began to suture the skin, so, so carefully, but every time she would thread the ragged skin, it would rip away like ancient paper, cracking and disintegrating right before her very eyes. Looking up, Alex saw Nate's expression, so calm and so patient, so much so that he was oblivious to the fact that his blood was quickly pooling on the oak floor. Her feet were barely visible as she attempted the sutures again, and again, and again with no avail. As Nate sat cool and reserved, believing his sister would stop the bleeding, it took all of Alex's stoicism not to give in when panic climbed into her throat, trying to constrict her very life. The blood had reached to just below her knees, as she continued to struggle to close his wounds. The odd thing was that the bleeding had stopped dripping from his wrists, yet the room continued to fill with blood. It was now deep enough to sweep Alex from her feet, causing her to have to tread the thin red liquid. While Alex swam, Nate did not, as he was statue-like, still sitting on the edge of the bed, submerged in his own blood. The crimson water was up to the tops of the windows, giving her just enough air to breathe. Alex touched the white popcorn ceiling, leaving red handprints everywhere. She took a deep breath and held it, as she dived down to grab Nate, pulling him upward by his shirt, now orange. Getting Nate's head above the surface of the water, Alex demanded him to breathe. Every time she yelled at Nate, he cried that he couldn't hang on anymore, sinking under the water's surface. She pulled him up again and with his eyes so forlorn, he begged Alex just to let him go, let him go, let him go. Suddenly the water was turning pink, giving her a better chance of locating Nate. She dove down into the water, searching for him; he was nowhere to be seen. Coming up to the surface for air, her lungs were taking in oxygen as fast as humanly possible before searching again and again, but still, Nate was nowhere to be found. The water became still and clear. Alex screamed, as she cried for mercy.

Struggling to catch her breath, Alex sat up straight, clutching her throat. A few seconds passed before she realized it was all a nightmare that had finally released her from its awful grips. Daylight was sneaking in between the windows and their white wooden blinds, providing Alex with enough light to find the hallway, and then the back door in the kitchen. Finding the outside, Alex sat on the edge of an Adirondack chair, with her bare feet in the dew of the green grass, and practiced how to breathe once again. Looking toward the ground, Alex didn't realize

Jay was before her until He knelt, placing His hands on hers, quietly reminding Alex that she was okay. She gazed into His calming, gentle eyes and heard His words. Sliding back into the chair, under an Eastern Redbud tree, her breathing slowed, and she fell back to sleep.

Hearing the screen door slam, Alex finally awoke, still shaded by the Redbud. Opening her eyes and looking upward, she found Joshua, holding her iPhone. She attempted to rouse herself fast.

"Your phone was going off a minute ago," Joshua spoke kindly. "I hope it's okay I brought it out to you."

"Yeah, yeah Josh—it's okay." Readjusting herself in the Adirondack chair, Alex took her iPhone. "Thank you, Joshua." She watched him start to walk away. "What are you up to today?"

Turning around, Joshua first looked toward the ground, then he looked up. "Me, huh? I'll probably go over Tad's again."

"Working on some big project?"

A tiny grin emerged across Joshua's face. "I do all the math for the project we're doing."

Alex replicated Joshua's grin. "You're not building a nuclear reactor over there, are ya?" she asked, jokingly.

A quick chortle paired with a low snort arose from Joshua. "No, you can't buy plutonium," Joshua said matter-of-factly.

"I'm just kidding, Joshua," she replied, as she stood up and stretched her back.

"I gotta get going," announced Joshua, already rushing toward the screen door.

"See you later," Alex spoke, not sure if he heard her. With her iPhone in hand, she walked leisurely back into the house, and into the bedroom where she had slept for the last two nights. Suddenly, inside the white bedroom which didn't resemble the bedroom in her harrowing dream, Alex remembered Nate, calm and resolute, believing she could save him. She remembered the bloodied water, rising around them, without mercy and without a purpose, as she gasped for air after every dive.

Alex went into the bathroom to relieve herself; it was 8:05 a.m. Returning to the bed, Joanne FaceTimed her.

Joanne's image popped up. "Good morning, Sweetheart! I didn't wake you, did I?"

"No, no—not at all," Alex stated with half of a smile, "did you have fun last night with Lila?"

"Of course, we did. Your father held her for an hour after we ate!" Joanne announced, wearing the biggest smile.

In the past several days, Alex had learned to laugh and cry almost simultaneously. With her fisted hand in front of her lips, she looked away, as a tear escaped her eye. "Really?"

"Oh Al, what's the matter, Honey?" Joanne solemnly asked.

Repositioning her chin between her thumb and index finger, she revealed her entire face. "Just another bad dream, that's all."

The dispirited expression cast upon her daughter was gut-wrenching. "I can tell it was a doozy." Joanne managed to hold it together, desperately wanting to embrace Alex. "Do you want to tell me about it?"

"Nope," she quickly uttered, gazing at her mom. "You don't have to know about it."

"How did I get such a brave daughter?" Joanne knew exactly how to get her daughter's attention.

Alex started to giggle. "Me? Brave?" she abbreviately asked. "I'm not brave."

"Are you fucking kidding me?!" strongly Joanne stated. "You are the bravest person I know!"

Still trying to process her mom's first statement, Alex hardly heard the second. "Mom, you just dropped the F-Bomb," Alex reminded her, laughing.

"I've been known to do that sometimes," Joanne admitted, grinning, and then laughing.

Not being able to speak due to her unimpeded laughter, Alex head's was in her one free hand, while the other tried to hold her iPhone steady. "Oh man!" She heard her dad's voice.

"What's the matter?!" Michael frantically asked, as he saw his wife vibrating with tears, and on her iPhone screen, his daughter was in the same condition.

Knowing that if she didn't say something right away, her father would be even more panicked, "Mom dropped the F-Bomb," Alex hysterically announced, clapping her hand to her bare knee.

"Oh geez," he said, relieved. Walking behind his wife, Michael grabbed her chin, planting a big kiss on her cheek. "Did she use it in the right context, Al?" he asked, fixing a cup of coffee for himself before returning to Joanne's side.

A few more giggles escaped from Alex before she answered. "I think so, Dad."

"So, what brought on this F-Bomb explosion," humorously asked Michael.

"Well," Joanne uttered toward her husband, "your daughter doesn't think she's brave."

"What?!" Michael expressed, puzzled, looking at Alex on the small screen. "No wonder your mother dropped the F-Bomb. You're the bravest person we know."

"See, it's our consensus," spoke Joanne, gesturing her hands between her and Michael, "and we made you."

Highly amused, and slightly embarrassed, Alex looked away and smiled. "I love you guys; you're a trip today. I heard you played golf."

Michael was humbled. "Yeah, it went okay. I'm a tad rusty."

Seeing her dad's reticence, Alex wanted to be positive. "You just have to get out and play more; practice makes perfect."

"That what they say, but I don't think I'm PGA material," said Michael, smiling.

Alex laughed quietly. "What did Conrad and Justin feed you last night?"

"Oh, they made a pork tenderloin, potatoes, and green beans, and we brought a strawberry cheesecake," narrated Michael, sipping on his coffee from his white mug.

"Oh, yum," Alex blurted out. "Dad, Mom also told me you held Lila last night."

Instantly, her dad smiled. "It has been a long time since I've held a baby—especially a baby girl."

Knowing what her father was surmising, Alex dipped her head, sensing his love. "I know, Dad."

"So, what do you have planned today?" Joanne inquired, so lovingly hanging onto Michael's upper arm.

"Mary and Joe asked me to stay for Sunday dinner, so I figured I would get on the road after that," answered Alex, as she straightened up her spine.

"Where are you headed?" asked her father.

Shrugging her shoulders, Alex also wondered. "I don't know, but I'll let you know when I land somewhere."

"Okay Al," Joanne initiated, "call us later. I love you."

"I love you, Al."

"I love you too," Alex said softly, "I'll call you later." And with that, she ended the call, taking a deep breath knowing she had many miles to go before she could hug her parents again. Feeling slightly melancholy, she FaceTimed Conrad, recognizing his unique ability to lift her spirits. "Hi Con," Alex began with a smile. "I heard last night was a big success."

"Hi Sweetie!" Conrad nearly shouted. "Your father was so cute with Lila; he held her for a very long time. I could tell he really misses you—your mom too."

Tears flowed easily now. "I really miss them too, and you and Justin." Alex wiped her dampened face with the bottom of her Pearl Jam T-shirt. "I really want to come home, but I know I'm not ready."

"Honey, you just gave me a tit shot," Conrad announced, breaking out in laughter.

"Oh my God, what has gotten into you people this morning?!" stated Alex, as she returned to laughing. "My Mom just dropped the F-Bomb, and you with my titties. What did you drink last night?"

"Wine," Conrad swiftly replied. "None of us are breastfeeding."

She couldn't manage not to smile and giggle. "Oh man, we are funny today." Alex scratched her nose with the palm of her hand.

Conrad sighed. "Seriously…If you want to come home, then come home," he spoke, generous with his kindness. "Although I know you, and if you don't finish this trip, wherever it takes you, you'll always regret it."

Knowing his words were true, her head started bobbing up and down before she combed her hair back. "You know me so well, Con."

"It goes both ways Al," he reminded her. "Just don't lose sight of what this trip is all about." Watching his best friend struggle from a thousand miles away was agonizing, especially knowing how badly she ached to hold his baby girl. "You'll be home soon enough to hold this little one."

Seeing Lila's little face meant everything to Alex. "Awww…She's so cute."

Conrad had his daughter in his arms. "Say 'thank you Auntie Alex. Now I must go have my diaper changed because I'm a good pooper,'" Conrad narrated in his pretend baby voice.

She chortled. "Alright Con, go change her," Alex pressed. "Thank you for being my voice of reason."

"No problem, Al," he replied, as he started walking with Lila. "You'll be my voice of reason when this one starts dating."

Giggling quietly, Alex looked forward to holding Lila when she returned home. "I'll talk to you later."

"I love you."

"I love you too, Con." The called ended and Alex knew she had to move forward.

There wasn't any shop talk at the Sunday dinner table. It was a day to be free from the stresses of the world. Football, baseball and essentially any kind of sport were allowed to invade the Jaffery's household on Sunday afternoons. Since the NFL preseason had just gotten started, there was no need for football enthusiasts to get too crazy. Bob was one of those football enthusiasts when the regular season began. Bob's team was the Kansas City Chiefs ever since the Rams returned to Los Angeles in 2016. Again, Alex found herself discussing Tom Brady when she really didn't care to—she never really cared to. Bob believed Brady's good days were behind him; Alex didn't put up an argument. He also believed Patrick Mahomes would be the future of the Chiefs franchise. Again, Alex did not argue with that perception. Looking at her funny, Bob inquired if Alex was any kind of sports enthusiast. With a wide smile and a devilish gaze, Alex expressed how much she loved to play Ping Pong. Hearing this, what he deemed as a silly response, all Bob could do was laugh and shake his head, while taking another heavy sip of beer.

Figuring Mary might need a hand in the kitchen, Alex left Joe and Bob to be the phantom quarterback or coach every time the Chiefs messed up a play, which was infrequent. Mary was keeping close tabs on the sausage and peppers cooking in the oven, as the penne was cooking on the stove. Alex hovered over the boiling pot of water, mesmerized by the tiny explosions of steam, and the soft sounds of the popping beads of water vapor. Alex felt Mary's hand on the back of her right shoulder; the warmth returned, healing in so many ways. Mary spoke so tenderly, as she explained how she still occasionally had bad dreams, haunting her sleep, and horrifying her soul. Mary quickly added that with the hands of time, tick, tick, tick, these bad dreams seemed to occur less and less, giving the receiver more peace. Soon, with the warmth and peace having calmed Alex again, even after Jay's comfort earlier that morning, Mary gently urged her to expose her dream for what it was—a bad dream. Mary wasn't her mother, and she didn't know Nate, so Alex knew she could narrate the events of her dream without concern. She recalled the frantic search for the sutures, attempting to stitch Nate's paper-like skin together, swimming in the crimson water that soon turn clear, and the most frightening part of all, the failure to save Nate, as he disappeared. Mary asked Alex if she ever had good, positive dreams about Nate. Most were good, Alex answered, and then smiled, at once recalling the incredible dream in which she embraced Nate, feeling that warmth and peace more intensely than the other times. The pasta was ready.

It had been some time since Alex had Sunday dinner, even before Nate's death; it seemed to be all consuming for the Romas to come together. Getting Sundays off from the hospital was futile. Another Herculean feat to overcome for Sunday dinners was if Nate was in the middle of a psychotic episode. Alex recalled several Sunday evenings grabbing something quick to wolf down in the hospital cafeteria. Physically, Michael, Joanne and Alex sat at the same cafeteria table, possibly even eating the same bland hospital grub, but all their focus was on Nate's condition four floors up. On this Sunday, Alex had the ability to taste all the flavors combining with each other—how the savor of the red and green peppers interweaved perfectly with the juices of the Italian sausage, as they seeped into the grooves in the penne. Even though the Italian bread was not the same quality as they had in Boston, or even Providence, it still did its job by soaking up the juices, with a delicate layer of butter. Alex enjoyed it all, remarking to herself that she looked forward to making this meal for her parents, Conrad, and Justin. They would probably lovingly laugh at her, wondering where she picked up her domestic skills along her journey. It brought a quiet smile to her face when she knew the answer would always be St. Louis.

Time was running short before Mary had to leave for her shift at the hospital. This was the first time in the last twelve days that Alex had a heavy heart leaving the comfort of Mary's and Joe's home and their unwavering support. She was enlightened by meeting Bob and understanding his introspective personality, seeing herself in him, even more than she was comfortable accepting. Alex enjoyed the brief, although meaningful, exchange she had with Joshua that morning. Opening the contacts app on her iPhone, Alex passed it to Mary, who put her and Joe's information in, and then she passed it on to Bob. Smacking his lips together humorously, Bob mentioned he gets his best sleep between three and four in the morning. Alex smirked, resisting the urge to laugh because it was probably true. Joshua took Alex's phone from his uncle, adding his contact information, just in case Alex needed any math questions answered. A tiny tear collected in the corner of her eye at Joshua's kind gesture, realizing she had had an impact on him over the last 48 hours. What little she brought into the house was already in the Camry. Outside, they all gathered on the worn and crumbling asphalt driveway, each one embracing Alex, making her promise to keep in touch through her road trip and beyond. She promised she would. As she closed her car door, sliding the key in the ignition, she caught a glimpse of Jay, sitting quietly in the passenger seat, ready to guide her to her next destination. He directed her to I-70W—headed toward Kansas City.

It was a change of pace to be getting on the road in the evening, and driving for an extended period, figuring it might be an easy drive not to be battling with the sun and the blazing heat. Alex thought she might be able to drive with the windows down, feeling the wind blow through her hair. She did just that.

No words needed to be spoken. Alex just allowed thoughts to run around in her brain, sneaking in and out of the valleys and hills of the gray matter. In front of her, she watched the red fireball that was the sun sink below the horizon, signaling it was the end to another day. Highways were beginning to look all the same, just with different cities and towns plastered on green traffic signs. She figured it would be a good time to throw on one of her playlists that would take her the rest of the way to Kansas City. The chosen playlist was years old, and it spanned the gambit of those little gem songs that most people have forgotten about, those little treasures that would remind her of Nate. Soon, she concluded everything would remind her of Nate, whether she lived in the Amazon, or at the North Pole. Memories would not escape Alex, nor did she want them to leave her, understanding memories were gifts no one could ever steal. They were hers and hers alone, no matter how good or bad those memories tended to be. As each song played, certain memories triggered along this concocted, manifested timeline she held in her head. She knew exactly what she was doing and where she was when a particular song was released or when she first heard it. After 2011 was when songs took on a new existence, a new perspective to her new reality that was Nate's illness. When *Time After Time* started to play, Alex instinctively gasped when the kick drum accompanied that very 1980s keyboard timbre. She choked back tears listening to the profound lyrics sung by Cyndi Lauper, reflecting whether she could have done more. Recognizing she was heading down that dank, dark rabbit hole she wanted to avoid, Alex took a few deep breaths to not enter that self-loathing zone. Flipping to the next song on the playlist was the easy way out, and she didn't know if the next song would try to take her down that same rabbit hole. She fortified her heart and soul with nanoscopic stone and mortar, building it with only her imagination, being so careful

to keep a running bond straight and tight. It was an exercise for her mind;
the playlist was still playing, as Alex continued with her invisible masonry work, keeping her eyes on the almost-empty highway, avoiding that rabbit hole.

Kansas City was a few miles away, as time approached 11 p.m. She looked forward to sleep—any kind of form of slumber she could come by, stopping at a Motel 6 south of the city. The humidity was thick and putrid, like nothing she had felt before on this trip, hitting her directly in the face getting out of her car. It was like walking straight in front of those massive heaters somebody would see on the sidelines at a Green Bay Packers' home game in the dead of winter. It wasn't winter—it was the dog days of summer in the Midwest. When Alex looked across the top of the Camry, having Jay within her sights, wearing in his hoodie and jeans, she imagined she would melt into a puddle of hot, messy goo if she wore His garb. Only grabbing the essentials, Alex checked in and went directly to her single room.

After flipping on the dull ceiling light, illuminating not much but the queen-size bed dressed in the usual autumn, orange, red and yellow leaf pattern, Alex searched out the air conditioning unit and flipped it on high, but high brought an obnoxiously loud, mechanically deficient noise to the room. She left it on for a few extra minutes to see if it cooled the room any. It did not. She shut it off and opened the warped windows as far as she could. The air remained dead still. Alex texted Mary that she made it to Kansas City okay. Given the late hour, Alex decided to put on the lightest thing she had and lie on top of the autumn bedspread. She was asleep within five minutes.

Either it was the bright, early morning sun that woke her, or the subtle commotion happening outside, nearby. Alex rose and threw on her flip flops, grabbing her iPhone inherently. Stepping onto the second-level, concrete portico, Alex looked down and saw two officers, one female, one male, trying to coax what seemed like a young girl into a big yellow school bus, which appeared to be recycled from any part of the country. The letters *I.C.E.* were plastered on its side, giving Alex enough information to make conclusions. She made her way down to the ground level to see if she could provide some assistance.

Extending her right hand, she introduced herself. "Hi. My name is Alex Roma. I'm a doctor."

Only the female officer extended her hand. "Hi, Alex. My

name is Officer Lindberg, and my partner is Officer O'Keefe over there."

When Alex looked his way, as he stood leaning on the side of the bus, he barely lifted a brow to acknowledge her presence. She imagined giving him the finger, but again, her better angels took control. Turning her attention to the young girl sitting on the wooden steps, thankfully in the shade, Alex studied her despondent, saddened demeanor. "And who do we have here?" Alex immediately crouched down in front of the girl.

"This is Inez," Officer Lindberg offered. "This morning she started her menses."

"The first time?"

"We believe so," replied Officer Lindberg, very unsure.

Lindberg's unassertive answer and tone piqued Alex. "How long has Inez been in custody?"

"Oh, Ma'am," clipped Lindberg, "we don't refer to it as 'in custody.'"

"What would you call it then?" Alex snarked back, giving Lindberg a look that would sink a thousand ships.

Lindberg, speechless, found the ground beneath her feet, studying the specks reflecting off the sun.

Moving slowly, Alex sat on the step below Inez, and delved deep to remember her Spanish. "Hola, Inez. Me llamo Alex. Soy doctor," she spoke, as clearly as she possibly could. "¿Te sientes bien hoy?"

Inez rested her beautiful olive-complexion face on her stacked arms that bridged her kneecaps. Her semi-frizzy, long dark hair was in a ponytail. She wore a yellow short-sleeved shirt with white shorts and had blue plastic flip flops on her feet. Inez didn't respond to Alex's question.

"¿Algo duele?" Alex softly pressed Inez.

The young girl lifted her head, as tears fell from her big, brown eyes. "Mi corazón," Inez woefully spoke, jabbing at her sternum with all four of her fingers. "¿Donde está mi madre?"

Taken aback by her own sudden emotion, Alex noticed her parched lips and looked up toward Lindberg. "Inez wants to know where her mother is," she announced to Officers Lindberg and O'Keefe. "Can anyone help me with that?"

"I don't know where her mother is," O'Keefe gruffly replied. "Why don't you call my boss, the President?"

Even if O'Keefe had a direct line to the President, Alex surmised he didn't want to hear all that she had to say. "This is not helping Inez."

Alex pushed out a long, frustrated breath. "Where are you heading with Inez?"

"We can't tell you that location," Lindberg answered.

Alex became more infuriated. "Can you tell me any more about this particular child?" Now her hand gestures were displaying her frustration. Her iPhone began to ring. It was Joanne. "Hi Mom. Can I call you back in a few?" Her mother was fine with that arrangement. "Okay Mom, I'll talk to you soon." The call ended.

Inez looked intrigued at Alex. "¿Tu madre?" the young girl asked, pointing at Alex's iPhone.

Gazing between Inez and her iPhone, Alex understood what the girl was inquiring. "Si, esa es mi madre."

Inez's big brown eyes filled, as they looked to Alex. "¿Donde está tu madre?"

"Ahhh...Mi madre vive en Boston. En el norte." Alex hoped she wasn't mangling the Spanish language.

"¿Puedo decirle hola?" Again, Inez pointed to the iPhone.

"You want to say 'hi' to my mom?" Alex confirmed with the girl.

"¡Sí, Sí!" Inez said with glee, sneaking her small hands around Alex's upper left arm.

Whether it was out of respect, or acknowledgment of their authority, Alex looked toward Officers Lindberg and O'Keefe for permission. As expected, O'Keefe just rolled his eyes, losing what was left of his patience, which could occupy a pinhead. Lindberg was unresolved. Alex FaceTimed Joanne. "Hi Mom," Alex spoke with her usual exuberance. "Quiero que conozcas a Inez. Meet Inez."

Joanne began to smile and wave within the tiny frame. "Hi Inez! You're so beautiful!"

Alex turned and smiled at Inez. "Mi mamá dice que eres hermosa."

Inez sat straighter, although never letting go of Alex's arm. "Gracias, Gracias."

"She's so cute," Joanne uttered to Alex. "So, what's happening there?"

"Well," Alex initiated, "I'm staring at this recycled yellow school bus from looks like 1972, and instead of 'First Student', it has 'I.C.E.' stamped on it."

"Gotcha," Joanne quickly replied.

"This little one won't get on the bus," Alex narrated for her mom. "She doesn't know where her mother is. I don't quite know what to do next."

Joanne thought for moment or two. "Do you have anything that you can give to her like a little trinket or something?

Since she was living out of her Camry, Alex tried to think of every item she had with her. She thought about plastic Jesus. For a split second, she thought about not giving him up because she thought he was something Nate had her stumble upon, but she had the real Savior. "I do," she directed to her mom. "Inez, espera aquí. Volveré."

Inez's hands weren't strong enough to keep Alex beside her, as her brown eyes welled up again.

Alex caught her small hand in hers and knelt in front of her. "Volveré ahorita. Estoy sacando algo de mi coche." She pointed to the Camry, parked ten feet away.

The abandoned child stood on the step to watch Alex walk to the car, wondering if she would be abandoned again.

Reaching her car, Alex realized her keys were in her motel room. Instinctively, she looked up and saw Jay observing what was happening below, catching His hand gesture that the Camry was unlocked. Once in the driver's seat, hot as the day is long, Alex fumbled under the seat and found plastic Jesus, wiping him clean again against her white cotton shorts. Closing the car door, she walked back through the gauntlet of O'Keefe's and Lindberg's eyes, prying and impatient, as she crouched in front of Inez. "Sabes quien es?" Alex handed Inez plastic Jesus.

The girl took it in her hand and surveyed for a moment. "¿Es Jesús?" Inez asked, looking straight into Alex's eyes.

"¡Sí! ¡Claro que sí, Inez!" Shifting her weight between both feet, Alex thought about what she wanted to tell Inez next. "Lo encontré hace unos días en Alabama. Creo que mi hermano me lo envió desde el cielo para mantenerme a salvo." Alex suddenly stopped, choking back tears. "Quiero que lo tengas contigo, así estarás a salvo."

"¿Tu hermano está en el cielo?" Inez asked softly, recognizing Alex's pain.

"Sí. Él estaba muy enfermo," explained Alex; her heart was heavy. It was up to her to keep that horrific night locked up somewhere, in a place nobody else could witness. "Puedes quedarte con él para poder rezarle. Él responderá a tus oraciones, Inez."

Inez looked up and wrapped her arms around Alex's neck, embracing her with all her might. "Gracias, Alex."

The unexpected admiration from this young girl almost overwhelmed Alex to tears. "Oh wow, Kiddo," she said, wrapping her arms around Inez small frame, holding her tightly. "Inez, siempre que necesites o quieras una oración contestada, puedes orarle. Puedes rezarle," Alex pointed to plastic Jesus. "Él responderá a tus oraciones."

Inez's big brown eyes gaped at Alex. "¡Es verdad!"

"¡Sí! ¡Sí!" Alex gleefully expressed. "Si le rezas y te subes al autobús, creo que verás a tu madre muy pronto."

Once again, Inez put her arms around Alex. "Te creo. Te creo, Alex. Gracias." The young girl with the beautiful features, and the long dark hair, began to make her way to the bus. Inez, with plastic Jesus in her hand, stepped up to the first step, and then turned to Alex. "Tu hermano está en paz."

Still on the verge of losing it altogether, hearing Inez's precious words made her crumble inside of her hidden chamber. Alex watched Inez take her seat, as she waved goodbye. The school bus wheels began turning and soon the bus was out of sight. Instantly, Alex felt a hand upon her right shoulder. Jay was to catch her when she fell into Him, shattered by grief, the same grief that was with her the night Nate took his life. The frustration of that same, initial grief, hitting Alex like a deluge, angered her. "Why can't I get a handle on this?" she cried into Jay's shoulder.

"Hey, hey, hey—look at Me; look at Me," gently demanded Jay, raising her gaze up to His sacred eyes. "Believe it or not, and I know you doubt yourself at every turn, but you are thriving every day."

Amid taking control of herself, Alex chortled. "You call this thriving?" She sat back down on the step. "I'd hate to see what not thriving looks like." Alex cleared the tears from under her eyes.

Jay followed Alex down and sat beside her. "There's the young woman I know and love," He humorously uttered, winking.

Alex smiled at Jay and flipped back her hair with her hand. "It probably didn't help that I sent that beautiful little girl off to God-knows where, and who knows if she will ever see her mother again."

"She will," Jay quickly interjected. "She'll see her mother again."

There was no reason to doubt Him. "What about the other five thousand kids we have locked up at the border?" rhetorically asked Alex. "Will they ever be reunited with their parents again?"

"Some will," Jay admitted.

"Oh man," Alex spoke, discouraged at the world, and maybe with Jay. "I'm going to go up to take a shower."

Alex stopped at Harvey's at Union Station for breakfast. The situation earlier that morning frustrated her—unable to shake Inez's young face from her mind, unable to shake the news video clips and the picture stills of the thousands of children in cages in abandoned, big-box stores which were put out of business by online retailers. Alex found it difficult to respect the government in recent days.

Alex and Jay sat on the upper mezzanine in Union Station, gazing at the Gothic Revival architecture, much like several large train stations in other American metropolitan cities. Alex had been through Boston's South Station hundreds of times; Union Station was a very similar structure where people had a purpose to be, whether it was to find another destination, whether to gather with friends over a meal, or whether to do something else. The Monday morning was palpable with all the hustle and bustle of getting from one place to another. It seemed like nothing slowed, as Alex peered down from the mezzanine, studying how people moved amongst one another. She saw the waitress return and sat back down.

"Thank you," Alex spoke to the older waitress, as she presented Alex with her Chamber Light Omelet. Seeing it, her stomach growled.

"Hungry?" Jay asked, seated across the faux, gray marble table.

Raising her eyes, taking the first sip of tea, she looked up at Jay. "Funny," Alex initiated, "every time I eat, You seem to always be off sitting with somebody else. Why not today?"

Looking past Alex, Jay observed this young fellow, sitting alone at another of those tables. "You're angry; you don't need to be angry."

"Yeah well..." She stopped, catching a glimpse of the huge American flag, hung on the opposite building, framed in the window outline that punctured the wall above the mezzanine. She leaned back in her chair and stared at it. "America. Do you like America these days, Jay?"

He was surprised at her rare indignation. "If I didn't like America, I wouldn't like you."

Alex crooked her neck and stared at Him. "Sometimes Your answers are weak."

Never did Jay lose His patience but she was testing Him. "What do you want to hear, Alex?"

Aware of where she was, surrounded in a public area, it probably wouldn't look favorable if she had an audience witnessing her having a conversation with nobody. "Later," she spoke under her breath. In record time, Alex finished her omelet. "Where are we headed?"

"Omaha," Jay replied while watching her quickly spring up from her chair, drinking the last of her tea.

"Omaha? Fields of wheat. Can't wait," she quipped. She paid her tab and walked outside to her Camry. Soon they found themselves on I-29 North.

It had been about ten minutes before Alex looked at Him. "I know you want to talk."

With both hands draped over the steering wheel, she figured she could use the traffic as an excuse not to speak. "Talking is overrated."

"Oh wow!" Jay suddenly expressed. "Didn't you say just that same thing to Conrad back in April?"

Alex turned to Jay with a look of bewilderment. "You were there listening on our conversations?"

"Well...yeah," Jay admitted.

"That's just creepy," Alex said, trying to keep her eyes on the road.

"How can it be creepy if I'm here to guide you," Jay pointed out.

Alex was unable to think of a quick comeback. "Do you regret taking me on?"

"Taking you on?" Jay needed to confirm rhetorically. "No, not at all. I have been with you since that night."

"The night Nate died?"

"Yes. I was there."

Her look bordered on an icy glare. "That's interesting," Alex said with the same kind of icy tone, altogether resentful of this latest revelation. The obvious question ricocheted in her head for what seemed like forever, but she wasn't that brave to ask Him, because she knew it would come with unrestrained emotions she wasn't prepared to confront yet.

"I understand your anger," Jay reflected. "You had it within you since that night, burying it far down."

These words rang true, although Alex didn't have the ability to acquiesce. There was no doubt it—the anger she was burying was slowly igniting, like magma stirring within a volcano that had been dormant for a thousand years. "You sound like you're channeling Darth Vader or something." Deflection was her security blanket.

Jay was almost exasperated. "If you don't want to talk, that's fine, but I have no doubt it will come out sooner rather than later."

Alex didn't have any quick comeback—she knew Jay was right. He's always right. Saved by the call coming through on her iPhone. "Ben!" she exclaimed, relieved she didn't have to walk that very thin line with Jay. "How was your weekend?!" She continued paying attention to the traffic in front of her.

"It was just an average weekend at the Samuels' household," he explained. "And what did you do?"

"I spent the weekend in St. Louis with a very lovely couple and their son," Alex narrated. "The wife is a nurse at the children's hospital there, so we got along really well."

"No doubt about that," replied Ben with a flicker of a chuckle. "I can't imagine you, of all people, would ever get under anyone's skin."

A rogue giggle escaped from her lungs, as she desperately tried not to look toward Jay. "I don't know there, Ben—you might be surprised who I can piss off, pardon my language."

Ben's previous chuckles turned to full out laughter. "Yeah, yeah—I can see you doing that to someone also."

Scratching an itch upon her nose, Alex continued observing the traffic. "How's our Ruby girl doing?"

"Oh, she's doing great! Eating up a storm and sleeping like a baby," spoke Ben with such pride and gratitude. "We owe you everything."

"You don't owe me anything," graciously Alex uttered. "Have you heard back from Memorial Health?" Turning on her blinker, she changed into the middle from the left lane.

"Today they called, and they told me they can't evaluate Ruby until January."

"January?! Are you kidding me?" Disappointment entered her voice. "Did they give you a reason why?"

The heaviness of Ben's sigh spoke volumes about his frustration. "They told me they are down two clinicians and have a waiting list a mile long."

Whether it was an idiosyncrasy or a habit, her left hand combed back her dark hair, as her fingertips scratched her head. "Oh man, Ben. I don't know, I don't know." It wasn't in her comfort zone to feel like she couldn't solve a problem. "Let me think on this for a day or so, and I'll get back to you."

"Oh Alex, you have done so much already. I'll continue to call Memorial to see if they can place us on the cancelation list."

Alex made sure there was an audible, dispirited sigh coming from her lungs. "I'm sorry, Ben."

"Everything will work out, Alex," Ben said confidently. "Life wouldn't be life if we didn't have our challenges."

Trying to put a good spin on it all, Alex smacked her lips, not exactly knowing what to say. "I know, Ben." She felt defeated. "I'll talk to you soon."

"God bless you, Alex," softly Ben spoke.

"Thank you, Ben," she returned. Air came out of her lungs like a slow burn. Sensing Jay's eyes settle upon her, Alex continued to keep her eyes on the road. "Can I start this day over again?"

"I'm sorry," Jay began, "that's not the way things work around here."

Lifting both hands off the steering wheel and then pounding her palms back onto the wheel again, Alex demonstrated her frustration with the day. "Can't blame a girl for trying," she said chuckling, on the verge of crying.

"What would you change if you could start the day over?"

Grabbing a tear before it hit her bare leg, sniffling all the while, Alex snickered. "Well, I probably would have slept in a skosh longer," she returned, cocking her head, and lifting her right hand, putting emphasis on the sliver of space she left between her index finger and thumb.

Gently mocking her, Jay did the same with His fingers and smiled. "A skosh?"

Quickly, Alex looked at Him and returned His smile. "Yeah, a skosh." Bringing her eyes back to the road, she combed back her hair once again. "How is it that this world can be messed up, and 95% of the world believes in You, in some type of God, and we conduct ourselves like morons?" Her fieriness was gradually seeping back under her skin. "How can people rip kids away from their parents? That's just cruel!"

Turning more to face her, Jay grinned one of those silly grins sometimes Alex catches. "And she returns!" Jay exclaimed happily.

Finding that silly grin, Alex just shook her head at Him. "You're such a goofball."

"It's better to be a goofball than a jerk," He determined.

"Well, you have a point there," returned Alex, still grinning, as she watched the road.

The Karner Blue

She didn't know what to expect to see once they reached Nebraska: a few corn fields? Maybe a whole lot of wheat on wide open prairies. She thought hard and long if she knew anyone that visited Nebraska just for fun or had even gone on vacation there. Not one person came to mind. She didn't even know anybody who had a friend of a cousin who was from Nebraska. All she knew was that Bruce Springsteen titled one of his albums *Nebraska*. Driving on I-29 North, into Omaha, was flat, with a few sporadic, short trees, lining the two-lane highway. Maybe beyond the trees were the corn fields and the wheat on wide open prairies. Alex wondered if anything exciting happened in Nebraska besides Corn Huskers football. She wondered if *Friday Night Lights* was recorded here, because Omaha seemed to have that kind of vibe.

They found a little hole-in-the-wall restaurant on the outskirts of the city so Alex could grab something to eat. She ordered a grilled cheese sandwich that was stuffed into a wide-slotted toaster—inventive but weird. It tasted weird too. Hospital food provided a smorgasbord of not-so-tasty food, but at least it had a hint of the correct flavor. This grilled cheese mystified her tastebuds, so much so that she dissected it. She pulled apart the two pieces of Rye bread only to find a bunch of parsley flakes embedded in a thick layer of mayonnaise. Alex didn't complain because she was the only one in the place, figuring she may have been his only customer for the day. Sitting at the counter that was covered in a Grey Poupon mustard-colored Formica that seemed to be original to the restaurant, she couldn't help but stare at the heavyset, older man, vacantly peering out the small window next to the side entrance. His thin gray hair was slicked back with Vitalis, as his folded arms rested on his tire-formed belly, seemingly waiting for his next customer. Of course, Alex wanted to strike up a conversation with him, although oddly enough, she was hesitant to do so. She wasn't having good luck so far interacting with people; she was hard on herself when she struggled to help them, and she didn't want to wreck this man's day. She ate her very bizarre-tasting sandwich and paid the $1.99 cost for the lunch. Alex left the owner, cook and waiter a ten-dollar tip. He did not speak the entire time she was in the restaurant. Maybe that was the last day the man planned to stay open; maybe that was why the man didn't have the will to speak. She looked to Jay for some guidance. Jay stood and walked over in front of the vacant shell of a man, putting His hands upon the man's arms, and prayed. Only this time, there wasn't any brilliant light; there wasn't any warmth to be felt, or peace to be experienced. Jay sat back down next to Alex, recognizing her confusion. He explained that the man was a non-believer of Jesus Christ—an atheist. Jay attempted to pray with him, nearly breaking down the walls of his ideology, but he pushed back at the last moments. Suddenly, Alex felt such sadness for the man whose name she would never know, whose voice she would never know the sound of, and whose disposition she would never truly see. She was of the belief that every soul needed to be understood by somebody else. She wanted to know if he had a somebody else.

Ruminating his circumstances was only bringing her down—she had to leave. Again, the solemn man didn't acknowledge her presence— no "thank you," no "have a nice day." She left the restaurant without saying anything kind, which was very unusual for her. Back in her Camry, she leaned her head back to take a deep breath. Once Jay was in the car, Alex started the engine and got back on the road.

She was itching to go for a long walk, recognizing her brain needed some housekeeping. Jay mentioned Standing Bear Lake had a walking trail that would suit her. Welcoming His suggestion, she found the park. Rifling through the backseat, Alex found her walking shoes and laced them up. She slathered her darker-than-usual white skin with sunblock, grabbed her full water bottle, and began her trek. It was another hot day, although the humidity was bearable. The activity of walking, moving just about all the muscles in her body, woke up her soul in ways she could never explain. She missed the ocean. She missed her parents, Conrad, and Justin more and more every day, so much so, that it started to shake her to her young bones. She desperately wanted to go home but she didn't know what to say to Jay. The interest of seeing how this journey was going to end dwindled with every mile she drove.

As Alex saw the lake ahead, she walked onto the grass and crouched down, looking out across the still water. There were people out in a few boats. Tears began to run down from her eyes as all the frustrations inundated her without mercy. Tucking herself farther away from anyone who might walk by and discover her weeping, Alex found a clearing closer to the lake. She cried until she couldn't cry anymore. Sitting quietly at the water's edge, she didn't want to appear weak to Jay, but she did want to head home. So sure that she was going to head home as soon as she could, Alex nearly called her parents to let them know, but she wanted to broach the idea with Jay first—He deserved that courtesy. Apprehension rose in her stomach when she imagined how that conversation would transpire. Alex was sure she knew what He would say, almost sure He would try to talk her out of going home. Figuring there was no time like the present, Alex chugged down a good amount of water before finishing walking the rest of the trail.

Approaching the Camry, Alex saw Jay leaning on the trunk. "Hey."

"That was a quick walk," He commented, looking at her with concern. "Is everything okay?" He knew what was on her mind.

Alex leaned on the truck beside Him. She took another gulp of water. "I want to go home, Jay." Her stomach clinched. "I want to head home as soon as possible."

Jay continued to look forward at the trees across from the parking lot. "Is everything okay at home?"

"Yes," Alex answered, noticing He wasn't making eye contact.

"Are you going back to work?"

Not prepared to answer this question, she stumbled over it as she might stumble over a rock in the middle of a walking path. "Uh...I don't know."

"What will you do once you are back home?" Jay continued to gaze ahead.

This was another question she didn't prepare to answer. "I'll do something."

Finally, He turned to look into her solemn eyes. "You're not ready to go home, and you know it, Alex."

With a heavy sigh, Alex looked away, contemplating His words. "Are You going to make me finish this trip?"

"If I make you, you'll resent Me, and that won't be productive for anyone," uttered Jay with conviction. "I also know if you don't finish this journey with Me, you'll regret it for the rest of your life. You'll never know what you missed, and you'll never know what could have been."

"What would I miss?" Alex inquired, fully knowing that He probably wouldn't divulge anything.

Jay chuckled. "Nice try, girly." He folded His hands upon His legs. "Why do you want to go home so bad?"

Scratching the side of her temple, she recognized that her answer might sound a bit juvenile even though it was the truth. "I miss everybody; I'm homesick."

Jay breathed in quickly. "Yes, I get that, I get it," He muttered, straightening up His spine, "but you do recognize everybody misses you too?"

The hesitation was evident even though Alex didn't recognize it herself. "Yeah."

"How would they feel knowing you came all this way: you are in Nebraska, the middle of the country, just to tell them that you are cutting the trip short because you're homesick." Jay didn't take His eyes off Alex as she pondered His question. "Your parents, Conrad, and Justin all know how important this trip is to you. They all have sacrificed so much for you to go on this trip. Finish it. Finish it for them."

Processing Jay's logic was easy; it was the feeling of longing to be home she had to overcome. "What happens if at the end of this whole trip I still feel stuck where I am now?"

Jay quickly interrupted her. "Wait a minute, wait a minute—you can't honestly tell Me you haven't felt the tremendous strides in yourself?" He stepped around to face her. "Haven't We been on the same trip?"

Never had Alex seen Jay's gaze so serious. Quickly, she looked away from Him. "You didn't answer my question," Alex said boldly.

Lifting His arms slightly, they fell limp to His sides again. "No, I can't guarantee you will have some miraculous revelation at the end of the trip," He spoke with confidence. "All I ask is that you finish this trip with Me."

With her arms across her chest, bending over slightly, Alex gazed down to her shoes, as she waited for them to do something spectacular, like transport her to another dimension, or bring her home by some Beam-Me-Up-Scotty way. It wasn't happening. She wasn't going anywhere. Realizing that she had to make this consequential decision herself, Alex was forced to rip open her soul and scrutinize every corner of her heart. Again, she waited for any sign at all to tell her what to do. She really wanted a sign from Nate. She trusted him with just about everything she had. She waited for another sign. Suddenly, she felt something on her arm, a tickle-like sensation, maybe a stray hair upon her skin. Before she haphazardly swept whatever it was off, she looked down to her left bicep, seeing a beautiful blue butterfly, enjoying the sunshine in that very spot. The creature was mesmerizing, as it held Alex's attention like nothing else had that day. "What type of butterfly is this? It's so small."

Stepping forward, He leaned over to study it. "This little guy is what you call a Karner Blue Butterfly. This butterfly was on the endangered species list several years ago, but they're coming back strong. They're usually native to the northeast, the Great Lakes regions," Jay explained, looking over the immediate terrain. "He's far from home."

Switching her eyes between Jay and the butterfly, Alex was stunned by the beauty of it all. Struck by the symmetry of each half of the butterfly, with its vibrant blue, deep orange dots, metallic-like silver flares and black outlines, so perfectly spaced, Alex marveled. "How do You know it's a male?" Her voice became soft.

Lifting His index finger, slowly and purposefully, Jay got as close as He could to the butterfly. "His body is narrower than the female's." Jay turned His eyes to get a different view. "And can you see the silver color on the wings?"

"Yeah," Alex replied, intrigued.

"The silver is exclusive to the Karner Blue male," Jay narrated.

The butterfly seemed settled upon Alex's arm, and then the tiny creature, with his thread-like legs, climbed up and resettled on her shoulder to get a better view. Slowly, he flapped his wings, but not to fly away, but to signal he was content. Bending her neck down and to the left, Alex strained her eyes to try to see this tiny, beautiful creature clearly. She brought her right hand close to her left shoulder and tried to coax him onto her index finger. As if she was trying to lure a kitten close to her, using a soft but high-pitched cadence, Alex was completely amazed when the little blue fellow climbed onto her finger. "Are you seeing this, Jay?"

Hearing the excitement in her voice made Jay smile. "I am, I am."

Like a flash of lightning, one of her packed away memories emerged, as she gasped when it surfaced. "Oh my God, Jay," Alex fervently uttered, finding His eyes again. "I remember it was five or six years ago, Nate took the standard high school art class," she recounted with her eyes widening at every thought. "Nate painted this same butterfly in that class!" Staring at the butterfly, Alex swore the amazing, little blue creature stared back. "What if this is..."

"Do you think Nate reincarnated into this butterfly?" Jay asked, puzzled.

"No, no, not at all," she spoke unequivocally, "but what if this is another sign from Nate? What if he's trying to tell me something?"

Jay returned to leaning on the trunk of the Toyota. "What do you think he's trying to tell you?" He challenged her.

With her eyes still glued to this tiny butterfly, Alex didn't put much thought into thinking. "I don't know." Straight away, the Karner flew up into the air four feet high, his tiny blue wings flittering what seemed like a hundred miles an hour and landed in the palm of His left hand.

For a few moments, Jay was transfixed on all the colors upon this small butterfly, positioned over His ancient, brutal wound before He turned to looked toward Alex. "What is he trying to tell you?"

Spellbound by His kind and generous gaze, Alex trusted all that Jay was. Before she had a chance to answer, the Karner quickly landed on her wrist, moving her to tears. "He's saying I should complete this road trip."

"Are you positive you want to finish this trip?" Jay inquired with the softest voice.

Raising her wrist up, taking a long, all-embracing look at this precious creature, noticing all the colors he displayed, the very familiar colors, Alex was presented with the decision. "Yes, I'm positive I want to finish this trip," she answered, staring into His eyes.

"Okay," He delivered easily. They remained at the rear of the Camry for the better part of an hour until the Karner finally moved on. He could tell by Alex's solemn expression she wondered if she would see the butterfly again.

Plains

Jay insisted Alex grab a good dinner after she didn't eat particularly well that entire day. They found the Upstream Brewing Company on the east side of Omaha, a two-story, tan brick building with a non-descript façade. Alex chose to sit outside on the patio under a grid of stringed, clear, round lightbulbs swaying in the light breeze. It was just about dusk, and the sky had turned a red-hot orange hue with purple streaks everywhere. She didn't quite know why more people weren't sitting outside on this beautiful night; if this night was transplanted back in Boston, Alex was sure there would crowds of people clamoring for a seat. A few minutes later, the waiter appeared in his formal garb of black dress pants, a black vest, and a shiny, crimson dress shirt. He couldn't have been more than 25 years of age, with his small, dark brown pompadour, perfect in every way, and with his skinny face to complement his thin structure. He wasn't tall although his lanky appearance indicated otherwise. His name was Patrick, and Alex addressed him accordingly. She ordered a Sam Adams and sipped in her usual style. Patrick left her with a plasticized five-page menu, most of it comprised of beer and wine selections. Looking through it, she spotted the "Blonde Pizza," which was a Margherita pizza, but with Alfredo

212

sauce. *Interesting*, thought Alex. She wanted to be daring.

The pizza surprised Alex—it was better than she had imagined. She ate the entire thing. Jay did His customary roaming around the restaurant to see if there were any lost souls who might require His immediate attention. This gave Alex time to mull over the day that seemed difficult; she didn't want to relive it and she knew she couldn't forget it. Sitting quietly, sipping on her beer, Alex drew her eyes up to the darkening, clear sky to see if she could spot the Karner. All she saw were the ever-present constellations that she couldn't quite name. She wished she had paid more attention to Nate when he would try to get her interested in astronomy. Memories rushed back of that Christmas Nate got his telescope; Alex surmised he must have been 12 or 13. Nearly every night, unless there was a horrendous storm, Nate would be looking through that telescope until their parents insisted he go to bed. Most nights, Nate would stay up all hours of the night searching deep space for anything extraordinary. Those were good memories; the bad memories came after Nate had experienced one or two psychotic episodes and launched the telescope out of his second-floor bedroom window, as it smashed into a million pieces on the concrete driveway below. Alex remembered the look of devastation on her father's face, heartbroken and without words, as she helped him pick up the million little pieces in silence, wondering how many peering eyes were watching. She wished she had learned the constellations.

Patrick returned and asked Alex if she wanted anything else, maybe another beer. His question rattled her. *Do I look like I need another beer?* she asked herself. Alex couldn't recall the last time she looked at her reflection. The Vietnam Wall rang a bell. She turned down another Sam Adams and asked Patrick for her check. Not too long after, Patrick recognized she wasn't a local, or even from middle America. With her experience from this trip, all she wanted was for Patrick not to ask her about Tom Brady. Thankfully, he did not. He did ask her if she was from the northeast, but nothing about football. From the few minutes they talked, it was evident Patrick wanted to leave Omaha, to live anywhere else. He was envious of her—boy, if he only knew the cold hard truth, he probably wouldn't be so envious. She paid her tab and included a generous tip. She returned to her car and waited for Jay.

Hearing Jay speak her name suggested she had caught some needed shuteye. As she tried to get back to a level of consciousness she could recognize, Alex noticed Jay chuckling, aware that He was chuckling that she could sleep anywhere. Prepared to take off to another campground to close this day, Alex discovered that Jay had other plans. Driving just a short distance to a rather empty parking lot, Alex followed His lead and followed Him to the Omaha side of the Bob Kerrey Pedestrian Bridge. Alex enjoyed walking, but this day seemed to have taken all that she had. Darkness had already set into the night, although the red and blue uplights on the outer edges of the curvy walkway lit up the three columns and the tension ties, which held everything together. Instantly, the pedestrian bridge reminded Alex of the Zakim Bridge in Boston, but on a smaller scale. There were some people on the bridge taking a late walk; whereas some, mostly teenagers, were finding all the dark spaces so they could discover lust, love, or heartbreak. Alex walked quietly next to Jay until they found an empty bridge overhang to look out over the Missouri River, which was incredibly tranquil. City lights from Nebraska and Iowa reflected off both sides of the Missouri, displaying its natural curvature.

"Has God given mankind all we need to figure things out for ourselves to live here on Earth?" she blurted out.

Jay rested His arms on the teal metal railing. "How so?"

She thought for a moment or two. "For instance—the microscope," Alex presented, "if inventors didn't have the skills, the knowledge and the materials to construct a microscope, modern medicine just wouldn't be."

Nodding, He clasped His hands together. "What do you think?" Expecting some off-the-cuff comment, she compiled her answer.

"We come up with answers to complex issues on a daily basis," Alex began, "we build, build, and build upon the things we know that are true and that work; why wouldn't God give us everything?"

"He has given mankind everything," stated Jay confidently. "There is math, biology, chemistry in everything that surrounds us. There is a reason for everything God has created; it is up to mankind to discover and use each morsel of discovery in the correct manner."

"I bet He flipped over the atomic bomb."

Standing straight, Jay grabbed the railing before Him. "People just have to think and ask themselves if their creation is going to harm their fellow man."

"First, do no harm—primum non nocere," uttered Alex, looking onto the quiet Missouri, clasping her hands. "Being a doctor means sometimes cleaning up the aftermath of a situation that went horribly wrong for some reason or another; sometimes I lose faith in people."

Alex was thinking out loud. "But literally, twenty minutes later, someone can do something amazing, and then my faith is restored."

"Do you still have your faith?" Jay asked directly.

She turned to Him, wanting some clarification. "Faith in You?"

"Sure," Jay settled.

Shifting her stance at the railing, Alex looked out into the night. "I have faith in You—how can I not; You are here with me."

"Yes, but My presence should not determine your faith. You need to feel it in your soul," He explained.

Alex nodded, as she took in a swift breath, mulling over her next words. "My soul, my soul, my soul—it's hard to gauge my soul these days." Disrupting her line of thought was the swell of commotion coming from the direction of the parking lot. In between the din of the swell, Alex heard a voice break through, announcing someone was stabbed. She looked into Jay's eyes for some explanation, but He had no answers.

There was a tear in the corner of Jay's eye.

Alex took off running. As she got to the parking lot, she saw just a few people standing around a man lying lifeless on the hard asphalt. The switch flipped and Alex knew what she had to do. "Excuse me, excuse me! I'm a doctor," she shouted, pressing through to get an initial assessment. "Can someone call 9-1-1 for me please?" She kneeled and investigated the victim's face, and then looked into his still, brown eyes. Life was draining out of him, much like the blood draining out of the slit in the left side of his upper chest. It was easy to locate the wound because the light fabric of his shirt was already drenched in his blood. Instantly, Alex ripped open his shirt, exposing the deep, hemorrhaging laceration. Hurriedly, Alex rolled up the tattered material of what was left of his shirt and firmly pressed it against the wound. "Can somebody give me a hand?!" she demanded over the chaos of the dispersed crowd.

Somewhere in the background, a harried voice could be heard: "Don't save that thing! He's a Muslim! He's a Muslim!"

These cruel words ran through Alex's brain, hitting every nerve she had, evoking her deep friendship with Justin. Refocused, she had a job to do. She couldn't make this personal. Looking out over the people surrounding her, nobody seemed to want to assist her. Alex even looked for Jay. Again, He had disappeared. "Where the hell are You?" Alex muttered under her breath. She felt the man's carotid artery; he didn't have a pulse. At once, she began CPR. Without assistance, Alex got creative and put her knee against his wound, keeping pressure on it all the while doing chest compressions. Without any medical instruments or even another set of hands, all she was able to do was buy time for this man. Reality set in that the last time she did chest compressions, vigorous compressions, was on Nate, in the final minutes of his life. She knew she could not go there; she could not revisit that gut-wrenching night, not then. All her attention had to be on the individual that was in her care. While her adrenaline had kicked in already, she started to feel the burn in her arms and thighs. Realizing that her energy level was fading, Alex had to find a way to regenerate that strength she required to continue. Feeling her anger building and building from the situation she was in, without any aid, without any sign of Jay, pissed off someone did this heinous act to another human being, she felt isolated. "Can somebody help me, please!" she screamed on the brink of exhaustion. "Jay, please help me."

In the distance, she heard sirens approaching. Alex didn't think she could hear a more beautiful sound, as loud and obnoxious as it was, at that very moment. She knew help was near, and suddenly Alex found a hidden pocket of strength that exploded. Finally, she saw the two paramedics approaching with the stretcher. Alex didn't stop compressions until she knew the paramedics were prepared to take over. Moving swiftly, Alex sat with her legs crossed, a safe distance from her patient. Taking a few deep breaths and shaking some life back into arms, Alex returned to give assistance to the two paramedics. "I'll do the Ambu bag."

"What, are you a nurse or something?" the young clean-cut man inquired hastily, as he assessed the victim.

"I'm an emergency room physician," she shot back, trying to be respectful in this tense moment. "He has been down for at least seven minutes; he's probably in hypovolemic shock." Alex controlled the Ambu bag precisely, without a thought.

"He doesn't have a pulse, Ma'am," the other paramedic stated like he was stating a score in a baseball game.

"Let's shock him," Alex demanded. Without discretion, she seized the defibrillator from the paramedics' gear, placed the pads on the man's chest, charged up the paddles, and ran 200 volts through his chest. Immediately, Alex felt his carotid, sensing no pulse. "I'm turning it up to 300."

Still no pulse. "Ma'am!" the clean-cut paramedic shouted. "The victim is deceased!"

Hearing his solid declaration, Alex ignored him. "Clear!" she announced and ran 300 volts into his chest. Again, she felt his carotid artery—no signs of life. Looking into the man's motionless eyes, Alex knew that mien on the dead all too well. She saw that his stab wound had stopped bleeding, as his blood had stopped flowing through his veins. Already, the dead man's skin was turning ashen. Still holding the defibrillator paddles in her hands, not aware she had an audience, Alex gradually processed the scene, staring at all the strangers staring back. It sunk in. Purposefully returning the paddles back in the paramedics' gear bag, Alex rose to her feet. "I apologize," she directed to the paramedics. After that, she picked a direction and just walked, not having a destination. At that time, she didn't need a destination, Alex just needed to walk. Her pace was faster than a relaxing stroll on a walking path; the last thing she wanted to do was to talk to another human being. She didn't want to give a statement to a police officer; she didn't want to answer any questions because she didn't have any answers that would make any difference. All she wanted to do was walk.

Twenty minutes went by, and Alex came upon an empty baseball field. The dim lights were still on overhead. She entered the small gate to the ball field and climbed up a few levels of the metal bleachers and sat. Looking downward, she was still covered with the blood of the victim and realized she didn't even know his name. What kind of person was this young man she tried to save, Alex wondered? What kind of life had he led and who did he love? Who was going to grieve for him? The wind picked up some, bringing Alex a refreshing breeze, but she couldn't do anything with it, feeling uncomfortably numb. Something caught her attention; she gazed toward the gate and saw Jay. Her numbness was replaced by anger, as she stood up and started descending the wide-open bleachers while He ascended them.

"Where are you going?" Jay inquired, watching her every move. He stopped climbing.

She didn't answer, as she continued to walk.

"Alex!" He exclaimed.

She stopped and turned toward Him. "What?!" screamed Alex. "I don't know what You want from me anymore!" Touching her head with both hands, interlocking her fingers, she gazed to the cloud-filled, midnight sky. "Why couldn't you help me save that kid? You were right there with me, and then You weren't. Where did You go?"

"I never left you, Alex," Jay stated, slowly walking toward her.

At the same pace, she walked backwards; her arms fell to her side. "That's a crock of shit, Jay!" Alex said, incensed. "You disappeared!"

"You couldn't see Me, but I was there," He assured.

Spreading her arms out, she finally stood still. "What were You doing while I was trying to save him?" Her anger gradually turned to sadness.

"I was guiding him into the Kingdom of Heaven."

These words halted her where she stood. Bewilderment engulfed her expression. "You were working against me?" Alex interrogated Jay. "We could have saved him, Jay! We could have saved his life!" she vigorously pleaded.

"He couldn't be saved, Alex," Jay stated, unwavering. His eyes were locked with hers.

Clenching her fists, a rage in her core ignited. "You are Jesus Christ, aren't you? Can't You do anything?" She gazed at Him with a curious eye.

"I can't save everybody, Alex," Jay gently uttered, "I cannot save everybody."

Shifting her weight from side to side, almost like she was prepared for a showdown, she didn't take her eyes off Him. "I don't believe that for a minute, Jay!"

"As a doctor, with all your medical knowledge and expertise, can you save everyone?" Jay challenged her.

With her swift gaze, she didn't like this question. "You know I can't save everybody," she spoke with rage. "Why didn't You save Nate?! Why couldn't You save Nate?!" Her voice grew louder, more bitter with each syllable. "I saw You fix that little boy with autism. How come you couldn't fix Nate before his schizophrenia developed?!"

Jay glanced at Alex with mercifulness. "Nate's illness was one of those abnormalities that couldn't be fixed; he gave it his all until he couldn't manage his thoughts anymore."

"Why, Jay?!" she begged.

Seeing the pain in her eyes was almost unbearable. "It was God's judgment to pull Nate into the Kingdom of Heaven, to relieve Nate of all of his mortal pain, and to give him a purposeful existence in Heaven."

"He was my little brother and my parents' son!" Alex shouted. "We could have managed him!"

"Nate didn't want to be managed, Alex," Jay stated in a gentle voice. "He knew that he was failing with every psychotic break; he saw it in all your eyes; the fear that grew within him—Nate knew it would always be a struggle. You know this, Alex."

Maybe Alex knew it, but she didn't want to accept it. Pacing back and forth, simmering with anger, she couldn't deny she didn't know her brother. "Dammit!"

Jay allowed Alex to work through her thoughts, long enough that she began to understand the brutal essence of Nate's mind. "You said 'a purposeful existence'," she interrogated, slightly curious. "What is he doing?"

He walked closer to Alex. "Nate's composing his own music, with a little help from a few of the greats," Jay revealed, smiling. "Today, he had a short jam session with John Lennon."

She didn't know what to believe. "Are you kidding me?"

"I never tell a lie, Alex." Jay stepped forward. "Here, hand me your phone."

Giving Him an inquisitive glance, she slowly reached for her iPhone in her back pocket and handed it to Him. Quietly, Alex watched His thumbs key in her security code and then He started searching for something on the Internet. It took a few minutes before He found what He wanted. "Listen to this." Holding up her iPhone, He started playing a recording.

It started playing, and instantly Alex recognized Nate's beautiful voice, singing a section of a song he was working on a week before he died. Her heart started racing, as she heard Nate's lyrics—his completed lyrics and guitar harmony. As she carefully took back her iPhone, Alex crumbled to her knees, covering her mouth with her hand, and began to sob fervidly. Her body quaked, as if the ground shook, but it did not. Knowing she had to breath, Alex looked up at Jay and somehow, she took in oxygen, as she continued to sob, so sustained that her stomach muscles began to get sore. "Nate's okay?" she barely got out.

Jay crouched down and held Alex tightly. "Nate's okay." All He could do at that moment was to let her cry for as long as she needed. He was relieved that Alex finally showed her pent-up anger toward Him; that was what she needed to begin to live again. She had to recognize the fact that she wasn't to blame for Nate's death. Several minutes had passed, and Jay noticed Alex was settling a bit. "Come on," He initiated, "let's get you off this dirt and sit on the bleachers." Jay helped Alex to her feet and guided her to the first level.

Exhaustion had set into every niche of every muscle. Using the bottom of her powder-blue tank, Alex dried her entire face, and realized the extent of her grungy appearance, as she was covered in dried blood and fresh dirt. "I'm a mess."

He crooked His neck toward her and nodded. "I bet you wish you had driven your car over here?"

Between the residual tears that continued to flow, Alex expelled a brisk chuckle. "No doubt." She used her fingers to clear her tears. Scanning her eyes around her surroundings, an empty baseball field, gradually she worked hard to settle herself, settle her breathing. Thoughts of Nate jamming with John Lennon brought an unexpected smile to her heartfelt expression. Again, Alex listened to the divine recording, choking back a few more tears. "Can I let my parents hear this?"

Resting His elbows on His knees, Jay's hands were clasped together. "How would you explain that to them?"

Stretching her neck upward toward Heaven, two of her fingers scratched the side of her temple while Alex understood the point He was trying to convey. "I understand, but I have all this wondrous news about Nate, and I can't share anything with them," she said between sniffles.

Jay was giving Alex His Divine, undivided attention. "Someday, a day will come when you'll know when you can tell your parents. They will believe you wholeheartedly."

"They will?" Alex asked, needing assurance.

"Yep, they'll believe you," Jay confirmed.

Alex folded her arms into her lap and leaned forward, looking out upon the world with her tired eyes. "Has Nate met David Bowie yet, because he loves Bowie." Recognizing how silly her question sounded, she broke into immediate laughter.

With her laughter being so infectious and needed, Jay dropped into her laughter, enjoying Alex's ability to find humor after a very difficult day. Gently, He bumped His shoulder with hers. "I'll make sure I get right on that," joked Jay. They giggled for several more seconds.

Alex became subdued once again. "You're leaving me soon, aren't You?"

Glancing into her eyes, He saw her apprehension. "We have miles to go, Alex," Jay promised, mollifying most of her angst. "I'm not going anywhere until our last stop."

Gazing at Jay with pure trust, studying His eyes, Alex was satisfied with His response. "Okay." She stood. "Want to start walking?"

Looking relieved at Alex, Jay knew she was going to be alright. "Sure, sure."

For a few minutes, Alex walked in silence, and tried to find the way back to her car. Once confident she was on the right course, and once she felt she was grounded, Alex began to talk. "What was his name?"

"Whose name?" asked Jay, walking beside her through some overgrown trees.

"The victim, as people refer to them," she clarified.

"His name was Seth Pashia," Jay led off in a quiet tone. "He was born in America. His parents immigrated here from Syria in 1993, and Seth was born in 2001 a little bit west of Lincoln, Nebraska, and planned to start college in three weeks."

"Okay, okay, okay—please don't tell me anymore," she said, shaking her head calmly. "I don't think I can handle much more tonight."

"You do realize the police are going to want to ask you questions?" He prepared her.

Glancing upwards, grabbing the side of her tired neck, Alex massaged it on her own. "I know the drill, but all I want to do is sleep, and I didn't reserve anything tonight."

"When We were at the restaurant, I reserved a site for you at Lake Cunningham," He announced.

"You did?"

"I did," Jay replied, smiling, and walking beside her.

Looking down at her feet continuing to propel her forward in more ways than one, Alex grinned. "God bless You."

Sleep had taken a hold of Alex, as she slept into the early afternoon. She had already seen the wee hours of that morning when she answered questions about the Seth Pashia case. The two paramedics who had contact with Alex gave identical accounts of the medical care he received. Before she left the Omaha Police Department, a young female officer who was at the scene, had offered Alex the use of the officer shower facilities, for which Alex was very grateful. Now, lying in her tent, her iPhone called for immediate attention; it was Joanne. It had been more than a full day since they had talked, although it wasn't one of their usual conversations. Rolling onto her left side, she pressed the FaceTime icon and saw her mother's beautiful face. Without warning, and without reason, Alex began crying. She sat up on her sleeping bag. "I'm fine, I'm really fine," she promised a concerned Joanne. "Overjoyed to see your face, that's for sure." She cleared her tears.

"Oh Al," Joanne spoke with a break in her voice. "Tough day yesterday?"

Pulling herself together quickly, she inhaled through her nose, eliminating the mucous from her sinuses. "Yeah, you could say that."

"Do you want to talk about it?" in a caring tone, asked Joanne.

At that very moment, Alex's demeanor changed; strength awakened in her guise. "Actually, I don't," she began. "I realized there are things I can't control, no matter how much I try. That's what I learned last night, Mom."

Placing her praying hands against her lips, nodding, and shutting her eyes for a moment or two, Joanne exhaled freely. "I prayed for this day," she admitted. "I wanted you, my sweet, loving daughter, to stop blaming yourself for Nate's death, because it was never your fault—it wasn't anyone's fault." Joanne paused to catch tears that attempted to run down her freckled cheek bones. "The disease took his life."

Alex had her own tears to tend to. "I realize that."

"Realizing that still doesn't make the pain of losing him any less, does it?"

Smacking her lips together, Alex shook her head back and forth. "Nope, it doesn't, although you have to know Nate is in a better place…without the disease controlling his every thought…his every action. He's free from all that."

Joanne rested her chin in the palm of her hand, still staring adoringly at her daughter. "That's about the only thing that brings me comfort, and you and your dad, of course."

"Where is Dad?"

"He is at the office preparing for Fall semester," spoke Joanne with great composure. "He misses you, Al."

Alex bobbed her head up and down. "I know he does," she replied. "I'll call him once I get on the road. You and Dad can keep me company if you're not doing anything."

"Where are you headed?"

"I believe I'm going to drive straight through until I get to Colorado—make up a little time," confidently Alex spoke. "I'm looking forward to seeing Colorado."

"It's beautiful, Al—you're going to love it," Joanne affirmed. "We would love to keep you company on that long drive."

It was easy for Alex to see how much Joanne cherished her daughter and all she was. "Thank you, Mom," she said, smiling. "Let me get ready so I can get going. Talk to you later?"

"It's a promise," Joanne retorted, blowing Alex a kiss.

"I love you and Dad," Alex proclaimed, same as every other time on this trip.

"Oh, we love you too, Al—to the moon and back. Be safe."

A huge grin plastered all over Alex's face. "I will." She closed out the call, very motivated to do what she needed to get back home.

Stopping at a local sandwich shop before the highway ramp, Alex ordered two of the same sandwiches, veggies and oil on a wheat roll, which would survive an eight-hour drive in an air-conditioned Camry. All she had to figure out was bathroom breaks along the way. Once she got on I-80 West, Alex ate the first sandwich within ten minutes. Jay had already prepared her tea prior to leaving the campground, as He usually did throughout this trip, making plenty for this long leg. The day was warm, but the humidity was down, and she imagined she would roll down her windows in a few hours. I-80 was just another two-lane highway with not much traffic. Population was low in middle America; green space was everywhere, especially away from highways and truck stops. Being out here, seeing all the 18-wheelers, Alex understood the gravity of automation in the trucking industry, the prospect of men and women losing their jobs to machines. Understanding both sides of automating the trucking industry, Alex tended to side with the truckers, who would lose their jobs, lose their ability to feed their families, lose their healthcare and lose their purpose. Alex knew all too well what being employed means to people. She saw it in her residency, as people begged her not to force them out of work, even if for a few days, because if they miss work, they wouldn't get paid. They had children that needed to eat; they had children that needed a roof over their heads. This was the reality of a good percentage of her patients.

Three hours in, Alex pulled off the highway to find a restroom. Around this part of the country, the golden arches of the 1970s and '80s remained the golden arches of 2019, as time stood still in the most remote counties of the nation. This was one town where nothing changed. Entering the McDonald's, Alex noticed a man sitting out front on the curb. She was struck how dirty the man was, as he looked like he had taken a bath in a sandbox. Even his skin was a gritty taupe. The restaurant was adjacent to a concrete and sand distributor. He had a full head of wavy hair, but again, Alex couldn't tell what color it might have been. Once Alex had used the facilities in the almost-empty restaurant, she went up to the counter and asked the woman server about the man outside. Judging the woman to be well into her seventies, her hair was a single shade of white. Alex was disturbed by her skeleton-like frame. It took an extra second or two for the question to register with the fragile-looking woman, but she finally explained to Alex that the ash-like man had been sitting outside for the last twenty-or-so years. Customers, especially out-of-town customers, buy him food daily, to sustain him, until his next meal. He wasn't homeless, although all his government benefits go toward rent because this small town doesn't give housing vouchers. Alex wondered how he gets food on major holidays, although she didn't want to assume he didn't have any family or friends, but from his grubby appearance, her assumption was that he did not have many supports. Not being one to eat much meat, she tried to determine the heathiest item on the menu. They were out of fish, and had been out of fish since 1982, which didn't surprise Alex. She decided to get him a hamburger and a small root beer because there were few other choices. Before leaving, she thanked the stick-like server for her assistance. Opening the door, as a cloud of sand particles flew up in her face, Alex heard the woman start talking to someone, but someone who wasn't there. Outside, she tried to block her mouth and nose to prevent the sand from entering her lungs. It didn't work; Alex barked up some sediment, holding onto the bag of food and the root beer. Once Alex got her bearings back, using her upper right bicep to clean what sediment she could from her face, she found the dusty man just where he was sitting ten minutes before. As she approached the man, she crouched, introducing herself.

"Hello Sir, my name is Alex," she began, "I have some lunch for you." Handing him the white paper bag and the root beer, she carefully observed him. "What is your name, if I might ask?" She watched him open the bag to discover what was about to fill his belly.

Reaching in the bag, he pulled out the hamburger, instantly started eating it, skillfully avoiding the crinkly yellow paper. "I'm Roger," he said, scarfing down what seemed to be his first meal of the day.

"Hi Roger," she said, sitting on the curb.

"Hi," Roger murmured quickly, putting all his concentration into eating.

The heat of the day was finally diminishing. "Is that the first thing you've eaten today?" An urge grew to go grab a facecloth from her car, run it under the water in the restaurant and clean the many layers of silt from his face, although she resisted.

Roger took a big gulp of the root beer, quenching his undeniable thirst. "Probably," he replied, not making eye contact with Alex.

"Do you live close by?"

Engaged with a couple walking into the small rundown hardware store on the opposite side of the street, Roger took another bite of the hamburger. "It's not far."

"Can I buy you some groceries?" she directed at Roger.

This grabbed his attention. "You want to buy me groceries?" he asked, looking straight at Alex. "Why?"

Alex grinned. "You seem surprised by that."

Eating the last of his hamburger, licking his thumb and index finger to get the taste of the savory ketchup, mustard, and pickle juices, Roger replied, "Well, it's not an offer I get every day—actually, not ever. It just seems strange." He looked at Alex with deep gratitude. "Rarely does anyone talk to me."

Alex tried to figure him out. "Why are you out here, sitting in the boiling-hot sun, covered in dirt?"

"That's my mother in there," Roger said, cocking his head toward the restaurant. "She has the beginnings of Alzheimer's. Doctors say if she does something familiar to her, that it might delay its progression," he explained.

Seeing the distance in Roger's eyes, reality set in. "She doesn't know who you are."

His head dropped, as disappointment consumed him. "Sometimes she recognizes me, but those days are very few and far between," Roger finished, looking up into the cloudy, gray sky. "Today, I'm that bum sitting outside of her McDonald's. By the end of a three-hour shift, she's so tired, she doesn't care who I am. I take her home and put her down for a nap until it's dinnertime."

Sensing his sadness, Alex didn't press him hard. "Do you have any support taking of her?" Quickly, she realized she didn't know her name. "What is her name?"

Roger turned to Alex and smiled. "Her name is Rose," he spoke with an uplifted voice, "Dr. Rose Leigh McGovern."

"A doctor?" Alex asked with enthusiasm.

"Yep, she was an OB/GYN for nearly forty years," Roger uttered proudly. "She delivered thousands of babies, and she also got many threats for doing the other part of her job."

"Oh wow," Alex commented, looking back through the restaurant windows. "Was she ever scared?"

"She always said she wasn't scared, but I knew she always carried a handgun," Roger narrated, taking another gulp of the root beer. "Even today, if somebody sees her and knew what she did, she gets nasty comments, but they don't register with her. Some people say she got what was coming to her when she got Alzheimer's. It has gotten much worse in the last few years." Looking back through the window, Roger checked on her. "What they don't realize is she saved many more lives than not."

Alex understood the growing divide of the country. "She was very brave."

Roger nodded his head in agreement. "Mom never understood how people could be so pro-life one minute, and then issue death threats the next, you know."

"I know; it doesn't make a whole lot of sense," Alex retorted, interlocking her fingers on the front side of her knee. "Do you have any siblings?"

Gazing up to the cloudy sky, Roger exhaled heavily. "I have a younger sister who doesn't come around much anymore; if she does, she leaves a casserole on the front step. If the neighbor's dog doesn't eat it before I grab it, then I don't have to cook."

"So, you are your mom's sole support?"

"Yes. Me and my wife," answered Roger, biting the corner of his bottom lip. "Dad died five years ago this past June. He was a meat packing manager."

She nodded out of appreciation of his openness. "And what do you do when you're not portraying a bum?" she inquired with a chortle.

Reciprocating Alex's quick wit, Roger grinned in her direction. "Believe it or not, I write suspense thrillers."

"Really?!" she blurted out. "Would I know any of your works?"

"I don't know—do you read suspense novels?"

"Not too many, but I will now."

Roger started to laugh, switching his weight to the opposite side. "And what do you do, Alex?"

Silently, Alex giggled for a hair of a split second. "I'm an emergency room doctor in Boston."

Roger scoffed, shaking his head and grinning. "I should have known," he said, still smiling. "Are you on vacation or something?"

Putting her hand through her black hair, carrying it out of her face, Alex prepared her words. "No, it's not exactly a vacation," she initiated. "I lost my brother about six months ago, so this is kind of a cross-country restoration road trip."

Lifting his head back up straight, Roger gazed forward and then looked at Alex again. "I'm very sorry to hear about the loss of your brother," sincerely said Roger.

Bobbing her head up and down like an average bobblehead, plastic figure, Alex appreciated his words. "I thank you very much."

"Is it working?"

Alex shifted her eyes back and forth. "Is what working?"

"The road trip."

Leaning slightly back on the concrete curb, Alex realized his question. "Oh! Oh! Oh! The road trip," she voiced at a higher volume. "Umm...Yes, it is working." Confidence extruded from her tone, as she recalled the difficult day before.

"Where does the trip end?" Roger curiously asked.

This was a good question for which Alex didn't have a concrete answer. "I don't know. Probably California."

"That's a very vague answer. California is a pretty big state," Roger humorously pointed out.

Alex begun to laugh, mostly at herself. "I don't know, I just go where the wind takes me." She left out the fact that her wind was Jesus. Looking into the restaurant, she saw Jay sitting with Rose.

"That's pretty 'nomad' of you," Roger said, laughing. "Where are you headed now?"

"I'm supposed to make it to Colorado by ten or so."

Instinctively, Roger looked at his watch. "Oh boy, you'd better get going," Roger said, getting ready to get up. He succeeded. "I have to get Mom home soon also."

Standing up, she brushed off the back of her denim shorts. "Sure, sure."

"I must say this has been the most enjoyable time I have spent hanging out in this parking lot," he expressed heartfeltly. "Do you want something from inside before you take off?"

"Oh no, I'm fine," Alex replied graciously. "I would like to say goodbye to your mom if you wouldn't mind."

Her request caught him off guard, as a solitary tear rolled down the left side of his face, scrubbing a thin line of silt from his skin. More silt vanished when he wiped it away from his cheek. "Absolutely!" Like a gentleman, he held the consecutive metal, glass doors for Alex, as they both went inside. He saw his mother get up from a table. "Mom, I would like you to meet Alex," he spoke clearly for his mother. "Alex is an emergency room doctor up in Boston."

"Oh my, that's terrific, Alex," Rose said excitedly, grabbing her hand. "Boston—I was in Boston a number of times for medical conferences."

So brightly, Alex smiled at Rose, as her old eyes were suddenly alive again. "Boston seems to be the hub for medical conferences." Noticing Rose was tiring on her feet, with her hand, contorted by arthritis, in Alex's, she persuaded Rose to sit back down at the same red table she had stood up from. Alex held onto Rose's arthritic hand as she herself sat across from Rose. "I heard you delivered lots of babies."

"Oh yes, lots of babies," Rose uttered proudly. "Have you ever delivered a baby?"

With her hands occupied holding Rose's, Alex tossed back her hair with a quick jog of her neck. "I have assisted with many births, but I haven't delivered a baby by myself."

"Oh, you will, my dear girl. You will have to when you least expect it," Rose uttered, putting all her focus onto Alex.

Smiling adoringly at Rose, Alex relished this moment. "Rose, when I do deliver a baby by myself, what is the best advice you can give me?" Something on her left caught her eye. Taking her eyes off Rose for a moment or two, glancing to her left, Alex watched Roger in a full-on stare, not believing what he was seeing and hearing from his mother.

"The most important thing for you to do is to stay calm and in control. If you are not, the mother is going to see it in your eyes and panic, and that doesn't help anybody," Rose said without blinking an eye. "And don't be hesitant about the decisions you make in difficult births; common sense goes a long way to making the correct decisions."

Mesmerized by Rose's collected manner and acuteness, Alex was filled with gratitude, as she listened to her sagacious knowledge. Gazing into Rose's eyes, Alex knew she was all there. "I'm pretty tough." Looking slightly to her left, Alex smiled at Jay, knowing it was He who had made this moment possible.

A wide grin permeated Rose's entire face, while she pulled her hands over Alex's and squeezed them lovingly. "I can see that in you," Rose spoke ardently. "Your strength is undeniable; it's hidden under that surface you protect so well—people need to see the warrior you really are!"

These words got to Alex's heart, as fast as a lightning bolt reached the ground, and made tears fall from her eyes. Turning her head to the right and upward, gently Alex pulled her right hand from Rose's grip to wipe the tears away. "Wow…You're very insightful, Rose."

Rose studied Alex's guise, noticing the speck of doubt she had in herself. "I'm a very wise, old woman," she spoke with assuredness. "Never doubt yourself; you weren't born with doubt—it will never suit you, Alex." Suddenly, Rose turned to her son. "Roger, can we go home now?"

With his tear-filled face, Roger stood up quickly. "Of course, Mom," Roger said softheartedly.

Before Roger got to his mother's side, Alex stood and readied to help Rose to her tired feet. "Here, let me help you up, Rose."

"Oh, thank you, Honey."

With Roger on his mother's opposite side, he found Alex's kind eyes. "Thank you, Alex."

After they got Rose comfortably in his 2004 red Toyota Corolla, Roger reached into his back pocket to pull out his Android. "Can I have your e-mail or cell—I'm going to send you some money. Do you have Venmo?"

"Yeah, but you don't have to give me money," she pressed.

Deep into his Android, Roger finally found his contact app. "Yes, I do. You bought me lunch under false pretenses."

With her hands on her hips, Alex turned her head and giggled. "Roger—you don't have to pay me back."

"Just let me do it, please," playfully begged Roger.

"Okay, okay," Alex acquiesced. She gave him her cell number. Within two minutes, she had received $50 from him. "Your hamburger didn't cost fifty bucks."

"Buy some of my audiobooks to listen to in your car," he suggested. "It's still a long ride all the way to California and back home to Boston."

Alex gazed down at her phone. It wasn't about the money, it was about another friend she just made, appreciating the gratitude Roger showed her. "Please call me if you need any advice regarding your mom. She's a very cool lady."

He extended his hand. "Thank you, Alex."

Once Alex shook his hand, the familiar warmth and peace engulfed her, giving her that incredible feeling once again. "I did nothing."

"You did a great deal for my mom today," Roger clarified before he started walking around the Corolla and opened the driver's side door. "Who knows," he began, smiling, "I might write a book about you some day." Watching Alex chortle at his silly offer, he waved and got into his car. Before driving away, Roger made sure Alex got in her car safely.

Alex gave him a final wave, and then he took off down the road. She couldn't help but wonder what his life was like day to day, and hour by hour. Alex got back on the highway to make it to Colorado at the late hour she hoped.

Stars

Colorado was still about three hours away. Dusk was just settling on the western horizon, displaying a brilliant, fiery orange hue, surrounded by a clear sky of gentle palettes of mild magentas and vivid violets that could make anyone gawk at God's masterpiece. Still wearing her sunglasses, Alex slid them down her nose to view the occupied piece of canvas that was the sky. Returning her sunglasses to their proper position upon her nose, she turned and saw Jay asleep. It was common for Jay to sleep while she drove; she often wondered if Jay stayed up all night keeping watch and answering prayers from His followers. That was a whole lot of homework for a night. Alex remembered all those nights during medical school, cramming for exams, and cramming all the information she could find about schizophrenia. Alex let Him sleep.

With her sunglasses now off and the windows down, the Camry ran steady on the dark, mostly empty highway. Alex phoned her parents.

"Hello, my darling," Joanne gleefully uttered.

"Hi Al!" Michael chimed in. "It feels like days since I've talked to you."

"I know; I apologize, Dad," Alex spoke sincerely. "I have missed talking to you too."

"I know you've been driving a lot."

"Yeah, especially today," narrated Alex, getting her second wind.

Clearing his throat, Michael chuckled. "You know what that

means, don't you?"

The decision had to be made whether she wanted to be humorous or subdued. Humorous won out. "A 3,000-mile oil change?"

Instantly, Michael laughed with his adored daughter. "Well, that too, but I am talking about you coming home soon." Silence pervaded briefly. "I can't wait see you, Sweetheart."

"Me too, Sweetie," reiterated Joanne.

Catching herself, Alex held back her unexpected emotion. "I miss you two, unbelievably so." Exhaling, she combed back her hair. "I'll be home soon." Keeping her eyes fixed upon the road, she knew just how much her parents ached to have her home safe and sound. "Did you have a nice walk this evening?"

"Yes, but it's kind of muggy here," Joanne described.

"I bet you haven't felt humidity like you do in the south."

Michael chortled. "It can remain there too." Listening to his daughter laugh was enough to sustain him for the rest of his life. Alex was his light, joy, and his true essence. "What exciting things did you see today?"

"Today?" she verified gently. "Well, a little bit ago I stopped at a McDonald's to use their facilities, and I saw this man sitting outside, covered in this clay silt stuff, looking pretty raggedy."

"Was he homeless, Al?" inquired Michael.

"I thought he was at first, but I was talking to the server, an older woman, and she told me the man outside wasn't homeless, but he didn't have money for food," Alex carefully narrated. "So, I bought him a burger and a root beer…"

"Healthy, Al," Michael jested.

A chuckle snuck out from Alex's diaphragm. "I know, right?" With more giggles, she went on. "I was going to buy him a fish sandwich, but they hadn't had fish since 1982."

"1982?!" Michael playfully repeated.

"Yeah, 1982," Alex asserted, still snickering. "Maybe it was even back before 1982, I don't know." She kept her eyes on the road. "So, I started talking with this man, Roger, his name is Roger, and it turns out that he is the son of the older woman at the counter."

"Are they both homeless?" asked Joanne, trying to piece together this convoluted Nebraskan tale.

"No, no, Roger's mother has Alzheimer's. Roger stays outside of McDonald's so his mother, Rose, can have a routine every day," recounted Alex. "Rose was an OB/GYN for nearly 40 years."

"And Roger—what might he do?" Joanne pried.

"Actually, Roger is an author. He writes thrillers."

"Al," Michael prompted, "what is Roger's last name?"

Something in her father's voice seemed curious. "McGovern. Do you know him?"

There was a slight hesitation. "Yeah, I do," Michael realized. "Last summer, I flew out to St. Paul for a conference. I must have talked to him for an hour or more about his mother. Nice guy."

"Wow, that's random," Alex retorted. "Before I left, I asked Roger if I could say goodbye to his mom. That brought tears to his eyes. And then I was talking to Rose, or I should say she was talking to me…" She stopped to gather herself.

"What did she tell you, Honey?" Michael pressed gently.

After a long exhale, Alex breathed in again. "Rose said she could tell I had a lot of strength…and umm…and umm…I shouldn't keep my strength hidden." Again, she exhaled hard.

"That's our girl," Michael said proudly. "Everyone can see your strength."

"It's becoming obvious," she returned confidently.

"Did you ask Rose anything?" Joanne jumped in.

"Yeah," Alex began. "I asked Rose what was the most important advice she could give me about delivering a baby."

"Haven't you delivered babies before?" Michael inquired.

"Not yet on my own," clarified Alex.

"What was Rose's response?" Joanne pressed with curiosity.

"Rose told me I had to be calm and in control," Alex relayed to her engrossed and loving parents. "She also said whatever decisions I make are the correct decisions, and common sense goes a long way, especially during difficult births."

"Rose is a very wise woman," remarked Joanne.

Listening to her mom's sparkling voice, Alex knew she was smiling. "She is very wise."

"Who would have thought—my baby girl delivering babies," Michael gloated.

"I haven't delivered a baby yet, Dad," chuckled Alex.

"Have I ever told you about the day you were born, Al?" he softly posed.

Like a million times. Quietly giggling, Alex settled in to listen to her dad's celebratory tale about her arrival into the world. "I haven't heard your account in a while Dad."

"Good, good, because I will tell it anyhow," her father laughed.
Joanne joined in his laughter.

"It was around midnight on September 27th, 1993. It was a particular chilly night. I suddenly felt the bed get damp."

"Eww…" Alex playfully embellished, keeping her eyes on the road.

"Your mother was asleep!" Michael exclaimed.

"I was half asleep," joyfully corrected Joanne.

Alex, giggling loudly, loved what she was hearing. "Mom was getting some shut-eye before she had to push me out."

"Yeah, well—it didn't change the fact that Mom's water broke."
Both mother and daughter giggled uncontrollably.

"I was freaking out!" Michael expressed jocularly. "I just wanted to get your mom to the hospital, but she insisted there was no rush."

"What did I know—I had never had a baby before," Joanne joked. "I didn't have any contractions."

Alex continued to giggle.

"I managed to change the bed, and your mom came back to bed and fell back to sleep. I sat in a wooden chair, staring at your mother, panic-stricken. I so, so wanted to put my hands on her stomach to see if you were moving in there."

Alex heard her parents kiss. "Aww…"

Michael continued. "Three hours later, your mom woke up with her first contraction followed by many thereafter. You came quick," he reported. "You came out before I could call 9-1-1."

"Your father was so infatuated with you at first sight," Joanne lovingly reminisced. "Dad put you in my arms and I was in total rapture with my little girl—our little girl. We just stared at you until the ambulance arrived."

Somewhere between her father sitting in the wooden chair and her parents ogling her when she was only minutes old, Alex allowed some happy tears to run down her cheeks, knowing she was very loved. "Thanks for telling that story again, Dad."

"Aww…Honey," Michael said gently. "The favorite moment I have about that early morning, and I have many favorite moments, is when I was holding you, Mom was sleeping, and dawn was breaking. Your fresh new eyes were wide open, looking back at me like you were saying, 'what are we going to do now, Dad?'"

"Yep, he didn't want anyone to hold you, Baby," Joanne confirmed.

234

Leaning her head back on the driver's seat headrest, feeling the wind in her hair, she wept quietly, as she felt just how much she loved her parents. "Have I told you just how much I love you two?"

"Oh, Babe, we love you too," cried Joanne.

With a cracking voice, somehow Michael held it together. "We can't wait to see you."

Taking in a quick breath, Alex got through the next few moments. "I know, Dad, I know. I'll be home soon."

For the next hour or so, Michael and Joanne continued talking to their dear daughter, as she got closer to the Colorado line. They would have talked to Alex all night if it was necessary. They spent much of the time talking about Conrad, Justin, and Lila, and how they were bonding as a family. Alex was hard on herself because she hadn't spoken to them in a couple of days. As parents almost always do for their children, Joanne reassured Alex, promising her that the guys had their hands full with Lila. Alex was sure she would make it her top priority to FaceTime with Conrad and Justin the next morning. It wasn't a big secret that Joanne and Conrad texted daily, comparing notes on Alex's status, making sure she was doing okay. Having that second check-in person was critical, as they had urged Alex to take this road trip. Alex thought back to the incident in Myrtle Beach and recognized how everyone must have been going out of their minds with worry. She put money on the reality that someone in her group—Mom, Dad, Conrad, or Justin—was ready to buy an airline ticket to Myrtle Beach to drive her home. It had been a few nights since she had given that terrifying night a thought. The chills going up and down her spine lessened when that tense moment popped into her brain. It would be with her for the rest of her life, in one form or another. Of course, Alex avoided bringing up the incident on the beach with her parents so far from home. Suddenly noticing the time, and doing some quick math, Alex realized the time in Hopkinton, urging her parents to turn in for the night. After a few minutes of the usual back and forth, as concerned parents do, Alex promised to text when she got where she was going. Michael and Joanne agreed, but everyone knew that sleep probably would be impossible until they knew Alex was safe for the night.

Once I-80 turned into I-76, Alex realized she had reached Colorado. It was dark, so she couldn't see much of the scenery. To Alex, everything outside seemed flat and mundane. She expected to see

mountain ranges, but everything was just flat. She had to remind herself
that the topography of one state might just roll over to adjacent states, chocking up this nonsensical thinking to just being tired. Twenty more miles to go until she reached the campground site she had booked earlier. It wasn't out of the question that she might just sleep in her car instead of setting up her tent and gear. Once she got to the campsite, she would gauge her level of motivation. There was a tiny possibility that she might develop a second—third?—wind, but she wasn't banking on that.

A few moments later, Alex noticed Jay coming out of His deep slumber. Not surprisingly, He awoke quickly, unlike the average human being. A question popped into her mind; she wanted to know if Jay had the ability to dream. In all His two thousand years plus, nobody had posed this question to Him, which shocked Alex, as she felt privileged to be the first. She supposed it was the doctor in her to make her wonder. Switching her weary eyes between the road and Jay, she waited patiently for Him to answer. This question made Jay think, as He took His time to ponder His response. Going back to the beginning when He was a mortal, yes, He had dreamt. After His death and resurrection, Jay's dreams ceased because He had a higher duty to fulfill the dreams of others, the believers, and the non-believers. Alex asked how nightmares manifest. Simply, Jay explained nightmares were generated from our own experiences, our own fears, and our own minds. Through the dark night, Alex recalled her bad dreams, especially in the wake of Nate's passing, understanding that that awful night would never leave her. She then asked Jay if she prayed before going to sleep, would she more likely have good dreams instead of bad ones. Jay supported that theory wholeheartedly. Accepting His word, His sacred word, Alex felt in her emerging, rebuilt soul, a new comfort with the bedtime prayer. Jay challenged Alex, asking her if times became difficult, would she continue with her faith and prayers. Even if her tiredness from a long day seeped deeply into her muscles and bones, she concluded she would hold onto her faith. Then, Jay found her right hand that was loosely situated on the bottom half of the steering wheel and held it for several seconds, reminding Alex He would always be with her, whether she would be able to see Him or not—He would always be with her. She smiled at that very notion.

Her iPhone called for her attention; she barely opened her eyes to answer the caller.

"Good morning, Sleepy Head," Conrad said, holding little Lila in his arms. "Say 'good morning, Auntie Alex'." His voice was as sweet as the morning dew.

"What time is it?" she inquired, as she rubbed her eyes. The first thing Alex noticed was that she was inside her tent. "Oh, she's so cute."

"By my calculations, it's almost 8:30 a.m. where you are," clarified Conrad. "I talked to your mom a little while ago; we talked a bit."

"Did ya?" Alex sat up to assist with waking up. "I'm sorry I haven't called you in the last few days."

"No, no—don't worry about it," Conrad spoke gently, as Lila was content with looking up at her dad. "Your mom said you sounded well, but she also said something happened that you kind of blew off, which made her worry a little." Conrad paused to gauge his friend's spirit. "Want to talk about it?"

Flipping her hair back, Alex scratched the back of her head and looked vacantly forward. "The other night in Omaha, this young man, a Muslim, got stabbed in a parking lot—just because he was Muslim," she began, biting her bottom lip. "He looked like Justin."

Conrad sighed heavily. "Oh, Al."

Returning her eyes to her iPhone screen, Alex continued. "Yeah, yeah—it was bad. I had it in my head I could save him, but I kind of knew he was too far gone." Briefly, she took a breath. "When the paramedics arrived, I kind of hijacked their paddles and shocked him a couple times, but that didn't work."

"You hijacked their paddles?" Conrad repeated, making sure he heard her correctly.

"Oh yes," Alex reaffirmed, looking away. "I felt like an idiot afterwards; everybody around was standing and staring at me like I was losing my shit—it wasn't one of my finer moments, you know."

"Were you losing your shit?" Conrad asked straight-out.

Exhaling the air out of her lungs, reassessing her actions, Alex remained steady. "Maybe just a little," she replied, demonstrating that tiny sliver of space between her thumb and index finger.

"I'm sorry that happened to you, Al."

Alex flipped back her hair again. "Yeah, well…I accept it as a valuable learning experience," she spoke confidently.

"Are you okay?" pressed Conrad.

"Yeah, I'm okay, I'm okay," Alex uttered with the same steadiness. "I'm tired of everybody hating and killing each other. It's freaking ridiculous."

"I hear ya, Chica," Conrad remarked in agreement.

Flexing her neck sideways, she concentrated on the bundle of joy in Conrad's arms. "How is she doing?"

"Oh, she's bound for Harvard," he stated without doubt.

"Really?" Alex quietly chortled. "What did Lila do that was so amazing?"

"Well yesterday, she was lying in her crib. We were in there just standing on either side, and she was turning her head back and forth, studying the both of us, like she was trying to figure us out."

"You know she can only see big, shadowy blobs," Alex stated, giggling.

"Are you raining on my parade…because it sounds like you're raining on my parade," Conrad expressed with a jovial tone, followed up by a gigantic smile.

Justin entered Lila's room where Conrad sat with their daughter. He was drying his hair with a jade bath towel. "Who's raining on your parade?"

"Alex," replied Conrad.

Popping his head over Conrad's tablet, Justin caught a glimpse of his good friend he missed so much. "Alex, Girl! How are you?!" Gently, he grasped Lila from Conrad.

Unexpectedly, Alex lost her breath for half of a second, as the image of Seth Pashia's still, deceased guise came rushing back, trying to disrupt her. She breathed and realized her friend was home in Boston, safe and sound. "Justin! I'm good, my friend!" she nearly roared. "How's Daddy life treating you?"

"Oh, this is the best thing I've done in my entire life, Al," Justin uttered, gazing down at his infant daughter. "Who knew I could love someone, this little human, so much."

She couldn't help but to smile broadly, so much so, it had the ability to light up New York City on the darkest of nights. "I've been hearing that a lot lately—about fathers and daughters," Alex professed earnestly, recalling the previous night. "I was talking to my Dad last night, and he was reminiscing about the night I was born." Looking away for a moment, Alex was grateful. "He has told that story hundreds of times, but last night, it was different somehow—I don't know."

Conrad came back into Lila's room and handed Justin her warmed-up bottle. "Things are different for your dad, your mom and for you too, Al," uttered Justin keenly. "You all are seeing life from a new perspective—you're all trying to regroup after the loss of Nate. You're their only child now, and you are their everything."

Tossing her hair back again, and appreciating Justin's unvarnished ideas, Alex's eyes were fixated on Lila sucking on the bottle, settled, and gazing up at him, listening to his every word as if she had known him for centuries. "Yeah, I know," Alex assented softly, nodding. "Look at her—she's so content, Justin."

The new father gazed down at his daughter and marveled over the fortune that was bestowed on them. "Yeah, she's pretty awesome," he said, kissing her soft forehead. "She can't wait to meet her Auntie Alex."

Discreetly giggling, her grin said it all. "Yeah, I know, I know. I'll be home soon."

"Where are you headed today?" Conrad asked, entering the conversation once again.

"I'm not really sure," she offered. "I'll probably find some hiking trails. I've been walking a lot lately." She knew full well that Jay had the last say over the activities of the day.

"That's fantastic, Al!" expressed Conrad vivaciously.

"Yeah—when I get home, I am determined to keep up with Mom again on the track, and you can tell her that too!" Alex exclaimed, falling into hysterics with her best friends. The laughter that had been hidden away for so long, hidden around corners, and hidden under layers and layers of sorrow was finally emerging, and it felt good.

Whether it was from the notion of Alex's physical resolve to challenge Joanne, or whether it was the cackling his dear friend was exhibiting, tears came to Conrad's eyes, realizing Alex was in a good place. "She's going to love that—she'll love that."

Noticing the tears in Conrad's eyes, she welled up too. "I know she will." Alex cleared her face. "I thank you both for sticking by me these past six months or so, I know I haven't been too cheery to be around. You guys mean the world to me."

"Now you are really going to make us cry," easily admitted Conrad, knowing Justin was on the verge of blubbering. "Al, we have been your friends for eight years—where are we going to go?"

"Yeah, I know," Alex confessed quietly, as she dried her face. She looked around her tent, feeling the warmth of a new day. "You think I should get out of this hot tent and go do something?"

Without a pause, both Conrad and Justin answered, "Yes," in unison.

Alex broke into uncontainable hilarity; she caught her head in her hand. "Alright, alright—I'll get going with my day."

"Be safe," demanded Conrad.

"Yep—I will," she promised unequivocally. "I love you guys."

"We love you, Al," Justin announced, still feeding Lila. "Talk to you soon."

"Absolutely," Alex extended. The next second, she ended the video call, and missed them already. It was time to start her day.

When she returned from the shower, Alex saw Jay looking out onto a very flat, brown plain; there was nothing definable about it, just brown and expansive. On the ground, she found her usual hot cup of tea waiting for her, but there was no fire burning. Knowing Jay could do possibly anything, she didn't challenge how He warmed up the tea, she just accepted it. Knowing she would have nothing left to eat, she had saved the last part of her sandwich in her cooler from the previous night. The land was so bland, arid, and sandy, Alex quickly ate and broke down the tent within five minutes. With everything in the Camry again, suddenly Alex felt something tickling her right forearm, recognizing that she should look before she shooed anything away. It might be something special; it might even be the blue Karner again—and it was. She hardly could believe what she was seeing, questioning if it had followed her from Nebraska. Like the last time encountering the Karner, blue and exquisitely beautiful, Alex studied it keenly, wondering if it was the same one. It had to be, Alex thought, although it seemed out of place in this arid climate. And the same as the last time, the Karner lingered on her arm. Would she dare to pull out her cell to take a photo of it? She wanted to—she wanted to show this beautiful and delicate creature to her parents. Slowly and methodically, Alex pulled her iPhone from her back pocket, making sure she didn't make any jerky movements to scare away the tiny butterfly. Desperately, Alex worked her iPhone with her left hand, moving so cautiously, capturing the image of the Karner. Sliding the phone back in her back pocket, Alex allowed the butterfly to remain for as long as he wanted. In her mind, Nate's spirit occupied this small creature.

Returning from His reverie, as He looked at the sparse, dry land, Jay walked over to Alex to check out the little creature perched on Alex's arm. He leaned over to get a closer look; indeed, it was the same Karner. Alex's eyebrows jumped at this awe-inspiring revelation. If the tiny creature wanted to hang out all day on her arm, then so be it. She wasn't about to disturb him from his comfortable perch, but if only she could have some way of communicating with him, that would be something. As soon as that concept left her, the Karner fluttered upward about two feet in the air and settled on her left shoulder. Alex wondered if this was a form of interaction, as he had landed on her left shoulder just like this, days prior. The little creature didn't make it easy for Alex to study him or his movements. Maybe he didn't want to be studied; maybe he just wanted to be. Just to be. Her brain suddenly kicked in. Could it be a possibility that Nate had just wanted to be? As a doctor and a sister of a paranoid schizophrenic, she knew his illness had to be dealt with medically, for his wellbeing and for his safety. There were several times when she had had long conversations with Nate about what it was like to be a paranoid schizophrenic. These conversations usually occurred after psychotic episodes when his meds were adjusted. Nate described the voices, the voices, the voices which seemed to never stop talking in his head. Nate realized the voices were in his head when symptoms began when he was 15; hearing the voices at first, he would look over his shoulder, but nobody would be there—nobody was ever there. Over time, the voices became more frequent and crueler, telling him how worthless and stupid they perceived him to be. After listening to these voices day in and day out, for months, Nate explained to Alex he began to believe it—he believed the voices. Alex recalled the many times during these unfeigned discussions that she was on the edge of tears, but she couldn't for Nate's sake; he needed her to be strong, unwavering. She was unwavering. By the time Nate reached his 20s, he stopped talking about the voices, for they were almost unmanageable, even when he was on five different psychosis medications, dulling all his other senses, as if he was a masterpiece cruelly painted over in monotone gray. Impermissible by medical professionals, Nate chipped away at the gray by skipping a variety of his psychotic medications, revealing his bright colors. Slivers of gray slowly collected below, exhibiting a patchwork of color, but allowing the unrelenting voices to return. Nate confessed he experimented with cocaine and heroin a handful of times although nothing quieted the voices—nothing disrupted the paranoia. He described for his sister all the times people stared at him, thinking he was some kind of freak on a verge of a psychotic break; if only they could listen to the voices, the merciless voices telling him that he had no reason to live because nobody could ever love him, then they would understand the anguish of schizophrenia. Alex and her parents constantly told Nate how great he was and how much he was loved. Once, Nate explained that for each positive compliment he received from Alex or their parents, a thousand more voices told him negative things. Nobody could compete with the voices; they always won.

The Karner suddenly took off into the air, giving Alex a show, fluttering and flying in no particular direction, staying in front of her, so she could watch him in all his glory, displaying all his happiness. She found herself enthralled with his enthusiasm, as he danced in the sun, colorful as could be. Within a second, the Karner disappeared into thin air, leaving Alex to look all around. Finding Jay's comforting eyes, He promised her she would encounter him again. She smiled and prepared to start her day, wherever it brought her.

The freeway was ahead of her, waiting to take her to some new destination, get her closer to home even if she was heading toward California. It was an easy drive on a two-lane highway. There was not much scenery to mention; everything was still brown and relatively flat, with a sprinkling of almost-green bushes on the occasional berms that flanked the freeway. Twenty-foot-tall poles with horizontal boards at the top carried power lines paralleling the freeway. Alex surmised that one very strong windstorm would shred the power lines; she silently wondered how long it would take to repair them, to get power back to the tens of thousands who relied upon it.

The last few days would stay with Alex all her life, let alone the entire trip. Thirty minutes into the drive to Aurora, Jay was awake.

"Did You get a good sleep last night?" asked Alex.

Jay chuckled quietly. "You know I don't sleep."

"You could have fooled me," she announced. "You were passed out like a toddler on a long car ride…imagine that." Looking toward Him, she grinned.

"I was resting My eyes," Jay replied.

"Oh my God, did You start that whole male excuse for taking a nap?!" Drollery punctured her question.

"Of course not, I adopted it," answered Jay, reflecting her humor.

"You are a funny guy today," she concluded. Pausing to take in the scenery around her, which wasn't much scenery at all, Alex was happy they were on the move again. "What are we going to do in Aurora?"

"They have a beautiful park there; I thought you would enjoy going for walk."

"You know I would never pass up a long walk; I really miss walking on the beach," she easily admitted.

"I know you do," Jay spoke. "I thought We could end this trip on Baker Beach in San Francisco."

Something in her made a shiver go up her spine. "We are ending the trip in San Fran?" Even though she had the ability to hear and understand His words, she needed that confirmation.

"Yes," Jay confirmed, sneaking a peek at Alex. "Is it okay that We end it in San Fran?"

Her split second of hesitation was palpable. "Yeah, yeah, of course," Alex portrayed. "San Fran is not too far away, you know."

Turning His head to gauge her disposition, Jay examined her with a keen eye. "I feel like you are apprehensive about the last stop."

She looked to her left, remembering He could see through her, as if she was made of glass. "I don't tend to like goodbyes."

Again, Jay chuckled quietly. "Hey Kid, I will never leave you," He spoke, grabbing her attention. "You won't see Me every day, as you do now, but you'll see Me."

This answer calmed her to the bones. "Can I talk to You whenever I need to?"

"Absolutely," Jay acutely emphasized, "you can't get rid of Me that easily."

Alex gazed at Him and smiled. "As if…" Putting her eyes back on the road, Alex realized if she had any pressing questions she wanted answered, she had better use her time wisely. "Rose?"

Jay looked toward Alex inquisitively. "Rose? What about Rose?"

"Will she go to Heaven?" Alex blurted out. Quickly, she looked at Him.

He clasped His hands together upon His lap and looked downward. "All those soldiers at Arlington—they had a duty to do, and though I strictly condemn all acts of war, I understand soldiers follow orders and act with great regard for their country. The soldiers who take life often, very often, live in a hell all their own," Jay narrated. "Soldiers can go to Heaven. God evaluates everyone's life, hearts, motives, and the overall humanity of a soul, and that dictates if they are bound for Heaven. Doctors like Rose fit into the same category as soldiers, scientists, and the like—their professional duties are separated from their personal beliefs."

"Is Rose bound for Heaven?" Alex pressed.

Jay sipped in some air between His teeth. "Most likely, yes."

"You don't sound very convincing," interjected Alex.

"Ultimately, it is God's judgment," asserted Jay, "I can only present My beliefs about an individual to God."

"It really works like that?" Alex inquired, as she considered this method of ascending into Heaven.

"In some cases, yes," Jay put forth. "Many cases are already settled when the soul reaches Heaven. If an individual conducts their lives respecting the humanity of their fellow man, they ascend to Heaven without question."

"Does purgatory exist?"

Caught a little off guard, Jay gave Alex a quick glance and smiled. "We are full of questions today, aren't we?"

She silently giggled. "I just figured while I have Your ear, I might as well ask these pressing questions we Catholics have." She paid attention to road ahead.

This time, His laughter was audible. "So, what can I say about purgatory?" Jay thought out loud. "Not all religions believe in purgatory; some believe the idea of purgatory was conceived by man in the twelfth century."

Alex wanted the facts. "But does it exist?"

"Purgatory does exist, although it is not a place, it is a process," Jay explained, "and I manage the process for certain souls."

"Will I be in purgatory?" she asked honestly.

Immediately, Jay began to laugh. "You do know you are only 26 years old?"

Alex grabbed a glance of Him laughing. "Yeah, I know, but I just want to be prepared, you know."

Laughing again, but only louder, Jay sat sideways. "Alex, all you have to do to ascend into Heaven is to help your fellow man, live in the light of Me. If you can do those things, you will be fine."

Flipping back her hair, she smiled out the left window at His answer. "I just want to see Nate again," she confessed, keeping her eyes upon the road.

"I know you want to see Nate, and you will," Jay promised with conviction.

"I will?" She looked for confirmation once again, as she gazed directly into His unwavering eyes.

"Yes, you will."

Her heart leaped with happiness once again, the fourth time in the past two days. Alex didn't need any more validation; she knew the

Man who had sat beside her for the last 2,400 miles. Her trust in Him was almost overwhelming to her, an idea that was foreign to her less than three weeks ago. Finally, she knew the truth because her eyes had witnessed His miracles firsthand—nothing could be questioned anymore, not His principles, not His devotion, and not His love. This gift she had was miraculous. Some people win the financial lottery, but she had won the spiritual lottery—something far more valuable than anything money could ever buy. Alex knew this trip had changed her although she wouldn't know to what extent for a time.

They stopped at Doug's Day Diner so Alex could extinguish her immediate hunger with an Italian toast open-faced omelet, brimming with tomatoes, avocado, and melted cheddar cheese. She must have been hungry because practically every morsel vanished within ten minutes. While she sipped on her hot tea, Alex had a chance to send her mom and dad the pictures of the blue Karner, giving them the context of their encounters. Once she typed the last words of her paragraph, Alex was as excited as a schoolgirl at the thought that she'd bring them happiness, so much so that she sipped her tea a little bit slower with the hope they would respond, even if it was a single heart emoji. She knew both of her parents were at their respective offices, preparing for the fall semester, preparing for life to continue after Nate's death. Disappointment filled Alex's chest when she looked back on her last six months, essentially failing to remain in life, wallowing in grief. Suddenly, she felt Jay's hand upon her shoulder. Gazing at His face, Alex saw Him shaking His head, indicating that the last six months weren't in play anymore; what she did from this moment forward counted. His words resonated with her, lifting the self-doubt off her. With that reassurance, Alex stood up and went to pay her tab. It was time to move on.

Cherry Creek State Park, a sprawling recreation area, was minutes away. It wasn't too busy for a Wednesday afternoon, which was surprising to Alex because it was such a beautiful day. Before she entered the park, she lubed herself with sunscreen by her car. Her iPhone buzzed; it was Joanne texting her daughter a long tender message, thanking Alex for churning up that memory which seemed to have been buried under a couple inches of water-logged sand. Joanne wholeheartedly believed that Nate embodied the spirit of the blue Karner, so much so that she rushed home and went up into their sweltering attic and dug out Nate's painting of a very similar blue Karner, dated in 2014. Receiving a photo of Nate's curled up artwork, as two of her mom's books held it down upon the oak dining room table that had served no purpose for over six months, and finally had a use, Alex beamed. It was just as she remembered it; if she could only touch the painting, the painting that Nate created, and which he had touched. At least her mom was touching it. No doubt Joanne would keep it safe until Alex got home. Alex texted her mother a quick message and promised she would call later.

Walking a little distance, she searched to find the hiking trail that would bring her around the reservoir; Jay pointed her in the right direction, and Alex thanked Him. Walking side by side, They set off on the hiking trail; sometimes the banter was light, sometimes they just walked saying nothing at all. Alex's mind wandered back to the ascension into Heaven; she wondered out loud about all the physicians in the first half of the twentieth century, when the act of sterilization on people with developmental and intellectual disabilities was widely accepted, which today, most people found altogether criminal. Alex thought the acceptance of sterilization was deplorable, especially amongst medical professionals. Did these physicians ascend to Heaven? She wanted to know Jay's thoughts and views, on the subject. Walking by her side, Jay put His hands in His pants' pockets, as the dirt kicked up from the ground with every step He took, and explained the inadequacies of man. Man, He began, very frequently do not think for themselves, especially in their formative years, depending on others for knowledge and answers. But some of those knowledgeable men, and women, had some old ideas that might have been archaic and Draconian for their times. Minds were and still are hard to change without strong persuasion. Sometimes persuasion doesn't work; sometimes minds won't change at all. Other times people must see the evidence right in front of their faces to make them change their perspectives. Sometimes people just must step a few inches to the right to see something at an undiscovered angle. Sometimes if someone just takes a few steps forward, up that hill, they might see the great ocean that holds the answers to life. Jay wanted individuals to think out of the box a little bit more and make situations better for the greater whole of mankind. Alex understood.

Again, They walked a little without exchanging words; They took in the beauty that surrounded Them, especially the shimmering blue reservoir that sat in the center of the park. When They reached the place where They had started, having encircled the reservoir, They spotted someone sitting on the black wrought iron bench, set back about ten feet off the trail. Alex stopped and observed their body language, clearly uncomfortable wrapped in their own skin, looking anywhere but forward. Not wanting to be too obvious, Alex approached at a slower pace.

"Is it okay if I sit here?" Alex gently asked, already positioning herself to sit.

Breaking out of the reverie he was in, the young man, with short black hair, wearing a black Metallica concert T-shirt and khaki shorts, replied, "Oh sure, sure," as he moved further down to give Alex more room on the bench.

"Oh, thank you very much," Alex replied, crossing her legs. "What a beautiful day."

The clean-shaven young man squinted, as he gazed up at the clear, blue sky. "This has been the best day of weather we've had in two weeks."

"Really?"

"Yup," replied the young man, scrutinizing the sky again.

Nodding along with his perceptions, Alex gazed upward. "My name is Alex," she announced, extending her hand.

He was slightly surprised by her gesture, although he extended his hand to meet Alex's. "Oh, my name is Dan."

"Nice to meet you, Dan," Alex said. "Are you a local?"

"Yeah, yeah—I've lived here all my life." Dan lifted his lower left leg and rested it on his right knee. Sandals adorned his feet, as he pulled back on his shin.

"I'm from Boston."

"I've never been to many places out of Denver," Dan scarcely admitted. "It's sad, isn't it?"

Turning, Alex gazed at the sad individual. "I don't think so," she said confidently. "I'm 26 and the farthest I had travelled was to Philadelphia until just a few weeks ago—now that's sad."

"What brings you here?" Dan asked, meeting her kind gaze.

Alex adjusted herself on the bench to give Dan her full attention. "My brother, Nate, passed away in February, so I'm on this kind of quest, driving across the country, to get myself pulled back together."

Dan listened intently. "I'm sorry to hear about your brother."

"Thank you, thank you, Dan," she spoke softly, nodding her head. "What do you do?"

Once again, Dan looked upward to see if any lonesome clouds were in the sky. None were present. "I come here a lot," he explained with some trepidation. "Can't really deal with being around many people at once, you know."

"Do you need me to leave?" Alex asked, sitting straighter.

"No, no," Dan passionately begged, "actually, you make me feel safer. Please don't leave."

Alex relaxed, retuning to sit idly on the bench. "I should let you know that I am a physician."

Dan looked at Alex with admiration. "You are?"

"I am," confirmed Alex. "I am an emergency room physician." She observed him closely.

Leaning forward, Dan clasped his hands upon his lap. "Oh wow," he said under his breath, looking vacantly out into nothing.

"Can I ask what makes you feel afraid?" gently asked Alex.

Dan bowed his head and laughed quickly. "Practically everything," he admitted, making eye contact with Alex for a split second. "I...I...lost my cousin in the movie theater shooting back in 2012." Dan caught a tear with his right thumb before it even thought about falling into the dirt and the few blades of grass. "I was 12 at the time; she was 16. I was sick that night, so I didn't go—if I had gone, we would have seen a different movie, and she would be alive today."

The words Dan spoke were all too familiar to Alex, all too real, as the horrific night that she found Nate close to death came flooding back. "My brother had severe paranoid schizophrenia, and he took his life by slitting his wrists," she quietly narrated, taking a deep breath. "I found him and attempted to save him, but I couldn't." Alex gazed up to the sky, on the brink of tears, but the tears didn't come. "I spent the better part of the last six months just wallowing in my own grief, not doing much of anything but visiting his grave almost every single day, and I dropped out of my residency," narrated Alex, as she bowed her head. "I wasn't doing anybody any good, least of all myself."

"I hear ya," Dan retorted, completely understanding her perspective. "My cousin understood me, you know...she, ah...she, ah...she stood by me when I told my parents that I felt like more of a male than a female, that I'd rather be their son, instead of their daughter." Swiftly, he looked at Alex, and then stared down to the ground. "That was six weeks before Polly got killed."

Hanging on his every word, Alex clasped her hands together upon her knees and glanced at Dan studying the ground beneath his feet.

"I'm so sorry, Dan," she expressed with a consoling tone. "May I ask how your parents reacted?"

Sitting back against the bench again, Dan looked far out into the distance. "Mom wasn't surprised at all, but Dad thought it was my tomboy phase and I would grow out of it as soon as I met a boy," he confessed. "When that didn't happen, Dad moved out—left my Mom, left me," Dan explained, as he slowly rubbed his palms together. "I blame myself for everything."

Alex glanced up to the electric-blue sky and breathed deeply. "Oh, the dreaded concrete room of blame—it's damn hard to break out of. Sometimes you spend days and days in there doing absolutely nothing. Other days, you might see light through a pinhole in the mortar, and you think maybe, just maybe, you can get out of this concrete room and live some kind of life—maybe you have some worth for this crazy world."

"Have you broken out of your concrete room yet?" Dan pressed Alex.

Flipping back her hair from her face, she revisited her last three days. "I believe I have," she confessed. "It hasn't been easy—far from it. Of course, my situation is different from yours, but the pain remains the same." Alex looked skyward again. "I believe that God just knows the people we need in our lives, for some reason or another. Everyone experiences loss in one way or another. Some people, like us, have experienced significant lost, and I believe God has given us greater strength to see that the people we have lost are around us, always."

Dan sat quietly and attempted to make sense of what Alex said. "I don't believe in God," he revealed. "I mean, what kind of God would let people continue to murder each other?"

Alex had asked herself that question hundreds of times. She figured that spending the past two and a half weeks with Jay might have brought her a little closer to understanding the human-being psyche. "God created humans with free will, but He didn't supply humans with a gene that prevents us from harming ourselves, or others; He didn't supply us with a gene to cure diseases or disorders—it would have been nice if He had. The only difference between us and animals is that we can rationalize…"

"For the most part," Dan quipped.

She looked at him quickly and agreed. "Yes, for the most part." Returning to her prior thought process, Alex reassembled her words. "What He did give us are all these amazing abilities that make us unique, such as the ability to love, to be compassionate, to find the beauty in the littlest things."

"All those things have opposite actions: to hate, to be selfish, and not to give a crap about anything," Dan said, exasperated. "What's the point of it all?!"

Keeping her voice low and gentle, she remained so focused, as if she was an arrow coming off a bow, heading straight toward an imaginary bullseye which only she could see. "If we lay down our swords now, what are we doing—who will we be fighting for?" Alex asked with vigor. "Not Nate or Polly."

"Yeah, well…I don't want to fight anymore—sometimes I don't want to breathe anymore," Dan admitted with his jaw clinched to match his fists.

Again, she observed Dan closely without being too obvious. "Have you ever thought about harming yourself, Dan?" She was becoming a doctor again.

Needing something to occupy his hands, Dan rubbed his palms together and squeezed parts of his fingers. "I have thought about it at times, but I don't like pain," he chortled in his throat. "Anyway…I couldn't do that to my mom."

"Are you close to your mom?" inquired Alex easily.

"She works a lot, so we don't spend much time together." Dan looked up to the sky and stared at nothing but blue. "I don't want to worry her too much."

Out of instinct, Alex clasped her hands together. "I guarantee that if you're not talking to your mother a lot, she's worried. She needs to know you're okay."

"How often do you talk to your mom?"

"I talk to my mom, and my dad, daily, sometimes twice a day," she uttered, smiling. "It has been crazy, and strange, and wildly satisfying," she continued. "When Nate got sick, I was 18, and all our focus was on him. I never felt slighted, probably because I was older. Now, it's just me, and I'm getting to know them all over again. I sort of feel guilty of their attention. I know they love me, and I love them." Happiness grew in her heart. "Do you have anybody you can talk to, Dan?"

Staring vacantly out onto the blue reservoir, he pondered her inquiry; he worried that he thought about it a little too long. "All I have is my mom." Embarrassment hijacked his stone expression. "Nobody wants to be friends with someone like me. If you didn't know, I'm a little bit of a freak."

"Why do you say that?"

He chuckled at the obvious. "I'm a transgender young man and everything paralyzes me. I'm not friend material."

"I don't think that's true," surmised Alex. "I think you're very down to Earth and easy to talk to…I just believe you need someone you can talk with and whom you can trust."

"Like a doctor?"

"It can be a doctor," Alex uttered, "or it could be a therapist, or even a support group." Seeing that his reaction didn't change, Alex hoped her words were sinking in. "I could make a few calls for you."

"You'd do that…for me?" Dan asked, stunned.

"Of course, Dan," Alex replied with a comforting voice.

As if his eyes were frozen in time, Dan appreciated Alex's offer. "I'd rather talk to you, to be honest—it's easy to talk to you."

Scratching the corner of her eyebrow, she took the compliment seriously. "I thank you for that," graciously she replied. "The most important thing I can do is listen to people; if they cannot express how they're feeling verbally, I have a knack for reading people through their body language."

"Did you learn that from being around your brother?"

His question surprised her a bit. She did a brief study of the years Nate was sick and figured there was some truth behind Dan's perspective. "I guess I did, actually, plus my training in med school."

"Is med school hard?" Dan inquired unexpectedly, but with conviction, looking directly at Alex.

She glanced back at Dan. "It's not for everybody," she admitted genuinely. "Do you have an interest in going into the medical field?"

"I think I do; I'm coming to the realization that there are more of them than there are of us out there," Dan said, smirking briefly. "The world needs more grounded people."

Alex looked away and smiled. "I can't disagree with that statement." Leaning forward, she closed her hands together. "What will you do now?"

The breath Dan took seemed to cleanse his soul. "Are you still willing to make some calls on my behalf so I can get into therapy?" His eyes locked on Alex's.

"Of course…of course," she said, unwavering. Before she stood, she touched his shoulder, demonstrating her commitment. "Do you mind waiting here a few minutes while I make some calls?"

"No, no, not at all," expressed Dan. He had a lift within his usual low voice.

Making sure she didn't move too far away from Dan, Alex found a boulder nearby and leaned on it. The first call she made was to Conrad to retrieve the proper people and numbers to call. Conrad gave her some helpful suggestions through their effortless conversation, offering to make some calls himself. Alex recognized that the tone of her own voice, strong and determined, was making her best friend's heart leap through the phone. Any reason to keep talking to Alex was happiness for Conrad. Selfish? No. He just wanted to know Alex was recognizing her worth. Even though she knew she would be talking to Conrad several times more, Alex always ended the call with 'I love you'. Glancing in Dan's direction, while waiting for somebody to pick up on the opposite end, she noticed Dan standing, pacing around a little. She returned near him to reassure him she didn't plan to abandon him. "I'm on hold with the local LGBTQ Support Affiliate," Alex informed him, still on hold. "They have one-on-one counselors."

Dan perked up and gazed at Alex, observing her steadfast patience. "Thank you," he said softly, genuine in his voice.

Staring into Dan's beholden eyes, somewhere deep within, she saw her own pain, recognizing the value of lifting another person up from their darkness. "You don't have to thank me, Dan."

Tears began rolling down his face, stunningly overwhelmed by her kindness. "Today is the first time in several years that anybody has showed me any kindness...at all."

The lump in her throat suddenly made a reappearance. "You're a human being, Dan," Alex said ardently, "don't ever believe you're anything less." At last, someone picked up on the other side of the call. Alex soon was a doctor again, advocating for Dan, advocating that he receive one-on-one and group therapy. She knew she was advocating to save his life. The phone call ended. "Do you have a car?"

"Me?" he replied, embarrassed over his meager assets. "I don't have a car. I usually walk everywhere."

Fast on her feet, Alex had the presence of mind to not let Dan feel shameful. "I didn't have a car up until a few months ago."

"Did you just get your license?" Dan asked, curious.

"I have had my license since I was 16, but once I began college, it was easier not to have a car since Boston has a variety of public transportation options," Alex explained. "Do you have your license?"

Before he answered, Dan bowed his head. "Nah...I haven't

found the courage to go through with the driving test yet."

"Well, that's okay…I know you will be able to take it soon," Alex spoke confidently. "I found you a counselor; he's right here in Aurora. He's a friend of a good friend of mine." Alex watched Dan sway on his feet, as he mulled over this opportunity. "He can talk to you today if you want."

Dan raised his grateful eyes to Alex. "Really?"

"Absolutely," she said, "I can take you there—that's if you are comfortable with that."

Continuing to sway, Dan's fingers began to twitch, as if they were bathing in a pool of anxiety. "I guess that will be okay."

She recognized Dan's nervousness. "You're sure?"

"Yes," Dan answered swiftly, "I have to do this."

Straightening out her back, Alex locked eyes with his. "Let's do this, okay?"

"Okay," he uttered with more confidence.

"You can just follow me to my car—it's not far." Within a few seconds, she was walking slowly toward her car, always mindful of where Dan was behind her. She tried to be keen to Dan's breathing patterns, listening closely to whether he was becoming nervous at any point. Through their short walk, Alex didn't notice any out-of-the-ordinary breath patterns other than the slight uptick of inhaling air due to the physical movement, especially at altitude. Trying not to be too obvious, Alex attempted to locate Jay, although she didn't spot Him. She could sense He was in the vicinity. It amazed her that she had the intuition to divine Jay's presence—Spidey senses of a different kind. She reached her Camry and unlocked it. "Where would you like to sit, Dan?"

He scoped out the interior of the Camry, as he stood about two feet away.

"I apologize for the messy back seat," Alex murmured, as she hurried to throw an armful of clothes in her trunk.

"I'll sit in the back on the right," Dan answered, biting his nails.

Looking quickly at Dan, Alex began to clear a space for him to sit. "Do you have enough room?"

"Oh yeah, Alex. Thank you."

She stood and watched Dan slouch in the back seat, resisting the urge to close the door. Sweeping around to the driver's side, Alex got in and shut her door and looked back, seeing Dan pull the door closed. "Ready?" she asked, as she prepared to buckle herself in.

"I'm ready," he announced, appearing a bit timid.

One click and she was fastened in. "It'll be okay, Dan," Alex said, glancing at Dan in the rearview. Returning her eyes to the dashboard, she noticed that Jay had materialized in the passenger seat. Giving Him a nimble look, she smiled, confident the day would proceed as it should. Alex started the Camry and continued her mission for the day.

"Thank you, Alex," Dan expressed with increased emotion.

Her eyes found Dan's in the rearview mirror again. "Of course, Dan."

The drive to Curt James' office was less than fifteen minutes from the park; Alex surmised if the ride had been any longer, Dan might have gotten out and derailed the plan. No words were exchanged during the brief ride, indicating to Alex that Dan was anxious. She kept glancing in the rearview; most times Dan was staring out the right side of the car, mesmerized by all the things and people they passed. It seemed Dan enjoyed the wind in his face just as much as she did—it was the perfect day to feel the air flowing around. Alex turned the GPS' voice off to keep Dan's nerves from fraying. A few minutes later, Alex pulled into a rear lot and parked at a small, two-story brick building. Before they could get out of the car, a man stepped out of the building, casually well-dressed, with jade green shorts and a white, jade pin-striped short-sleeved shirt. He appeared a little older than Alex, possessing that certain swagger that she lacked. He had short, dark curly hair and an accompanying very well-maintained beard. Alex exited her Camry and met Curt with an extended hand. "You must be Curt."

Curt had a smile that seemed to spread over most of his face, revealing his perfect set of teeth. "Alex! I'm so glad to finally meet you. I've heard so much about you!"

"It's so good to meet you too," said Alex, trying to get the attention back on Dan, as she turned and saw his head rise above the Camry. Walking around the rear, she introduced Dan to Curt. "Curt, I'd like you to meet Dan," Alex said, making room for Curt to step forward to shake Dan's hand.

"It's very nice to meet you, Dan," Curt enthusiastically spoke.

"You too," Dan strained to murmur, looking at the ground. He appeared to be having second thoughts, but leaving would be much more of an effort.

"Do you want to come inside so we can chat? Whatever you want to do," Curt said easily.

Setting his eyes on the brick building, Dan mulled over his next move. "I can come in," Dan said quietly.

"Okay," Curt replied in the same, calm tone. "You can follow me inside."

Dan gave a nod toward Curt and immediately looked at Alex. "Can Alex come too?"

Curt exchanged glances with Alex. "Oh, sure, sure, Dan, whatever you're comfortable with." Curt led their way inside, entering through a metal door with a key. Inside, a small white foyer greeted the new visitors; Curt made sure the door was locked nonchalantly. What was a drab foyer opened to a great two-story space, where sunlight reached every corner. Artwork adorned all the walls, full of color and full of life. Curt noticed Dan's intrigue. "Are you artistic, Dan?"

Still spellbound by all the paintings, sketches, and pieces of sculpture, he nearly neglected to answer the question. "I can draw a little bit, but not like any of those," Dan replied, pointing to a couple of different pictures.

Curt, with his arms effortlessly crossed, smiled, and gazed at Dan. "You'd be surprised how many see this art for the first time, and I always ask them that particular question and everybody says they don't have any artistic ability or very little, and suddenly they create this."

Dan continued to gawk at all the things that surrounded him. "No judgment," he said softly.

Curt peered at it all. "That's right…no judgment."

Alex already was getting an up-close look at all the artwork, as she walked around the space, giving some room for Curt and Dan to chat. Coming across an etching of a Monarch butterfly, she stopped in her tracks and carefully studied it. It depicted its profile view with such amazing detail, Alex couldn't help but to think about Nate's painting of the blue Karner, remarking how incredible butterflies were, even in an artistic impression. "Incredible," she whispered.

"Can Alex join us?" Dan asked Curt.

Glancing toward Alex quickly, Curt returned to Dan. "If she's comfortable with that, sure."

The word, 'she' got her attention. She returned closer to Curt and Dan. "This artwork is incredible."

"That it is," Curt concurred proudly. He cleared his throat. "Dan would like for you to join us while we talk."

Seeing Dan nod, almost with his eyes begging, Alex was on board. "Absolutely, Dan."

"Thank you, Alex," Dan expressed, almost smiling.

"Just follow me up to my office," Curt directed toward Dan and Alex. They ascended the painted-black metal staircase echoing noise from each of their steps. Once they all got up to the second-floor level, the metal echoes stopped. As Curt led Dan and Alex down a narrow hall, he swiftly ducked his head into his secretary's office to relay a message, and then he was off to an adjacent office, most likely his own. "Can I offer anyone a drink?"

Dan passed on anything, but Alex welcomed a bottle of cold water, and sat down on the small sofa, crossing her legs. "Thanks, Curt."

"Sure—I can't get you anything to drink, Dan?" Curt pressed.

"Oh, I'm good for now," Dan confirmed, not saying anything more.

"So, Alex told me a little about your circumstances...I'm terribly sorry about the loss of your cousin, Polly," Curt said in a caring voice. "That's still tough, isn't it?"

"It's always tough," Dan replied, not lifting his head very high.

Curt listened while he observed Dan's defeated posture. He glanced at Alex. "Would you categorize yourself as depressed?"

Dan struggled to look up. "I guess so."

"Have you had thoughts about hurting yourself?" Curt navigated this with precision, as his arms relaxed on his chair's armrests.

"I told Alex I have but I couldn't do that to my mom," explained Dan, as he looked away, searching for some hole to crawl into.

"How long ago was this?" Curt asked without pause. There could be no pause when dealing with life and death.

Dan took a cleansing, deep, but heavy, breath. "Maybe four or five months ago, when I saw my dad." Raising his head, Dan found a corner of the ceiling he could focus on. "I was walking home...it was pouring, and he...he didn't stop to give me a ride." Like a thunderstorm, heavy tears poured out from Dan's core, releasing the frustration that had built up for so long.

It was difficult for Alex to remain on the sofa and not console him as he sobbed. Alex knew the feeling all too well. She uncrossed her legs and sat intently with her arms on her legs and stared at Dan.

"I swear, he knew it was...he knew it was me!" Dan cried out. "It has been seven years and he still can't accept me."

Curt reached for the light-blue box of tissues on his desk and handed it to Dan. "Sometimes it takes people, especially parents, a long time to come to grips with their children being transgender," Curt explained. "Your dad probably never experienced anything similar growing up. Maybe his religion prohibits the belief that individuals can choose their own gender, that it's against God's will."

Dan chortled through his tears. "My father? My father doesn't have a religious bone is his body." Dan pulled out some tissues out of the box and wiped his eyes. "I'm nineteen and my dad can't stand to be within five feet of me."

"How was your relationship with your dad before you told him?" Curt inquired with care.

Dan was able to gather himself, reeling his emotions back in. "I thought we had a great relationship," he stated confidently, "we loved to go fishing and camping, you know…normal stuff fathers do with their daughters."

Before asking more questions, Curt pondered Dan's situation. "Have you ever sat down and really talked to your dad to explain how you feel as a person, to give him your perspectives?"

It took Dan several moments to dissect this question carefully. "I was only twelve at the time; I mean, what twelve-year-old has the capacity to verbalize clearly what they're feeling?" This was a rhetorical question. "Did I fail myself?" begged Dan.

"You never failed yourself, Dan," Curt promptly said. "You hoped for your dad's acceptance, and when he was unable to provide it, you shut down." Waiting for Dan to grapple with the day and days past, Curt gauged where his thoughts were. "Did you ever think about writing him a letter?"

This was a possibility Dan had never considered. "It would have to be one hell of a long letter," Dan remarked with a quiet chuckle.

Again, Curt and Alex exchanged a hopeful glance.

"Curt, would you help me write it, or just look it over after I write it?" asked Dan with purpose.

"Absolutely, Dan," spoke Curt, assuredly. Curt sat straight in his chair. "Dan, I would like to set you up with a mentor, if you'd like."

"What does a mentor do?" Dan asked. He held his head higher—more confidently.

Curt smiled inside. "Our mentors are support systems for individuals like yourself who might be feeling alone; you can ask your mentor anything. If they can't answer a question, they have a team of professionals, including myself, they can ask anonymously, on your behalf. Mentors can assist you with finding employment, mental health resources, housing, grants for college, assistance with food, legal assistance, and things of that nature."

"Will I need to pay anything?"

"No, you don't have to pay anything," Curt rendered. "We mostly rely on private donations."

Dan took a moment to consider the sudden support system he had just found with Curt James and his organization. "This has been quite a day," he said, almost breathless, but thankful.

"I am so proud of you for having the courage to come here today, Dan," announced Curt.

Shyness engulfed Dan as he looked down. He raised his head up again. "The credit belongs to Alex."

Alex inhaled quietly, not expecting Dan to make such a proclamation for something as simple as her kindness. "Dan, you did this," Alex confirmed, smiling.

Dan chuckled. "Okay then, you started the process of saving my life today. Can you accept that much?"

Barely taking a breath, Alex stood and embraced Dan with everything she had. "You'll be fine," she whispered, "Polly would be so proud of you right now." Tears welled up in her eyes.

"Nate would have been proud of you too. You saved a life today," said Dan, not missing a beat.

Hearing these words made Alex weep, as she continued to embrace Dan. "Thank you...thank you for saying that," she expressed, gushing gratitude. "I needed to hear those words." As the embrace ended, she wiped under her eyes and saw Curt's inquisitive look upon his face. "I lost my brother back in February; he committed suicide."

Like a jackrabbit, Curt jumped up to his feet. "Alex, I had no idea," he said softly, grabbing both of her hands. "I'm so, so sorry for your loss."

Squeezing his hands in return, Alex cleared her throat. "Thank you, thank you, Curt...It has been a tough year." Alex sat back down on the sofa, being sure not to take the attention away from Dan.

"Anything I can do for you, let me know," Curt said, taking Alex's lead and sitting back down. Dan followed and sat as well.

"Just make sure Dan's in good hands," asserted Alex, and glanced toward Dan.

"I will certainly call you every week to tell you how this young man is doing," promised Curt, wearing a mile-wide grin.

Dan piped up. "Will I be allowed to keep in touch with you, Alex?"

"Absolutely, Dan," Curt said. "I'm sure Alex has an e-mail

address."

"Oh, I do…I will leave it with Curt, if that's alright," replied Alex.

"Sure…sure," Curt said with vigor. There was a quiet chime coming from his mobile. He read the text message. "Ah yes…Marty, your mentor, just arrived. Would you care to go meet him, Dan?"

Shuffling his body a bit, Dan prepared to stand. "Oh, okay."

Curt popped up from his chair. "I'm just going to introduce Dan to Marty, and I'll be right back up."

"Okay," said Alex.

"Promise you won't leave before I say goodbye," Dan instructed, grinning.

Crossing both of her hands over her heart, she found Dan's enlivened eyes. "I promise, I won't leave without saying goodbye."

"Okay," Dan said, still grinning.

Still sitting, Alex watched Dan follow Curt out of his office. After taking a big gulp of water, she stood and readjusted her shorts and tank top. She grabbed the water bottle from the light-gray carpet and took another sip. The office was small, so she didn't have to walk far to see all the framed pictures on the walls. Sometimes she looked closely, sometimes she didn't. Sitting back down on the sofa, Dan's words came back to her: *You saved a life today.*

"Pretty incredible, isn't it?" Jay's voice emerged from the doorway.

She followed the voice, finding Jay leaning on the outside doorjamb. "Holy shit, Jay," Alex said, startled. "I swear You enjoy scaring me." She saw the silly smirk upon His face.

"Maybe a little," Jay confessed, chortling. "I have to have some fun." He entered Curt's office and sat down in his chair.

"Such liberties," Alex playfully ribbed.

Jay giggled. "How did it feel to save a life today?"

Straightening out her spine, she had her arms crossed, relaxed, piled upon a single knee. "It felt pretty good," Alex answered, stretching with an exhale.

Crooking His neck, Jay continued with His questions. "You think you're ready to return to work?"

Examining her own heart, Alex knew the answer. "I feel like I am ready, yes," she said without hesitation.

Jay scrutinized Alex's guise, mannerisms, and her eyes. He already knew what was in her heart. Taking a moment or two to consider everything that made Alex who she was, He smiled. "Are you sure you're ready?"

"Yes, I am ready," Alex said with more authority. Suddenly, Jay became more serious. "What's that look for?" Alex felt her stomach tense.

Jay contemplated if it was appropriate to tell Alex what was on the horizon. He displayed human tendencies like rubbing His temples, twirling His mustache hairs, and looking aimlessly around the room.

"Am I going to die?" she blurted out.

"No, you're not going to die, not anytime soon anyway," Jay assured her.

She breathed a little easier. "Do I have to worry about my parents?" Alex asked with a bit of a tinge within her voice.

The answer ran across His eyes. "Everyone will worry about their parents, and everybody else."

Her neck, along with her head, pitched forward, as if Alex expected to see more in His vague answer. "An epidemic?" Her eyes squinted.

Jay remained quiet, not giving away any more clues as to what would be on the horizon. "You must remain strong and committed to your profession."

Alex continued to inspect Jay's staunch expression, as He revealed nothing else. "When?"

Again, Jay stayed quiet, disclosing nothing more. "I will always be at your side."

Continuing to attempt to unearth more answers, thoughts and questions ricocheted around her skull. "Why can't You stop it?" she begged.

"It's too late," He barely revealed. "Are you ready to return to being a physician?"

"Yes," Alex answered without a thread of doubt. "Can I go home?"

Jay chortled. "San Francisco awaits." At once, He gently clapped His hands together and grinned like a child keeping a big secret.

What was His plan? Alex knew she trusted Jay and His glorious plan. "Okay."

They all gathered: Dan, Curt, and Alex, outside by the Camry.

There was a sense of peace that surrounded Dan that wasn't present a couple hours prior. Alex had even more of a reason to get back on the road, the road to get to San Francisco, even if she didn't know what awaited her. Getting to San Fran meant that she would get to go home where her parents anticipated embracing her with everything they had, and where she would get to hold Lila Alexandra for the very first time. Home was where she would begin her life again. She didn't worry about what was on the horizon that Jay was hinting about. There was no time for that—she had saved a life today.

Dan was tearful saying goodbye to Alex, although very hopeful they would stay in touch. Curt promised to keep in touch as well. After Alex got into her car, they waved as she drove away. The day was bittersweet, as she knew the trip was drawing closer to its finale.

Atmosphere

It was less than an hour to Colorado Springs where they would finish the day with a hike through the Garden of the Gods. These natural rock formations, tall and aberrantly shaped, mostly red clay in color, were eye candy for the soul. Where Stonehenge was a marvel in human ingenuity, Garden of the Gods, was the unique creation of Gods. They had no time to waste—dusk would be setting on Pikes Peak to the west in the mountain time zone in a few hours. The park visitors were gradually leaving while Alex and Jay were entering the grounds. There were very few times that Alex used her iPhone for anything other than a communication device—a broadcasting amenity to let her loved ones know she was safe. It had been a transcendental medium when she got to listen to Nate jam with Lennon. Today, her iPhone would capture beautiful shots of these awesome rock formations, as they seemed to rise to reach the Heavens, and God.

Looking west, a full moon had placed itself over the disappearing Pikes Peak ridgeline. Alex took copious photos of this, God's indelible artwork, memories of which she would hold onto for years, even sending the photos to her parents and then to Conrad. Her day began with, and ended with, a hike. The hike around Garden of the Gods was tactile, for Alex could climb and touch these grand red rock formations and view the different layers of some of them. People were allowed to climb the formations, no higher than 20 feet off the ground, unless it was wet or icy. Alex didn't have much experience with climbing seriously, except for the occasional visit to rock-wall facilities in and around Boston, where she always donned a harness, with a big cushy mat below. Here, she was content remaining three feet from the ground.

Being in the night air was exhilarating and crisp, as the air was the coolest it had been throughout the trip, understanding the elevation of Colorado Springs was nearly six thousand feet higher than Boston. It was always an enticement to imagine the stars were within an arm's length being at such a high elevation, even though they were millions, even a billion million miles away. What struck Alex the most was how bright and distinctive everything was skyward. Light pollution didn't exist amidst the rock Gods. Alex found an empty bench, lied down and just immersed herself in everything that was above her, shocking all her senses alive again. There was a second bench, about 15 feet away, where Jay perched Himself to clear His mind for a while. There wasn't any need for discussion, or even small talk; it was time to just be in the moment. Her eyes switched from one constellation to another, desperately wishing she had paid attention to Nate's interest years before, but she realized she couldn't dwell on the past. She had to get passed all her what-ifs, because it wouldn't change the present going forward. Nothing ever would change the past. Time travel only happened in movies, very far from reality, although it pushed the human imagination in ways that betrayed hearts and minds. There wasn't any rewind button for time. Alex understood why time was so precious.

The Garden of the Gods would be closing in 15 minutes; Alex would have liked to remain, staring at the stars for the entire night. Jay happily informed her that He had already reserved her a campsite about ten miles away. She looked at Him and smiled, slightly embarrassed that she had neglected to think about taking care of her lodging. Of course, she thanked Him profusely. When They reached her car, Alex tried to reach her parents, but cell service was sporadic at best. She sent the same text message to her parents, Conrad, and Justin in the hopes that it would be plucked up by a cell tower and be catapulted to Boston to let everyone know she was safe.

It was the first night of the trip that Alex got to sleep under the stars, with no protection of a tent. It was daring, although this campground encouraged sleeping under the stars. Plus, she had Jay to protect her from the rare chance that some wild animal would eat her alive. When she awoke the next morning, the only seemingly wild animal Alex encountered was a very energetic, bouncy, and lovable Chocolate Labrador puppy that had gotten away from its owner. The vivacious puppy seemed to have had a predestined path thought out before his child-like escape—a beeline to Alex's accessible face. Barely awake, Alex felt a small, but wet, coarse tongue licking near her right ear, as she instinctually put her arms up, discovering it was a puppy, and not an animal that would do any damage. On the contrary, the little excitable puppy began to gently gnaw on Alex's fingers and hands when she sat up from her slumber, softly giggling.

"Boy oh boy—you're a cute one," Alex said, holding the spirited pup to her chest. She started scratching behind one of its ears. Seconds later, Alex saw a young girl sprinting toward her. Swiftly, Alex crouched, barefoot, on her sleeping bag. "I take it this little cutie is yours," said Alex, smiling while the puppy treated her neck like a lollipop.

The little girl, who looked to be eight or nine, stopped short five feet in front of Alex and just stared, plucking a strand of blond, slightly wavy hair from the corner of her mouth. Wearing oversized gray shorts and an ill-fitting magenta short-sleeved shirt, the girl was barefoot. "Yes," she barely whispered.

Something within the little girl's eyes seemed off, and somewhat desperate. Alex resisted making assumptions that quickly, but her gut was telling her differently. Still holding the puppy, Alex rose to her feet and met the girl where she stood. "Here you go, Sweetie," Alex said, handing over the puppy to the little girl. "What's his name?"

Again, the little girl stared through Alex instead of at her. "Can't talk to strangers." The girl ran off as fast as she had chased down the puppy.

The strange interaction with the girl left Alex a bit dumbfounded, as she paid close attention to what direction the girl and her puppy headed. Alex just stood and contemplated the angst she continued to feel. She turned back to her sleeping bag situated less than four feet from the Camry. Opening its door, her cell was just below the driver's seat; there weren't any missed text messages or voice messages, which indicated hers didn't get through the previous night. Worry crept into her core, as Alex imagined her parents and Conrad having had radio silence from her for nearly a day. Figuring there weren't any cell towers anywhere close, she wanted to get on the road as quickly as possible. Alex found the shower facilities and did her usual morning routine when camping. Back at the Camry, not surprising, she found Jay leaning on it. "Hi." Opening the back door, she put her duffle bag inside.

"That woman over there was looking for you," Jay said, pointing over His left shoulder.

Her eyes followed where His finger was directed toward. "Oh, okay…I see her. Thanks," replied Alex. The woman stood about 15 feet away, as she approached the woman. "Hi, my name is Alex Roma," she politely said. "You wanted to see me?"

"Oh, Alex, hi," began the woman, "my name is Melanie Bruno, I own Dispersed Campgrounds."

"Oh, hi, Melanie—it's good to meet you," kindly said Alex, fixing her clothes once again. "Can I help you with something?"

Melanie, with her frizzy red hair, tied up in a ponytail, seemed to be preoccupied. "We are looking for a little girl with a puppy. Someone said you were talking to her a little while ago."

"She's missing?!" Alex said, agitated. "Yeah, yeah—her puppy started licking me awake. Not a minute later, she came toward me, and she stopped and stared—a very distant stare," she described.

"Did she talk to you?" asked Melanie.

"Yes," Alex opened, "I asked her if the puppy was hers and she said 'yes', and then I asked her what the puppy's name was, and she said she wasn't allowed to talk to strangers, and ran off." She visibly exhibited confusion over the girl's answer. "She darted off in that direction," said Alex, pointing up a little hill toward the left.

Melanie, wearing khaki shorts, a sky-blue, button-down shirt, and hiking boots, stepped forward to gaze carefully up the hill. "Is that all she said, Alex?"

"Yes, Ma'am." Alex met Melanie where she stood. "Are you going to call the police?"

Clearing the sweat off her red forehead, Melanie threw her hands on her hips. "I can't right now," she stated with authority. "When this happens, which is not very often, I call in my guys who are on call."

"I will start looking right now," Alex pressed. "I am a physician."

Immediately, Melanie glanced at an eager Alex. "You're a doctor?"

It always confounded Alex when people's jaws drop she revealed her profession. She believed that if she told people that she was a coal miner, it wouldn't usher in as many jaw drops. "Yes, I am a doctor," she spoke confidently, without self-doubt, without hesitation.

As the words seeped into her consciousness, Melanie realized the asset she had in Alex. "Would you like to search with me?"

"Sure, sure," Alex concurred. She watched Melanie jump on her phone to organize the pending search. Once the search was executed, Melanie concentrated on walking her land with efficiency. "How long have you had your campground?"

"Oh, this land has been in my family since before the 1920s," narrated Melanie, as she hiked up a knoll, blocking the strong sun while glancing down on a good chunk of land below. "Over the years, we've sold off ten acres. Made some decent money. We have about three acres left."

Standing next to Melanie, Alex scanned the area, searching for any sign of the girl. "Do we know the girl's name?" she asked, stepping down about a foot to get a better look.

"Not yet," Melanie said, as her voice dripped frustration. She looked at her phone to see if she had any text messages. There were none.

"Her parents didn't say what her name is?"

"Not yet," Melanie replied, dragging out the phase like a flat lyric. She continued walking.

"Don't you find that a little strange?" Alex dared to ask.

"I do," Melanie admitted. "You never know what is in people's heads these days. Last week, I had a guy here, brought his pet Python—this sucker was huge," Melanie said, using her hands to demonstrate its girth. "That night, he decided to take it for a walk. Of course, it was freaking everybody out. Yeah—I told him he had to leave."

"Wow—talk about ballsy," Alex easily commented. Her eyes kept scanning the arid brush and dirt before her.

"Yeah—people just think anything goes these days. It's ridiculous," said Melanie, stepping upon a knoll.

"Oh yes," Alex agreed. When Melanie stopped and looked over the land. Again, she didn't see any sign of the girl, or the puppy.

Melanie kept walking. "Where is home for you?"

"I am from Hopkinton, Massachusetts, right outside Boston," Alex returned, "very New England-ish."

"Are you on vacation?"

"Not exactly on vacation," she said, hesitating a split second, "it's more of a restoration trip. I lost my brother back in February." No more words were necessary.

"Oh wow, Alex, I'm truly sorry for your loss of your brother," sincerely Melanie expressed, still walking and scanning. "What was his name?"

"Nate," Alex spoke, smiling. It was then that she heard a high-pitched bark and stopped. "Do you hear that?"

Melanie stopped and listened. "I do," excitedly she uttered, as she took off in the direction of the barking.

Alex followed Melanie down a long slope, where there were some ten-foot, half-bare trees coming out of a flat area of sandy dirt. Practically in the center, sat the girl, holding the twitchy puppy that wanted to be anywhere but there. "You have her?"

Melanie took a second to mull over her approach to the girl. She nodded and crouched down near the girl. "We have been looking for you, Honey. Are you okay?"

Kneeling beside Melanie, as the last of the question left her lips, Alex surveyed the girl's condition from a short distance. Physically, the girl seemed okay, although that vacant, strange gaze remained caked on her face; she was silent. "Can you tell us what your name is?" Melanie asked in the gentlest tone. A half a minute passed as the girl's expression didn't change, so stagnant and still, as she had a death grip on the puppy's collar.

"Are you hungry? Do you want something to drink and eat?" Melanie offered, trying to get the girl to emerge from the cluster of defoliated trees. "You must be uncomfortable in there." Melanie extended her right hand toward the girl.

Alex watched the girl's face and eyes dart downward to survey the surroundings. At once, the puppy got free and ran straight to her, reconnecting again.

"My puppy!" the girl screeched, standing up and stepping closer to Alex.

With the puppy already in her arms, Alex made eye contact with the girl. "I have him—he's not going anywhere," she promised. "Do you want to sit beside me so you can pet him?" She watched the girl move in to pet the exhausted pup. "What's his name?"

The girl's eyes were bolted to the puppy, as she petted his head. "Dutch," she replied faintly.

"Dutch? That's a great name," returned Alex, holding him tightly. "Did you pick him out yourself?" Alex was skillfully searching for ways to gather the answers they needed.

The girl shook her head. "Jimmy got him."

"Wow, that was very nice of Jimmy to get you a puppy," Alex

said, gaining her trust. "Is Jimmy here with you?"

The girl barely nodded.

Melanie was observing quietly, texting her team that the girl had been found.

"Don't you think Jimmy is worried about you and Dutch?" Alex asked the girl. When the girl had to mull over the question, Alex grew tense. "Is Jimmy a family member, or a family friend?" The puppy was asleep in her arms, as Alex saw the girl's face go white as the clouds above. "Do you feel like you're in danger?"

Melanie stopped breathing as she waited to see how the girl would answer.

The girl locked eyes with Alex for what seemed like an eternity. Alex didn't press—she waited for her to speak. She prayed the girl saw the truth in her eyes; she hoped the girl felt safe with her. Before taking another breath, the girl fell into Alex's arms, in a heap of tears—in a ball of emotion. Melanie acted fast in grabbing the puppy, as the child took its place within Alex's arms. All Alex was able to do was to rock her, as she cried, holding the girl's head to her chest. "You're safe, I promise…" Alex repeated. She looked at Melanie with great trepidation. During the ten-or-so minutes that the girl sobbed in her arms, Alex looked up and just prayed to God, with all the strength in her heart and soul that the child would be okay. Alex had to believe she would be—she had to be. Noticing the girl was calming down, Alex slowly attempted to get her to talk. "Do you think you can tell me your name?" Alex said softly.

The girl's chest heaved with each irregular breath she took. Slowly, she sat up on her own, trying to calm herself down enough to speak. "Samantha, Samantha Shea."

"Samantha," Alex recited. "That's a beautiful name."

Samantha's breathing became more balanced as she looked upon the peaceful land. "They were calling me Elizabeth when they took me."

Alex looked at Melanie, astounded. "Who took you, Samantha?"

"Jimmy and his wife, Brenda," Samantha revealed, realizing she was safe. "At their house, they had pictures of a girl who looked like me."

Melanie stepped away to call in the authorities.

It was a feat for Alex to get her head around what was happening. "When did they take you?" Her eyes never left the girl.

"February," said Samantha, as she took the puppy back.

Alex swallowed hard, as she looked away for a split second, realizing that since Nate's death, she had been grieving while Samantha was kidnapped, while her parents were probably frantic all that time. "Samantha, where do you live?"

"Maryland."

Looking up toward the gray-filled cotton sky, Alex fought back tears, imagining what this child must have gone through. She gently placed her hand back on Samantha's and held her close. "You're safe now, Samantha Shea." Unexpectedly, the girl kneeled and wrapped her arms around Alex's neck. Innately, Alex coiled her arms around the girl, vowing to never let her out of her sight until she was with her parents.

"Thank you," Samantha whispered before she fell asleep on Alex's right shoulder. "You're very welcome, Samantha." Continuing to rub the sleeping girl's back, Alex silently wept, as relief, sadness, frustration, and indignation hit her without mercy. Her body vibrated, sobbing much like the way the little human who now slept soundly in her arms sobbed ten minutes prior.

"Alex, are you okay?" Melanie asked, noticing her crying. "Do you want me to take her?"

Nobody was going to take Samantha from her until she was confident the girl was safe and with her parents. "No...no...I'm really fine," she retorted, gathering herself up again off the ground. "I have Samantha."

"The police should be here very soon," Melanie announced with relief exploding from her voice. "Are you sure you don't want me to take her?"

"No, thank you though," said Alex, surveying the land. "Where's the puppy?"

"He's right behind you." Melanie smiled. Just then, Melanie's staff escorted the Colorado Springs Police to where they stood with Samantha. Their priority was to get the girl to a safe place while they searched for Jimmy and Brenda. They determined Melanie's cabin would be safe.

Alex suddenly had four or five Police officers offer to carry Samantha for her; she resisted handing the scared child over to strangers even if they were the authorities. Soon, the Colorado State police were notified of Samantha's plight. Once they came upon Melanie's cabin, police cleared it to be safe, allowing Alex inside. Melanie directed her to the living room where a wooden couch with tan, red and green plaid cushions sat. Gently, Alex laid the sleeping girl down on it, putting a small couch pillow under her head. Alex crouched and then sat on the floor, exhausted, as she rested her head on her hand, as her elbow rested on the couch cushion. She found it difficult to take her eyes off Samantha even if police were everywhere. As she gazed at Samantha sleeping soundly, Alex neglected to notice Melanie approaching with a glass of cold water.

"Here—drink this," Melanie kindly demanded. "Can I get you anything else?"

Taking the water straight away, Alex took a huge gulp of water. "Thank you, Melanie," said Alex, feeling more alive. "Do you have Wi-Fi? I just wanted to text my parents to let them know I'm okay."

"Oh sure…sure," Melanie uttered in a caring tone, as she proceeded to share her password.

"I greatly appreciate it, Melanie." Alex entered it into her iPhone. The phone connected at once, as Alex breathed again. Immediately, she sent a brief message to her parents and Conrad, letting them know she was fine. As fast as she sent the message, within a minute, she received thankful messages back. Unaware of how thirsty she was, she quickly finished the water.

"Alex, let me make you something to eat," Melanie prodded her new friend. "Samantha is sleeping—she'll probably sleep for a while—and police are everywhere."

Surveying the living room, a very rustic room, filled with a camp of law enforcement men and woman, Alex recognized the girl was well-guarded. "Okay." She stood and followed Melanie into her very rustic, old kitchen. The stove must have been from the 1940s, black and with the curved flue pipe going directly into the interior brick wall. She watched Melanie grab four pieces of kindling and threw it into the stove. "Can I help with anything?"

"No…no…Please sit," said Melanie, as she carefully checked the temperature of the stove discs. "Do you like eggs?"

Already sitting at the round, Mahogany table, Alex glanced out the large, picture window that showed more of the beautiful views of Pikes Peak. "I love eggs, thank you."

Melanie grabbed a bowl of eggs from the white 1940s refrigerator and brought it to the stove. "Are you a coffee or tea drinker?"

"Oh, tea is good, Melanie, thank you," Alex kindly expressed.

"Were you able to text your folks?"

"Oh yes, thank you, Melanie," Alex replied warmheartedly. "They worry about me driving by myself, you know."

Cooking the scrambled eggs, Melanie chortled. "Oh boy, I know the feeling. My son and daughter are both truckers, so I know the anxiety." Pouring the hot water into a white mug, she brought it over to Alex. "Milk, cream, or sugar?"

"Oh, thank you, this is fine, Melanie." Alex bobbed the teabag in the boiling water and watched it turn amber. "Do they enjoy it—being truckers?"

"I think when they started, they had visions of driving for big-time musicians and rock bands, but now, ten years in, the industry is pushing the drivers to drive further on less sleep. I get the feeling they might be looking for a change," Melanie narrated.

"Yeah, I can't imagine that'd be an easy profession," remarked Alex. Out of the corner of her eye, she noticed a tall man wearing a light-blue shirt with beige trousers walking slowly into the kitchen.

"Ma'am," the Colorado Patrol Officer spoke.

Melanie gave him her undivided attention. "Sir."

"I am Officer Skip Matteson," he began. "We have confirmed Samantha's story. She was kidnapped on February 26th in Rockville, Maryland while walking home from school."

Alex had no idea what was going on within the officer's gut, but she felt instantly queasy listening to Samantha's confirmed story. "Shit," she mumbled under her breath.

Officer Matteson glanced at Alex. "Her parents have been notified and they will be arriving at Denver International in about five hours. We would like to escort Samantha to Denver to reunite with her parents," Officer Matteson detailed, veering his eyes between Alex and Melanie. "I would like one or both of you to come along with Samantha, since she seems comfortable with both of you."

"Sure, sure…anything for Samantha," Melanie spoke first.

"Absolutely," Alex stated. Before Officer Matteson excused himself from Melanie's kitchen, the big, obvious question leaped out from her lips. "Have you caught Jimmy and Brenda yet?"

Officer Matteson stood tall and strong, looking at the age he might have a couple of grand kids. "Not yet, Ma'am, but we have some good leads already."

Alex listened with her neck crooked, but he had her undivided attention. "Thank you, Sir."

Touching his hat rim, Officer Matteson slightly bowed. "If you need me, I'll be out front."

Samantha slept for two more hours. While she slept, Alex was able to enjoy her scrambled eggs that her new friend, Melanie, cooked. Like a Cuckoo clock, Alex popped her head into the living room every ten minutes to make sure Samantha awoke to a familiar, trusted face. Sometimes Alex just stood with her arms crossed, leaning on the dark-stained door jamb between the kitchen and the living room, ruminating what the last five months were like for Samantha—such a sharp change from her normal life, being in third grade with her friends, being at home, feeling safe and loved by her parents she had known all her life. It must have seemed like a bad, horrifying dream that she wasn't able to wake up from. It made Alex's spine shudder contemplating what abuse Samantha might have suffered at the hands of her captors, knowing how people's minds could betray them, making them do unspeakable acts. Sometimes it was too disturbing to think about. Tired of standing, Alex returned to sitting in front of the couch where the puppy snuggled upon her lap.

For the second time that day, the puppy awakened her with wild licks to the face. Alex opened her eyes and saw Samantha staring at her from the couch.

"Where am I?" Samantha inquired softly.

Alex got to her knees swiftly. "Hi Samantha," she began, matching the girl's soft tone, "do you remember the woman I was with when we found you up on the hill?"

Samantha nodded, as she took a prolonged look around the rustic living room to try to get her bearings.

"Her name is Melanie, this is her house, and all kinds of law enforcement are here, outside, keeping you safe. They are working on getting you back home," Alex explained to Samantha.

Her eyes brightened up wide. "I'm going home?!" Samantha nearly exploded out of her skin, as she collapsed back into Alex's arms and wept with happiness.

The girl nearly took Alex's breath away. "Aww...Baby Girl," she said sweetly, "what are you doing to me?" Alex whispered and grabbed her tightly. It was hard for her not to cry along with Samantha, having totally captured her heart. What seemed like hours turned out to be just a few minutes. Tears fell down her cheeks, as she tried to wipe them away.

Samantha pulled away, curious to witness Alex crying. "You're crying. Why?"

Looking up at the popcorn ceiling, Alex smiled, taking in an exhilarating breath. "I'm just so happy that you are going to see your parents today, after such a long time not seeing them," said Alex. "These are happy tears, and then later, when you see your parents, they'll have happy tears too, because they missed you so much."

The girl locked eyes with Alex and knew what she spoke was truth. "Happy tears?"

"Oh, most definitely happy tears," Alex gleefully conveyed, holding onto Samantha's smaller hands. "Are you hungry—can I make you something to eat?"

Staring around the room, Samantha was deciding what her small body needed. "Milk."

"You want some milk?" excitedly repeated Alex.

A tiny giggle emerged from the girl. "Yeah."

"Yeah?! Yeah?!" Alex said enthusiastically and stood. "Do you want to follow me into the kitchen?"

Samantha did a big nod.

Alex's heart leaped. "The kitchen is right in here," she said, pointing in the direction of the kitchen. Alex observed Samantha lean to see the entrance to the kitchen, gingerly taking just a few steps forward. What she didn't expect was when Samantha snuck her smaller hand into hers. Alex fought not to look downward to confirm what was true, as her heart skipped a beat. All that Alex needed to do was to squeeze Samantha's hand, signaling she was safe in her presence. Hand in hand, Alex ushered Samantha into Melanie's rustic kitchen.

It was about an hour and a half before Samantha needed to be in Denver. Officer Matteson coordinated every part of this unification, including the vehicles and security, and he even sent one officer to the nearest department store to buy new clothes and shoes for Samantha. Melanie and Alex, along with a female officer, remained within feet of the upstairs bathroom while Samantha bathed herself. Alex kept on high alert if she needed anything. Soon, Samantha emerged from the bathroom looking nervous but happy at the fact she would be reunited with her parents soon. Now her clothing consisted of well-fitted long denim shorts, a white short-sleeved shirt, white knee socks, and new, white, Reebok sneakers. Samantha was very thankful for the new clothes, although she looked forward to getting back in her normal clothes.

Once they got back downstairs, Officer Matteson and his force of ten escorted Samantha, Alex, and Melanie into a Colorado Patrol gray SUV. The puppy sat on Samantha's lap. It was already coordinated by

Officer Matteson that one of his officers would drive Alex's Camry to Denver; after Samantha was reunited with her parents, Alex's plan was to continue on her way. She assumed They would be going to Utah next, but she wasn't going to assume anything before talking to Jay. In the SUV with Samantha, Alex, and Melanie safely in the back, Alex glanced at her Camry to see if Jay was in the passenger seat, and He was, to Alex's relief. It made her quietly chuckle when she imagined Jay, invisible and hushed, and most likely, sleeping, His presence unbeknownst to the police officer next to Him. She thought that the officer who got to sit next to Jay was a very lucky individual.

With Officer Matteson at the wheel, it was altogether different to be driven, whereas Alex had driven herself for the past two and a half weeks. She had more than enough time to really take in the scenery that surrounded her. But she didn't allow her attention to be shifted away from Samantha, who sat stoic, looking at Pikes Peak out the left window. Alex sat on Samantha's left, observing her often. Did she dare to ask Samantha what she was feeling? Alex wanted to, although she didn't want to disturb the girl in any way. To Alex, Samantha appeared anxious.

"Are you feeling alright, Samantha?" Alex asked, watching the girl stroking the sleeping puppy.

Samantha glanced left to notice Alex's eyes upon her. "What if my parents don't remember me?"

It was a stunner of a question that jarred Alex a bit. "Ah, Samantha, I can promise you your parents have been looking for you day and night since you were taken in February," she expressed sweetly. "Whether children are gone for a day, or forty years, parents don't ever forget their children."

"Never?" Samantha needed to be sure.

"Parents never forget their kids, Sweetheart," confirmed Alex. Looking into Samantha's resigned, blue eyes, it was clear it wasn't enough. "Do you know what?"

"What?" the sweet voice answered.

"I have been driving across the country for more than two weeks now, and I know when I get home in a few short weeks, my parents will probably be crying happy tears when they see me," Alex proclaimed with the widest grin. Glancing over Samantha's head, Alex noticed that Melanie was smiling along. "Melanie has a son and a daughter who make their living driving trucks across the country. I bet she sheds happy tears every time they come home safe and sound."

Samantha turned her head to the right toward Melanie. "Do you cry happy tears?"

"I do, Sweetie," Melanie answered, her voice so caring and wondrous. "When they come home, I usually cook them all kinds of good food, like pasta and meatballs, meatloaf and potatoes, cookies, brownies, cakes and things like that." Melanie paused and caught Alex's gaze. "What is your favorite thing to eat?"

Alex smiled.

Samantha had to ponder that question for a bit, as she seemed to want to come up with something she remembered before she got kidnapped. "Umm...Macaroni and cheese."

"Oh boy, I love macaroni and cheese," Alex said, smiling at the engaged girl.

"Me too," Melanie chirped.

"Me three," Officer Matteson chimed in with enthusiasm.

Nobody in the back seat expected him to speak; they all laughed. Everybody thought about something else besides the cruelty of the last six months. This was indeed a happy day: a missing girl was about to be reunited with her parents. It was hard to get life much better than that. For the rest of the ride to Denver, everyone tried to keep Samantha in jovial spirits.

Two miles away from the police station that Officer Matteson had designated as the location the reunification would take place, he spoke to Samantha directly, detailing every step that was to follow. His voice was soothing and clear, leaving no detail a secret. Listening to the officer, Alex surmised he had reunified hundreds of times, but in reality, Samantha would only be the third reunification of his career. These were rewarding slices of his career, although he hated the knowledge of how reunified children were considerably wrecked by their fearful detention. Reunification was always euphoric at first, maybe lasting for a week or two, but what a victim experienced during the time when their life was out of their control, many suffering unspeakable cruelty and isolation, makes reentering their 'normal' life difficult, as if swimming in a pool of anxiety and fear. Children who have been torn out of their families and deposited in a synthetic family lose a part of their identity that might not always return, as they might habitually look over their shoulders, frightened to be taken once again. The act of kidnapping any human sickened Matteson to his core.

Officer Matteson ordered the media stations off-site if word got out that the reunification was in process. Just as Matteson had informed

Samantha, he drove the SUV down an incline that led to an underground parking lot. The accompanying police vehicles parked, flanking Matteson's vehicle. Within seconds, Matteson stepped out and opened the rear, left door, allowing Alex, Samantha and Melanie out of the vehicle. To get on Samantha's level, he perched himself down on one knee, and informed the obviously nervous girl that her parents were just inside, waiting in a room. Matteson asked Samantha if she was ready— she was. Instinctively, Samantha slipped her hand into Alex's for the second time that day. Alex's heart leaped, as she steadied herself for what was about to take place. Alex was curious if Samantha's legs were as wobbly as hers. She concluded that Samantha's legs were stronger at that moment. Following Officer Matteson through the garage, and then, the entrance door, the anticipation was palpable on everyone's faces and probably embedded in everyone's chests as well. Taking about five steps forward, Matteson turned around and ushered Samantha into the room where her parents waited, hardly breathing, yearning to hold their child who had been gone for six months. Once she laid her eyes on them, Samantha dashed toward their open arms, as her parents' love reclaimed her. Alex steadied herself with the painted-white, cold, steel doorjamb and watched the explosion of love, relief, and euphoria rain down on them. Never before had Alex bore witness to such a validation of devotion, as she believed Samantha's parents would not let her out of their sight.

At that moment, Alex stepped back and went back out into the underground garage to fetch some air. To her right, Alex found a curb to sit on, as she rested her arms over her knees, dipping her head. She took some deep breaths before she wept, considering the heaviness of the day, realizing just how much her parents missed her, and how she missed them. At times, she sobbed, realizing how much they wanted her back home, and recognizing parents' sacrifices for the children, how they would give their lives for their children. Michael and Joanne never had the ability to save Nate's life; he decided that for himself. Alex knew how it felt—to feel hopeless trying to save Nate, although she was just his big sister. Nate was their child—a child who had a severe mental disorder that robbed him of so much.

"Hey," Melanie whispered loudly, as she approached Alex. She sat on the same curb. "You doing okay?"

Trying to clear her eyes from tears, Alex chortled through her emotions. "Yeah," Alex voiced while she sniffled. "Parents are really brave to have kids, aren't they? I mean, so many things can go haywire, like kids being kidnapped, and kids getting sick. How are you not overwhelmed with worry all the time?"

"Oh God, it's not easy by any means," Melanie admitted, resting her chin on the heel of her hand. "But once you hold your child in your arms, you truly know you can stand up to anything to protect them, and that never goes away."

Listening, and hanging on Melanie's every word, Alex understood the idea, although she knew she wouldn't know the true feeling of being a parent until she was one. She took in a sizable breath and then let it go. "My friends just adopted a baby girl, and they are simply enthralled with her."

"Yep, their lives will never be the same, in every great way possible," Melanie said, smiling. "The Sheas would like to meet you, if you're ready."

Suddenly, Alex panicked over her disheveled appearance and her puffy face, as she quickly stood, drying her eyes and face with all the surfaces of her hands. "Ah, geez."

Melanie rose to her feet and stared at Alex. "You look fine," she exclaimed passionately. "They don't care what you look like—you found their daughter!"

It was hard to argue with that. "Okay, okay, okay." Alex followed Melanie back inside the building, and into the room where the Sheas hadn't let go of Samantha yet, if they would ever again.

"This is Alex," Melanie said, introducing her to a very grateful Mr. and Mrs. Shea.

Before Alex could utter one word, she was clutched by Mrs. Shea. Alex was engulfed in that familiar sensation of peace and warmth that she had come to know on this road trip. Instantly, Alex was revived once again. There were no words to be said. Slowly, Alex reciprocated Mrs. Shea's embrace. "She's safe."

Pulling away, a poignant Mrs. Shea glanced at Alex with profound appreciation. "Words can't express how grateful we are for you finding Samantha today."

Words escaped Alex for a few moments, as she gazed at Samantha, wrapped in the love and security of her father's arms; the anxiety had disappeared from her beautiful face. "You have a very strong daughter." Alex was bowled over from how much mother and daughter resembled each other. The only difference was the length of their blond hair. Mrs. Shea wore a sage-green sun dress and white sandals. Her porcelain face was gaunt. "She looks just like you."

"She's my girl," said Mrs. Shea, choking back tears. She motioned her husband to come to where she stood with Alex. "Alex, this is my husband, John."

"This is Alex, Daddy," Samantha announced, as her father still held her up, bracing her legs on his chest, as she looked downward upon him.

This was music to her ears. Grinning at Samantha, Alex extended her hand. "Hi, John."

Out of courtesy, John extended his hand. "Thank you for taking care of Sam today—we really appreciate it," he said, barely trying to meet his hand with her hand. He let Samantha down, as she went back to her mother.

Something in Alex's gut told her that something was off. As Samantha passed in front of her, Alex softly scratched the top of her head. "We were in the right place this morning," commented Alex, surreptitiously glancing into his still, black eyes. It took everything Alex had not to look back to check if Officer Matteson was close by.

John said nothing and then stepped back a few steps. Seemingly a few years older than Mrs. Shea, maybe several years older, John had a head full of salt-and-pepper, crimpy hair that touched his shoulders. He was tall and lanky, dressed in black jeans and a black button-down short-sleeved shirt. Returning her attention to Samantha and her mother, she crouched low. "How are you doing, Kiddo?"

Samantha wore a smile as big as the moon. "Good," she chortled, with her hands playfully in motion in front of her mouth.

Mrs. Shea knelt on the floor and Samantha melted back into her lap. "Is there anything, anything at all, that I can do for you?" begged Mrs. Shea.

"Oh, no, no, no—I'm just happy Samantha is safe and going home." Alex grinned brightly. "Samantha was a little worried that you wouldn't remember her, and I said parents never forget their children."

Mrs. Shea immediately clutched Samantha's blond head to her chest. "Oh Baby, we would never forget you," she promised, kissing Samantha's head. "Never, never, never, Baby."

Alex looked on, feeling relief. "I have to get going," Alex announced. "I want you to continue to be brave, as I know that you are."

Samantha stood and wrapped her arms around Alex's neck. "I'll be brave."

"Oh Kiddo, I know you will," said Alex, as she embraced Samantha one last time. Alex stood. "Make sure you take good care of

Dutch."

"I will," Samantha said purposefully, looking at the sleeping puppy on the metal bench.

"Goodbye Samantha, goodbye Mrs. Shea," Alex sincerely uttered before bowing to John. As she turned, she heard Samantha and her mother respond but not John, as Alex surmised he didn't like her for some reason. She found herself in the underground parking lot, finding Melanie. "Have you seen Officer Matteson?"

"Sure, he's over there," Melanie pointed. "Why?"

Spotting Matteson, Alex walked toward him. "I have a bad feeling about Samantha's dad." Breathing out, she approached Officer Matteson. "Sir."

"Alex," Matteson responded.

She breathed in. "Mr. Shea is under the influence of something, but I'm not sure what."

Matteson glanced at Alex. "I saw that as well," he said, clearing his throat. "Are you going back inside?"

"No. I was going to get on the road." Alex's heart ached for home.

Matteson stepped forward. "We have Jimmy and Brenda in custody. They are saying Mr. Shea paid them to abduct Samantha."

Alex and Melanie looked at each other, dumbfounded. "What?"

"We're currently working with the FBI to verify their claims. Apparently, Mr. Shea and Jimmy worked together, and without giving away too much, Mr. Shea, who is Samantha's stepfather, got into financial problems and Jimmy and Brenda paid Mr. Shea."

It felt like someone had punched Alex in the stomach. "Please tell me Mrs. Shea wasn't involved."

"Our preliminary investigation indicates that she had no involvement in or knowledge of the crime."

"Oh, thank God," uttered Alex, sinking to her heels. She took a few deep breaths before standing back up. "What's going to happen now?"

"We'll take them upstairs to interrogation. In an hour or so, we should have more evidence; we'll separate them, and we'll see where the cards might fall," Matteson presumed. "Where are you headed?"

"I was going to try to make it to Utah tonight," Alex retorted, attempting to disguise her exhaustion.

"You should get a room for the night and set off early tomorrow morning," suggested Matteson, reaching for one of his cell phones. "My brother-in-law owns a few hotels in Denver—I'd be happy to cash in a few favors."

Sound had barely escaped Alex's vocal cords before Matteson reached his brother-in-law. A few minutes passed, and her reservation was already arranged. Then, Alex allowed her tiredness to flow into her physical body, as all her muscles unwound. "I thank you, Sir."

Matteson smiled. "Please, call me Skip." He pulled one of his official business cards out of the back of his cell. "If you ever need anything at all, call me."

Feeling undeserving of Skip's attention, she took the card and stared at it. "Thank you, Skip." Alex saw him walked back into the building to do what was required. She returned her eyes to Melanie. "How are you getting home?"

"Oh, one of the officers from Colorado Springs is going to bring me home; he's a friend of my son's, so I'll be in good hands," Melanie joked. "Will you be okay?"

"Oh yeah, I'm good…I'm good," Alex said confidently, thankful for her support. "I appreciate your hospitality."

Melanie grinned and went in for a warm hug. "I thank you for all your help. I couldn't have done it without you."

With her chin upon the notch of Melanie's shoulder, Alex hugged her in return. "Yeah, okay, like I believe that. You're a badass." Alex retracted her arms.

"Yeah, but you are the doctor," Melanie reminded Alex.

As planned, at least since Skip's suggestion, Alex restored herself with a good night's sleep in one of the more upscale hotel rooms. She had to conclude she must have made more of an impression on the lead officer than she realized. It was now 6:24 a.m. in Denver, which made it 8:24 a.m. in Boston. Her iPhone was perched on the bedside table within arm's reach; she picked it up and FaceTimed her mother. Leaning on her right elbow, Alex flipped her untamed black hair back out of her young face.

"Hello," Alex said excitedly, giggling.

"There's my beautiful daughter who I miss so much," spoke a gleefully Joanne. "Where are you—are you still in Denver?"

"Yeah," Alex said easily. "I'm going to jump in the shower and get on the road. I want to drive all day."

Joanne smiled. "You are not going to stop anywhere and just ricochet off the California coast and come straight home?"

Laughter filled the quiet hotel room, as the sun presented itself through the white, patterned curtains. "That's exactly what I'm going to do!" Her laughter was abundant with strength and joy.

"Have you heard anything about the little girl yet?"

"No, not yet," replied Alex, more serious. "I'll probably touch base with Melanie later on today."

"It's so hard to wrap my head around the fact that someone would do something as horrid as selling their own stepchild. It doesn't make sense," Joanne said, contemplating the tough circumstances.

"I know," injected Alex. "Is Dad working?"

"He is working, but he should be home around one," said Joanne. "I know he misses talking to you."

"If he wants, and if you want, you can keep me company when I'm driving," proposed Alex, sitting up on the edge of the full-size bed.

"I'm in, Babe, and Dad will definitely be game," Joanne answered, as she couldn't stop smiling.

Alex laughed quietly. "I don't know if you had any plans or not."

"Please, we like staying home these days," her mother admitted.

A pang of guilt swept through Alex like a gust of wind coming down an empty valley, when she tried to conjecture whether her parents were staying in because she was on the road, or if going out was a game of how many eyes were going to stare at them with pity. "You should go grab lunch somewhere," mentioned Alex.

Scratching the corner of her eyebrow, Joanne considered her idea. "Maybe we will."

"Do it," Alex pressed. "Let me get this day going and I'll talk to you later."

"I love you," Joanne voiced, infinitely confident.

"I love you too, Mom," returned Alex, blowing Joanne a kiss through the small screen, and then watched her beautiful mother return the virtual kiss. She ended the call, which was becoming more challenging to do. Alex jumped in the shower.

Prior to leaving her complimentary hotel room, she found a small pad of paper in the side table and composed a gracious note to a man whose name she didn't yet know. Alex got a little bit of cash out of an ATM nearby and folded it into the note. Back inside the hotel lobby, bright and contemporary, Alex walked up to the white marble desk and made sure the concierge got it to the hotel owner, who she discovered was Doug Manning.

Finding the Camry in the parking lot, she also found Jay. She smiled at Him and They got into the car. While inside the hotel, she had grabbed a cup of tea and an egg sandwich to scarf down in the first 15 minutes on I-70 West. Like any other leg of the trip, Jay got comfortable in the passenger seat and fell asleep. Again, it came to her mind what He did when He wasn't in sight. He was Jesus Christ, sought-after by so many on Earth, to fulfill their wishes, to make the people they loved whole, healthy and safe. It was a 24/7 obligation which He took on willingly, as He never complained. He saw everyone equally and saw each living spirit worthy of His love. He shed tears when humans failed each other in the most brutal of ways, even if their weapons were words. He shed even more tears when humans didn't respect the Earth, and all it had to offer, even the aspects not yet realized. He was sitting in her car while He had every reason to go tend to something else that needed His attention. There were 7.9 billion people worldwide and He was going to see her through to San Francisco.

Alex stopped in Grand Junction to gas up and to grab more food. The sky brightened up a little when They crossed into Utah. She was making good headway to reach St. George, right before the border with Arizona, by nightfall. San Fran was two days away, she figured. She fought her feelings of excitement being so close to San Fran, and feelings of apprehension of saying goodbye to Jay, even if He would always be in earshot; they gnawed at her gut. If she didn't see Him every day, would she have the same strength she had then and there, driving 80 miles per hour on I-70 on two lanes of highway? She hoped she would. The scenery was mostly flat, although low mountain vistas seemed to pop out of the ground, putting dimension into the distance. I-70 hovered around 4,500 feet in elevation—a far cry from the 400-foot elevation she was used to in Boston. The sun seemed closer, and the sky seemed intensely blue. Traffic was light, as Alex frequently had the road to herself in scattered intervals. Sometimes she would see semi-trucks along the way and wondered if the driver was one of Melanie's children. Alex decided to call Melanie to see if she had heard anything about Samantha's father. If she hadn't heard anything from Skip, she would certainly have heard something from her son's friend. Word was John Shea had been arrested on conspiracy to commit fraud and accessory to kidnapping. He would be extradited back to Maryland the day after next. Mrs. Shea and Samantha had already returned home. Alex and Melanie continued to chat easily, considering the time they spent the previous day tending to a child, newly freed and extremely vulnerable. Alex would never forget the words Melanie left her with at the police complex: 'You are the doctor', expressing to Melanie how much she appreciated hearing those words. Melanie had to get back to running the campground, while Alex had to continue making her way west. They promised to talk soon.

It was nearly one in the afternoon, Mountain Time—three o'clock in Boston. Alex instructed her iPhone to call 'Dad'; it obeyed, as she wondered if there were any cell towers in the area to catapult her call to Boston. There were.

"Hello Al," Michael nearly cheered, "how are ya, Girly?!"

Alex giggled loudly. "You're so cute, Dad." She needed to change lanes momentarily. "I'm good. How are you?!"

"I'm good, Al," returned Michael. "Preparing for the Fall semester; it's kind of busy. Where are you?"

Something in his voice seemed diminished. "I'm driving through Utah—I'm almost to interstate 15," perked Alex, knowing she was days away from San Francisco. "Is everything okay, Dad?"

"Yes, why?"

"You seem down." Alex paused to ruminate over her mom's tone earlier that morning. "Mom seemed down too."

"We just miss you, Al," uttered Michael, his voice breaking. "I never thought going to work would be so difficult, and Mom can tell it's difficult for me, you know."

Tears welled in Alex's eyes listening to her dad's struggling voice. "Yeah, I know." Sniffling back droplets of nose mucus, Alex flipped back her hair. "Things will be awkward for a while until people realize we don't have to be handled with kid gloves—people must know that they can still talk to us like normal, you know. Yes, we have suffered a great loss in our lives losing Nate, but we are still here."

Michael exhaled, hanging on her every, incredible word, as his spirit leaped with happiness. "Do you know how fuckin' incredible you are?!"

"Dad!" Alex blurted out and then, she laughed. Looking over at Jay, she found Jay still out like a light.

"What?!" her father exclaimed. "I'm stating the truth, Al. I'm just in awe of how brave you are."

"Aww, Dad…I don't feel brave…I feel like I've abandoned you, Mom, and my life," Alex admitted; tears filled her eyes.

"You didn't abandon us, Al, you just needed to do what you had to do to heal, and to grow," Michael spoke honestly.

Alex squeezed the mucus out of her nose, as she blindly hunted down a tissue in her center console. "Do you think I'm healed, or whatever you want to call it?"

"Absolutely, Al," Michael said with conviction, without an inkling of doubt. "How do you feel?"

Even though she wasn't expecting this question, it didn't scare her. "I feel good, Dad...I mean I have learned so much about myself on this trip that I probably wouldn't have learned otherwise. I have met so many incredible people along the way," Alex narrated, pausing to take a breath. "And the most amazing aspect of this trip is you, Mom and I have become so much closer, which really means everything to me." Alex fought hard to keep it together.

"You are everything to us, Al," Michael lovingly reiterated. "What's the most incredible thing you have seen so far?"

Breathing in and out as deeply as she could, Alex felt a tug at her heart that she wasn't able to tell her father all of Jay's miracles she had witnessed. "The other night, in Colorado Springs, at the Garden of the Gods, it was just after dusk, and the sky...the stars were so bright, I felt like I could almost touch them...I couldn't help but remember how much Nate loved astronomy, all the planets and constellations."

"Pretty cool, isn't it?"

"Yeah," Alex uttered, reserved. "We should take a trip out here next summer."

"We would love that, Al," Michael returned sweetly.

"Maybe I could be the tour guide since I know the area," Alex joked.

"Very true."

Suddenly, Alex remembered a question that was on her mind. "Dad, did you and Mom go out to lunch today?"

"Yes, we did, because our brilliant daughter, who also is a brilliant doctor, told us to go out for lunch," Michael dutifully described.

Alex laughed out loud, changing lanes again. "And where did you go?"

"We went to Ko Sushi and Grill," answered her dad. "Mom had the 'MOM Burger'."

"How fitting," Alex said, chortling, watching the road.

Michael mirrored her laugh. "And I had the tuna burger. It was nice."

"Oh, yum," Alex said with transparent tastebud-envy. "I miss Northeastern cuisine. I'm figuring California cuisine must be pretty good." In the far distance of the call, she heard her mom's voice.

"Hi Sweetie. Where are you?"

Listening to her dad give his wife her location was very sweet. "Yeah, I just got on I-15, headed to St. George."

"Will you stay in St. George tonight?" Joanne asked.

"Yeah, I already have a reservation," she announced for her parents. "I think there's a pool."

"No gators?" Michael kidded.

"I think I'm pretty sure that hotel pools are gator-free, Dad," Alex laughed out loud. For the next hour or so, as the sunlight of the day faded, Michael and Joanne remained talking to their daughter, keeping her engaged. Like all the times before, the conversations were easy. Michael and Joanne wanted to keep the conversations upbeat, because going backwards was non-negotiable. Some evenings, Michael and Joanne would stream a movie they had previously watched together, some with Nate, and her parents wouldn't recite the movies, but do commentary on them—especially comedies and thrillers. Often, the conversations would turn to Nate, and how he would react to certain scenes, as he was very keen on how characters were feeling in their hearts. Talking about Nate was healing for the family who loved him so deeply despite his challenges. They celebrated Nate's memory whenever they could. They even dared to discuss having family and friends over on his birthday in November to celebrate his spirit and all that he was on Earth. They all got behind the celebration of Nate's life, even though surely different emotions would be everywhere, much like the stars in the night sky. It would be alright to laugh; it would be okay to cry.

At 8:48 p.m., Alex pulled into the parking lot of the Red Lion Hotel in St. George, less than 10 miles from the Arizona border. Nevada wasn't that much further. She stepped into the hotel foyer, and the space was high and open, with rust-red-painted steel beams and large glass panes. The floor was a shiny black marble, but Alex wasn't sure it was real marble. She found the reception desk, checked in, and dared to ask if the pool was still open. It was open for another hour, which propelled Alex to hurriedly dig through the backseat of her car, looking for her one-piece navy bathing suit with only the dim light from the parking lot light. It took a few minutes to dig through her dirty laundry, reminding her she had laundry to do.

After changing in Room 67, her designated room for the night, Alex found the pool facilities, quickly walking into the humid, chlorine-dense box of air. There were two teenage boys in the clear water, clowning around like teenagers do, as a woman observed, sitting on a bench. The two designated lap lanes were unoccupied; Alex sat down on the concrete edge, and slipped down into the 85-degree water, enlivening every muscle of her body. Dropping below the water, she finished getting the rest of her body wet, as she started swimming back and forth at a relaxed pace, trying to give her muscles something different to do, working out the ten-hour car ride. Swimming was relaxing and would induce her to sleep well. The hour passed quickly. She got out before the pool closed, dried herself off, and walked back to her room where she showered and snuck into bed. She was a day closer to heading home.

Her iPhone woke her from a sound sleep. With her eyes still closed, Alex felt for her iPhone on the side table, which was a little challenging because nearly every morning she awoke in different accommodations. When she had turned more onto her front, her face squished into the fluffy pillow, Alex picked up her iPhone, and managed to force an eye open just to see it was Conrad. She touched the accept icon and put it on speakerphone.

"Dude!" Alex spoke with force.

Conrad chuckled. "Are you still sleeping?"

Taking a swift breath between her teeth, she realized she was more conscious. "Technically—no, but do I want to be? Kinda." She repositioned her head upon the pillow. "What time is it?"

"In Boston, it's almost nine. Lila has already had two bottles," Conrad said. "What time is it there?"

"Where am I again?" she posed to herself, beginning to keep her eyes open. "St. George, Utah? I believe it's seven here."

Conrad continued to chuckle at his best friend. "You sound like a strung-out musician on the last leg of a world tour!"

Alex sat up, sliding backward against the pillow and the wooden headboard. "Funny." She laughed, flipping back her hair. "How's the baby girl?"

"She's just perfect," Conrad spoke with exploding love in his voice.

"Never let her out of your sight, Conrad," Alex almost demanded. "There is too much craziness in the world."

"Yeah, your mom told me about the little girl in Colorado," Conrad divulged. "That must have been crazy."

"It was, it was," she admitted, imagining Samantha's petrified face, trying to hide in the cluster of bare trees. "Who would have thought a stepfather could do such a thing?"

"A very greedy, drug-hungry bastard, that's who," Conrad quickly answered. He changed the subject. "What do you have planned for today?"

"I'm not sure," Alex muttered, as she rubbed her eyes fully awake. "Vegas is not far; maybe I should go play some slots to try my luck," she quipped, giggling.

"The Grand Canyon is not that far from you," Conrad reminded her. "You should go check it out."

"I was checking out how far it was from here. Technically, Grand Canyon-Parashant, the north side, is only about 30 miles, but the road there takes almost four hours on a dirt road," Alex explained. "I'm not feeling that."

"Okay," Conrad accepted, not giving up on getting his friend to seeing the awe-inspiring Grand Canyon. "Vegas has helicopter tours of the Grand Canyon—go on one of those."

Arguing that she was too afraid to fly in a helicopter wasn't going to work. Alex knew she had the money, especially if she didn't have to drive eight hours to have only one view of the mammoth canyon. "Yeah, okay. Can you send me the links?"

"Sure."

Before she could search for helicopter tours on her own, the links came through from Conrad. "Okay, I'm looking at them," Alex narrated for him, scrolling through the different trips. "They have a sunset tour."

"Well, I hope you fly out of the Canyon before sunset," said Conrad.

Continuing to scroll, reading the description, Alex began to fiddle with her bottom lip with her free hand. "Actually, the sunset tour happens when we fly back to Vegas, which seems more logical."

"That sounds wonderful," he spoke, his voice uplifted from what Alex was going to see. "Book it. Take lots of pictures."

"I'm booking it…right…now…for tonight," Alex confirmed for Conrad. "We are going to have a birthday celebration for Nate in November."

"You and your parents?"

"Yeah," Alex quietly replied. "We think it'll be good to get our family and friends together to celebrate his life."

"Are you ready for that?" Conrad wasn't one to weave around a topic—he went straight in.

"Yeah, I believe I am," she spoke softly, but confidently. "No doubt it will be emotional…but we'll get through it."

"Yep, you will," Conrad agreed unequivocally.

There was a sliver of a pause, as she recognized her newfound strength and resolve. "Where's Justin?"

"He's on a diaper run," Conrad admitted, slightly embarrassed. "We're still figuring out numbers; it's all about the numbers, Al."

She busted out laughing. "Yes, it is, Con." Alex stood and looked out her room window and found West Mountain Peak staring back at her. "Scenery is incredible here, Con." She clicked a photo of the massive formation and sent it Conrad.

"Wait until you see the Colorado River cutting through the Grand Canyon…Magnificent!"

"I bet," returned Alex. "I'd better get ready for my day in Sin City and in a chopper."

"Just remember," began Conrad, "what happens in Vegas stays in Vegas."

Laughing out loud, Alex started looking for appropriate clothing to wear. "Where have I heard that before?" she jested.

"Have a great time today," uttered Conrad. "I think Lila is awake."

"Okay, Con. Great, big kisses to Justin and that cute little baby." Alex smiled brighter than the sun.

"I love you, and I want pictures!" Conrad reminded her.

"I love you too," expressed Alex, closing out the call.

Once she checked out of the hotel, Alex threw her duffle bag in the Camry. Jay was nowhere to be found, which wasn't unusual. She decided to take a leisurely walk around the exterior of the hotel, seeing if she could locate Him. By the time she got to the west side, she looked across the road and saw Jay coming from the direction of West Mountain Peak. The air was already nearing 95 degrees in the shade. Alex observed Jay walking across the road, still wearing His jeans and hoodie. Obviously, He didn't have a need for a suitcase, but looking at Jay made Alex want to liquify in a puddle of sweat. Jogging across the mostly abandoned road, He met Alex, hardly winded.

"Did you climb all the way up there?" Alex posed to Jay, feeling the sweat forming on the back of her neck. She lifted her hair up.

"I sure did," He acknowledged with the air of gallantry. "You should have joined Me."

Looking up to its peak, judging the temperature of the day, still early, Alex smirked. "Yeah...no." Turning around, Alex let her arms fall to her side, as she started to complete the circle back to the Camry. "What did You do up there on the mountain?"

"I was listening to prayers," Jay said.

She opened the driver's side door and dropped into the warm seat. Closing the door, Alex watched Jay get in. "Do you ever get overwhelmed with all the suffering in the world?" she asked. She started the car engine.

"I carry a good part of suffering on My back—My Father gave Me that resilience to do so," Jay recognized. "I welcome people putting their hardships on Me because it gives them a chance to hope, and then, flourish."

Now, she wondered how much suffering He carried for her, especially in the last six months, while she knew there were so many more serious crises happening in the world besides the death of Nate. She pulled out of the parking lot and headed to get back on I-15. "How much did You carry for me?" asked Alex, contrite, glancing at Him.

"You don't have to ask Me that," Jay remarked. "You carried your fair share." Catching Alex looking at Him again, He smiled, signaling there was no need to worry about what He carried on her behalf. "I hear We are going to tour the Grand Canyon in a helicopter?"

Chortling while paying attention to the road and other cars, Alex nodded. "We are."

"Good choice," Jay revealed.

Sand

Traffic coming in from the north of Las Vegas was bumper-to-bumper—brake lights as far up as she could see. It reminded her of Boston traffic each morning that she would see from the T going to work. She was at a standstill, with views of Vegas which she imagined she could reach out and touch. Hotels of silver, gold, white and glass, popped out of the ground as if a gigantic child had put the city together with glittery Lego pieces with an imagination that ran wild. Her copilot was fast asleep, giving Alex a chance to touch base with her parents. In the little amount of time since she had gotten off the phone with Conrad, her mom and dad already knew about the Grand Canyon tour, leaving her to the whim of their worry; but oddly enough, they were excited that she was going to see one of the majestic sights on Earth, although they had Alex promise them she would call or text as soon as she got back on solid ground. Of course, she would. It was hard to not relieve their stresses by telling them she was in good hands with Jay always by her side. She promised she would call them later, ending the brief conversation with I love yous.

Having moved ahead only one hundred yards since calling her parents, she had two more miles to creep until she got to her exit, which seemed to be everyone's exit. Jay awakened as if He just had a five-minute nap. The absurdity of going to Vegas, Sin City, with Jesus, was almost comical, as she immediately went to asking Jay if she was going directly to hell for driving Him into what some also called Gluttony City. She didn't want to spend eternity in an icebox. Jay was never bored spending time with Alex because she had the ability to make Him laugh, quite a lot. This time was no different. He posed the question to her if she was planning on doing anything depraved while in the city of vice. Her answer was a definite no. Then what did she have to worry about, He countered. When He put it that way, she had nothing to fear.

It was close to 2 p.m. Pacific Time. Twenty miles back she had left Mountain Time behind. Besides the annual daylight savings time flip ahead and flip back occurrences, driving westward was something she was still managing to keep straight. Reaching the Pacific Time Zone was epic compared to where she had been just three weeks prior. She had just over 550 miles to go until she was in San Fran—one or two days away. Every time Alex thought about arriving home, seeing her parents with mile-wide smiles on their faces, feeling them embrace her so tightly and lovingly, and returning their embrace, she would smile, almost giddy. She couldn't wait for that moment.

Getting off I-15, They embarked into the city where some people come to exploit their vices, whether gambling, drinking, sex, or anything else deemed seedy or sinful; this city in the desert served up all kinds of tantalizing offerings. Alex wasn't visiting Vegas for anything other than a helicopter excursion to the Grand Canyon, and maybe a little sightseeing, gawking without judgment. Up ahead, Alex spotted a place to get a bite to eat. They entered the parking lot of SkinnyFATS, next to an establishment called Beer Zombies. She thought the name was interesting although it did not prompt her to step inside. The growling from her stomach was distinct. Inside was a little crowded but the line was moving at a good pace. The menu was easy to see and she mulled over her choices. Since she was going to be in a helicopter for at least two hours, she wanted something filling. She ordered the Cranburkey sandwich, which consisted of a turkey patty, arugula, tomato, onion and cranberry yo on a wheat bun. She filled up her water jug and just sat at a table by the window. Jay sat across from her and let Alex devour her lunch. Within His view was the Mandalay Bay hotel, sheathed in gold, mirrored veneer panels. Leaning His chin upon the heel of His hand, His elbow on the table, Jay was deep in thought, at times closing His eyes. Alex, quiet, listening toward the window, looked in the same direction, understanding His absorption. It was less than a year since a gunman had killed 58 souls and injured hundreds more, as they were enjoying a country music festival. Alex grew angry thinking back on the horrible and brutal, unspeakable act, like all the mass shootings in previous years. It was one of those savage acts that needed ineradicable memorials to commemorate the dead; where loved ones could visit and touch the engraved name of the tragically lost, cry, swear, and pray. Jay still had His eyes closed, probably praying, Alex guessed, sitting quietly for a while.

She found a parking lot not far from the Mandalay Bay hotel which the shuttle for the helicopter tour designated as the pickup spot. The sun was getting less intense, as the afternoon wore on, changing the angle of the sun's rays hitting the atmosphere of the Earth, dropping the temperature a slim five degrees. Alex found a shaded area on the concrete curb in front of the tan brick one-story building. Jay seemed to be still detained in His soul, locked in sadness, reflective and resolute, as He rose to His feet, walked about a hundred feet southeast and sanctified the hallowed ground. Immediately, the ground quaked for a second or two, disturbing Alex and nobody else, compelling her to jump to her feet. She wasn't quite sure if the vibration was caused by a geological event or by Jay's Heavenly powers. Not taking her eyes off Him, as He walked back toward her, from the relief set upon His face, Alex was almost positive the Earth jolt was His doing. Like nothing had happened, like nothing had disturbed Him, Jay sat back down on the curb, feeling Alex's eyes upon Him. He was confident He didn't need to explain Himself or His actions; Alex knew His intentions. Less than a minute later, Alex sat back down on the curb, forcing Him to make eye contact with her. It was the first time Alex saw Jay shed a tear; it wasn't a sign of weakness but, rather, a sign of strength. Something unexpectedly prompted Alex to graze His cheek, where the tear descended, absorbing it into her mortal skin, and, at once, pulling back, as if she had crossed some forbidden line. Jay swiftly grabbed her purportedly unlawful hand and forgave her impetuosity, rather a human reaction. Alex's eyes didn't waver from His, as she took her hand back, still guilt-ridden, subduedly apologetic, and swiftly looked away. Jay, keenly aware she wasn't settled, unable to forgive herself, reiterated she was free of sin. She had to believe Him because He was who He was—Jesus.

Other people started to gather, fellow adventurous, thrill-seeking nature lovers who wanted to see the Grand Canyon, or least parts of it from the air. She stood up and joined the rest of the standing guests.

One of them, a woman, suggested it might be a good idea to visit the little girl's room before hopping on a helicopter. Alex thought it was something she should do also, asking the woman if she may follow her, having no idea where the bathroom was located. The woman, pleasant enough, was around 50, decked out in a black blouse, white knit pants, and high-heeled d'Orsay shoes. Her hair, long, thick and platinum blond, complimented her two-inch, pearl, fake nails and the overpowering flowery perfume she had seemingly bathed in. Her whole persona screamed *Las Vegas, Baby!* Alex presumed, and rightly so, that this woman probably had never held a laborious job in her life, although she never wanted to make off-the-cuff judgments about anyone. Alex tried to make small talk with the woman, but she presented herself as not so chatty. Maybe it was the way she dressed, very casual, as she wore her usual denim shorts and various colored tank tops. Today, it was a very pale yellow. Alex didn't have to impress anybody. The woman remained nameless, as she left the bathroom first, leaving Alex to find her way back outside.

The shuttle bus had arrived by the time Alex made it back outside in the afternoon swelter. Jay had disappeared again. Taking a swift glance around, Alex didn't spot Him before boarding the shuttle bus next-to-last. She sat next to a gentleman.

"Got enough room?" he asked, trying to embed his hip into the side of the padded black side panel.

"I've got more than enough room, sir," Alex said gleefully.

"Hi," the man twisted, "please call me Charlie." He extended his hand.

"Hi, Charlie," Alex said, smiling, "it's so nice to meet you. I'm Alex."

Charlie chortled. "My granddaughter's name is Alex." He reached for his cell phone and brought up a picture of her. "There she is."

"Oh, she is cute," sincerely she said. With a gentle jerk, the shuttle bus began to roll, headed the short distance to Harry Reid International Airport .

"Thank you, thank you," Charlie returned in a soft voice. "Will this be your first helicopter ride?"

"Oddly enough...no," Alex laughed, clasping her hands together, "about three weeks ago, I went on my first helicopter ride in Myrtle Beach."

"So, you are a helicopter junkie now?" Charlie prodded

kiddingly.

With her hands around one knee, she looked downward and smiled. "No, not at all," she began. "I was talking to my friend this morning and he told me I had to check out the Grand Canyon, so here I am."

"Driving across the country or something?"

Grinning widely, she nodded. "Something like that, yeah."

"Alone?!" Charlie barked.

Feeling like she was about to be scolded for being like a devious teenager, she cringed. "You could say that, yeah?"

"So, where is home for you?" He possessed the sweetest voice.

"I'm from Hopkinton, Massachusetts…near Boston," Alex uttered easily.

"Marathon starting town?!" he said excitedly.

"Have you been to the marathon?"

"I have…I have…," answered Charlie, as he was transported back. "My brother ran it back in 1976, because he was in college, and he was kind of a jock, you know. Somebody dared him and it took him seven hours to complete. He never did that again." Charlie's belly was jiggling with contagious laughter.

Alex caught his laughter bug.

"Have you ever run it?"

The very thought of herself running a cool 26.2 miles gave her the giggles. "Oh no…I could never run that far at one time, oh no—I would need about four days, with sleep in between, to finish the entire marathon." The giggles continued. "My mom ran it a few times though."

"Congratulations to your mom," expressed Charlie, in a higher tone.

"Yeah," she chortled, as she thought about seeing her very soon. "She's a running guru—very enthusiastic about running."

"The running thing didn't rub off on you, uh?"

With her head on the back of the shuttle seat, Alex shook her head. "Nah, I would much rather hike or walk than run any day of the week." Before they knew it, the shuttle pulled up to the helicopter area at the airport. "Are you from Vegas, Charlie?"

Giving a minimal sigh, he pushed up his silver-rimmed eyeglasses upon his nose. "No, no," Charlie drew out. "My wife and I live in Orange, California. Actually, this trip was scheduled for last year, before my sister was killed in the shooting." Charlie paused, gathering himself. "My wife is with my sister's wife now because she's dying of pancreatic cancer."

"Oh Charlie, I'm so sorry," Alex said, feeling horrible for this poor man. Their conversation was interrupted, as it was time to get off the shuttle bus and onto a sleek, red helicopter. Alex stayed close to him.

"My sister-in-law, Lu, insisted we come on this helicopter tour, but my wife wanted to stay with Lu, because my wife is a nurse, and finding the right kind of care is difficult."

A pilot directed their group to the second helicopter.

"Is Hospice involved with her palliative care?" Alex inquired. They boarded the second helicopter and listened to the pilot give his four passengers instructions to buckle themselves in and put their headsets on. Since Charlie had flown before, probably more than twice, he gave Alex helpful tips on the seatbelt harness. She felt safe and secure, tied to the tan leather seat for all eternity it seemed.

"We are all set back here, Jack," Charlie spoke to the pilot through the mic.

"Thank you, Charlie," Jack returned, monitoring the whirling of the rotors. "Here we go."

Maybe Charlie had flown a lot more than twice, most likely a half dozen times, Alex recalculated. When the helicopter started rolling forward to advance to the liftoff area, Alex was all-in, anticipating the striking tour to come into view. The helicopter finally lifted, as all eyes viewed the glittery city from above, leaving it behind for a while. It wasn't long before the bulk of the city was out of sight, just leaving widespread, untouched land below, as it slowly became more flora. The ground gradually turned into solid rock in tan and burnt orange tones. Heading southeast, far in the distance, mountainous ranges could be seen, in gentle purple hues—purple mountain majesty. Alex grabbed her phone from her back pocket and began snapping photos of the beginnings of the Grand Canyon. Charlie pointed out dramatic scenery that would wow people who never set eyes of the Grand Canyon. Alex even dared to take short video snippets of the approaching land masses.

"Hoover Dam will be coming up on our right," Jack announced into his mic and ran through everybody's headphones. All at once, four sets of eyes shifted to the left and downward, waiting for the great feat of the 1930s to come into view. From three thousand feet above the structure, it looked small, but, the concrete dam was massive, compared to the tiny cars that drove on the rim and on the bridge that straddled the girth of the Colorado River. The water of the Colorado was a bright and brilliant teal blue, shimmering from the afternoon sun, contrasting so well with the hard, rust-orange gorge the water carved out through millions of years, unfathomable for the human mind to fully comprehend. A lifetime remained a blip in time compared to 5.5 million years. It was tremendously beautiful to see what time and nature could do. It was also tremendously frightful how humans, ingenuity and time could take such a toll on nature, proven by the low level of water in Lake Mead, revealed by the white swathe of rock and sediment that had been under water. People wanted to deny science when science stared them right back in the face.

Alex was taking in everything around her—all the breathtaking views of the Canyon, and the magnitude of it all, were just incredible. Charlie pointed out things without speaking, not wanting to interrupt Jack's explanations. The other two people on the helicopter, clearly newlyweds, young and starry-eyed, kept to themselves. At times, when something in view arose, too good to pass up, Charlie grabbed his mic, muting his voice to everybody but Alex, he would put his own narrative on an area of the Canyon worthy of it. And Alex listened to his every word, as he temporarily adopted her as one of his own. Imitating Charlie, before Alex asked a follow-up question, she covered her mic and spoke in a hushed voice. Charlie was directly to her left, while the sweeping views of the massive formations of the Grand Canyon with only fiberglass and Plexiglas between, were to her right. For the rest of the flight to the designated landing plateau, Alex remained speechless, enthralled with all the beauty of one of the most astounding creations of nature on Earth.

The specified Canyon plateau welcomed the two helicopters like it did every weather-perfect day. Alex felt fortunate that the weather on that day was nearly flawless, only for a few, very few clouds that decorated the velvet blue sky. Once she got out of the helicopter, Alex felt the need to touch the ground beneath her feet just to see what 5.5 million years felt like, believing it would feel different from the rocky terrain of New England. There was more silt and dust in the Canyon, but rock felt like rock anywhere, she presumed. In her own world for a few minutes, Alex walked slowly around the plateau to look in every direction available to her; she didn't want to miss anything. Walking around the edge of the plateau, Alex stayed about 18 inches away from the very edge, thinking of her parents constantly. With her iPhone in hand, she clicked a dozen, two dozen, three dozen, four dozen photographs of the many layers, alternating in sand, rust, and taupe, as many small sprigs of green attached themselves all the way around the Canyon like barnacles would attach to a shipwrecked vessel under the surface of the sea. Alex looked in one direction and saw the Colorado River flowing easily at the bottom of the Canyon. The waters were calm where she glanced, but she knew in certain areas of the Canyon, the waters could be roaring and vicious, as if the river was trying to expel something that was unworthy to be there.

"Incredible, isn't it?" Charlie put forth, approaching Alex on her left.

With her arms crossed in front of her, Alex twisted her torso to acknowledge him. "Truly incredible," uttered Alex, still in awe.

Charlie gazed at it all, squinting his eyes. "I believe Jack is about to pop open the champagne bottles, if you want some."

Turning to see what was happening, people started to mingle around the picnic tables the helicopter tour guides had already placed on the plateau. "Oh, okay," Alex returned. Finding an empty side of a table, Alex sat down, facing out from the table. Charlie followed her lead and sat effortlessly on the picnic bench. Gauging Charlie to be around 60 years of age, the biggest thing on him was his stomach, covered in a maroon T-shirt that hung over his gray cargo shorts. His socks were white, and his sneakers dingy-white due to overuse. On his head was salt-and-pepper hair that covered most of it. His nonchalant appearance perfectly matched his easygoing personality.

Clear plastic cups were set up on the table, with Moët & Chandon champagne in them. She watched Charlie reach around to grab two cups of the bubbly and hand one to Alex. "Here you go."

"Oh, thank you, Charlie," Alex said, taking a tiny sip. "This is good—I haven't had bubbly in a while."

"Yeah, this is a good brand, and not too expensive," he spoke, sipping on his own cup. It was clear that he wanted to continue their conversation from before takeoff although he didn't want to be a bother.

Alex made it easy for him. "I'm a physician."

Hearing those words, Charlie cranked his gaze back to Alex, as if he just won a million dollars at a slot machine. "Somehow I knew you had something to do with healthcare from your question about Hospice," he confessed. "Yeah, we are lucky if they come once a day. My wife and daughter are just exhausted."

"When did Hospice begin?" Alex took another small sip of champagne.

Looking downward, Charlie scratched the top of his head, trying to come up with a date. "I think it has been like three weeks," Charlie surmised. "Lu hasn't been conscious for a few days now."

"She's a fighter," said Alex, stating what was obviously true.

"Oh, you have no idea," Charlie shared keenly, chuckling to cover up his hidden despair. "After my sister was shot, Lu, she just wouldn't give up on my sister, even though the doctors gave my sister a less-than-five percent chance of survival, and survival meant 24-hour care in some kind of long-term facility. I couldn't do that to my sister."

She was all too familiar with losing a sibling. "What was your sister's name?"

Exhaling his breath, Charlie took a bigger sip of champagne. "Her name was Casey," Charlie said, "Little Casey Louise, who just loved life."

In the spectacular environment she found herself in, surrounded by the beautiful layers of rock and silt, Alex realized why she was there. "I lost my brother, Nate, back in February," she expressed, without restraint, and without flinching. Lastly, she looked in Charlie's eyes.

Everything fell into place within Charlie's mind, instantly understanding what brought her to this place. "I am so sorry, Alex," Charlie mourned, because he knew how to mourn.

Breathing in the clear air of the Canyon, she held herself together. "Does it ever get easier?" Again, she turned to Charlie.

He shrugged, indicating that he didn't have any concrete answer. "I don't know, I don't know," Charlie began. "We just need to do the best we can while we are on Earth."

Alex couldn't argue with that. Flipping back her hair, Alex conjured up a plan for Lu in her final days. She saw it as her responsibility, and in her heart, she felt it. "Charlie, if it's alright with you and your wife, I'd like to assess Lu, and determine if she could benefit from anything else."

Words escaped Charlie at that very moment, lifting his eyeglasses, rubbing his tears away with his plump thumb and forefinger, he was overcome. "That is very generous of you, Alex."

Clasping her hands together upon one knee of her crossed legs, her head bobbed up and down. "Don't worry about it...Don't worry."

More tears welled in his eyes. "Thank you, Alex," Charlie expressed with bursting sincerity.

"Of course," she said softly, as she felt a gentle breeze surrounding her.

The stay on the Canyon plateau was ending; they had to get back to Vegas before dusk. Everybody got back into their assigned helicopters and kept to their seating choices as they flew out. After landing to fuel up, Jack, along with his colleagues, took off and headed back to Vegas, but not before passing over the Bowl of Fire, a very large crater of red-orange, dusty spires of rock, erupting out of this divot, enhanced by the setting sun. Alex needed pictures—she needed to show her parents, Conrad, and Justin.

Vegas came into view, as dusk remained minutes away. Seeing Vegas from above, with its lights turned on, the city didn't seem any different from all the Hollywood flicks and shows filmed there—Vegas was just another city to Alex. To Charlie, Vegas was a place entirely different; it was a sacred place where his sister, Casey, lived, loved, and died. As they passed over the golden-glittered exterior of the Mandalay Bay hotel, Alex observed Charlie choking back tears. Even though she wanted to, Alex resisted putting her hand on his shoulder to comfort him. The sun just disappeared below the western horizon without too much fanfare.

The shuttle dropped the Grand Canyon guests off where they had been picked up. Serendipitously, Alex's and Charlie's cars were parked about twenty feet apart. Alex would follow Charlie to Lu's townhouse, northwest of the city, as he avoided city traffic and took all the back roads, which were minimally lit, as all the businesses were closed for the day. Within ten minutes, Alex followed Charlie into one of several entrances that led to the middle section of a sprawling townhouse complex, which could have stretched half a mile, north and east, every townhouse looking the same. It was hard to tell what shade the beige was, because it was everywhere; the only difference within all these sets of condos was what each resident hung on the front door, if anything at all. Charlie pulled into an empty space. Getting out of his silver Nissan sedan, Charlie waved her into the space next to his. Alex, turning off the Camry, got out, opened the trunk and began to look for her stethoscope and blood pressure cuff. As she dug through all her extra clothes and camping gear, not in any organizational order, it hit Alex that she hadn't used these very common medical instruments since before Nate died. Before leaving Boston, it occurred to her that it might be wise to bring her stethoscope and blood pressure cuff, not knowing if she would encounter any situation in which they might be needed. It was easy to berate herself for the past six months of wallowing, although it was even easier to let it go. The lost medical instruments were found, in the

capable hands of a young doctor. Closing her trunk with authority, as
the typical sound echoed within the square of indistinguishable condos,
Charlie was impressed with Alex's physical strength.

Alex followed Charlie through one of the doors nearby, into a
small lighted foyer, painted white, as it led into a living space, and beyond
that, a moderate-sized kitchen. Alex saw a woman, pretty, but obviously
tired. She was watching television on the cushiony, blue fabric couch.
Wearing casual khaki shorts and a light-pink blouse, she got to her feet
to hug Charlie.

He kissed her easily on the lips. "Jane, I would like you to meet
Alex."

Jane, with her blond hair that surrounded her spherically shaped
face, kindly shook Alex's hand, giving her a light embrace. "Oh Alex, it's
so generous of you to come. It's so nice," Jane uttered through her
tiredness. "Can I get you something to eat or drink?"

"Some water would be great, thank you," Alex returned, as she
walked further into the living room, putting her palms together. "May I
use your facilities?"

"Oh yes, of course," Jane expressed, directing Alex to the
downstairs bathroom just around the corner.

"Thank you very much," Alex extended politely. She quickly did
what she needed to do and rejoined Charlie and Jane. "May I assess Lu?"

"Absolutely," said Jane, relieved and more relaxed.

Alex grabbed her stethoscope and her blood pressure cuff she
had placed on the nearby side table.

"Ever since Lu became unable to walk, we had to move her
bedroom downstairs," Jane explained, as she walked toward a room, of
which the door remained opened. A wheelchair, folded, was set against
the wall next to the doorway.

Remaining quiet, Alex entered the interim bedroom behind Jane.
Before Alex got a view of Lu, she noticed the countless pictures and
photographs, some Scotch-taped to the wall, especially the photos that
were taped to the light-gray painted wall over Lu's head, which lied still
on a white pillow. Lu lay on her back. "A lot of pictures," she
commented in a low voice, studying several images carefully, matching
up the smiling face to the sedated woman. A dog, maybe weighing
between 60 and 70 pounds, with a brindle pattern on his back, and a
white underbelly, put his head up, gazing at her.

"That's Justice."

Hearing his name created something to pang in Alex's stomach, not knowing if he was friend or foe, although if he had a tendency to be aggressive toward strangers, she surmised Charlie and Jane would have placed Justice in a safe place. There was a folding chair at the side of the queen-size bed. "May I sit?"

"Sure, sure," Jane said, as she sat on the edge of the bed, paying attention to Alex's next move.

To begin, Alex gently touched Lu's exposed arm and hand to gauge her body temperature. Lu's skin was soft and cool. Alex took into consideration the air conditioning was on, and reached under the dense handmade quilt, with turquoise, burnt orange, maroon, black and white, in a traditional Native American pattern. Lu's legs and feet were a little bit warmer.

"This morning her legs were kind of cool," Jane remarked, clearly in tune with what Alex was doing.

"Do you want to give them another feel?" suggested Alex, preparing to check Lu's heartrate, as she made sure the stethoscope temperature was warm. "Lu," quietly began Alex, "my name is Alex; I'm a physician, and I'm going to listen to your heart. Will that be okay?" She gazed down at Lu's face, slightly pale with her eyes closed. There was a slight layer of gray hair that had grown back since her last chemotherapy treatment. Through looking at the photos on the wall, Alex knew that before the cancer diagnosis, Lu's hair was long and thick, with streaks of black and gray—a beautiful woman that her wife, Casey, loved so much—a love which radiated off the walls of photographs. With no evident response from Lu, Alex went ahead and placed the stethoscope on her chest and listened. Lu's heartbeat was fast although weak.

"Her legs and feet are somewhat cooler than they were this morning," Jane reported.

Charlie came into the room with Alex's glass of cold water and handed it to her. "How is she?"

Alex grabbed the water from Charlie, taking a sip or two. "She's comfortable." Standing up, Alex walked out of the room and into the kitchen, placing her glass on the counter. Charlie and Jane followed. "May I see her charts from hospice?"

"Sure, sure," Jane said, and fetched them off the round dining room table, noticing Alex followed.

Sitting at the table, Alex began to peruse the charts, carefully and methodically. She was most interested in the last few days. "Have you noticed if Lu became anxious at all in the last few days, because I don't see any anti-anxiety drugs prescribed?" Looking up, Alex saw Charlie scoff in frustration, as he looked at Jane.

Jane rubbed her palms together. "I did mention that the other day to the nurse because Lu was agitated the previous night, all night," narrated Jane, "but the nurse said anxiety drugs weren't necessary for end-of-life care."

"Do you use anxiety drugs for end-of-life care at your hospital in Orange?" Alex asked Jane.

"All the time," said Jane, sitting down and becoming emotional.

Out of the corner of her left eye, Alex caught Charlie approaching Jane, putting his burly arms around her, kissing her on the cheek. "I'll call the nurse first thing in the morning and see if I can get anything prescribed for Lu."

"Alex, please can I get you something to eat?" begged Charlie.

It was hard for Alex to ignore her growling stomach. "Okay," she surrendered.

"We have some pepperoni pizza that our daughter left earlier. Jane made potato and leek soup the other day—it's delicious," Charlie paraded.

"Oh, soup sounds really good right now," Alex said, thinking it was an odd craving when the temperature still hovered around 85, as it neared 10 p.m. It must have been her New England bones that craved the hearty soup, or it was the sense that she was going to eat something homecooked. Whatever it was, she needed to eat.

"Charlie tells me you are from Boston," Jane presented, sitting three feet away.

"I am, I am," Alex answered, her voice lifted.

"I'm assuming you went to med school there; it's the best area to study medicine." Jane stood to help Charlie bring bowls of steaming-hot potato and leek soup to the table.

Alex rose to her feet and grabbed a bowl from Charlie, as he also had in his hand a bag of rolls to share. "I went to Tufts Medical School, and I started my residency, but had to pull back a little bit after I lost my brother," Alex recounted, realizing it was becoming easier and easier to talk about Nate, to anyone, really.

"Charlie told me about that as well," Jane said with a kind tone—caring and soft. "I'm so, so sorry for your loss."

Sitting back down, she was truly grateful for all that she had at that moment. "I thank you, Jane," returned Alex. "I'm sorry for your loss, too. Charlie told me about Casey. I can't imagine."

Charlie sat. "Can we discuss something else besides death for the moment, please? Let's talk about how spectacular our trip was today."

With her eyes downward, buttering her roll, Alex looked up and smiled. "It was a pretty awesome helicopter ride."

Charlie, Jane, and Alex enjoyed sitting down over a meal and being present, talking easily because they understood each other's pain, past and in the moment. Jane needed sleep, evident from the dark circles under her weary eyes. Alex offered to stay with Lu, in the oversized, sage chair in the corner of Lu's room. Jane, feeling the guilt rise within her, resisted Alex's offer until Charlie demanded his wife get a full night's sleep, knowing she hadn't had one in too many nights to count. Jane surrendered and went upstairs. Charlie cleaned up the kitchen from dinner. What he had to do would just take ten minutes, and with Alex's help, it would take even less. Before retreating upstairs with his wife, he made sure Alex had everything she needed: pillows, blankets, towels, and Charlie offered her anything in the kitchen that Alex would ever care to drink or nibble on. After three weeks on the road, dealing with setting up and breaking down her tent, in rain or shine, dark or light, fighting off mosquitos and undetermined insect species, she kind of welcomed not worrying about all that stuff, and instead, cared for a dying human being, giving some relief to her exhausted family. Charlie let Justice out one last time for the night.

Checking the time—11:14 p.m. Pacific Time, and too damn late in Boston—Alex just sent a brief text to her parents, figuring her dad would see it first in the middle of the night. For a short time, Alex fell asleep on the living room couch, wearing the same clothes, although barefoot. A wet nose touched her exposed arm, sparking Alex awake. It took a fraction of a second to orientate herself to where she was, as Justice continued to nudge at her arm until she moved. With only the light from the large television on the wall that abutted the staircase, Alex forced her eyes open to see Justice bouncing backwards with his eyes glued to her. As Alex sat, fairly certain Justice wasn't in attack mode, she followed him into Lu's room, where she found Lu agitated, with her extremities in constant motion. Out of compassion, Alex stroked Lu's anguished face and whispered her presence. An hour and a half had passed since the last course of midazolam strengthened with a fentanyl patch on Lu's upper right arm. Lu had one last bolus to be administered. *First, do no harm*, Alex reminded herself. She hurried to get Lu's chart from the dining room, and dashed back beside Lu's bedside, comparing how often Lu received her boluses in the 24 to 48 hours. Boluses had increased, although the level of midazolam hadn't. It was 2:48 a.m. and the nurse from the hospice local branch was not arriving until 7 a.m. Alex decided to administer Lu's last bolus and immediately got on the phone with Hospice. Out in the dimly lit kitchen, Alex impatiently waited for her call to be answered, as she was unable to stand in one place. Through the low light, Alex noticed Jane coming down the stairs in her lighter colored fluffy robe, reaching the kitchen.

"On hold?" Jane asked, without really having to ask. She took a seat on a barstool across from Alex.

"Yep," Alex returned, holding her cell to her right ear. "Is this a common occurrence?"

"Yep," Jane ricocheted back, watching Alex's annoyance sprawled over her face.

"Can't sleep?"

Jane shook her head. "I saw Lu was agitated again—I wanted to help."

"I was hoping you would get more sleep," said Alex softheartedly, still holding her cell.

"Yeah, sleep is kind of nonexistent at the moment," said Jane, stretching her arms out across the island, recoiling them back, as one bent, supporting her head. "I have known Lu for the better part of thirty years; when I met Charlie, Casey and Lu were already together," Jane narrated memories that delighted her. "Lu was a communications specialist during the Gulf War, and then was hired by a private company here in Vegas; Casey was an executive manager of MGM."

"Oh wow," Alex uttered.

"Yeah," replied Jane, as she looked vacantly into the corner of the kitchen. "When Lu became sick, she took early retirement, which didn't amount to a heck of a lot. Then Casey began working part-time to be with Lu for all her appointments, her chemo and of course everything else that goes along with a cancer diagnosis. They went to the country music festival last year, and Casey was killed. I don't think worse things can happen." In the deep, dark hours of a Monday morning, Jane wept for what was lost, and who was soon to be lost.

Alex looked upon Jane, recognizing her grief, that vacant space in her chest that might be filled on day. It was a challenge for Alex to hold it together, but she had to, because she was a professional, and professionals cry when nobody is around. "Does Lu have any other family?" Alex asked quietly.

Jane cleared her round face of tears. "Lu only has us," she said. "Way back when Lu and Casey got together, her parents disowned her because she was gay. Even when Lu's parents died, she wasn't allowed to attend the memorial or the burials." Jane went on, "I believe if her mother had passed after her father, she would have reached out to Lu."

The iPhone now rested on Alex's shoulder, as she hung on the line waiting for somebody to answer—anybody. "Oh God, that's so sad."

"Exactly," Jane professed and jolted her arms forward in disappointment. "I mean, what parents could disown their own child?"

Shrugging her free shoulder, Alex looked at Jane without an answer. "My two friends just adopted a baby girl." Handling her iPhone, Alex shuffled screens around and brought the newest shot of Lila with her dads, showing it to Jane.

Happily gasping, Jane smiled at the image. "Oh my gosh, she's such a doll! What's her name?"

"Lila Alexandra," Alex gushed—her heart leaping.

Jane glanced at Alex. "Aww…she has your name as her middle name. So sweet."

"I haven't held her yet, but soon," Alex said, still gushing.

"Are you heading home soon?" asked Jane.

"Once I reach San Francisco, I'm going to head home."

"What's in San Fran that you want to see?" Jane followed up.

Looking downward, Alex scratched her temple. "I'm not sure, really," she easily confided. "It has been a while since I've walked on a beach. I really look forward to doing that."

"You should drive up the Pacific Coast Highway; it's just so beautiful, especially at this time of year. It'll take longer, but it is totally worth it," Jane suggested, forgetting for a split second that death was approaching in the adjacent room.

Alex heard Jane, acknowledging the recommendation, but she knew she had to play every route by ear. "That sounds nice," Alex remarked, smiling, as the frustration rose from her chest—nobody was picking up her call after 45 minutes of waiting; Lu was comfortable now, at that very moment, but nobody knew what the next moment had in store. A fight was approaching, but Alex and Jane didn't know when or what tools they would use to defend Lu from pain. Alex retreated to the oversized chair three feet away from Lu, while Jane went back upstairs to attempt to get more shuteye before the enemy invaded once again. Alex got comfortable in the chair and quickly drifted off to sleep.

The sun, off the white sand, bounced off the inside walls of the small shack with triangles of bright light, waking Alex. She immediately got up and walked out onto the beach, looking to the right, and to the left, only seeing one person—a woman, dancing on the beach, so singularly and brilliantly. It was Lu dancing, wearing a mini black halter dress, the top of which was made from lace, and wearing her hair down, long and thick. Lu had no notion that anyone was watching her dance like a ballerina, nor would she have cared. Continuing to watch Lu's beautiful, solitary dance, barefoot in the sand, someone walked up on her left side, joining her in this private production. Looking to her left, Alex saw Nate. Nate wore a bright white short-sleeved shirt with matching white casual pants, barefoot as well. Nate's arms were crossed in front of his chest, with an ease she had never witnessed; she was unable to see the inner sides of his wrists. Alex began talking to Nate, as if she had already talked to him only an hour before, so tied up in his expression and how happy he looked, gazing at Lu dancing upon the sun-drenched white sand. Daring to look at Nate's face for longer than a millisecond—young, bright, and handsome, with his hair like it always was, brown and slightly wavy—and as Lu's elegant movement kept his attention, Alex inquired what he thought Lu was doing. Once he spoke, Alex almost lost her breath, never imagining she would hear his voice again. So sweet and light, as Alex remembered it, Nate explained that Lu was doing the Dance of the Soul's Flight, where the soul prepares to move onto the next kingdom. With her eyes fixated on Lu's fluidity, Alex crossed her own arms, and posed to Nate if he did the Dance of the Soul's Flight, turning toward him. Nate didn't answer right away, still enthralled with Lu. As he swayed a little, twisting his hips leisurely, Nate explained that he indeed did the Dance of the Soul's Flight, albeit, abbreviated, due to the suddenness of his death. His Dance of the Soul's Flight wasn't compromised, described Nate to a riveted Alex, although he would have enjoyed a longer duration to dance. She wasn't quite sure what the Dance of the Soul's Flight brought to the dying, but she just reveled in standing beside Nate and in standing on the white sand beach, feeling the warm sun and the breeze that accompanied it. Sister and brother stood side by side, enjoying the strengthening sunlight and the bright blue ocean in the background, transfixed on Lu performing her Dance of the Soul's Flight without a thread of trepidation.

She heard an unfamiliar sound, a buzz of some sort, jolting Alex awake, as she sat up on the oversized chair, grounding herself of her location. Instead of watching Lu dance, she saw her incapacitated in the bed. The buzz went off again, and Alex threw the blue-and-gold Afghan off her legs, rising to her feet. Exiting the room, Alex found Jane descending the staircase, and going to answer the door. Alex stood back and allowed Jane to communicate to the young nurse, maybe around the age of 30, all her concerns, which were Alex's concerns, about Lu's current state. Before the nurse assessed Lu's condition, Jane introduced Alex to the nurse, Laurel—stating Alex's profession. Alex watched Laurel's eyes, steely with a touch of blue, inspecting her, probably believing she couldn't possibly be a doctor, dressed like an oaf. Laurel barely shook Alex's hand and went on to assess Lu. Laurel's blond ponytail and electric-blue scrubs disappeared into Lu's makeshift bedroom. Alex took advantage of the moment to use the bathroom, and to reflect on the dream she had just left two minutes prior. Still in a sleep fog, Alex kept sitting on the toilet even though it wasn't necessary anymore. A smile came across her face when the image of Nate entered her mind. Alex wanted to know if the dream was more of an indication that Nate was assuredly okay. She wanted to believe that—she needed to believe that. Two more minutes passed, and Alex washed her hands and left the bathroom. Jane was leaning on the kitchen island because sitting on a chair would just make the nervous tension that much worse. Alex joined Jane at the kitchen island, not knowing that just her presence eased Jane's mind.

"Can I make you some coffee or tea?" Jane offered, needing to keep her hands occupied.

"Tea would be great," Alex gratefully replied. "Were you able to sleep a little?" She watched Jane walk around the island, fill the kettle, and place it on the range.

"I think I may have gotten two hours or so—better than any other night," Jane said, throwing her hands in her robe pockets and leaning her backside against the counter. "How 'bout you? Were you able to get some sleep?"

Already propping her chin on her palm, curling her fingers outside her bottom lip, Alex shuffled her weight between her bare feet on the Rushmore Rock porcelain tile, azure in hue, cool and refreshing. "I must have slept because I dreamt."

From Alex's calm eyes, Jane couldn't imagine her pain. It wasn't a nightmare, but she didn't want to assume. "Good dream?"

Alex took in some cool air between her teeth. "Compared to

other dreams I've had over the last six months or so, this dream was okay…it was okay." Bowing her neck to the right, she smiled.

Jane was on the verge of asking a follow-up question, but Laurel emerged from Lu's bedroom. "How's Lu?" Jane knew it was a ridiculous question to ask, but she asked anyway.

"At the moment, she's resting…" Laurel said, and abruptly stopped.

"Lu was not comfortable last night; she was very agitated," Alex said, advocating for Lu. "She has no order for an anti-anxiety med. Can I ask why?" Once this question leaped from her lips, Alex saw the resentment in Laurel's eyes.

"I believe Lu should be on anti-anxiety meds also," Jane injected, siding with Alex. "At my hospital in Orange, anti-anxiety drugs are protocol for end-of-life care."

Laurel shifted her eyes between Jane and Alex, not knowing who to address first. She addressed Jane first. "Lu's medical history doesn't specify she was ever prescribed anti-anxiety medication. Introducing anti-anxiety at this stage might not prove beneficial."

"What if they do prove beneficial?" Alex rebelled, so confident in her knowledge.

Laurel stood in place, not wanting to be second-guessed in her profession. Taking her gritty eyes off Alex, Laurel switched to Jane. "Do you agree with her suggestions?"

Alex did not appreciate Laurel's brushing over her name and profession.

"Yes," Jane answered with authority, "I wholeheartedly agree with Alex's assessment." It was then that Jane saw Charlie come downstairs, wearing the gray cargo shorts and a lighter-blue short-sleeved shirt, with tan slippers.

It was easy for Charlie to notice the stress that lay upon his wife. "Morning, Laurel," he spoke. Charlie hadn't experienced a 'good morning' in a year or so, since Lu was diagnosed. It didn't get better. "How's Lu?" He watched Laurel's hard eyes transitioning between Jane and Alex.

"Are you okay with me calling the doctor to see if he will prescribe an anti-anxiety medication for Lu?" asked Laurel.

"Absolutely…absolutely," Charlie replied, aware what the plan was all along. He trusted his wife, whose medical ideology paralleled Alex's.

The count was three to one, with Laurel being the one. This

wasn't a competition, although Laurel might have felt like they wanted to win. "Excuse me, I'm going to call the physician."

Alex dared to make another order. "I feel Lu needs an increase in the midazolam dosage. Her pain will increase."

Laurel stopped, and then turned. "Would you like to talk to the physician yourself?" she inquired in a cutting tone.

Alex was taken aback, as was Charlie.

"Here's what I'd like you to do, Laurel," snapped Charlie, "I would like for you to call the physician, tell him Lu Benally's family wants another nurse, and that he should call me immediately after he gets off the phone with you. He has my number."

Locked in a stalemate stare with Charlie, fully knowing she didn't have a defense of her rudeness, her impatience, would ever right the ship, Laurel acquiesced. "Of course," Laurel spoke, indifferent and without emotion. She walked out through the door when Charlie opened it.

Closing the door gently, Charlie looked back at Jane and Alex, questioning if he had done right or wrong by Lu. "Now we wait," he announced, coming back into the living space and joining Jane and Alex at the kitchen island.

"I'm going to check on Lu," announced Alex, aware that Jane and Charlie might need time to talk about what decisions needed to be made next. Entering Lu's room, Alex noticed she hadn't been turned to reduce the chances of bed sores. Alex turned Lu at 5 a.m. that morning, and she would do it again. Justice still lay on the left side of the bed, where it butted up to the wall. Like at 5 a.m., Justice hopped off the bed when Alex changed Lu's brief. Alex would do all that and more; judging by the way things hadn't been moved, Laurel had done the bare minimum in that five-or-so minutes she was with Lu. Alex took great measures, positioning everything meticulously, to ensure nothing would get caught up in the repositioning. From the collection of pictures all over the room, Lu was a small woman; pancreatic cancer had diminished her muscles and skin. Little by little, Alex tugged gently on the cloth bed pad until Lu was in a satisfactory position. Lastly, Alex repositioned Lu's head on the pillow, making sure her neck was always supported and her airway not contorted, so breathing wouldn't be cumbersome. It already started to be cumbersome. Reaching for her stethoscope on the oversized chair, Alex listened to Lu's lungs and heart. Compared to the night before, she noticed more fluid in her lungs. Her heart rate had slowed somewhat but hadn't weakened. Stepping back, she caught a glimpse of the doorway, seeing Jane looking on, crying.

"I was watching you for a few minutes," Jane admitted easily, weeping. "You're pretty great at what you do, and we can't thank you enough."

Not taking compliments easily, which was nothing new, Alex allowed her neck to tilt and smiled. "I'm just doing what needs to be done."

Pushing herself off from the doorjamb, Jane walked to the oversized chair and sat. "Her color is a little off today," she remarked, staring at Lu's peaceful expression. "The only comfort I have is she'll be with Casey soon. If two people were meant to be together for eternity, it would be them."

Tingles sped up and down Alex's spine as she looked at some of their pictures on the wall, now drenched in sunlight. One photo captured Lu and Casey, dressed to the nines, in celebration, allowing Alex to see all the love for herself. "Great picture," Alex said softly. Stepping back, Alex sat carefully on the edge of Lu's bed. "When was that taken?"

Jane repositioned herself on the oversized chair, as she pointed to it. "That was their second ceremony, taken overooking Lake Mead, when same-sex marriage became legal in Nevada. That was a fun wedding," Jane said, grinning. Once she turned her head back toward Alex, she glanced at Lu, smiling. "Look," Jane whispered excitedly.

Alex followed Jane's eyes to Lu's smiling face. As Jane stood, Alex followed her lead, switching places with her. She watched Jane pour her love over Lu, stroking the top of her head, telling her that she was loved. Sitting back on the oversized chair, Alex just observed the precious moment between family. It was often believed by many people that the dying person, especially if potent pain medication flowed throughout their bodies, were unheeding to everything, including every conversation happening around them. The last sense to wane before death was hearing. If Casey couldn't be the voice heard in the last moments of her life, Jane wanted it to be her and Charlie's voices when Lu left this Earth. Alex recalled that she was the last voice Nate heard, although she wasn't positive about it, she would like it to be true. She recalled that the last moments of Nate's life were chaotic, irrational, brutal and sudden, with no time to be accepting of his inevitable death when she was fighting like hell to save him. That was her job. Maybe she failed at just his final moments, Alex thought. Had she said enough to him? Had she made him feel loved and accepted, as his blood drained from his body? Alex told herself she did what she was capable of while frenzied and completely overcome.

Settling into what might be an undetermined amount of time, Alex was asked to stay until Lu took her final breath. Charlie and Jane insisted on compensating Alex, but she refused, believing it would be wrong of her to do so when she had proposed the plan. In a city where money changed hands, probably every five seconds, for items or services most mankind thought seedy, even criminal, Alex could not have accepted compensation. Jay wanted her to come to Vegas. Whether it was to assist Charlie and Jane with Lu, or some other reason, Alex was content with what Jay wanted her to do.

Charlie spent about an hour on the phone trying to convince the Hospice manager that Lu needed a new plan, and subsequently, a new lead nurse to work closely with Jane and Alex to develop Lu's comfort plan. The manager agreed. It would be a few more hours before the nurse came. Alex ate breakfast with Jane and Charlie, and then showered in the upstairs bath. The sun was strong, as it brought another hot day to the southwest. Alex wanted to go for a walk, but it was much too hot. Even Charlie just stepped down the front stairs to let Justice do his business. Justice was content keeping vigil beside Lu. Charlie and Jane decided to go to the store to pick up some essentials, leaving Alex to tend to a sleeping Lu. She took advantage of this time to call her parents to let them know she was fine and explain what she was doing. They were proud of their daughter although so anxious to have her home but remaining quiet on her account. Trusting Alex was easy to do. Since her father was a professor of Gerontology, Alex picked his brain about end-of-life care, and what approaches were the most prudent. It was simply exultant for Michael to discuss medical topics with his daughter, even though the talk about dying could be heavy at times. Michael showered in eternal guilt daily, knowing his daughter had found her brother, minutes from death, in a pool of blood. Michael only saw the aftermath of his son's death in Alex's then apartment the next morning, refusing to allow Joanne to see it. If he couldn't protect his daughter, Michael would surely protect his wife. There on that cold, late February morning, Michael had sat on the hardwood floor in front of his son's blood, tracking from the small bath to the kitchen, and had cried without mercy for a straight hour. Death was something father and daughter shared professionally, and so personally.

Joanne worried Alex was spreading herself too thin, but she promised her mother she was doing very well. Being preoccupied with Lu, Alex had forgotten to send the Grand Canyon pictures, which she did right there and then. Joanne was grateful for the gorgeous pictures of the canyon, and some pictures of Alex. Any picture of Alex was gold to Joanne; hearing her voice was priceless. Trying not to be overly transparent with wanting her daughter to come home as quickly as possible, to throw her arms around her and not let her go, to shower her with all the love she possibly could, Joanne posed questions about Lu, knowing full well that Alex may not be able to divulge much information. What she was able to reveal was the dream she had had that morning. Alex made sure she didn't gloss over one little speck of detail of the dream since it was their late son and their daughter starring in the unconscious film. She started at the beginning, describing waking up in some beach shack and walking out on a sun-filled beach full of white sand. Alex switched the call to FaceTime and sunk into the couch, relaying the actions and her observations, especially what Nate was doing, saying, and wearing. There were laughs and smiles than tears of sorrow. They thoroughly enjoyed watching their daughter's face sparkle like fireworks when she described how she felt just standing beside Nate; even if it was just a dream, he was well and happy, as contentment absorbed into his skin from the rays from the sun. His eyes were profoundly tranquil, as Nate watched Lu's choreography on the beach with the ocean behind her. Alex couldn't help but to notice her parents' eyes blossom at all that she revealed about the gratifying dream. Whereas Lu neared the last days of her life, Alex was realizing she had her whole life ahead, and she wasn't about to surrender.

Charlie and Jane returned to Lu's townhouse well before the new Hospice nurse arrived. It was going on four hours since Lu had gotten her full bag of midazolam. Charlie and Jane brought back food essentials: milk, bread, chicken, eggs, and other various things to munch on. Alex guessed it might be a challenge to know how much food to buy, not knowing when that time would come. In the past few hours, Alex noticed that the rattle had started in Lu's throat, indicating she was losing her ability to swallow or clear secretions. This prompted Alex to turn Lu more on her side, so Lu wouldn't struggle, placing a towel beneath her cheek. She informed Jane of this development, and Jane told Charlie. When they went into her room, the rattle couldn't be overlooked. Alex stood in the doorway for several minutes, watching Charlie and Jane sit quietly, holding Lu's hand. Jane found the tube of body lotion and began to massage in the lotion onto Lu's hands and arms while she talked slowly and tenderly to her, reminding her she was loved—always loved. Alex had to wonder if Lu was still dancing on the beach, as she saw her do in her dream. She wondered if she had an audience. It didn't matter if the audience was of one or of many; Alex wondered if Nate was still watching Lu dance in the realm Alex had been transported to in her dream.

The doorbell rang again, alerting all who surrounded Lu, reminding them that the visitor would bring the cruel reality back to what was about to happen. Charlie, Jane, and Alex sat with Barbara, a veteran nurse older than Jane, probably ready to retire. Barbara stood tall and steady, dressed in the same electric-blue scrubs. She had black-rimmed eyeglasses which sat under her pulled-back gray hair. Whereas Laurel just carried a yellow legal pad, Barbara had a leather bag, filled with notepads, pamphlets, and pens. Whereas Laurel was brisk, Barbara was kind, and listened. Barbara had already reviewed Lu's charts, and asked Charlie and Jane what they wanted for Lu, altogether knowing their options were very limited. Jane spoke for them both and told Barbara they wanted Lu to be as comfortable as possible, emphasizing the use of anti-anxiety meds. Barbara agreed to that, and also agreed to increase the midazolam, which she had with her. Before Barbara entered Lu's room, Charlie fetched Justice and took him for a short walk in the brutal, Nevada sun. It took Barbara about twenty minutes to switch out the midazolam IV bags and program the infusion pump. Since Lu already had a central line from her chemo regiments, connecting the IV was quick. Alex watched Barbara do all this, and everything came back to her—all the hours she had spent in clinical learning the protocols of each drug, and how to calculate how many milligrams to administer for a specific weight for each patient.

With Lu set, with an increase of midazolam running through her veins, repositioned in her bed, and with her brief changed—the old brief hardly damp—Alex needed to go for a walk. In the last hour, clouds had collected in the southern, Nevada sky, dropping the temperature a miniscule two degrees. Alex lubed herself with sunscreen, and dared to take on the suffocating heat. Charlie suggested she visit Centennial Hills Park, where she could walk freely. Alex thanked Charlie and promised she would return in a few hours, leaving her stethoscope and blood pressure cuff as collateral. Centennial Hills was a mere five-minute drive from Lu's townhouse complex. Alex parked and got out, as she walked leisurely into the park, seeing children playing on colorful slides, monkey bars, swings, tunnels, and other various playground equipment. People sat at picnic tables under porticos that provided some necessary shade.

Alex sought out the paved walking trail and walked on the dirt path beside it. Within time, Jay started walking beside her, as she was expecting His arrival.

"Are you doing alright?" Jay pressed, matching her easy stride with His hands in His pockets.

Looking to her right, as Jay walked on her left, Alex breathed in the warm air. "Yeah, I'm doing alright," she stated with confidently, looking back at Him. "It's tough to watch someone pass away, but I know what cancer does to a body. My job is to keep dying patients as comfortable as possible."

"Oh wow," Jay said, "I thought you were going to read Me the riot act, and tell Me how I could save Lu, and how I'm not doing My job."

Letting free a giggle, Alex gazed back at Him. "Nah…Something tells me she wants to go be with Casey."

Holding His face to the sun, Jay walked proudly. "You're probably right."

With Jay by her side, Alex walked a few minutes without speaking. The peace cleared her mind, as she tried to think about nothing in the moment, which was hard for Alex to do for more than five minutes. "Am I doing right by Lu?"

"You're the doctor—you tell Me," He bounced back on her.

"Why can't You just give me Your opinion?" she pressed with gentle frustration. "Why do You always want my opinion? You can be so squishy sometimes."

Jay laughed hard, snapping back His neck. "Squishy? That's a new one. I don't think I have ever been called 'squishy' before."

"You know what I mean."

"Of course I know what you mean, but it's not My job to reveal how to feel; you have a mind of your own. All I ask of you, and every human being, is to have humanity and kindness for others, but you knew that already."

Alex took a sip of her water. "I just want Lu to be as comfortable as possible, you know?"

"I know, Alex, and you are doing well," Jay confirmed.

After He spoke these words, Alex was able to breathe a sigh of relief. She still wanted to do better, and she vowed to do so. "What have You been up to around Vegas? Have You helped anyone win a lot of cash?"

"Maybe, maybe not," Jay teased, smiling mischievously.

Looking at Him, she smiled and shook her head. "You can't even tell me that?" Alex begged.

"Okay…Okay…Maybe I did," He confessed gleefully.

"So, You don't consider that cheating, not even a little bit?" said Alex, very animated in her expression.

"I would refer it to as luck," Jay concluded, laughing hysterically, clapping His hands together.

"Oh my God," Alex began, giggling. "Ever think about going on the stage?" Obviously, this wasn't meant to be a serious question, but an observation.

"Come on, laughter is good for the soul, even on the darkest of days; if someone can laugh about anything, anything at all, then the bad days might be manageable," Jay said.

"I don't think I laughed for three or four months."

"It was four and a half months," clarified Jay, as this preciseness threw her back on her heels.

"Really—You know that?!" Alex looked toward Jay, astonished. She continued to walk.

"Well, yes."

Flipping back her black hair, sweaty and untamed, Alex glanced at Jay. "Still a little creepy, Dude—I'm just saying."

He smiled because she smiled. "Forgive Me for My appearance of being 'creepy'," said Jay, actually using air quotes. "You had Me worried."

Alex gave Jay an inquisitive glance. "Why?"

"You were so lost in your grief that I wanted you to get home every afternoon from the cemetery," Jay reveled. Another inquisitive look came in His direction.

"Why didn't You make Yourself known then?" asked Alex.

"You weren't ready," Jay started, glancing at her. "Things were still very raw for you, and I knew you wouldn't accept Me." As They continued walking on the path, Jay observed Alex, reflective, in her own silence. "I needed you to get away from home."

Standing a little bit straighter, Alex had a question of her own. "What if I never left Boston when I did?"

Jay smiled. "I knew it was inevitable that you were going to get away—you had to; it was in the stars."

Alex investigated the deep-blue Vegas sky. "In the stars, ay?" she rhetorically repeated. "Lucky me." Ten minutes went by, and They found themselves back at the entrance of the park. The crowd had grown at the park within the twenty minutes since she had run into Jay. Pulling out her iPhone from her pocket, she checked the time. "I'd better get back to Lu. Will You be around?" Alex asked Jay as if He was just one of her guy friends who she might meet for a drink after work.

Jay silently chortled, giving her a silly look. "I'm always around, Kiddo."

"I know, I know," Alex giggled. "Walk me to my car."

"Yes, of course." Jay followed her the short distance to the Camry. "This thing might need an oil change soon."

"Yeah, I know," she said, easy in her tone. "I thought I'd wait until We got to San Fran to change it." She opened the door and got in.

"Yeah, that's fine," Jay said, hanging His fingers over the top of the car door. "See you soon."

From His voice, she sensed that was more a statement than a question. The statement meant more than just seeing Him, it meant He would guide Lu's spirit into the Kingdom of Heaven, much like He had done with Seth in Omaha, and Nate in Boston. "Yeah, I'll see You soon."

The solemnness in her voice pierced Him, shattering Him like crystal. Once Alex started the engine, He closed the car door, giving her a gentle wave.

Unexpectedly, Alex's chest heaved a few times, as tears filled her eyes. It was difficult to pinpoint exactly what it was in her heart that was causing her to be melancholy; she felt certain it was that she would need to say goodbye to Him soon, very soon indeed. As swiftly as the sadness had surged over her, it was gone.

Nobody seemed hungry when the evening came across Vegas, not even Justice. Charlie begged him to eat, even enticing him with fresh green beans in his kibble, but he just wouldn't eat. Alex covertly had the pizza in the refrigerator, picking off the pepperoni. She felt guilty that she was so hungry, although being hungry meant she was focused and calm, able to do the task she was asked to do. It was another long and emotional day for Jane and Charlie, advocating for Lu much like Casey would have advocated for Lu, or so they hoped. Completely drained from the day, Jane and Charlie retired for the night; whether they would sleep, no one could say, but they needed to retreat. Alex took up her position in the oversized chair to the right of Lu's bed, keeping the small light on so she could see Lu. Quietness seemed to ooze from all corners, making everything still and reverent, as if angels had descended. The only sound really audible was the rattle in Lu's throat, indicating the length of pause between her shallow breaths, all of which took on different attributes with each lengthening gap. Alex got comfortable in the chair, as she propped herself up, leaning her head on the back cushion of the chair. Looking right, Alex had a clear view of Lu, lying so still, except when her lungs managed to take in and drive out air. Rolling over to her right side, Alex threw her left arm over the bolster of the chair and observed Lu. She kept a close eye on the rise and fall of her rib cage. The slow motion of her breaths lulled Alex into a deep, warranted sleep that lasted until the sun came up.

Feeling something behind her knees nudged Alex's eyes to barely open. Putting her left hand back behind her, it encountered Justice's hindleg, as he curled up beside Alex. This jolted her awake. First, Alex looked at Justice, then at Lu, seeing Jay seated on the edge of Lu's bed, as He held her left hand with both of His. Suddenly, Alex sat up, ready to run upstairs to alert Charlie and Jane, but Jay gestured that that wasn't necessary. Even though she grappled with His injunction, Alex acquiesced and sat quietly, looking on. Enraptured, Alex sat motionless, gazing at Jay as He guided Lu's spirit into the Kingdom of Heaven, and at that exact moment, a brilliant surge of light filled Lu's room, leaving behind her mortal body. For a moment, Jay remained, making sure Alex was okay with what she had just witnessed—more grace than sadness, more light than darkness, more harmony than silence. As Jay was about to leave, Justice military-crawled onto Alex's lap and relaxed his head on her knee. Glancing perplexedly at Jay, holding her arms in the air, Alex didn't quite know what to do. It wasn't like she hadn't owned or known dogs before, but it was a dog that had never seemed to pay any attention to her in the past two days, and now he was snuggling up on her lap—or at least the top half of him. Still staring at Jay, slowly Alex brought her hands down upon Justice, scratching his tan fur on his head and back. Jay smiled and left the townhouse. Alex settled into scratching Justice, as she looked upon Lu's body, wondered if she was finally with Casey. She hoped that she was.

Having one last task to do, Alex started going upstairs to tell Charlie and Jane. Justice tore up the stairs like a bolt of lightning, scratching at their bedroom door, which relieved Alex somewhat, being uncomfortable encroaching on their space. When Alex stepped up to the landing, the bedroom door opened, and Jane was face-to-face with Alex; no words needed to be spoken. Jane read everything in Alex's eyes.

Reality steamrolled Jane, as she succumbed to embracing Alex because that was all she could do. Seconds later, Charlie emerged and grabbed Jane, hugging his wife with all his might. Alex retreated downstairs, and so did Justice, her new pal.

A few minutes later, Charlie and Jane came downstairs and sat with Lu for about twenty minutes. The previous night, when Jane and Alex had sat before going to bed, they had talked easily about how many people rush to make all the arrangements immediately after an individual has passed. Jane explained that in her recent experience, people are becoming mindful, just being present after a person dies, reflecting on the person's life and what they meant to them. People should just be present. Alex hung on Jane's every word, appreciating her years of experience in the field. Alex wanted to be great—a great doctor, and she knew how important it was to listen to all medical professionals so she could put together her game plan.

Alex decided to take it upon herself to take Justice out to do his first morning business. Like the day before, Vegas was already hot at 7:14 a.m. It was amazing to Alex that Justice went along with her, without balking, and without a single whimper; he just sniffed around like it was any other day in Vegas, on his bright yellow leash. Alex didn't walk him too far out of the front yard because she didn't exactly know where to walk him. Once he did his business, Alex appropriately picked it up with a plastic bag and carried it back inside. In the kitchen, Charlie and Jane sat quietly together, looking forlorn but relieved that Lu's suffering had ended. Feeling stupid, for she didn't know where to discard the bag o' poo, Alex started to head back out the front door, but Charlie caught her attention before she stepped out.

"Do you need something, Alex?" he questioned kindly.

She turned, still holding the bag. "I didn't want to bother you all; I just was searching for where I can dispose of this."

Charlie started to walk toward her. "Let me take that, Hun." His voice was sweet and kind. "I didn't show you the garage before." He opened another door and stepped down, putting the bag in a trash receptacle. Stepping back into the townhouse, he closed the garage door. "I bet you're hungry; come eat something."

Alex followed Charlie into the kitchen where Jane was sitting, still tearful. "I'm terribly sorry for your loss, you and Charlie," Alex muttered. "Can I do anything for you?"

Jane reached for Alex's left hand, pulling her closer. "You have done so, so much for us already," Jane said with her red tearful eyes locked into Alex's eyes. "We can't thank you enough for doing what you did for us, truly…truly. You are a Godsend."

Visibly moved by Jane's sentiments, Alex cleared a few tears from her eyes. "I wish I could have known her before."

"She would have loved you," tearfully Jane spoke.

"I can't deny that," Charlie affirmed. "Casey would have loved you as well." He lifted his glasses to clear his own eyes.

"The funeral home should be here shortly to take Lu," said Jane, blowing her nose.

"Alex, can I make you anything?" begged Charlie.

"Oh no, Charlie, I'll wait," countered Alex easily. "I might go shower, if that's alright."

"Yes, of course, Alex," said Charlie, getting Justice's food ready in the white ceramic bowl.

"I won't take long," Alex spoke, feeling like she had to announce she wouldn't use too much of the hot water. Climbing the stairs again, Alex entered the guest bathroom she had used the day before, using the same towel and a new facecloth. Turning on the shower, letting the water warm, Alex used the bathroom and then undressed. In the shower, rather a tub and an enclosure, Alex let water spray upon her head, neck, and shoulders, as the rest poured down the rest of her fit body. Feeling the water on her face, warm and fluid, something got to her; out of the blue, Alex began to cry hard, but quietly, hunching downward. It was the absurdity of it all—life. One minute, it was there. The next, it was gone. Her chest heaved in and out, as her breathing was staggered, not quite knowing what was causing this bout. Balanced on the back, blue-tiled wall, the warm water soothed her, bringing calm to her. Alex knew she was close to heading home and she wanted to get there as soon as the wind could get her there. At last, she stood, finished her shower, and got dressed. When she opened the door, Alex was startled to see Justice lying on the beige, tiled floor, as he almost blended into it. What gave him away was his woeful, but beautiful, ice-blue eyes, which she really hadn't noticed before. Even though her hands were full of towels and such, Alex crouched down and scratched his head. He quickly rolled onto his side, looking up, inviting her to scratch his belly.

"I think you have a new buddy, Alex," Charlie said from the living space down below.

Meeting Charlie's gaze through the wrought iron spindles on the upper railing, Alex smiled. "I think so too." Descending the stairs, Justice followed Alex. She stuffed everything, towels aside, into her duffle bag beside the couch.

"Let me take those towels, Alex," said Jane.

Alex noticed Jane's eyes were still bloodshot, and suddenly she wondered if hers were too. "I can start a load of laundry, Jane."

"Don't be silly," replied Jane, taking the towels from Alex. "Charlie is going to make you something to eat."

Whether that was a demand or a suggestion, Alex made her way to the kitchen island and sat. "Are you and Jane going to eat?"

Charlie sighed, appearing beat-down. "I think we are going to wait a little while. The funeral home just left." He flicked a lone tear from his cheek and readjusted his eyeglasses.

"I'm so sorry, Charlie," Alex spoke mournfully, her eyes locked with his.

Breaking the gaze, Charlie cleared his throat. "Thank you, Alex." Puffing out his burly chest, he exhaled heartily. "I'm so thankful Lu is with Casey now." That admission nearly toppled him. "What can I make you, Alex?"

Taking a few seconds to judge his emotional state, Alex saw he was okay. "Eggs would be great."

Charlie smiled, grabbing the black spatula. "Any special way you like your eggs?"

"You can surprise me," said Alex, flipping back her damp black hair. It was easy to see that Charlie needed something to do, to keep him from dwelling on the double

loss of Casey and Lu.

"I have some laundry going," Jane announced, walking back into the kitchen. She sat beside Alex. "What's Charlie making you?"

"Eggs," Alex said excitedly, straightening her back. "He's going to surprise me. Is that wise?"

With one joke, everybody broke into laughter. "You're pretty safe," Jane kidded back, extending the jollity. "He's pretty good in the kitchen."

Hearing his wife's praise, Charlie gradually turned to smile at Jane. "Thank you, Honey."

The conversation lagged for a few, long seconds, which was not surprising given that someone had just passed away in the adjacent room three hours prior. The aura in the townhouse was disorienting, as if someone had noticeably dimmed the sun, where clouds were present, or if someone had added an extra second onto every second. Something had disrupted normalcy for an uncertain period. Life still had to continue for everyone Lu left behind, even though it seemed a little unwieldy, lonely, and very unfair. "Does Charlie cook at home?" Alex wanted to keep the conversation light.

Prior to answering, Jane lifted her chin and smiled in his direction. "He, like every other capable man, has the whole grilling thing down pat, I must say," she offered. "He always has dinner on the table when I get home, even if it's not until eleven at night."

Alex shifted her exuberance between Jane and Charlie. "Aww...that's really sweet."

"That's the kind of man I am," Charlie quipped with a goofy smile.

It was evident to Alex that Charlie rarely took himself too seriously. "It just occurred to me that I haven't asked you what you do."

Plating her eggs on a rustic blue wavy dish, Charlie was very pleased with the concoction of scrambled egg, tomato, red onion, and melted cheddar cheese. "I'm the executive director of a nonprofit that provides services for individuals who have developmental disabilities," Charlie spoke without any fanfare. "My cousin, Marie, has Down syndrome. She lives independently and she has a full-time job."

The plate of mouthwatering eggs were taking her attention away from Charlie's response for a split second. "I can see that in you, Charlie," Alex replied exuberantly, picking up the fork earmarked for her. "When I was in Savannah, I came across this very nice family with a child who has athetoid cerebral palsy—she's nearly five, and her grandmother was still feeding her just milk with an eyedropper while she held her on her lap." Picking up a fork-full of eggs, Alex blew on them. "I'm not going to lie—it kind of freaked me out a little."

Resting his forearms upon the kitchen counter, Charlie watched Alex take her first bite, giving her his full attention. "I can definitely see why that would scare you."

"Charlie, this is delicious!" Alex said, swallowing her first bite and taking another.

"Why, thank you," smiled Charlie, gently doing a victorious fist pump. "Yes!"

"You're such a goofball," Jane surmised, reflecting his great smile.

This levity was warranted even though it might last through the afternoon, night or even the next three days, although Charlie was confident he and Jane would settle back into life in Orange. "What happened with the little girl?"

Swiftly, Alex covered her mouth with a lightly closed fist to hide her closed lips as she swallowed. "It was obvious to me she had the ability to swallow milk, so I asked Yvette, the grandmother, if I could try something different," Alex explained to her captive audience of two. "Yvette was a little apprehensive, but her daughter-in-law urged her to allow me to try. I sat Ruby back in her stroller, and I discovered that Ruby was able to swallow the milk without coughing if I held her jaw closed. Her uncle tells me Ruby is eating some solid food now, has gained five pounds already, and sleeps through the night, which she wasn't doing before."

"She was hungry," Charlie deduced.

"She was hungry," repeated Alex, as she took another bite of her eggs. "I have been trying to have Ruby evaluated so she can get more than two hours of therapy a month." With the paper napkin in her hand, Alex wiped her mouth.

"Really, two hours a month," Charlie uttered, "that's not much at all."

"Definitely not," Jane interjected easily.

"Where did you say Ruby was from?"

"Savannah, Georgia," answered Alex. "Her uncle is a pastor down there—a nice man."

"Mom isn't in the picture?" Jane inquired.

"Mom had a drug problem. She passed a few months after giving birth." Alex continued enjoying her eggs.

Scratching his forehead, Charlie let out a long sigh. "Boy, that's tough." He stood up to fix his shirt, soon returning his arms to the countertop. "I have a friend in Georgia—in Atlanta, actually. He can help in this situation."

Alex quickly locked onto Charlie's eyes. "Really?"

"People don't call me 'Charlie the Wiz' for nothing," he said humorously. He got interrupted by his cellphone. "Yes, Jim, how have you been?"

Both Alex and Jane remained quiet as Charlie chatted with Jim, whoever he was. It was obvious Jane knew Jim, and as the very brief conversation ended, Jane didn't need any explanation as to what it was about. "He's not going to take Justice, is he?"

"Nope," sighed Charlie, defeated. "He didn't even ask about Lu."

Something made Alex look at Justice, who was lying to the left of her barstool. "I'll take him." *What the hell did I just say?* "I'll take

Justice," Alex said as if the words were just exploding from her mouth indiscriminately, and she didn't have the ability to reel them back. At that very moment, Justice looked up at Alex like he knew he was hers from then on out.

"Are you sure, Alex?" pressed Charlie.

"Oh Alex, are you sure?" Jane reiterated.

As Alex continued to look into Justice's eyes, she recalled all their interactions that morning. "This morning, he crawled onto my lap."

Charlie and Jane stared at Alex dumbfounded, but wholeheartedly grateful. "Alex, what can we say?"

"You don't have to say anything," Alex expressed easily, "just give me the lowdown on this cutie."

Charlie couldn't do much but gawk at Alex. "You're a Godsend."

Giving Charlie and Jane an unassuming glance, Alex just smiled.

In the hot Vegas sun, the fact didn't pass by Alex that the shower she had taken about an hour before seemed pointless, as she was bathed in sweat trying to organize her Camry to make room for Justice, his food and some of his toys. She hadn't been this organized since God knows when, figuring Jay might supply her with a specific date and time later. A little organization made the car not looked so packed, even with the addition of an average-sized dog in the back seat. Charlie and Jane couldn't help but give Alex the warmest of embraces, as they promised to keep in touch. Alex promised to do the same. With one more pet from Charlie to Justice, he knew he would have a good life with Alex. With a turn of the key in the ignition, she was off, on to her next destination, wherever that might be. Before she pulled out onto the main road, stopped at the stop sign, she noticed Jay was waiting on the curb; she waited for Him to jump into the passenger seat. They were off.

Getting back on I-15 South, traffic was light going out of the city, but heavy going in. Alex concluded this was a daily occurrence. Not seeing too much of Vegas didn't much matter to Alex; instead of coming away with a few bucks from a slot machine, she came away with a new furry friend with four legs and a cold wet snout that hovered over her right shoulder, and sometimes her left. Justice was relaxed as he watched cars and trucks travel northeast and southwest on I-15, like he had done this a hundred times before. No doubt he had. As traffic dispersed, it was hard not to scratch Justice under and around his jaw and ears, always preferring his ears. Jay looked on and smiled. After a while, Justice was lying on part of Alex's sleeping bag, enjoying the hums and vibrations of the ride. Quickly, Justice was asleep.

With every mile, California got closer and closer. On this day, Alex was more happy than apprehensive at the possibility she could be heading home in a day or so. Entering the Golden Gate state brought Alex to the realization that she had succeeded at accomplishing something through a very crushing point of her young life. She also realized she had many people who guided this long, arduous, self-actualizing journey—namely, Jay, her parents, Conrad, Justin, and the countless people she had met along the way. These people would remain with her for the rest of her life for all the lessons she was taught. There was one person who she couldn't deny had assisted her through her trip and that was Nate. His memory pushed Alex in every direction imaginable, forcing her to walk into places that were full of doubt, full of sharp edges, and full of darkness, trapping her soul from the sun and light needed for everything to grow. Humans weren't built to hibernate through the coldest of winters. Life had to continue; that held true from the beginning of time. People never became extinct like dinosaurs; people had endured so much suffering in modern history and life continued. In Nate's mortal absence, time would buff out all the jagged corners leaving smoothness that wouldn't hurt as much; although there would always be an empty crevasse in the heart, an empty room, it would never feel the same. It was like a lost key never to be found until they reunite in Heaven.

Almost three hours into the drive on I-15 South, Alex was starved for food and entertained the idea of a bathroom break. Before she determined the appropriate exit to take, Jay awoke, and then Justice popped up, breathing upon her right shoulder.

"I'm going to get some food in the next few exits," announced Alex to her passengers.

"You must wait to do that," Jay quickly injected.

Alex gave Him a puzzled glance. "Huh? What if I have to use the bathroom?"

Jay met her glance. "That'll have to wait too."

Switching back and forth between the two lanes of the highway, with speed limits ranging between 55 and 70 miles per hour, Alex's eyes narrowed. "What's happening, Jay?"

"You're going to have a small emergency to tend to a few miles up, to the left side, in the median."

Scared out of her skin, her adrenaline started to kick in, not because of the impending 'small emergency', but for the fact that she had to drive onto a median without knowing the terrain. Alex immediately looked in all her rearview mirrors to gauge if and when she could begin to slow down, as she was already in the left lane. "Shit...I'm going to piss a lot of people off, Jay," Alex said, flipping on her warning lights.

"They'll get over it, Alex," Jay spoke easily, like He had complete control over the situation—because He did.

The honking of horns started behind her, as she reduced her speed gradually down to 25. "Jay, You have to help me get onto the median," she begged, gripping the steering wheel so tight that her knuckles turned white.

"I am right here, Alex," Jay reassured her, giving her a confident stare. "See that car up ahead in the median?"

"Yep," Alex answered hastily, "that's it?"

"Yes," Jay answered just as quickly.

Instantly, Alex started her way into the median, slowing down her speed as much as possible, as not to damage her Camry or Justice. "Hold on, boy." Once Alex hit the sandy dirt, she quickly decelerated, kicking up a plume of dust behind the Camry, as it bounced on the uneven ground for about five seconds. Alex made sure she parked next to the fully intact, small, blue SUV, as she continued to assess the situation. Before turning off the Camry, Alex had the presence of mind to roll all the windows down. Getting out, she told Justice to stay. Jogging around the SUV, Alex saw the driver's side door was half open with a purple sneaker attached to a leg hanging out. Alex approached the door carefully, assessing more of the field, finding a woman in active labor. "Ma'am," said Alex, getting the woman's attention.

"I thought I could make it to the hospital," the woman spoke, winded from the contractions and the circumstances she found herself in. "This third one—he's coming early."

"Ma'am, my name is Alex, and I am a physician," Alex offered, opening the driver's side door to its limits.

"Really?!" the anxious woman exclaimed, trying to stay calm. "This must be my lucky day."

Alex crouched and held the woman's hand, ignoring the vehicles whizzing by in both directions. "What's your name, Sweetie?"

"Ellen," she barely got out when another contraction took hold, as she gripped Alex's fingers as if she was squeezing the last liquid out of an orange. "Oh my God...I'm so sorry."

Alex just smiled at Ellen. "It's okay, Ellen," she said, her voice uplifted. Alex rose a little from her heels. "I'm going to run to get my sleeping bag, my pillows and whatever else I have because you are going to have a beautiful baby here today."

"I tried to call 9-1-1 but I have no signal," Ellen spoke, winded.

Quickly, Alex crouched down, meeting Ellen's frightened eyes. "I've got you, Girl."

In the moment Ellen was locked onto Alex's soothing gaze, she was immersed in faith, becoming emotional. "Thank you."

Alex smiled. "I'll be right back." Darting back to the Camry, she grabbed what she thought would be helpful going into this maiden delivery. Oddly, Alex's entire being was calm; every inch of her knew just what had to be done. With her arms full of blankets, pillows and towels, Alex looked toward Jay, seeing His own calm eyes; she knew everything would work out with this new little life entering the world. Returning to Ellen, Alex put down the soft pad, the sleeping bag and two pillows for Ellen's head on the uneven ground. Before Ellen experienced her next vicious contraction, Alex helped her lie on the uninviting ground. "You're okay?"

The latest contraction overpowered Ellen, rendering her unable to answer Alex's question at that particular moment. "Do I have a choice?" Ellen said, trying to breathe, feeling the aftermath of another vicious contraction.

"I don't think so, I'm sorry," Alex said, draping a blanket over Ellen's bent knees. "Ellen, I'm going to take your pants off."

"Logical, isn't it?" Ellen quipped, as she tried to keep the humor in a very tense time.

Alex couldn't help but to chuckle. She quickly disrobed Ellen's bottom half of black leggings and flip flops. At first glance, Alex saw the baby's bottom already exiting Ellen's body, creating concern in Alex's gut. "How far along are you, Ellen?" Alex asked calmly while grabbing a few hand towels.

Still breathing like she was running a full marathon on her first attempt, Ellen had to think about her answer. "Umm...I'm 36 weeks. Why?"

"He's coming out breech," Alex spoke without apprehension, although she had hoped that her first delivery wouldn't be complicated.

Instantly, Ellen's back arched, as she started to cry, grabbing her face. "Is that why it hurts so much?!"

"Yes," Alex replied, as her adrenaline kicked in. "Can you push for me, Ellen?"

All she wanted to do was to push, and she did, grunting with all her might.

With her hands on the baby's backside, Alex observed him inch his way out a little more. "Good, Ellen!" Sweat was seeping out of her every pore at will, without attention from her occupied hands. "Can you push for me again?" Alex asked, shifting her eyes upon Ellen's crimson face for a second.

Ellen couldn't speak, she could only push, letting out a guttural scream, still crying.

Most of his tiny body was within her hands. "Good job, Ellen," Alex exclaimed quietly. Digging her finger between his extended left leg, Alex carefully plucked it out of the birth canal. Carefully turning him 180 degrees, Alex did the same maneuver with his right leg, and then his right arm, everything purple in color. With one more rotation, Alex extracted his left arm, only leaving his head. Observing the umbilical cord wrapped around his tiny neck, Alex worked quickly but methodically to extract his head, tucking her middle and index fingers below his eyes, upon his cheeks, angling his neck downward about a quarter inch, until she had all of him in her hands. It wasn't time to celebrate until she heard noise coming from his lungs. Gently, Alex laid him down on the sleeping bag, uncoiling the umbilical cord from his neck. She picked him up, and immediately the newborn started to cry. "There he goes!" Alex exclaimed, immediately laying him on Ellen's chest.

"Oh my God!" Ellen cried out happily, as she clutched the newborn to her rising and falling chest. "Thank you so, so much, Alex." Weeping easily, she was suddenly thankful for her fortune.

Standing up, looking back and forth at either side of the highway, Alex wondered how she would protect her patients until helped arrived. Crouching down, she took hold of Ellen's left hand. "Boy, will he have a story when he gets older," Alex said, chuckling, gazing into Ellen's very grateful eyes. "Let me go find something to clip off the umbilical cord."

Going into mother mode already, Ellen tried to block the baby from the brutal sun, putting one of Alex's folded blue bath towels on him. "There you go."

In the Camry, Alex was looking for anything to clamp off the cord, digging in all the crevasses of the car, searching for anything, and finally coming across one lone elastic. With her Swiss Army knife already in her hand, Alex looked up, catching Jay smiling at her. Reciprocating His smile, she took off to tend to her patients, rushing back to cut the umbilical cord and to apply the elastic to it. "Do you mind if I check him out?"

"Not at all," Ellen returned, very content to have this new life on her chest.

Putting on her stethoscope, Alex listened to his tiny back first, challenged by the roar of the engines passing by in both directions. Alex heard a miniscule amount of congestion in his lungs. The sound of his strong, fast heartbeats made Alex more confident. "There's a little fluid in his lungs, but his heart is very strong," remarked Alex, displaying a big smile. Suddenly, she heard sirens approaching. Getting to her feet, she looked in all directions, finally seeing a gray SUV approaching in almost the same tracks the Camry had set into the sand. The vehicle stopped, and an officer got out. "Boy, you have no idea how happy I am to see you."

The California Highway Patrol officer, with his beige short-sleeved shirt and pants and a dark wide-brimmed hat, immediately got on his radio and called for a bus—police lingo for an ambulance—once he recognized the scene. "I see your hands are full," he kind of quipped, which didn't settle with Alex well.

It seemed calling in a bus was the extent of his helpfulness. Alex didn't have time for idle chatter with this young officer; returning to Ellen, recognizing she had just spontaneously expelled the placenta, Alex cleaned her up as best she could with what she had, which wasn't a lot granted she had never imagined she would have to deliver a baby on this road trip. "How's the little guy doing?" Alex asked, as she crouched down to take all the brunt of the boiling hot sun upon her back.

"He's chilling out here on my chest," Ellen spoke easily, lightly caressing his back and head.

Looking over at the baby, Alex never tired of watching babies sleep, especially on the humans who were responsible for their creation. As Ellen described, he was just chilling on Mom's chest, seemingly trying to figure out the world already. "He's a little cutie," Alex happily commented.

Ellen smiled like the sun looking down at her precious new addition. "I think I'm going to name him…Alexander…Alexander Thomas," said Ellen, slowly glancing toward a very touched Alex. "Alex is a strong name."

Alex chortled. "So I have been told." A single tear fell from her left eye. "I think that's a great name, Ellen."

"Yeah?"

Humbled beyond words, Alex swallowed hard, nodding her head. "Yeah." In the far distance she could hear the approaching rescue vehicles, although she couldn't decipher how many. "Here comes the Cavalry," she commented, looking for the incoming rescue vehicles. Soon, police vehicles flanked I-15 South so that they could control traffic for the rescue vehicles to access the median. The rescue pulled up as far as it could, behind the California Highway Patrol SUV. Two paramedics stepped out, one female and one male, retrieving the stretcher—a school-bus-yellow one at that. Alex didn't move from her sun-blocking post until they were ready to move Ellen and the baby.

The paramedics made quick work of getting mother and child into the back of the ambulance. Alex carried the baby while they situated Ellen. After she handed the baby to the male paramedic, the female paramedic offered a bottle or two of antiseptic wash to Alex, as she noticed all the remnants of childbirth on Alex's limbs. "If you need more, we have more."

"Oh, thanks," Alex gratefully replied, pouring the clear antiseptic liquid over her arms, hands, and legs. She had a towel from the rescue. "How far is the hospital?"

"It's about five miles north in Victorville," the woman said.

"Would it be possible for me to follow you?"

"Of course."

"I'm so sorry, I didn't get your name," Alex said to the woman.

"Oh, my name is Skylar," she said.

"I'm Alex," she said, purposely not extending a hand. Skylar, a woman approaching her mid-thirties, wore her dark brown hair in a ponytail that reached down below her shoulder blades. She was a couple inches taller than Alex, and with broader shoulders and hips, matching her average, beautiful appearance.

"Hi Alex," spoke Skylar, as she closed the ambulance doors. "Follow us!"

Watching Skylar jump into the driver's seat, Alex put her hand up, thanking her. Jogging to the Camry, Alex got in and quickly glanced around to double-check that all her passengers were still present and accounted for. Starting the engine, she reached to scratch Justice's scruff. "I'll get you to some water as soon as we get there." Before she put the car into drive, out of the corner of her eye, Alex saw Jay gazing at her.

"Good job, Kiddo," Jay spoke, locked into her composed, obliged eyes.

"Thank you, Jay," replied Alex, her voice drenched in sincerity and grace.

"Let's go."

A bigger smile draped across her guise. "Let's go."

Alex followed the rescue to Victor Valley Global Medical Center in Victorville, a small town about an hour and a half east of Los Angeles. The medical center looked more like a high-end motel than anything else. Watching the rescue pull into the overhead bay, Alex pulled into a parking space close by. Grabbing her water bottle, Alex dared to ask Jay for a favor, asking Him to give Justice a drink of water and let him stretch his legs a bit. The worst Jay could say was no, Alex thought, but He did not. Alex told Jay she would be back as soon as possible. She entered the same door Skylar and her colleague had just brought Ellen and the baby through, immediately searching for the public restroom. It was less than ten feet away. Alex did what she needed to do, noticing how badly she needed another shower. At the sink, she washed up as best she could with commercial hand soap and brown paper towels. Looking into the mirror, she couldn't do much with her hair, already dried with sweat.

Back in the hallway, Alex began to search for Ellen and the baby, or maybe Skylar, because nobody said she couldn't. Using her sense of hearing, Alex listened for familiar voices, as she didn't see many people. Finally, turning left, she saw Skylar standing immediately outside the bay, as she picked up her pace. Skylar explained that the medical center wasn't equipped to care for premature babies and planned to transfer him to Children's Hospital Los Angeles. Although the baby was stable, it was the medical center's protocol. Ellen was within earshot of their conversation; she begged Alex to accompany Alexander Thomas to Los Angeles. Hearing Ellen's shrill voice, Alex couldn't say no—it was impossible to say no. Before leaving, Alex made sure she had Ellen's and Skylar's cell numbers, promising to contact Ellen when she reached L.A. While they loaded the baby into the bus, Alex jogged back to the Camry just in time to see Jay get Justice back into the backseat. Pretty soon, Alex jumped into the Camry, starting the engine, and thanking Jay for tending to Justice.

Sunset

Except for a scattering of tall palm and very narrow, almost arborvitae-like trees flanking the edges of the five-lane highway, I-10 West reminded Alex of driving on I-93 into Boston. Following the bright-red square rescue, with only its lights on for the past hour and a half, Alex did well keeping pace with Skylar. It became more challenging when they got into the city. It was obvious it wasn't Skylar's first time going to Children's Hospital Los Angeles on Sunset Boulevard, nor would it be her last. Before Skylar pulled into the ambulance bay, Jay directed Alex where to park, not too far from the emergency entrance.

As Alex slammed the driver's door shut, Justice's head popped out of the back window, reminding her that she indeed had a dog. She asked Jay if He could watch him for just five more minutes. He nodded, flicking His index finger for her to go. Jogging to where the rescue was parked outside the emergency entrance, Alex searched for Skylar, as she was exiting to look for Alex. As they met up, Skylar brought Alex inside and to the section where they had the baby, with doctors and nurses surrounding him, as if he had just emerged from Area 51. Suddenly, she heard someone say her name.

"Alex? Alex Roma? Is that you?!" asked a male voice.

Not exactly knowing where the familiar voice was coming from, it was then that the man stepped out of the circle, making her eyes open wide. "Chris!" Alex said, knowing exactly who knew her name, as she smiled brightly. Sensing he was coming in for a hug, Alex took a half step back. "I don't think you want to hug me right yet," she began, giggling. "I'm covered in sweat—sweat, and other stuff you don't want to know about." She looked at the baby upon the stretcher.

"Oh!" exclaimed Chris, glancing back swiftly at the baby. "You're the one who delivered him in the middle of I-15?!"

Shyness engulfed her, as she let her head drop while she haphazardly raised her hand like she had committed some kind of schoolhouse prank. "Yes, yes, that was me."

Chris gazed skeptically at her. "Why are you cutting yourself short, Alex?" He couldn't take his eyes off her. "That is the most amazing thing I have heard in ages, man." His arms expressed his enthusiasm. Stealthily, one of his hands found its way onto her right shoulder. "Hey everybody," Chris spoke, elevating his voice, "this is my good friend, Dr. Alexandra Roma; we went to medical school together back in Boston and she is the person who delivered this baby boy out in the middle of I-15!"

The team briefly stopped and applauded Alex. Once the spotlight was on her, she turned a bright shade of red, but she held her head up high. To her right, Alex saw Skylar clapping and smiling. "You're in big trouble, Mister," she said under her breath, smiling at Chris.

Chris just thoroughly enjoyed this moment and continued to clap and giggle, sneaking in a side hug. "Oh my God…It's so great to see you!"

She smiled up at Chris. "It's good to see you too!" Alex expressed freely. "How the hell did you come out here to L.A.? I thought you were still in Boston."

Before Chris had a chance to answer, Skylar had to interrupt. "I apologize, but we must get going. It was a pleasure to meet you. Good luck!" Skylar left her with a smile and a wave.

Unwittingly, Alex had put her left hand upon Chris' forearm, while directing her attention toward Skylar. "Thank you so much, Skylar!" She reciprocated her wave. In seconds, she disappeared. Alex refocused her attention back on Chris, still unaware of the placement of her hand.

The smile never left his face. "Yeah, so, I was asked to come out here to fill in for another resident for the five seven or six months, but he's back, and I get to go home in a few weeks."

"Wow, that's cool," Alex said. She quickly looked at her iPhone to check the time. "Is it really 3 o'clock?"

Chris checked the clock on the wall in the examination bay. "Yes, it's almost three. Do you have to be somewhere?"

She started texting Ellen. "Well, not exactly," began Alex. "I have my dog out in my car, with the windows down of course, so I have to get back out to him, and I have to text the baby's mother. Do you mind if I take a picture of the baby?"

"Sure, sure," Chris answered, understanding her motives. Walking over next to the clear bassinet now, Chris prepared to swaddle the little boy in the standard white baby blanket with blue and pink stripes. "He looks good, Al."

All the sudden, words escaped her, while she watched Chris make swaddling a baby a true art form, remarking how gently he held Alexander Thomas, and how much he loved his job. "You're pretty good at that," she commented, standing there awestruck.

Holding Alexander in his arms, Chris laid him back down in the bassinet. "He's ready for his close-up."

All Alex could do was smile, as she sauntered forward, squatting down on the opposite side of the bassinet, ready to snap pictures of the new baby boy. "Thank you, Chris," Alex conveyed with gratitude. "Does he have a bracelet on?"

Giggling came quietly from Chris' chest. "It's on, I promise. I'm going to have someone take him up to the nursery." Making a gesture to one of the nurses in the area, Chris grabbed her attention. "Erica, could you take him up to the nursery please?"

"Absolutely, Dr. Jacobs," replied Erica, who couldn't be older than 24.

"Thank you, Erica," said Chris, as he watched her wheel the bassinet out of the state-of-the-art exam room.

With her arms crossed in front of her, Alex walked next to Chris, also watching Erica exit the room. "Look at you, Dr. Jacobs," Alex quipped, smiling.

Chris laughed. "So…explain to me how you drove out here with a dog."

Alex started walking out, figuring the way outside. Chris helped her navigate through the emergency section. "Actually, I've only had the dog since this morning," she admitted.

As his eyebrows constricted from wonder, Chris' expression indicated he needed more information. "This morning?"

Outside, the warm air hit them like they were walking through a clothes dryer. "Yeah. How much time do you have?" Alex inquired with a rhetorical flare.

Chris looked at his watch. "As luck would have it, I was off at 3." He continued to follow her to her car. "I just have to go back and check out quickly."

Searching the front seat covertly, Alex didn't see Jay; she only saw Justice's head sticking out of the back window. "And this is Justice," she uttered, introducing Chris to her new furry friend, scratching his head, as he looked like he didn't have a care in the world, panting at a steady pace.

"Is he friendly?" asked Chris before he touched the mutt. "I don't want to lose a hand, you know."

"Well," Alex started, "he has been friendly with me for the past three days or so, so he should be fine."

"Are you confident with that answer?" he jested, cracking a laugh with his eyes upon Alex.

"Does he look vicious to you?" Alex put forward with the same humor.

Chris chortled. "I was attacked by a Chihuahua when I was ten."

Not even a second passed when Alex found herself laughing hysterically. "Really…a Chihuahua."

"He was mean!" Chris exclaimed, trying to hold his composure. Pretty soon, he was laughing uncontrollably with her.

Once Alex retained some semblance of a straight face, she begged him for his hand. "Give me your hand."

Without questioning her motives, he relinquished his left hand to both of hers. Soon, Justice was sniffing his fingers before she put his palm on Justice's head.

"Now, just scratch his head," she softly demanded, dropping her hands away from his.

Obeying, Chris began scratching Justice's head, driving his fear downward. "I think he likes me." Chris shifted his eyes to Alex once again.

"I think he likes you too," she uttered, smiling.

Chris switched his left with his right hand upon Justice's head. "Hey, are you hungry—do you want to grab a bite to eat or something?"

"I could eat," Alex said, as her stomach grumbled with ferocity. "I just have to get cleaned up somewhere."

"My apartment is just around the corner; you can get cleaned up there," Chris offered.

"Yeah, sure."

He smiled. "Just let me run back inside to get my stuff and I'll be right out."

"Okay," she acknowledged, returning his smile.

"I'll be right back," Chris began, as he started sprinting back inside the hospital.

While Alex waited for Chris, she opened the driver's side door and sat down. She had time to send a group text to her parents, Conrad, and Justin to announce her accomplishment for the day, and boy, oh boy, it was a big one. She even sent the picture of Alexander Thomas along with the text, and soon, her iPhone began exploding with praise and adulation from all. Delivering a baby in the median of a major highway didn't quite register with her as a big deal yet, but maybe in a day or two, she would recognize the magnitude of it all. Without warning, her eye caught Jay standing next to her. "Holy shit!" she exclaimed, looking up at Him.

Jay couldn't help but to laugh. "You are so funny."

"I'm glad I can make You laugh at my expense," she said, half kidding. Having her right leg in her car, she moved it out and sat on the edge of the seat. "What have You been doing?"

"I was sitting with Justice for a while, then I walked around for a bit, waiting for you," said Jay. "I think I'll hang out here for a day or so—hang out with the kids."

"Okay," Alex said, looking up at Jay, "can You keep an eye on Alexander?"

Jay smirked a silly grin. "Everybody is My flesh and blood, Alex. Of course."

"That was a silly question, wasn't it? I apologize," Alex offered.

"Apology not necessary, My friend. Just believe." With those words, Jay headed back into the hospital.

Alex watched Him until He disappeared into the hospital doors. He must have known Chris was on his way out because just then she saw him sprinting back toward the Camry. For some reason, Alex stood up just to get back into the driver's seat and unlock the car for Chris to jump into the passenger seat—Jay's co-pilot seat—which seemed a bit awkward, but the awkwardness passed quickly. "All set?"

"Yep," Chris said, snapping his seatbelt in, as Justice sniffed his bald head. "He won't chew my head off, will he?"

Alex busted out laughing. "No! The worst he might do to your head is lick it!" She started the engine. "Where am I going?"

"If you go out here," Chris pointed with his right index finger toward Sunset Boulevard, "you can take a right, and I live on North Commonwealth Avenue on the left, a few streets up."

Quickly glancing at Chris, Alex smirked. "North Commonwealth Avenue? Very fitting for a guy from Boston."

"I thought so too," Chris agreed, chuckling. "Wait until you see the house—very New England-ish."

"Really?"

"Yeah, it's a Garrison style; I have the upstairs and two other doctors have the downstairs," explained Chris easily.

Turning onto Sunset Boulevard, Alex absorbed what she could see, especially the tall palm trees; the trees made everything different—a totally contrasting vibe from the Northeast. A few streets down, Alex took a left onto North Commonwealth Avenue. "This is so not New England."

"This is the West Coast, Al," said Chris, chuckling.

"I know that, but everything's so different," she commented, her eyes starstruck at everything.

"This is my place up here on the left. Just park in front."

"Okay," she replied, parking the Camry in front of the white Garrison. They both got out. "Is it dog-friendly around here?"

"Yeah," Chris began playfully, "people have dogs in California."

Looking across the Camry top, Alex noticed Chris quietly laughing, as he shut the door. "Ha ha," Alex quipped. Once she opened the back door, Justice jumped out and stayed within five feet, which amazed her. With his yellow leash in her hands, she attached it to his collar and grabbed the duffle bag.

"Let me take that," offered Chris, walking around the back of the Camry, as the sun blazed down.

Her eyes met his. "Oh, thank you, Chris."

He put her duffle on his free shoulder. "Absolutely."

"I am just going to see if he'll do something," muttered Alex.

"Sure, sure." Chris sauntered across the front lawn, watching Alex with Justice, nose to the ground, in debate of whether he had to relieve himself or not. This dog wasn't stupid; he relieved himself quickly to get inside. With due diligence, Alex picked up his business.

"Where can I discard this?" Alex asked, holding the filled plastic bag.

Chris took it from her and brought it around to the left side of the house where the trash receptacles were placed. He walked back to the front, brick stoop and opened the door. "Welcome to my humble abode," Chris said, walking into the small foyer with another door and a staircase leading up to the second floor.

Alex crammed herself and Justice into the foyer with black laminate tile and an ordinary floor mat, as Chris closed the door. "Thanks."

"Please, go up," spoke Chris politely.

Starting to ascend the stairs with Justice, Alex noticed that the treads were dark walnut and the risers painted white, and she, too, thought the vibe was very New England. Soon, Chris caught up to her, and reached around her to unlock his apartment at the top of the landing. Once Chris opened the door, Alex and Justice walked inside. "Oh wow, this is so nice," she said, suddenly finding herself in the huge kitchen, open to the living area in the rear of the house.

Chris set down both bags on the dark hardwood floor. "Pardon all the boxes in the living room."

Standing on her tippy toes to see the boxes sitting on the living room floor, Alex leaned on the large kitchen island. "Do you mind if I give Justice some water?"

"Oh, sure," Chris replied, as he stepped around to the kitchen, opening the door of the white upper cabinets to retrieve a pale-yellow ceramic bowl. Filling it with cold water, he set it down on the floor. In his natural way, Justice investigated the contents and began to lap up the water with ferocity. "He's a thirsty guy." Chris filled the bowl again. "Let me show you where the shower is, Al."

Like all the other places she visited or stayed, Alex took everything in, observing things that caught her eye, like the small, silver-framed picture of Chris' mother on one of the side tables in the apartment. "Oh, your mom…How is she?"

"She's good…she's good," Chris expressed happily. "She's going to flip when I tell her I ran into you."

Shyness gripped her. "She's so kind."

Grinning, Chris scratched his nose. "Here's the bathroom," he said, pointing out the obvious, "and this is my bedroom." Popping into his room, he grabbed some towels from his closet. "And here are some towels."

She grabbed the towels and held them to her chest. "Thank you. I'll be right out. I have become the queen of the fast shower," Alex cracked.

"Take all the time you want."

"I'll be fast—I'm starving."

Chris began to laugh hard. "Lucky for you, I'm pretty hungry too, so I'll change out of my scrubs."

"Do you need the bathroom?"

"Nope, I'm fine," Chris stated with unparalleled certainty.

It was a three-block walk to El Cid, a Mexican restaurant on Sunset Boulevard. The façade looked like a typical Mexican outpost, with decorative curves for the frieze, decked out in black, with the exterior painted a classic mustard. The size of the front was deceiving, because once inside, the place seemed to expand miraculously. Alex and Chris were greeted by a young man of Mexican descent, with thick black hair and olive skin. The nametag on his electric-blue vest indicated his name was Jon, and he didn't possess any hint of a Spanish accent. Jon asked if they would like to sit outside on the back patio. It was just about 5 o'clock, well before the evening rush, so they decided that eating outside would be nice. Jon ushered them outside, down the white stone steps, onto a terracotta-tiled patio, which was practically empty, giving them options of where to sit. In one of the corners that abutted the lower steps, a dark wicker bench with a curved, tall back seemed to call their names, as it was well-shaded.

In gentlemanly fashion, Chris let Alex sit down first on the white cushion while he followed soon after. "Well, this is a nice surprise, having dinner with you," Chris spoke genuinely, clasping his hands together on the wrought iron table.

"May I get you two something to drink?" asked Jon.

"Water is fine for me," Alex replied.

Chris chuckled, glancing at Alex. "I'm going to have a beer."

"Corona?"

"Corona's fine, Jon," Chris said.

"I'll return with your drinks," said Jon, leaving the menus for them on the table.

"Thank you, Jon," expressed Alex, quickly grabbing a menu. Jon left to get the drinks. "Have you eaten here before? What's good?"

Just enthralled, Chris stared at her and giggled. "Shall we get an appetizer before you chew my arm off?"

"I'm a little hungry; I haven't eaten since this morning," Alex said, jesting right back.

Taking a quick look around, Chris noticed there was another waiter close by. He raised his hand, grabbing the waiter's attention.

"Excuse me, do you think you can ask Jon if he can bring us an order of Salsa Verde? This girl is ravished over here; this morning she delivered a baby in the middle of I-15." The look he received from the young waiter was priceless—a deer-in-the-headlights kind of gape. The waiter went tearing off to find Jon.

"You're still a goof," Alex pointed out, giggling.

"Yeah, well, some things never change," Chris said, smiling. "So, what brings you to California?" His tone turned more serious.

For a split second, she locked eyes with his striking crystal-blue eyes, and then broke away. "Umm…where do I start?" Embarrassment overtook her as her fingers fiddled with the sugar and Splenda packets. "It has been a very tough six months."

"Yeah, I can't even imagine," Chris said in a low voice. "I apologize for missing Nate's funeral."

"I didn't know you were in California," said Alex, looking up underneath their red sun umbrella. "Imagine my surprise when I saw you today!"

"I was probably more surprised seeing you," Chris expressed, engaged by her attention. "It blew my mind. How the hell did you end up here?!"

"Umm……" Alex murmured, contemplating where to begin. "After Nate died, I dropped off my residency and didn't really do much at all." Looking away, she continued. "My Dad was becoming annoyed with me, because of my residency, and Mom was too perky for me to understand, you know."

Chris was all in. "Got it."

Finding his eyes again, she knew he was listening. "So, one night, the guys, Conrad and Justin, and I went to Duxbury Beach, and somehow the conversation got around to me travelling across the country so I could get my head straightened out a bit."

"Oh wow, Al—I had no idea," Chris expressed, feeling tears gather in his eyes. "How were your parents about you driving cross country, by yourself?"

Readjusting herself on the bench cushion, Alex crossed her right leg over her left, nonchalantly, rubbing her shin. "Honestly…we have learned to communicate a lot better since I got on the road, if that makes any sense at all," she portrayed. "We talk every day, sometimes twice. Sometimes I'll catch a conversation with Mom or Dad, and we just talk, you know."

"They probably miss you like crazy," Chris easily presumed.

Before responding, Alex crooked her neck downward and grinned. "Yeah," she said, stretching the word out. "I really miss them too."

"So, now that you are on the West Coast, when are you heading home?" posed Chris, gentle on his pace.

"I'm driving up to San Fran, and once I get there I'll start heading home," she narrated softly.

Chris smiled, giving all his inquisitiveness to Alex. "What's in San Fran?"

She shrugged her shoulders. "I don't know exactly," she hesitantly replied. "The Golden Gate Bridge." Laughter sprang from her chest.

It didn't take long for Chris to get drawn into her laughter. "I guess it's Alex's Magical Mystery Tour?"

Her laughter jumped from second to third gear. "Yep...Exactly." The simplicity of smiling felt good, let alone the laughter.

At that minute, Jon appeared with their drinks and the order of Salsa Verde. "Are we ready to order?"

Chris' eyes switched to Alex again, as she was already diving into the tortilla chips and the Salsa Verde. "May I order for the both of us?"

Somewhat unsuspecting of his question, Alex scrambled to say something, swallowing what remained in her mouth. "Oh...I apologize. Yes, yes, go ahead and order." She took a gulp of water.

Holding back laughter, Chris returned his attention to Jon. "We'll have the seafood paella for two please, Jon."

"Certainly," said Jon, taking back the menus. "Is there anything else I can get you?"

Chris looked at all that was on the table. "I think we're good, Jon. Thanks." When Jon left the area, Chris popped the cap off the Corona and took a sip.

"Have some before I eat all the chips," demanded Alex, sipping her water. "The salsa is good."

Giving a nod to Alex, Chris stuffed his mouth with three chips drenched in green goodness. "I know."

She watched Chris pulverize the chips with his well-sculpted jaw line. "You said you're heading home in a few weeks?"

Taking another sip of his beer, he washed down what lingered inside his mouth. "Yes, like in two and a half weeks or thereabout."

"Are you flying?"

"Yep," he answered, trying to squelch a rising belch. "I fly out on the 4th, I believe."

Alex ate a few more chips. "Are you going back to Children's?"

"Oh yeah—it's the only place I want to be," Chris spoke with authority. "How 'bout you? Are you going back to Tufts?"

"If they'll take me back, I'd love to be there with Conrad and Justin," said Alex, uncertain of what the future held.

"Why wouldn't they take you back?" Chris asked, his voice filled with faith. "You're an incredible doctor."

Reaching for her water, she took a few sips. "Yeah well, the higher ups may not cut me much slack with me flaking out during my first six months of residency."

Resting his head in his left palm, just about all his upper arm laid parallel on the table. "That's just bullshit."

"It might be bullshit, but it's my reality," admitted Alex, noticing other patrons walking down to the patio. Glances came toward their direction. "I have no idea what I'm going to face when I try to get my rotation back."

"Have you asked your dad what you should do?"

This question made Alex think, as she studied the late afternoon, L.A. blue sky, cloudless and deep. "We really haven't discussed it; I think he just wants me home, so he can see that I'm good and safe, and put back together again, but I'll definitely, definitely ask him that in the next few days," said Alex, taking a few more sips of water.

"I think you'll be fine, Al," Chris uttered convincingly.

"Yeah?"

"Yeah," he reiterated, nodding, locked into her eyes again.

The reality was that she would get to be a doctor again, because that was what Jay said to be true, although He hadn't specified the circumstances of how that would happen. She just needed to put her trust in Him. She already had.

They enjoyed the seafood paella for two, filled with scallops, mussels, shrimp and oddly enough, Chorizo. Knowing Alex was not really into eating meat, but not declaring herself an official vegetarian, Chris didn't mind trading a bit of his seafood for all her Chorizo. Soon, they witnessed such a brilliant sunset, with the sun encased by streaks of hues of blues, pinks, and yellows in the western sky. Recalling the past three weeks, she reminisced for Chris all the sunrises, sunsets, and midnight skies she had witnessed, all spectacular at each location. So comfortable with Chris, Alex divulged how she chastised herself for not learning all the constellations and such when Nate was all about astronomy some time ago, as she believed she had cheated him and herself out of quality time together. Not that Chris was an expert in naming every constellation and star, but he offered to get her versed through his insights. His offer moved her in ways she never expected, although she kept it inside, not wanting to appear too covetous.

It was incredible how the crowd grew on the patio once the sun went down. Alex and Chris were catching up as old friends, surrounded by an electric vibe, which occurred when the crowd would anticipate when the live music might begin. As the darkness settled, a breeze kicked up off the coast, altogether refreshing after a day in which the sun was merciless. Alex realized she needed a haircut when the breeze continued to blow her hair into her line of sight, as she flipped it out of her face each time the wind kicked up. The idea that there was beach not too far away tantalized her like nothing else did at that time, but Alex remembered that Justice needed to eat and go for a walk—maybe a long walk—if Chris didn't object. She was certain he surely wouldn't.

After Chris paid the tab, they walked back to his apartment. Alex grabbed some dog food from her car that Charlie had given her before she left Vegas. They found Justice just chilling on the area rug in the living room. As soon as Justice got up and met them, Alex made sure she crouched down and praised him by massaging him around his scruff, becoming more attached, as if he was hers since ancient times, with her ancient heart. Chris picked up the empty bowl from the floor, placing it on the island. With the food in the bowl, Chris put it back down and they watched Justice wolf it down within a minute's time. Given the fact that they had been gone at dinner for the better part of three hours, Alex decided it was time to take him for a walk. There was no question that Chris would accompany Alex; of course, she had the ability to use the GPS on her iPhone, but she was his good friend, and he wasn't about to let her walk the strange city streets after sundown, alone.

"How far is the beach?" she asked, walking on the same sidewalk, in the same direction with Chris, beside her.

"It's about fifteen miles," replied Chris, glancing at her, smiling.

Fifteen miles sounded like one hundred miles—walking that far wasn't possible on any given day. It had been a long day, but a good day all the same. Before she had time to determine her energy level, her mom was calling. With a simple touch, Joanne and Michael appeared on the small screen. "Hello!"

Simultaneously, they both greeted their daughter with the same enthusiasm. "How are you, Love?!" Joanne spoke with adoration. "We are just over the moon about what you accomplished today! We are just so proud—so proud!"

"Congratulations, Honey!" Michael injected proudly.

"Oh, thank you Mom and Dad," Alex said, not feeling the gravity of the day yet. "I just did what I had to do with the tools I was given— mostly my hands."

"Spoken like a true doctor, Al," expressed Michael, overwhelmed with gratitude, nearly bursting from his chest.

"Thanks, Dad."

"Are you walking somewhere, Love?" Joanne asked, as she saw that Alex was outside.

"Yes," Alex began, "we are taking Justice for a walk. It's a nice night in downtown Los Angeles." It hadn't dawned on her that it was so late on the East Coast, given the fact they were on the couch in the den.

"So, who is this friend you met there, Al?" pressed Joanne, staring lovingly at her daughter.

Handing her iPhone to Chris, Alex gave him a smile. "Ta-da!"

"Chris Jacobs!" exclaimed Joanne. "Oh my God—we haven't seen you in like, forever! How have you been?!"

His smile consumed his face. "Hi Mr. and Mrs. Roma!" Gazing right, Chris saw Alex enjoying the moment. "I've been good!"

"Oh God, Chris, please call us Michael and Joanne," pleaded Alex's mother. "So, what are you doing in Los Angeles?"

Giving a slight chortle, Chris' smile never altered. "I was needed here for the last six months or so because I had to fill in for another resident. Yeah, so…"

"Do you like Los Angeles, Chris?" asked Michael, trying to hide a yawn.

"I mean, working at L.A. Children's has been great, but I can't deny I really miss Boston, my mom and everyone; yeah—I can't wait to get home, Michael, that's for sure."

"Yeah, I bet," uttered Michael.

"Did you two have dinner yet?" Joanne inquired like a mother would.

"Yes, we had a very nice, very relaxing dinner at this place called El Cid—Spanish food."

"It was great food," Alex interjected out of shot.

"That sounds yummy," commented Joanne. "So, I am going to

assume you two crossed paths at the Children's Hospital today?"

Chris smiled easily. "Exactly, Joanne! I was blown away when I saw Alex earlier."

Listening to Chris speak with such exuberance made her giggle. "Blown away, huh?"

"Yes, blown away," Chris spoke confidently, locked onto her eyes.

"Chris, how's the baby?" asked a very humbled Michael.

"Oh God, he's just perfect—just perfect, Michael," answered Chris with the same ecstatic enthusiasm. "He weighs a little over five pounds, his lungs are strong—he's just perfect."

Settling down, Joanne, abundant in grace and fortitude, hugged Michael's shoulders. "I'm so proud of you, Baby Girl," she said, tearing up. If there was some way to crawl through the phone to hug her daughter, she would have.

Chris handed Alex back her iPhone, completely enraptured by how much her parents loved her. Quickly, he looked away to clear his eyes.

"Given the fact it's past one o'clock here, Al, we're going to head to bed," stated Michael, "but we'll definitely talk to you tomorrow."

"I most definitely will talk to you tomorrow. I love you."

"We love you too, Al. Goodnight, Love. Goodnight, Chris!" spoke Michael for them both.

"Goodnight," Alex replied, "I love you."

"Goodnight, Joanne and Michael," Chris joined in.

"Goodnight, Chris."

"Love you," Alex repeated before she ended the call.

"Wow, Al, they really love you, you know," Chris said, as he put all his passion into his words with his physicality. "I haven't talked to my father in like seven years. And when I tell people, not often, that my father is a deadbeat, crackhead, white dude, they look at me funny, as if to say, 'I thought only black guys were deadbeat dads', and all I want to say is, 'pull your head out of your ass, man'. It drives me nuts. But I can't lose my shit, because I would ever be known as that angry black man."

Alex felt his frustration, his sadness. "Do you know where he is?"

Looking down at the sidewalk, concrete squares with cracks with fractures radiating in all different directions, Chris ruminated. "The last thing I heard, he was in New York, living wherever he could find. I heard he looked bad."

"Do you ever think about trying to find him again?" pressed Alex.

Chris doddered on his feet while he contemplated his response. "Not really, because every time I find him, I get him into a program, he might stay in for a week, maybe two, if we're lucky; he checks himself out, immediately inserts a needle into one of his non-collapsed veins, and then he calls me up to tell me what a piece of crap I am, along with Mom," he narrated, on the verge of tears. "I don't need that crap, Al."

Her fingers found Justice's head, scratching his soft head, as she processed the weight upon his shoulders. "I hear ya." Glancing at Chris, although her circumstances were different, she could tell that their pain was hauntingly similar. "How's your mom doing?" she asked in a soft voice.

Chris couldn't hold back his smile. "She's doing good…really good. This year, her real estate company was in the top five in Boston. She's seeing this guy friend now."

"This guy friend?" repeated Alex, chuckling. "Have you met him?"

"Yeah, I met him a few times," Chris said. "He's a nice guy—he treats her well. I think they are going to take a trip to that new Justice Museum down in Alabama."

"The National Memorial for Peace and Justice? I was there like two weeks ago. Powerful stuff."

"Really? Montgomery, correct?"

"Yes."

As Chris continued to walk, Alex and Justice walked in the direction he was leading. "I remember Mom and I watching a segment about it on *60 Minutes*. We were talking about going. Now she's going with Steve."

"Everybody should see it," said Alex. "It's truly spine-tingling." Right then and there, Justice did his business. "That's not spine-tingling, Justice."

Seeing Alex laugh, Chris laughed along with her. "Here, let me have the bag. I can get it."

Giving him a brisk look doused in humor, Alex got to the job at hand. "I can pick up dog poop, you know; I'm not a damsel in distress," she pointed out, pulling the poop bag over her fingers. "Don't forget, I did bring a life into the world today."

Standing in a casual stance with his arms relaxed at his sides, Chris watched Alex carefully pick up Justice's deposit. "Another week, and you'll be a pro at that," joked Chris.

"You are such a funny guy, Chris Jacobs," she jested back, as she twirled and twisted the brown plastic bag closed. Standing again, she surveyed the area. "Did we just walk around the block?"

"Pretty much," uttered Chris, looking around the neighborhood and seeing his place only a few houses down. "What's ya wanna do?"

She thought for a bit but not long. "Want to stream a movie?" Alex asked, contorting her face somewhat. "You pick."

With his hands in the pockets of his long sage-green plaid shorts, he weighed his choices. "Have you seen *Green Book* yet?"

It was as if a billow of embarrassment consumed Alex, as her head dropped a little bit. "I've heard a lot about it, but I haven't seen it yet."

Chris recognized the fleeting sorrow within her eyes. "Come on, let's go watch it," he spoke, walking slowly toward his place until she caught up.

Giving him a smile, she felt understood. "Thank you."

"You're very welcome," Chris said easily, returning her smile.

Once Justice was settled next to the couch, which only took a half of a second, Alex sat on the cushiony, midnight-blue, fabric couch, as she sunk into it comfortably. She watched Chris attempt to use the Fire Stick remote to find the movie but to no avail.

"Do you know how to work this?" Chris asked, uncommonly flustered. "I think I have it on Amazon." In that second, he stood, and headed toward his bedroom. "I'll be right back."

Flipping her head to watch him bolt to his bedroom, Alex turned her attention back to finding the movie, which took her under a minute to do. "I found it," she announced, as she glanced toward his half-closed bedroom door. "What are you doing in there?"

"I'm looking for something," Chris spoke with determination.

"Do you need help?"

"Nope."

"Do you want me to send Justice in there to help you?"

"No," Chris answered, a little louder than the last time, with a slight giggle in his throat.

Curiosity got the better of her, as she got up from the couch to saunter over to Chris' bedroom door, peaking her head around the door, observing him pulling stuff out his closet. The closet light was the only light on in the navy painted bedroom. "May I come in?"

Crouched down, Chris turned on his feet and gazed up at Alex. "Oh sure, sure," he said, settling down on the floor, continuing to rifle through thin piles of papers and envelopes.

Alex knelt on the floor, and then sat beside Chris. "Can I help you look for something?"

Still filing through papers, his fingers separated single pages to view each. "I'm looking for a letter. I think it's in one of these envelopes over here," said Chris, reaching for another pile of envelopes in the closet floor.

"Is there anything written on the envelope?" Alex asked, wanting to help.

A sigh left his chest. "I believe your name is written on it."

Quickly glancing at a resolved Chris, Alex didn't press him for information. "Okay, that should narrow it down a bit," she commented, as both her interest and heart rate increased.

At last, Chris finally held onto one lone envelope in his hands, staring at it as if he had just found the lost lottery ticket; he opened it just to double-check it was all there. It was. "Umm....before you read this letter, I wrote it on the second day out here," Chris said, pausing to collect his emotions. "It almost killed me when I found out what had happened with Nate; you needed me and I couldn't get to you." Wiping his eyes, he handed Alex the letter.

Her heart rate stepped up a bit, looking into his watery crystal-blue eyes. In slow motion, or so it seemed, she took the letter and began to read it, as it grabbed her attention at the first paragraph. Like Chris, she was gripped with emotion, as she painstakingly read every word, professing his deep feelings for her. When Alex peered his way tens of times reading his words, Chris sat nervously, looking vacantly into the practically empty closet. His written words proved to Alex that he understood her so well, being acutely aware that she had to give all her attention to Nate in every free moment she had. In his words, Chris declared he would wait for her until the end of time. "Remember that night you stayed with me when Nate had one of his psychotic episodes; you were asleep on the couch." she asked in a quiet voice, with tears rolling down her cheeks.

Hearing her speak was euphoric; Chris didn't have to look away. He was looking at the woman he loved. "I do remember."

Breathing, and looking upward, flipping back her hair, Alex swallowed hard. "Nate woke up and he was pretty lucid, and he told me I was going to fall in love with you because he could see you were in love with me," Alex admitted, breathing in more oxygen. "I didn't see it, but Nate did." Between laughing and crying, she shook her head. "I'm such an idiot."

Chris leaned forward and kissed Alex's lips. He didn't care what she looked like, he didn't care what was coming out of her eyes or nose, because he just wanted to kiss her—he had waited so long to do so.

At that moment, Alex came alive with his lips upon hers, as she kissed him back, putting her hands cupping both sides of his jaw line, pulling him toward her, as she kissed his lips repeatedly. "I'm so sorry, Chris."

Still amazed she had kissed him, as she so passionately displayed her love for him, Chris gazed at Alex with raw emotion. "You don't have to apologize for anything, Alex. You have been through so much. I watched you with Nate; you were amazing with him. I could never have done what you did for him. You are amazing."

Alex was finally feeling, instead of thinking, as she kissed Chris again. "This is the first time in so long I have felt alive, Chris," Alex said, locked into his eyes.

Slowly, Chris rose to his feet, holding Alex's hand, guiding her up with him. He held her tightly into his body, as he continued to kiss Alex with all the love he had for her, which could fill the world. With his big, but gentle hands, he began exploring her body until she slightly flinched. "I'm sorry."

She put her head to his chest. "No, no—don't apologize. I want this for us, but I haven't done this in a long time," Alex admitted freely. "I don't want to disappoint you in any way."

With his eyes upon her, Chris found her chin and held it up to gaze at her beautiful face. "Alex Roma, I don't think you could ever, ever, disappoint me," he said, smiling, gazing into her stunning soul that would surely keep his heart beating forever, he imagined. "It has been a while for me too."

Once again, Alex kissed Chris boldly, as her passion grew exponentially with his, exploring what was waiting underneath their clothing, which swiftly came off and gathered up in an arbitrarily shaped circle on the dark floor. His bed was mere feet away, as they used it to keep enjoying their own wonderland of skin and everything else that went along with making love.

The sun was bright in the eastern California sky, which hadn't reached into Chris' bedroom yet. He awakened first, having the notion that the greatest night so far wasn't a mere dream but a reality. Truly content to watch Alex sleep beside him, Chris didn't have a care in the world—besides her, of course. The urge to touch her became too great, especially when a stray piece of hair crossed over the left side of her magnificent face. Chris tested out the theory that he had skills to move that one hair back where it belonged without disturbing her. The task was nearly complete until Alex began to stir, opening her eyes a bit, gazing at Chris at first sight.

"Hi," Alex uttered, beaming at Chris, as she leaned over to kiss him.

Chris didn't need anything more at that moment; he had her love to sustain him in every possible way. "Good morning," Chris said, moving her closer to him, as her neck found the crook below his muscular shoulder. "Sleep well?"

"When we slept, I slept," she answered, trying not to giggle. It didn't work.

"You're very vivacious, Alex Roma," he said, laughing. Under the maroon sheet and matching light comforter, he found one of her hands to hold.

Kissing him again, she found his eyes tied to every move. "What do you have to do today?"

"Well," Chris began, adjusting his head on the pillow, "if I had my way, I'd spend the entire day in bed with you, but I have to work at three."

"Spending the day in bed with you sounds spectacular, but the world awaits," Alex spoke cheerfully. "Do you think I can come with you and see the baby?"

"Absolutely," Chris smiled, gazing at the woman he simply adored. "Yesterday, when I saw you at the hospital, I couldn't believe it was you—it was like a dream. I'm very blessed—very blessed indeed."

Lying on Chris' chest was a gold cross, significant to all Christians of the world. Alex held it from the bottom and stared at it. "Do you ever wonder if Jesus could walk among us and we wouldn't know it was Him?"

"Like that song, *One of Us*?" Chris questioned, as he tenderly stroked her temple.

"Yeah," she answered, shifting her eyes up to his.

"I guess anything's possible these days," Chris surmised, "look who's in the White House."

"Oh man, let's not discuss him," begged Alex. "I haven't had breakfast yet." At the mere mention of breakfast, Justice catapulted himself onto the bed and went back and forth looking at them both with a goofy expression.

"He's not going to eat our faces off, is he?" Chris asked, half joking.

Instantly, Alex was hysterical with laughter; she loved the way he could make her laugh. "I highly doubt he'll chew our faces off, but I'll feed him just in case." Justice jumped off the bed once she began moving over Chris' body. As new lovers often do, captivated by what their love could make them feel, wanting to feel that rapture of needing, wanting, Justice would have to wait a little longer for breakfast.

Having tea and a piece of toast on Chris' screened-in back porch, surrounded by trees, making it a glorious space, Alex's iPhone beckoned for attention. It was Conrad, and she knew it would be fated that he was bound to see right through her giddiness that would tip him off. Taking a deep breath, she tapped the accept button.

"Hello there," Alex said in the middle of taking a sip of tea from her large yellow mug.

"What's ya doing?" asked Conrad impishly, obvious that he had insider information.

"I'm having breakfast," she barely gave up. "What are you doing?" Alex took a bite of toast.

"I'm waiting for Justin to dress Lila, and then I'm going to feed her," uttered Conrad, getting things organized in their farmhouse kitchen.

Alex smiled. "Very domestic of you two," she commented, as she took another bite of toast.

"Were you domestic last night?" Conrad asked slowly and methodically, pronouncing every single syllable, as if his mouth was a word factory.

Raising her left brow, Alex gave Conrad a disillusioned glance. "Really, dude?"

Upon her answer, Conrad smiled, as he didn't need any more confirmation. "That's all I needed."

Alex gave him an eye roll along with a humorous snicker, knowing she was sunk. "And what are you doing today?" Aware this might be a longer than usual conversation, she positioned her wrist on the edge of the round glass-top table, iPhone in hand.

Nothing could wipe the smile from Conrad's face. "Umm, I

think we are going to just take Lila to the park," he said. "Are you headed home soon?" Before Conrad could hear her answer, Chris walked into the frame. "Hi, Chris!"

"Oh, hi Conrad!" Chris said enthusiastically. "Long time no see. How are you and Justin doing with your new baby girl?"

"It's so nice to see you, Chris," Conrad spoke with the same enthusiasm. "We are doing great with our new pumpkin pie. She's just great!"

"Conrad, Chris wants to see the little cutie," spoke Alex.

"Yes, Justin is bringing her out now," Conrad uttered with an overjoyed heart, as he took Lila into his arms. "Chris is there with Alex."

"Ohhhh, hi Chris!" Justin said with elation. "How are you?!"

Crouching down beside where Alex was sitting, Chris slid his hand onto her back. "Hi Justin! I'm doing great, just great!" he said undeniably happily, lightly squeezing just under Alex's rib. "How have you been?"

Kissing Lila's head in succession, Justin smiled widely. "Need I say more?"

"Not at all, man!" Chris stated with a tone filled with total bliss, staring at beautiful Lila. "I heard Lila's middle name is Alexandra."

"Yes, yes, that is true," Justin confirmed, grinning without reservation. "We wouldn't have had it any other way."

Humbled to her heart's core, Alex beamed outwardly. "I figure when she gets to be twelve or thirteen, she'll be cursing me out because she might be hearing her full name if she gets in trouble." Laughter filled the porch.

"Lila will be the perfect child and teenager, won't you, Baby Girl?" Conrad cooed while he fed her the bottle.

Again, laughter filled the room. "He's going to change his tune once the boys start flocking around," Justin quipped.

"Oh, stop," Conrad said calmly, feeding his little girl. "Lila is going to be perfect."

Chris was giddy over the fact he was talking to the home crowd whom he hadn't seen in months. "What's happening in Boston? I miss all of you back there."

"Yeah, I bet," Justin reacted. "We didn't know you were in Los Angeles until this morning." The words, 'this morning', were suspiciously glossed over.

Alex tried to be cool about Conrad's and Justin's newest revelation, as she scratched her left eyebrow that didn't need scratching.

"Boston is still Boston—nothing much going on here," replied Justin. "You're coming home soon, correct?"

This was another confirmation for Alex that they had talked to her parents, probably Joanne more specifically, before Conrad FaceTimed her. All eyes were on Chris, especially Alex's.

"Yes, I have about two weeks left out here, and I'm flying home," Chris said, almost jumping out of his skin. "Can't wait!"

Alex smiled at his eagerness, his warmth she could easily sense. A flashing thought crossed her mind that she could lie low in Los Angeles for the next two weeks so he could drive home with her. Although the idea sounded great, Alex knew she had to get back to her life, especially her residency she had to somehow get back. Life awaited her. "Well, guys, we are going to take off to see the baby I delivered, on the side of the highway, no less."

"Oh yes, congratulations, Al!" Justin exclaimed, very animated with his arms and hands. "Of course, it had to be you to deliver a baby first, in an obscure place."

Alex giggled. "Okay Sparky, calm down there," she said, still laughing. "I'll call you guys later to tell you all about it."

"Please do!" Justin spoke.

"Okay Al, we won't keep you any longer," Conrad spoke, holding Lila. "We'll catch ya later. Bye Chris! We love you guys! See ya soon!"

"Bye! Love you!" Alex spiritly uttered before closing out the call. Returning her eyes to Chris, they simultaneously busted out laughing with no immediate end in sight. Alex leaned on his rugged shoulder, taking hold of his opposite hand. "I hope you realize that we are the talk of all our friends, our families and anyone who might know us."

With his arms surrounding Alex, Chris kissed her forehead. "You know what I say to that?"

Putting her head back so she had a good look at his clean-shaven face, Alex happily grinned. "What do you say?"

"Let them talk," replied Chris, subsequently kissing her lips softly.

As Alex followed Chris through the entrance of the hospital, he led her to the nearest elevator bay, entering the first cab that opened its doors, as other people shuffled in behind them. On this day, Alex chose the only pair of black dress pants she had with her, along with the white short-sleeved shirt she hadn't yet worn. She was rather impressed nothing was wrinkled knowing they had been thrown in the back of her Camry somewhere. The elevator stopped at every floor to let somebody out; Chris and Alex got out on the third floor, stopping at the front desk to get Alex processed to enter the wing. Chris had some credence with security, as he was able to get her cleared rather quickly. Unlike the previous day, Alex took note of how Chris looked in his electric-blue scrubs, as if he was born to wear them. As the beige, heavy, metal door closed behind them, Chris and Alex walked together down to the nursery, where they found Ellen rocking a very content Alexander Thomas, and a man who they considered to be Alexander's father, in one of the quiet rooms. Chris gently knocked on the half, glass-paned door, as he opened it.

"Hello," he spoke in a soft voice. "My name is Doctor Christopher Jacobs; I was here when they brought your son in yesterday. "How is he doing?"

"Oh, hello Doctor Jacobs—it is very nice to meet you," Ellen expressed with genuine gratitude. "Alexander is doing pretty well considering the extraordinary entrance he made into the world yesterday."

Crouching down, Chris grinned, aware of everything that had transpired. "Yeah, I heard all about it. That was amazing!" It was almost impossible for Chris to take his eyes off Alexander, knowing who helped to bring him into this world. "I brought a guest who you might want to see." Chris stood back up and held the door open high, as Alex snuck under his arm.

"Hi Ellen!" Alex exclaimed very quietly, wearing the biggest smile.

Nearly jumping out of her skin, although resisting to do so, Ellen could hardly believe her eyes. "Oh my God, Alex!" she exclaimed a little bit louder. "I didn't expect to see you."

The gentleman sitting beside Ellen took cues and offered to take the baby. "Let me take him, Babe."

"Oh, thank you, Hon," Ellen said, giving the baby to the man who clearly had a vested interest in both mother and child. Once he had a secure hold on Alexander, Ellen steadily rose to her feet and extended her arms in preparation to give a powerful embrace to Alex.

Alex felt Ellen's arms around her back, as she easily reciprocated, instantly feeling that warm peace that was supplied by God's love and His spirit. "Oh boy."

Indebtedness kept Ellen hugging Alex for several more seconds than usual. "I can't thank you enough for what you did for me yesterday; you are a very brave soul. God bless you!" With one last quick squeeze around Alex's shoulders, Ellen released her, but held onto Alex's right hand. Ellen had a few stray tears she wiped away. "Alex, I'd like to introduce you to my husband, Mike."

Being a father of three now, Mike was well-accustomed to shaking somebody's hand while holding a child with a free arm. "It's so, so nice to meet you, Alex. I can't thank you enough for what you did for my wife and my son yesterday," said Mike, his voice drenched with sincerity. "It was incredible."

Flattered and humbled, Alex smiled. "Given the circumstances, I did what I could—I'm happy everything worked out." With all the attention upon her, she felt undeniably awkward. "Have the doctors said when you can bring him home?"

"Probably tomorrow, since he's doing so well," entertained Ellen. "His sisters are anxious to meet their little brother."

It took Chris all his strength not to reach out and put a supportive hand upon Alex's shoulder given Nate's recent passing, although there wasn't any reason to do so.

"Alex, would you like to hold him again?" Ellen offered.

"Oh, sure, sure," spiritedly Alex spoke. Readying her arms to take the precious infant, Alex waited for Mike to get in position to hand over his first son. Being a doctor, she knew how to hold a newborn properly, holding the head steady, which she had down pat. In her arms, the swaddled Alexander was very content, as if he was catching up on sleep from a hard day's work. "Hey, Little Man—you are very cute with your little beanie on." Swaying and bouncing gently, Alex was totally enamored with Alexander.

"I think he likes you," Chris uttered softly, as he was totally enraptured with her.

Twisting her hips slightly, Alex turned her neck to look at a captivated Chris. "You think?"

"Of course," Chris returned easily.

It was obvious to Ellen that Alex and Chris knew each other. "Do you work at this hospital, Alex?"

Still focused on the little bundle, Alex heard Ellen's inquiry and turned her attention toward her. "Actually, I'm from Boston," she began narrating. "Chris, I mean, Dr. Jacobs," Alex giggled, sneaking a quick glance of an amused Chris, "we went through med school together back in Boston, so…"

"Are you out here on vacation?" Ellen asked, sitting back down on the hospital's gentle glider rocking chair.

Following her lead, Alex sat down on the blue padded metal bench next to the rocker, always looking down at Alexander. "Umm…I took some time off because I lost my brother, Nate, back in February." She breathed a little faster, feeling her heart beat a little faster too. "So, I decided to drive cross country to clear my head out."

Chris looked on, simply amazed at Alex's strength. He loved her even more.

"Oh Alex, I'm so, so sorry for your loss," Ellen said, as she reached out to touch her arm, as if she knew the depths of her sorrow. "Six years ago, last week, I lost my sister to cancer—it was brain cancer." Ellen teared up easily.

Immediately, Alex grabbed onto Ellen's hand. "Oh God, Ellen, I'm sorry," softly Alex expressed, as her own tears filled her eyes.

Squeezing Alex's hand in solidarity, they understood each other. "All three of our kids were born after my sister passed," uttered Ellen gracefully. "I'd like to think she handpicked them for me; maybe they combined forces yesterday to bring you to me in my time of need."

Clearing her eyes, a huge grin came Alex's face. "They probably did just that—I'm sure of it."

"Yep," Ellen responded, holding tightly onto Alex's hand again.

"Yep," echoed Alex, gazing down at Ellen's gift from above. Intuitively, without reason, Alex glanced toward the glass window in the door and out of the corner of her eye, caught Jay, looking upon the room, namely her, smiling wildly, as she knew she was prepared to move forward, after travelling three thousand miles, after crying as many tears and after regaining herself by discovering who exactly she was along the way. She returned her indebted gaze to Alexander, still content and sleeping, thanking the grace of God.

Arriving at Chris' place to grab Justice, Alex desired to write a letter for him to read when he got home from work later that night. From his printer, Alex pulled a few sheets of copy paper out and sat at the kitchen island to pen something significant to Chris, as he had done for her months before. With her duffle bag on the kitchen floor, Alex retrieved the letter to reread it, wanting to sense his loving spirit again, taking time to absorb his words, worried she might have missed something reading it only once. Reading it for a second time, Chris' powerful words to her, written in his endearing, tiny, chicken scratch that she had gotten used to over the years, melted into her skin. It seemed like his words took on this blue metallic, almost three-dimensional kind of character to them, as some words sparkled, while others glimmered. It was the work of his incredible heart he possessed, his God-given heart, which he poured out on the four pages Alex held vigilantly in her hands. A few times, she had to absorb fleeing tears into the skin of her index fingers and thumbs that would transfer onto the letter, which would ultimately make it hers and hers alone.

Twirling the pen over and under the fingers of her right hand, Alex thought about what she wanted to convey to Chris, perfectly and honestly, for she knew she wasn't accustomed to writing such letters of the heart, only the hundred-or-so letters she wrote to Nate when she felt he needed her written word. Those letters were written on the premise that Nate might not read them, depending on his fragile psyche. Many times, Alex would watch Nate spitefully tear her letters into what seemed like a million little pieces, while she stood, heartbroken, very aware he never read one word. In those moments, disheartened and shattered, she always had to remind herself that it was the disease and not Nate. Other times, Nate was overjoyed to receive a letter from his big sister, sometimes to the point of shedding tears over what she had written. Oh, how she would love those moments—bringing Nate a little bit of levity and knowing he was loved before his mind betrayed him again.

Toying with the idea of calling Conrad for advice was like a flame instantly extinguished by another force in Alex's mind. She knew she had to write this for Chris herself, using her own thoughts, her own feelings, and her own heart—a heart that suddenly came back from a place it didn't want to go again. Maybe she should begin with that, she thought. She had to begin somewhere. After writing the date, and Chris' name, the words started flowing onto the page, like a deluge of ink that soon filled one, and then a second, page, and remarkably to Alex, it all made sense. She tried not to apologize too many times, very aware Chris didn't want apologies from her—he just wanted her honesty. Reflecting on the past three weeks on the road, Alex went in-depth on how everything she experienced on this trip changed her perspective on living a life God had given her with the best she had to give others despite her tremendous loss of Nate. Alex also went as fast as possible recounting the frightening night on Myrtle Beach, where she had felt so afraid. The grace of God saved her life that night, she revealed. If Alex wrote it, Chris would believe it. Alex explained with all the truth within how deeply she doubted herself and her worth as a doctor following Nate's death. Again, she mentioned how the grace of God restored her faith in herself, being an agent of faith and hope moving forward. By now, Alex was on the fourth page—granted, her handwriting was larger compared to Chris'. It surprised her as to the breadth of emotion she put into this letter; twenty minutes prior, she questioned if she could write more than a paragraph to Chris—evidently, she could. Lastly, Alex expressed the importance of her metamorphosis and how spirituality seeped into the complexity of her bones and tissues, which, she believed, would never be extracted. Being mindful of what Chris might have expected, as he hadn't communicated with Alex since before Nate's death, she stressed that she remained the person he survived med school with, day in and day out, but something out of the atmosphere, a wayward asteroid, had grazed her, realigning her orientation, although creating a strong individual. Alex expressed hope that he would accept all her transformations.

Meeting Chris back at the hospital, Alex returned his key to him, as he met her at her car. With the driver's door opened, she leaned on the side while Justice had a front row seat to their conversation.

"Do you have everything?" Chris asked, trying to block the sun from his eyes so he could get a good look at her before she headed up to San Fran.

"Yeah, I have everything," she relayed, as she ended her answer with a smile.

Stepping forward, Chris' two hands found Alex's hips. "Please be safe," he softly demanded.

Locked onto Chris' eyes, she didn't want to look anywhere else at that very moment, putting her arms upon his shoulders, kissing his lips. "I will," she promised, knowing Jay would keep a keen eye on her.

It was still breathtaking for Chris to have the attention of the woman he had for a friend for the last four years in his arms now, as he hoped it would never stop being breathtaking going forward. "Call me when you stop somewhere."

With one last kiss to give, Alex held his strong hands. "I will, I promise." Pulling away from Chris was harder than she ever imagined it would be, as she had to continue to remind herself she would see him in two weeks. Holding onto his hand, Alex sat back down on the driver's seat unwillingly, tossing back her hair. "I'd better get going."

Chris was crumbling inside, but he managed to carry a strong exterior. "I'll see you at home in about two weeks, give or take—alright."

He watched her move her legs into the car, as he helped close the door. Needing one last kiss to sustain him, Chris snuck his head inside the window to steal one more kiss. "Please, be safe."

There was no denying Chris' love for her, as Alex saw it in his soulful, beautiful blue eyes. "I have my beast in the backseat to protect me," she said, half joking. They were hand-in-hand when she witnessed Chris scratch Justice with his free hand. She turned the key in the ignition. "I left something for you when you get home tonight. It's on the island."

"Really?!" Chris reacted spiritedly, smiling. "Now I'm intrigued."

Alex giggled softly. "You should be intrigued."

"Yeah?"

"Of course," she said with a confident grin. With their hands still interlocked, she struggled to let go. "I'll call you later."

"Alright Girly, get going," Chris said, surrendering her hand. "I'll talk to you later."

"Oh yes," Alex said, preparing to put the Camry in reverse.

Chris waved, watching the woman who had captured his heart drive out of the parking lot, turning onto Sunset Boulevard. He had to go be a doctor now, lightly tapping on his chest where his gold cross lay under his scrub shirt.

At the intersection of Sunset and North Vermont Avenue, traffic stopped for a red light; Alex saw Jay waiting on the sidewalk until He made His move and got in the Camry. Alex, not skipping a beat, mentioned it was her first time picking up a hitchhiker. Jay, not skipping His own beat, reminded her that she did offer Him a ride back in Pennsylvania, when she had first encountered Him. This, Alex could not deny, as she thought back on what seemed like a quarter century ago, not forgetting to mention He had declined her kind offer. Turning left onto Fountain Avenue, the Church of Scientology of Los Angeles came into view. Alex knew very little about the religion other than what she had heard on the news and what she had read in psychiatry and psychology medical journals. In a couple minutes of stop-and-go traffic, she kept looking toward Jay, assuming He could still read her thoughts.

"You're not very talkative today," Alex commented, as she observed the infamous California traffic in every direction. Well past the church, Alex left it behind. "How was your night at Children's?"

Surprisingly, Jay let out a forlorn sigh. "Some good, and some very tough moments," He portrayed. "Anyone's suffering is hard to watch, but watching babies and kids suffer is especially difficult."

Alex glanced at a weary Jesus. "I believe all of humankind can get behind that belief," stated Alex, sighing on her accord. Getting on Route 101 North, she recalled a time with a child. "I think it was last May, I was doing a short stint at Boston Children's Hospital," she began.

"With Chris," Jay quickly interjected cleverly, knowing His timing was perfect.

Completely and utterly derailed from her line of thought, Alex glanced in His direction for a split second, returning her eyes back to another new highway. All she could do was clear her throat, more to give herself time to regroup than for any other reason. "Yes—with Chris." She glanced at Him again, realizing that Jay, indeed, knew everything.

"Okay, tell me the story," Jay nudged.

Out of habit, her left hand tossed her hair back, as she became settled with the traffic flow. "Well, we had this boy, seven years old and two days post-op from a Transtibial amputation from trauma from a car accident," she begun narrating. "Our job, Chris' and mine, was to clean and inspect the wound on a daily basis, sometimes twice daily, but more importantly, our job was to get this little boy accustomed to his new reality of not having the bottom portion of his right leg anymore, which was extremely hard some days, because he was just not having it."

"Some kids find it difficult to accept new circumstances, while other kids bounce right back up," stated Jay.

"Exactly, exactly," Alex remarked, paying attention to the gradually thinning-out traffic. "The parents were very nice and all that, although when the little boy imagined he felt his leg was still attached, they would give into that idea."

Jay unhurriedly crossed His arms in front of His chest. San Francisco remained a good five hours away. "So, what did you do?"

Sighing easily, Alex slid both of her hands to the bottom of the steering wheel. "Chris and I spent a lot of time after work brainstorming what we could do for this boy, to demonstrate that he had his entire life in front of him, to do whatever he wanted."

"What did you do?"

"First, we got him comfortable with just leaving his room, because he didn't even want to do that," she explained with vigor. "We made sure he had clothes he felt comfortable wearing, and all that." Thirsty, Alex gulped some water. "We were able to recruit, if You will, some other kids receiving prosthetic services from Children's to introduce to our little guy so he knew he was not the only one who had lost a limb or who had been born with a deformity."

"How did that go?" pressed Jay.

"That approach went extremely well," Alex spoke, stoked. "We were able to get him comfortable with visiting the prosthetic lab at Children's and eventually we were able to get him fitted for a prosthetic."

Jay glanced at Alex. "Do you want to know what that little boy did today?"

"Huh?" Alex asked, very curious. "What do you mean, 'what he did today?'"

Turning in His seat, Jay faced Alex increasingly. "Well, because we're driving, I can't show you the video, but your little man ran in his first race today, and he came in second."

Swiftly, Alex looked at Jay. "No way?! Seriously?!" Her voice raised an octave.

"Kiddo, really?" uttered an annoyed Jay. "Seriously."

"Oh no," she hastily replied, reaching out to touch His hand, "I believe You—I believe You wholeheartedly, Jay. I'm just thrilled beyond words at the moment." A single, happy tear, escaped from the corner of her right eye. "I can't wait to tell Chris."

Jay understood. "Yeah, I know." Now on Route 101 North, He sat quietly, watching the highway serpentine through the small green valleys and around hillocks, bringing them ever closer to San Francisco. Jay glanced back toward Alex. "Comparing the boy's story to this road trip, might you sense any parallels?"

"Parallels?" she spoke just to speak the word. "What do You mean, 'parallels'?"

"Just think about it for a little while," He gently urged. "I believe you'll discover some interesting similarities if you just consider things."

The curves of the highway didn't provide Alex more than just a few seconds to stare into Jay's eyes. As her mind relaxed, thoughts started emerging, becoming clearer with each mile, recalling being so lost in grief over the loss of Nate. She remembered their first encounter on the dark and winding road, where the Camry had stalled out. As the boy had to learn to trust her and Chris, Alex had learned to trust Jay, even though she resisted His guidance in the beginning. So did the boy. At every location They visited, there was a lesson to be learned, sometimes very difficult and poignant lessons that had to touch every shattered thread of her being to stabilize the injury to promote healing. Without all those hard lessons, without all those interactions with mostly very kind individuals, Alex didn't know what would have happened without

Jay as her co-pilot. Tears fell easily, as she glanced at Jay. "You put this entire trip together?"

Weighing her question, He wobbled His neck from side to side, pushing His lips out, looking out the windshield. "Pretty much." Jay returned His eyes to her. "I can't deny the fact that I had assistance with managing this by a lot of faith, prayers, and the tiniest bit of luck. I also had assistance from a few angels on Earth."

"Angels?"

"Ellen was one, Rob, Hope, Frankie, Yvette, Jeff, Mary, Roger, and Mrs. Shea were the others," Jay clarified, clasping His hands together. "They had healing powers you desperately needed."

Putting her right hand on top of His hands, Alex glanced at Him with the utmost feeling of gratitude, the kind of gratitude that not everyone feels during a lifetime. "What can I possibly do to pay You back for all this?"

"You don't need to pay Me back for anything, Alex," Jay spoke honestly, His eyes unwavering. "Just live your life fully, never doubting yourself. Live your life with humanity and kindness, because there isn't much of that going around these days, as you know."

Another tear fell without being caught. "Yeah, I know," she responded, as her eyes were firmly looking forward.

"And I want you to live full of happiness, joy, and above all, love, because I know you have a lot of love in that big, gigantic heart of yours," Jay portrayed with fervor. "Everyone should know it."

Lifting her hand to catch more tears streaming down her right cheek, she returned it to His hands. "Am I Mother Theresa caliber?" Alex rhetorically asked, as she laughed out loud.

Giggling, while sucking in air between His teeth, Jay issued Alex a big grin. "Boy, that's going to be a tough one to sell," Jay joked, being truthful.

"I thought so," playfully uttered Alex.

"And never, ever, lose your sense of humor," begged Jay, holding onto Alex's hand. "Your sense of humor will get you through a lot of hard, frustrating times."

Sighing, Alex believed Him. "That thing You mentioned in Colorado, right?"

"Yes."

"Is there any chance I could get You to expand on what is coming?" Alex figured it was worth another attempt.

"I wish I could, Alex, but…"

Finding His eyes, Alex knew she had to trust Him. "Okay," she uttered, fully accepting His answer without reservation.

"Like I explained before, if you ever, ever need Me, just call Me, and I'll be there," Jay recited. "It might take Me a couple hours or so, but I'll be there."

"Rush hour traffic on the Zakim?" she quipped.

Her witticism caused laughter, as Jay busted into fits. He appreciated her quick comebacks. "Yep, exactly, exactly!" There was no doubt in His heart that Alex was prepared to emerge again.

Justice was getting antsy, and Alex was getting hungry. They stopped in Morgan Hill to satisfy their needs. Finding the establishment, Noah's Bar and Bistro, Alex went in and ordered herself a grilled salmon sandwich to go and used the facilities. Not far from the restaurant was Britton Field, where there was more than enough space for Justice to run around after he ate. With the sun dropping slowly in the western sky, the weather couldn't have been better; it was so clear, with a little bite in the air. Before she ate, Alex made sure to alert her parents, and then Chris, that she was about 90 minutes away from San Francisco, her last official destination Jay set up for her.

But what was in San Francisco that He wanted Alex to see, she wondered. As the Camry was backed into one of the parking spaces that abutted the field so she could keep an eye on Justice, running back and forth, a typical canine at play, she climbed up and sat on the trunk of the Camry and dug into her dinner, but not before she offered Jay some food. Not surprisingly, He declined her offer. Jay leaned on the left side of the trunk and asked Alex for her iPhone and keyed in the code. It didn't take long for Jay to bring up the little boy running in his first race earlier in the day, overwhelming Alex to shed very happy tears. Taking a break from her meal, Alex sent the video link to Chris, her parents, Conrad, and Justin. The responses she received back were all very positive and joyful, especially Chris', which wasn't surprising. The idea of what she would see in San Francisco never abated, as Alex weighed the possibilities. Trying to be nonchalant about it, playing it as cool as possible, she nudged Him to reveal what San Francisco had in store. A detective she was not, and Jay even told her that, comically, of course. From the cosmic-sized smile He adorned on His angelic guise, Alex felt confident it wouldn't be bad, for she had successfully completed what Jay had intended for her to do. Maybe it was a prize of some sort, she pondered, as she enjoyed her grilled sandwich, watching Justice happily roaming and playing. At times, he would come back to feverishly lap up some water from his bowl on the ground. When Justice had had enough play, he lay on the ground not far from Alex.

While preparing to get back on the road again, getting Justice comfortable in the backseat, Alex's iPhone rang. It was Ben calling to thank her for connecting him with Charlie, moreover, explaining that Ruby would be evaluated by the best specialists in Georgia. This news was wondrous to Alex, as she started the Camry. She told Ben she would most likely be back in Boston in a week's time, gazing at Jay to get His confirmation on that belief. Jay gave it by nodding in the affirmative. Closing out the call from Ben, Alex promised to touch base with him when she got home. Alex asked Ben to give Ruby and the rest of his family her love. As a man of the cloth, Ben left the call with a 'God bless you', as she easily returned the same sentiment.

Once Alex saw the large green highway signs announcing San Francisco was within 30, 20, 10, and then 5 miles, she was able to allow herself to get excited. Off in the distance, the two international orange pillars stood tall against the dark amber sky. Lit up by bright white lights, it was difficult for Alex to look at anything else. Before getting to the bridge, Jay instructed her to take the exit prior to the bridge, as she trusted Him with all her soul. They drove through the Presidio of San Francisco area, south of the Golden Gate, and parked on Lincoln Boulevard, parallel to Baker Beach on the Pacific. Getting out of the Camry, Alex was met with a strong southwesterly breeze coming off the water which was almost chilly. She hustled around to the other side of the Camry and dug through the backseat to find her oversized, gray, pullover Tufts sweatshirt. The fact that she wore long pants on this one particular day wasn't wasted on her when the wind blew with a fierceness that might have scared the average person away, but not her—she was a New England girl through-and-through, as she had played in stronger winds as a child. Coming back to the driver's side of the Camry, Alex grabbed Justice and followed Jay into one of the beach's closed parking lots. They crossed over one of the boardwalks that led to the sand. To Jay's amusement, Alex stopped to take off her sneakers and socks.

"Really?" Jay broached, giving Alex a goofy look.

"Yeah, why not? The sand is still warm from the sun," she pointed out, holding her sneakers in one hand, and Justice's leash in the other.

Jay couldn't exactly argue with that logic. "Okay, go for it," He said, smiling. A few seconds later, Jay walked onto the beach, where a few others lingered quite a distance away from Them. Grabbing a glimpse of Alex walking slightly behind with Justice, Jay was sure they remained safe. "I thought you would like to see a beach again, since it has been a while."

Loving the feel of the sand surrounding her feet and toes, this was her happy place for her soul, a rejuvenating place. It didn't matter what coast she was on, being close to an ocean was her elixir. "Thank you. This is wonderful, Jay."

"Just don't get too close to the water; the riptide gets a little…gnarly…out here at night," He advised, as He attempted to sound cool.

"Did you just say, 'gnarly'?" Alex couldn't keep from laughing out loud.

"Why, yes I did," Jay admitted easily. "Didn't I sound cool?"

Still quietly chortling, she looked at Him. "You don't strike me as a surfer dude."

"Well, I thank you for your honesty; I will not say 'gnarly' again, at least in your presence," spoke Jay, demonstrating His comedic side. Approaching the place He had designated, He stopped and turned to Alex. "See the moon over the Golden Gate?"

"The moon?" she inquisitively uttered, sure that she hadn't noticed a moon prior to this moment. Turning to face north, Alex was struck to see a moon, the giant, amber and cream-colored sphere, positioned perfectly over the iconic bridge. "Did I really miss the moon before?"

"You could have been looking at it from a different angle," suggested Jay, pacifying her confusion.

Enthralled with its beauty, Alex stopped wondering about angles. "It's magnificent." It was several seconds later when she felt Jay gently put His hand upon her left shoulder, as she slowly gazed toward Him, but then returned her eyes to the moon. Her senses began to rise, as Alex recalled what transpired in Gettysburg. Eerily, the once-gusty breezes coming off the Pacific were suddenly calm; the stars in the sky were astoundingly prolific. Something caught her eye about 15 feet away, approaching her without fear. As if 2,300 puzzle pieces, suspended in a translucent, thick substance, all came together within a few seconds, suddenly she saw Nate, standing two feet away, wearing the same pair of jeans and navy-blue Champion sweatshirt he wore the night he passed. "Is it you?" she cried out softly, afraid to believe her own eyes. "Jay, can

I touch him?!"

"Yes, of course," Jay answered without pretense.

With that, Alex jumped to Nate to embrace him, and then broke down in sobs when he reciprocated her strong clutch. Everything about Nate felt familiar—his arms, the smell of him, and his love. "I miss you so much," Alex whispered in his right ear, as her chin lay upon the curve of Nate's neck.

Squeezing her shoulders tightly, Nate recognized her unconditional love. "I know you do, I know you do…and I miss you, Al," said Nate, managing to have Alex release her arms so he could look into her weeping eyes. "This was never your fault; it was never Mom or Dad's fault. I was dealt a lousy hand of cards, and I had to play them the best way I knew how. There wasn't anything anyone could do."

She couldn't help but to caress all his face, making sure it was him, and familiarizing herself with him again. "Are you okay?" Once the question slipped from her mouth, Alex knew it was a stupid inquiry.

"Yes, I am," Nate promised, as he took both of her hands in his. "I have been watching you these past six months, and you can't give up on life because I'm not around. To surrender all you worked for, all you have dreamt, and all you ever wanted cannot hinge upon my presence. Do you know why you cannot do that?"

It was amazing that she was staring into her little brother's eyes again, looking at his wavy brown hair along with his handsome facial features. "I'm guessing you are going to tell me."

Shifting his weight to his left side, Nate kept holding her hands against his chest. "Because I'm still going to be with you, every day of your life, cheering you on upon all your victories, and through the tough times, I'll be whispering in your ear, 'you got this'. You won't visibly see me, but I'll be with, and beside you." Holding Alex's hands, Nate held them a little tighter. "Please don't carry my death upon your shoulders."

Not sure how much time she had with Nate, Alex wanted to focus all her attention on him. "That was a very hard lesson to learn, but I understand that now," Alex confessed, as she continued to keep her eyes on Nate. "We miss you like crazy."

"I know you do," Nate repeated, giving Alex another strong embrace. "Who's your friend over here?" Nate crouched down and scratched Justice's head while his other hand still held his sister's.

This interaction solidified for Alex that Nate was indeed present and wasn't some weird delusion she was having. As Alex crouched down next to Nate, she cleared the tears from her face while small amounts continued to escape. "This is Justice."

"What a righteous name," Nate reacted exuberantly, as he overindulged the pooch with kisses and rubdowns. "By the way, Lu says 'thank you' for taking such good care of her during her last few days."

Stunned by Nate's last statement, she stared at him with utter amazement, having been caught off-guard. "Is she with Casey?"

Once he took his attention away from Justice, Nate returned his jovial glance to a gaping Alex. "They are together. They're very pleased that you have Justice."

"Oh wow," she uttered, as her spine tingled, completely amazed by how the Heavens operate.

"Our time is running short," Nate declared, standing up.

Shooting upward like a rocket, Alex followed, standing. "Will I see you again?" she pressed hard.

"Eventually—yes," Nate stated with certainty, taking her hands within his. "I'm told you have a long life ahead of you. Go be happy, go love like you've never loved before and go be a doctor, because being a doctor is who you are, my dear sister."

Tears were the name of the game for Alex when it came to her heart. "Can you hear me when I talk to you?"

"Yes, yes—of course I hear you when you talk to me!" Nate ardently confirmed. "Talk to me all the time. Mom and Dad do."

"Really?" Alex smiled.

"Yeah," confirmed Nate. "They want you home in the worst way. They always ask me to keep you safe."

One of her hands grabbed the few lines of tears running down her face, as her diaphragm heaved in and out. Alex studied his face before he had to leave. "I love and miss you, Nate."

He smiled widely. "I love and miss you too, Sis." Giving her one last hug, he kissed her on the cheek. "I was right about Chris," Nate remarked proudly.

Caught between crying and laughing, eventually laughing won out. "Okay, I'll give you that one."

Walking backwards, Nate slowly disappeared, all the while, repeating: "I told you so." Nate left her as she smiled.

Staring for a few long seconds at the spot where Nate had just stood, the wind picked up again, startling Alex out of her reverie. "Did that just happen?"

"It did happen, yes," Jay reassured easily. "Are you okay?"

Emotions ran high in her soul, processing the past several

minutes with Nate—a gift from the Heavens, and from Jay. Continuing to stare off in the area where Nate had stood, she freely wept. "That was amazing," spoke Alex, as her voice cracked. "Thank you."

Clasping His hands in front of Him, Jay bowed His head a trace. "You are very welcome, Alex." Nothing more needed to be said at that very moment. Knowing Alex was grappling with the past month spoke volumes to Jay to what she was able to accomplish for herself. He gradually saw her tears halted, managing well to gather herself back together. "You're heading back home tomorrow," plainly stated Jay. "What does that feel like?"

Shifting on her bare feet in the sand, Alex gazed up to Him. "It feels good...it really does," she said softly, on the verge of a grin.

"Are you happy you stuck it out until the very end?" Jay inquired, as He expected He already knew her answer.

The coldness in the air got to her hands, as she remembered she had pants pockets to stick them in. "I almost didn't but I'm certainly blessed that I did," she easily admitted. "Thank You for sticking with me." Humbleness emitted out from her bones, through her tissues and then, her skin.

"It's My job," He pointed out.

"Well, You should ask God for a vacation after dealing with me for the past month," Alex quipped, as laughter took over.

"Maybe I should," Jay responded with the same quick wit. "No, no...I just want you to live your life like Nate told you to do."

Alex nodded, and then looked into Jay's eyes. "You know I will," she uttered definitively. "Am I allowed to give You a hug?"

"Yes, but let Me walk you back to your car."

Smiling, Alex was ready to move forward. "Okay." Picking up her sneakers and Justice's leash, They walked back to the Camry, making a stop at the end of the boardwalk to get her shoes and her socks back on. It had gotten darker since they had arrived at Baker Beach. As Alex opened the rear side door, Justice jumped in effortlessly, realizing a snack might be coming soon. Alex closed the back door and opened hers. "Thank you, Jay, for everything really. You changed my life."

With open arms, Jay easily wrapped them around His latest graduate. "Remember, this isn't goodbye."

Alex wrapped her arms around His back, clutching Him with all her restored strength. "Oh, I know, but I'm still going to miss You." She released her hold.

"I hear you, Kid."

Getting in the Camry, Alex tossed back her hair, as she suddenly felt exhaustion seeping through her muscles. "What time is it?"

"It's 10:08 p.m.," He answered happily. "And as luck would have it, I reserved a room for you at the Inn on Folsom." Jay closed her door the rest of the way. "Get a good night's sleep; it's back on the road again tomorrow."

Finding the hotel on her phone, Alex placed it on her dashboard. "On the road again like Willie?"

Jay busted out with a giggle. "On the road like Willie—yes." Standing straight, He tapped on the car door. "Be bold."

"Oh, I will," she promised. Starting the engine, Alex grabbed Jay's hand one last time. "Thank You."

"Anytime," He reiterated genuinely. Letting go of Alex's hand, Jay watched her pull away, heading south on Lincoln Boulevard. "Don't forget to change the oil tomorrow!" Jay humorously shouted. After He saw her give Him the thumbs up out the left side, Jay knew it registered with Alex.

Through the rearview mirror, through the darkness of the night, Alex saw Jay waving. When she looked in the rearview again, He had vanished from sight. Her instincts told her to look toward the right, but He wasn't in the passenger seat. A few moments had passed—lonely and terrorizing moments—when the feelings of doubts emerged. Throwing back her black hair, Alex's right hand was met with Justice's tongue, indeed signaling to his new owner that he was with her. Alex couldn't help but to scratch the side of his snout to thank him for protecting her soul.

The Inn on Folsom was in the industrial part of the city, sporting four stories, with a dark-blue narrow façade. Across the street was a rug and carpet company, in a two-story, beige painted, expansive building. Alex was already up and checked out before 8 a.m. The skies were overcast, but bright, as the atmosphere was in the process of burning off the morning haze. They were both satisfactorily fed, Alex and Justice, when she had begun organizing her backseat and trunk for the 3,000-mile, give-or-take, trek back to Hopkinton. She had already booked a campground in Utah for that night, figuring she could drive twelve hours a day, including pit stops. Determining that she had organized as much as she possibly could inside the Camry, Alex got Justice settled in the backseat, loving him up with rubdowns just as she had witnessed Nate do the night before. All of the sudden, she heard a very familiar voice speaking rather loudly, as she popped her head out of the backseat to see Chris, wearing gray cargo shorts and a white shirt, standing directly across the one-way street, carrying a bright yellow duffle bag.

"Oh miss, miss, miss," Chris spoke, playing the role of the wayward traveler. "Is this the ride headed back to Boston?"

Being very happily surprised by his appearance, she played along. "Who wants to know?" she quipped, barely keeping her elbows on top of the Camry.

"Ma'am," Chris started.

"Ma'am?! Do I look like a 'ma'am' to you?" posed Alex uproariously while she kept her eyes glued to him as he walked closer, ever so slowly.

"You don't like 'ma'am'?" he kidded, approaching and kissing Alex.

Surprising Chris, she interrupted their kiss devilishly, smiling. "It's not one of my favorite names." With that off her chest, she resumed kissing Chris, as Alex. "How did you get here?"

"I hopped on the first bus I could find to San Fran, after I talked to my boss, convincing him to let me return home early," narrated Chris, "and it also helped a lot that I had accrued nearly two weeks of sick and vacation time, so I cashed those hours in."

"Yeah," Alex uttered, holding her hands upon his chest, mesmerized by his voice.

Holding onto her elbows, Chris continued. "And once I read your letter you left, I knew I had to come find you and take the long ride home with you." Chris kissed her lips once again.

"You weren't scared off by...by what I wrote?" Alex asked honestly.

Chris brought her head to his chest and just held her tightly to him. "Do you know what?"

"What?" she giggled, feeling completely safe within Chris' arms.

"I sort of like the new Alex," he offered. "I'm not saying anything was wrong with the old Alex, but the new Alex seems to be a badass, in the good way, of course."

"Of course," giggled Alex.

"You are so, so, strong, and so bold."

"I like bold," she said, as she looked up into his eyes. "Shall we hit the road, because somebody has taken the front seat over." Justice had moved into the driver's seat, displaying a goofy look.

"Absolutely," Chris uttered, kissing Alex. "Is my bag going to fit into the trunk?"

Opening her door, Justice returned to the backseat while Alex popped the trunk. "We'll make it fit." As such, they made it fit. "We just have to make one more stop."

Rounding the car, Chris opened the door and got in. "Where are we stopping?"

"The car needs an oil change."

The biggest grin overtook Chris' face. "Let's do it!"

Alex started the engine. "We're going home!"

Traversing the country for a second time was much different than the first time. Now Alex had a plan, and a single destination, which she knew was home. Instead of being guided by Jesus, she was guiding herself back to where she could begin the rest of her life, while all along carrying Jay and Nate in her heart. Seeing other parts of the country the second time around was even more grand and majestic than the first; she had the ability to observe more deeply because Chris did most of the driving. Alex and Chris made I-80 and I-90 E their main route home, all the while, stopping every night to sleep after driving 12 to 16 hours a day. Other than the first five hours of their drive back home, when Chris had caught up on sleep from his long bus ride to San Francisco, Alex and Chris were always talking through the miles and miles on the highway, at every meal and every night they shared together. Attending four years of medical school set the foundation of their friendship, while spending 46 hours together driving home solidified their love. Conversations abounded through their drive home with parents and their mutual friends, some of whom Alex hadn't been in contact with for many months, since before Nate's passing, as she now felt the need to apologize for her missteps during her grief. Every time Alex apologized, Chris sighed, as he tried to convey she didn't need to apologize, always holding onto her hand to make her believe in her whole self like he did.

Homecoming

Her alarm went off at 6 a.m., just as Alex had planned. They had found a motel in Albany in which to spend their last night on the road. She was already out of bed when Chris awoke, walking around the dark room, while the strong sun tried to flow through the brown flowery curtains. The alarm was even too early for Justice, as he was comfortable on the carpeted floor. He raised his head briefly only to put it back down again, going back to sleep. Alex searched for something appropriate to wear on this most momentous day she had been anticipating for a month. It was obvious to Chris that Alex was feeling a bit anxious about the homecoming, for it had been a long while since she had seen Chris' mom, other than in their numerous FaceTime chats they had had in the past four days. Chris lay in bed, with his head propped up on his arm, watching the love of his life, in all her naked glory, tear through her duffle bag, as she decided what to wear. Words alone weren't alleviating her unfounded jitteriness. Getting up on his knees on the full size, lumpy mattress, Chris gently reached for her bare hips and made her sit to take a deep breath, informing Alex that everything would be fine. It was amazing to Alex how just the sound of Chris' voice had the ability to settle her down, especially when he encircled her with his body. Reaching into her duffle bag, Chris picked out the same black pants she wore into

Children's Hospital Los Angeles, with a pale-yellow, button-down, short-sleeved shirt. Before Alex took a shower, she thanked and kissed Chris, energized.

Minutes away from home, both nervousness and excitement seeped into her veins, as she prepared to see everybody, especially her parents. Alex played that night on Baker Beach back through her mind a thousand times because she didn't want to forget one second of it as long as she lived. She knew she wouldn't. As Chris turned down Alex's street, he held onto her left hand a little tighter. No words needed to be spoken when Alex and Chris saw the few extra cars parked in front of her parents' house. Pulling up, the people most invested in Alex's homecoming were standing and awaiting her arrival. Any stranger watching this moment might have wondered if the young woman was returning from a tour of duty. It was a tour of duty rebuilding herself after such a devastating loss of her brother.

Once Chris put the Camry in park, with her parents only feet away, Alex jumped out, and put her arms around her mom, as her dad put his arms around Alex. She sobbed hard hearing her parents sob, vowing to never let her go again. "I never thought I could miss you so much," Alex cried.

"Oh, Baby Girl, don't ever discredit what distance can do to a heart," Joanne spoke solidly, holding onto her child so tightly that nothing would ever come between them. "Are you alright—tell me you're alright."

"I'm more than alright, I promise," assured Alex, clutching her mother just as tightly.

"Thank God you're safe," Joanne whispered in her beautiful daughter's ear.

"Nate kept me safe also," Alex revealed quietly.

Such a statement prompted Joanne to look into Alex's tearful eyes. "I knew he would." Joanne brought Alex close to her, studying her daughter's face with her fingertips, clearing away the tears.

There wasn't a doubt that she was her mother's daughter, recalling how she touched Nate's face on Baker Beach. Oh, how Alex wished she had the ability to share those moments with her parents.

Finally, Michael got his chance to hold his daughter. "Boy, did I miss you, Al."

Compared to the day she left, his embrace exceeded that ten-fold. "I missed you so, so much."

As her mother did, her dad didn't relinquish his daughter to the world quite just yet, while her mom kept her hands upon Alex's back. "All this love—wow."

"You deserve it, Kiddo," Michael stated with pure conviction, kissing her forehead.

Aware she and her parents had a captive audience, Alex turned her attention to Conrad, Justin, and little Lila. She hugged Justin, and then, Conrad, as he held Lila in the baby carrier. Boldly, Alex went ahead and unbuckled Lila and cradled her in her arms. "Hey Girly, hey Girly—I've waited so long to meet you, and hold you," Alex quietly spoke to the precious infant who was sleeping in her arms. "You're so cute with your very hip blue jeans and your pink shirt." Alex was instantly in love. The shade was plentiful in the front yard with the large maples and pines.

Everyone was completely enthralled with Alex holding a very content Lila for the first time. "I have had a lot of practice with babies in the last week, you know," she uttered, grinning wildly, sparking everybody to laugh.

"Want to babysit tomorrow night?" Conrad said on an impulse, as he chortled. "Justin and I haven't had a night out in three weeks."

It was hard to take her eyes off what Alex considered the cutest baby in the world. "If my arms weren't holding you, Sweet Girl, I would pull my tiny violin out and play your dad a concerto," Alex quipped in the sweetest voice. Again, everybody broke into laughter.

Gently pulling Alex's head toward him, Conrad kissed her temple. "I missed you, my friend."

The anxiety Alex had been feeling five minutes prior had all but dissipated. While she continued to hold Lila, Alex witnessed such a connection between Chris and her parents that it nearly made her heart leap out of her chest, realizing he was the one all along—all along through college and med school, all along through the occasional meals he had shared with her family, and his mother. The universe knew her heart before she had an inkling. Even Nate saw it and predicted their future. Chris was also formally introducing Justice to Michael and Joanne, where they were already enchanted with his easygoing disposition, or maybe it was the fact Nate had indulged Justice with rubdowns on Baker Beach, creating the truest connections. Right there, Alex quietly thanked Jay, God and Nate for this very day that brought her home to family and friends who loved her so, so much. A silver-blue Lexus SUV pulled up in front of the house and parked. Alex saw Chris motion for her. "Con, do you mind holding Lila? Chris' mother is here."

"No, no, not at all," Conrad spoke easily, taking his daughter into his arms.

Alex walked to where Chris met his mom, Dana, as she got out of her car to envelop her only child within her strong arms. Dana was just about four inches shorter than her son, making it all that much easier to hold his bald head to kiss it all over. Wearing neon-pink dress pants and a white blouse with low-heeled black leather sandals, Dana was slightly Rubenesque in her shape, sporting a dark, short bob cut with light-brown streaks. Once Dana released her son, Chris reached for Alex's hand. "Hi Dana," she said reservedly but smiling wildly.

"Come here, and give me a hug," demanded Dana, practically giving Alex no other choice.

Alex very happily embraced Chris' mother, as she hadn't seen Dana since before Nate's passing. "It's so good to see you again."

"I'm so, so sorry to hear about Nate, Alex," Dana spoke, holding onto Alex as if she was her own. "I'm so sorry we missed his services."

"You never have to apologize for anything, Dana," softly expressed Alex. Feeling Chris' mother release her so she could see her beautiful face, Alex smiled boundlessly. "You look so good!"

"And so do you!" Dana expressed with vivacity. "Love looks good on you, Girl, especially with my handsome son." Laughter exploded all around, as Joanne and Michael joined their daughter in greeting Dana.

"I'm so happy to see you again!" Joanne expressed joyfully, embracing Dana with ferocity.

Michael grabbed Dana's hand and elbow, as he landed a peck on her cheek. "Hi Dana! It's great to see you again!"

"Same to you, Michael," said Dana, taking stock of the gifts of this day, observing her son so happy with Alex, as his arm comfortably draped over Alex's shoulder. "I swear to God, they were made for each other."

"I totally agree," Michael spoke when a tear broke free.

"Let's go inside and eat!" Joanne announced, as she so lovingly grasped Alex's shoulders.

"I could eat," uttered Alex, laughing and finding her mother's hand to hold, as everybody made their way toward the house. "I have dibs on Lila for the rest of the day."

No one objected to Alex's wishes.

Epilogue

Inserting her key into the door lock of their apartment, Alex walked in after working 36 hours straight at Mass General, during the first wave of the COVID-19 pandemic. The world had been into the pandemic a little more than two months without any signs of it slowing down. The thing about a novel virus was that there wasn't any proven treatment, there wasn't any vaccine that would eliminate the symptoms, decreasing the spread of it, and it was an extremely contagious respiratory virus that could be deadly, even to people who were healthy, let alone to those who were immunocompromised. Alex couldn't recall all the patients she had lost in the past two months—patients who had no loved ones to be present in their last hours and minutes of life, only by video calls that were heart-wrenching for all parties involved. It was taking a toll on the strongest of doctors, nurses, respiratory therapists and practically everyone else in the medical field.

Kicking her comfortable shoes off that she had switched into after leaving the hospital, it was a few minutes after 7 a.m. on Tuesday, May 26, 2020. On the white wall, opposite the entry door, hung a basic wooden, Christian cross that Alex made a point to touch when she got home every time. Justice danced around her feet, full of excitement every time she arrived home. Even though her entire body was exhausted beyond what she thought possible, there was always time to give Justice a whole bunch of rubdowns. Alex entered their bedroom to find Chris sitting stoic on the corner of their unmade bed in front a bank of bay windows overlooking the Charles River. She approached him, climbing on the bed, finding him in tears.

"Babe, what's wrong," softly pressed Alex, wrapping herself around Chris with her body, caressing the back of his neck and head.

All Chris could do was to shake his head and cry, while he held his cell in his hand. "They did it again, Al," Chris fought to get out. "This time, they didn't use a gun, or any weapon, unless you consider a human knee a deadly weapon."

Moving around the bed, Alex crouched in front of Chris, seeing the magnitude of frustration upon his face. "Chris, what happened?" Justice lay down beside them.

It didn't take long for Chris to pull up the appalling video captured the day before, in broad daylight, on a street in downtown Minneapolis. Holding his cell for Alex to view, Chris remained stoic. "Eight minutes and forty-six seconds, Al," surmised Chris, vacantly looking out at the morning sky.

Alex watched the horrific footage the entire world was viewing. Everybody knew his name—George Floyd. As a doctor, she understood what was exactly happening inside the chest and brain of George Floyd, as he was being asphyxiated under the knee of a white police officer. Alex listened to all the pleading voices behind the cellphone, demanding that steely officer to get off Floyd's neck as he kept repeating that he couldn't breathe. With each minute that passed, Alex's frustration grew with Chris', as she frequently glanced up at him, seeing the tears stream down his face. Alex had seen enough and rose to comfort Chris, capturing back his attention. "What do you want to do?" she asked, holding his face.

Eye to eye with the woman he loved so much, Chris let everything out. "I want to scream like I haven't screamed before!" he exclaimed, as he bordered on anger and resentment. Still, his tears flowed easily. "I want to rip my chest wide open to show everybody that I have a heart, lungs and my blood runs red just like every other human on Earth!" Suddenly Chris' anger was replaced by incredible emotion, sobs, dropping his head downward. "I want...I want our kids to grow up in a world much different than all this."

It was the first time Chris had displayed such visceral emotion with her. Alex lifted Chris' face upwards, as she cried with him. "You want to have kids with me?"

His tearful eyes proved to be unflinching. "Of course, I do," Chris admitted easily, sneaking out a smile.

His smile led Alex to forge a bigger smile through their collective tears, as she kissed Chris so passionately. "I love you," Alex expressed inherently, like all the hundreds of times before, "and nothing will stop us from living the life we deserve."

"Promise?" Chris ventured.

"Yes, I promise."

Made in the USA
Middletown, DE
10 April 2023

28419779R00227